The author was born in 1945 and educated in Stourbridge, West Midlands. He married in 1968 and moved to Shropshire in 1971. He had four children, twelve grandchildren and one great-grandchild.

He passed away before the publication of this book at the age of 74 on 24 June 2019.

To my wife, Jane

Norbert Van De Hemn

THE ROYAL FALCONER

AUSTIN MACAULEY PUBLISHERS™
LONDON • CAMBRIDGE • NEW YORK • SHARJAH

Copyright © Norbert Van De Hemn (2019)

The right of Norbert Van De Hemn to be identified as author of this work has been asserted by him in accordance with Federal Law No. (7) of UAE, Year 2002, Concerning Copyrights and Neighboring Rights.

All rights reserved. No part of this publication may be reproduced, stored in a retrieval system, or transmitted in any form or by any means, electronic, mechanical, photocopying, recording, or otherwise, without the prior permission of the publishers.

Any person who commits any unauthorized act in relation to this publication may be liable to legal prosecution and civil claims for damages.

ISBN 9789948366751 (Paperback)
ISBN 9789948366577 (E-Book)

Application Number: MC-10-01-1935015
Age Classification: 21+

The age group that matches the content of the books has been classified according to the age classification system issued by the National Media Council.

Printer Name: iPrint Global Ltd.
Printer Address: Witchford, England.

First Published (2019)
AUSTIN MACAULEY PUBLISHERS FZE
Sharjah Publishing City
P.O Box [519201]
Sharjah, UAE
www.austinmacauley.ae
+971 655 95 202

England, 1235 AD

This story is set in the year 1235. It is twenty-nine years after the death of King John and his eldest son, King Henry III (1207–1272), reigns over England; Scotland is ruled by King Alexander II (1198–1249), and his wife Joanna is the illegitimate daughter of John and half-sister of the English king.

Wales is ruled by Llywelyn ab Iorwerth (1195–1240): 'ab Iorwerth' simply means, 'the son of Iorwerth', and he prefers to go by the title 'Prince of Gwynedd', or simply the 'Lord Llywelyn': He never held the title 'King of Wales*'.

Most of England's French-owned territory was lost under King John in wars with Phillip II of France in 1113–1114; thus the nickname Lackland, (Sans Terre). Yet, despite this and the passing of some one-hundred and seventy years since the Norman invasion, the French still hold some influence in court, and their language remains part of the legal system.

As far as further conflict is concerned these are rather benign years. If, however, there is to be one thorn in the English king's side, then it is the Gaelic speaking Welsh. Still fiercely independent, the Welsh fervently protect their borders, and raids and skirmishes into England, though infrequent, prove a constant reminder of their presence. However, away from these borderlands it is a time of peace and noble lords look towards sports, such as hunting, to rid themselves of any aggression.

Some twenty years after the signing of the 'Magna Carta' by King John at Runnymede in 1215, it is a time when all men have the right to a free trial. However, the laws of the land remain very much in control of the earls and barons, and vary throughout the land.

Ancient 'Dane Law', combined with the Christian 'Ten Commandments' form the basis along with Royal Decrees, and if there was any point needing clarifying, the church is normally consulted. However, the overriding and final say always remains the king's prerogative. The twelve men jury** we know today, did not come into existence until much later in history. Those accused were simply judged by their peers, and the number could vary from one to several depending upon the region and the circumstances.

The year 1235 is therefore a time when the landowners and nobility rule. A time when the overlords are very much in command.

*The title 'King of Wales' did not exist in this period of history, and probably never existed in its entirety, since prior to Lord Llywelyn Wales was, at best, controlled by three separate leaders, (or chieftains), in three distinct regions; (Gwynedd, Powis and Deheubarth).

**In 1730, the British Parliament passed the bill for 'Better Regulation of Juries', thus replacing the old haphazard system and laying down many of the basics we know today, including the establishment of the twelve men jury.

The Death of a Guard

A little after midnight on the fifth day of August, in the year of our Lord, twelve hundred and thirty-five, Richard, son of Frederick, man-at-arms to the Baron de Clancey, took guard duty outside the strong room to Lodelowe Castle. He would stand guard outside the steel door entrance until first light, when he would be replaced. This was a regular duty and something Richard did on average three times a week, and sometimes four.

The strong room lay beneath the baron's quarters in the West wing of Lodelowe Castle. There were two ways to get access. One was from the baron's reception room and the other, from steps in the corner of the courtyard. Both entrances were gated and always locked. A further steel door protected the strong room itself. This too was always locked and it was outside this inner steel door that Richard, son of Fredrick, took guard that night.

At about seven o'clock the next morning, Cuthred, the castle's sergeant-at-arms paid the guard a visit. Again, something that happened most mornings. But on this occasion, things proved very different. He arrived to find the guard lying on the floor in a pool of blood. Feeling his neck, he detected no pulse. Richard, son of Frederick, was dead. Furthermore, the door to the strong room was open, and by the look inside many valuables had been taken. An evil deed had been done.

When the Baron de Clancey got to hear of the robbery he was furious and vowed to track down the culprit and bring him to justice.

One week had passed since the murder of the guard and the theft from the strongroom of the Baron de Clancey. This story begins some fifty miles to the north, in the city of Salopsbury.

Chapter One

It was early morning and the inhabitants of the city of Salopsbury were waking up to the prospect of a fine day. Heavy thunderstorms overnight had left puddles in the patchwork of undulating cobbled streets, but as the sun began to rise, the skies had cleared and now there was not a cloud in sight. Where the late summer sun caught the puddles, thin wisps of glistening white steam rose, caught the light breeze and evaporated into the air.

Away in the distance, beyond the haphazardly constructed timber buildings that surrounded the market square, a hand bell rang. It tolled three times; clanging sharply and crystal clear, above the clatter of cartwheels on the narrow cobbled streets. Immediately, a flock of pigeons took to the air. A stray dog with a half chewed ear and feeding on garbage, tossed from a window, yapped loudly, then, upon seeing the approaching crowd, put his tail between his legs and scuttled away, to disappear down a side alley.

The hand bell tolled once more. Half a dozen sharp clangs this time, followed by a loud and resonate voice calling: "Oyez, oyez, oyez."

Those not already in hot pursuit of the briskly striding town crier, stopped what they were doing and looked towards his direction. Quickly, they dropped whatever they were doing and set off for the market square. Here they mingled with the gathering crowd and waited, now immobile and looking on as the town crier climbed to a vantage point, high atop a flight of stone steps. Round and ruddy was his face, and he wore the gold-braided black cloak and feathered hat of the authority invested in him. In one hand he clutched a scroll, tightly rolled; in the other, he intermittently swung his small hand bell. The scroll contained a message from the castle that stood high upon the hill that overlooked the market square. The scroll contained an important message that was to be delivered forthwith to the inhabitants of the city of Salopsbury.

The crowd was slow to gather, appearing in ones and twos. They stood in small groups, avoiding the puddles, and all turning their gaze to the top of the steps. The closely knit huddles had but one thing in common; each and every one of them waited in eager anticipation, all fidgeting nervously and making little or no sound. Only the ringing of the hand bell and the intermittent stentorian voice of the town crier was present to break the uneasy silence.

When enough people had gathered, the ringing of the hand bell ceased. The town crier was now ready to deliver his message. But he was not to be rushed. He never was. His experience of forty years had taught him how to handle the crowd. He cleared his throat, unfurled the scroll and raised it at an arm's length, high before his face. He paused and lowering the scroll a little, he stared down at the faces below. The wait seemed forever, but in truth, not long, just enough for a complete and total silence to befall the market square. The town crier could see that he had them in his grasp. He was ready and they, too, were ready, ready to listen to his every word. He knew this. He cleared his throat for one final time and began to read from the scroll.

His opening message was short, just a few words, but all the same, very much to the point.

"The Earl is dead, long live the Earl," he called, his voice resonating and echoing around the timber-framed buildings that encircled the market square.

The people absorbed the town crier's sad news in silence and then turning their heads, looked at one another. Eyebrows became raised and heads began to nod, and soon a hubbub of muted voices flared within each small huddle of the crowd.

The town crier cleared his throat yet again. He was nowhere finished; there was more to be read, and on realising this, the eager silence returned.

The crier waited for the crowd to settle once more. He was experienced enough to know when it was time to deliver. He would only continue when he had regained the crowd's undivided attention. He displayed his displeasure with a deep furrowed frown, accompanied by a steely glare. Eventually, the silence he demanded, returned. He played the moment for all its worth, delaying for several seconds longer than necessary, before continuing.

He read on, "Earl William Fitzgerald passed away peacefully in his sleep this very night. In observance of the laws of the good King Henry the Third of England and of the by-laws of the Council of the Marches, and in accordance with the line of succession, and at the behest of the late departed Earl William Fitzgerald, all titles, properties and lands associated with the fiefdoms and earldoms of Salopsbury and the Council of the Marches have, upon the Earl's departure, now passed to his cousin, Herbert Fitzgerald."

The crier paused and peered once more above the scroll. His glare on this occasion was met by a stony silence, not a murmur issued from the crowd. They wanted to hear more and desperately wanted him to continue.

The crier returned his focus to the scroll and read on, saying, "It is the new Earl's wish that following the death of his dear departed cousin, Earl William Fitzgerald, there will now follow a period of mourning. In two weeks' time, on the day of the market, in the year of our Lord twelve hundred and thirty five, and in the reign of the good King Henry the Third of England, Herbert Fitzgerald, the new Fourth Earl of Salopsbury and Earl Representative for the Council of the Marches, will appear before his subjects. Until that day, it is decreed that, a period of mourning be observed. All singing, dancing, revelry and merriment, along with all forms of gambling, the playing of games and the practice of archery are all strictly forbidden, by order of the Earl."

The crowd understood. No one objected. News of the late Earl's death had not come unexpected. He had been unwell for quite some time, and everyone knew this, and the town crier had appeared regularly to keep his subjects informed. They nodded to each other in silence and many bowed their heads in silent prayer. There was no argument, no disagreement, no protest, just prayers and perhaps a few tears. It was only right and proper that the inhabitants of the city of Salopsbury show a little respect for their departed lord and master. It was their duty to grieve upon his death along with the new Earl and his closest family.

With his message delivered, the town crier re-rolled the scroll, placed his hand bell beneath one arm and moved on to a fresh location. In every quarter of this haphazard and sprawling city his message was the same.

"The Earl is dead, long live the Earl …"

Chapter Two

The late departed Earl William Fitzgerald, Third Earl of Salopsbury and Earl Representative for the Council of the Marches, was in his sixty-third year when he passed away peacefully in his sleep. Twice he was married; his first wife, Catherine de Say, departing this life when William was fifty-eight years of age. After thirty-six years of relatively happy marriage, this first union had but one failure, Catherine bore no heir to the Fitzgerald line.

Upon Catherine's death, a hasty new marriage was arranged. From across the English Channel came the Lady Adela, youngest daughter of the Duke d'Honfleur, reviving fresh hopes that a son and an heir be at long last forthcoming. But alas, this second marital union also proved fruitless. For although the Lady Adela was young, a mature twenty-one when she wed and still a virgin by all accounts, once again the consummation came to nothing.

Therefore, upon the death of William, there were no sons, no brothers, nor any immediate family to continue the Fitzgerald line. Thus it was that the Salopsbury titles, along with all their associated properties, lands and estates passed back up the line and down again to William's cousin, Herbert Fitzgerald, his nearest and only living male relative.

Although late in coming, some say this was a blessing in disguise, for the new Earl had two sons, and both had further sons of their own. Stability had returned to the earldom, the future of the Salopsbury titles and estates was safe, and after nearly forty years of uncertainty, the scribes could now draw up a list of heirs that would last until the end of the century.

Earl Herbert Fitzgerald stood aloft the great tower of Salopsbury Castle. The city's new overlord was a short, stout man, forty-eight years of age, a paunch belly, neatly trimmed greying beard and receding hairline. Out of respect for his departed cousin, the late Earl William Fitzgerald, he was dressed in black, something he had done for the past two weeks. His attire supported a long black cape that fluttered in the breeze, and on his belt hung a short sword with an ornately decorative handle displaying the coat of arms of the Fitzgerald family.

As the sun rose, a cloudless late August sky signalled a fine day in prospect. In recent days the thunderstorms had returned, this time more ferocious than those experienced some two weeks earlier. Flooding was widespread and the rivers were swollen. But the worse had passed, and given a few days all tracks and roads would be passable once more.

The Earl leaned against the ramparts and looked around. The red disc of the early morning sun was partially hidden behind a ridge of low hills away to the east. The standard of the Fitzgeralds, with its gold-braided surround and the heads of three snarling lions emblazoned upon a pale blue and yellow shield, fluttered noisily at half-mast above his head. He loosened the ropes and raised the standard to the top of the mast. His mind was on other things, but he was aware of what he was doing and the significance of the act. It was necessary that this be done. He retied the ropes and managed a smile. Now, after two weeks of mourning, the standard of the Fitzgeralds had returned to full mast.

With this small but important task done, and without the courtesy the ceremony probably demanded, the Earl moved to the western ramparts and rested his arms upon the wide, red-brick walls that encompassed the high, square tower. His brow was furrowed, yet he still managed a smile. The sadness of the last two weeks was nearing an end, and it was time for the city of Salopsbury to go about its normal business. With head bowed and mind deep in thought, he found himself staring down from the high tower towards the long, horseshoe bend of the River Severn far below.

Salopsbury Castle stood on an outcrop of rock overlooking a great bow in the river. Within this vast loop stood the churches, houses, shops, taverns and stables that constituted the ever-expanding city of Salopsbury. Soon, no room would remain for settlement on the land bounded between the castle and the great bow in the river. But to move outside this pear-shaped tract of land, would be to lose the protection of the river and the castle, for within this vast loop there existed a safe haven in a land much threatened by raids from across the border with Wales.

Just two roads entered the city, one to the north and the other to the west. The northern road passed beneath the castle's portcullis, whilst the western road entered the city via an arched stone bridge that spanned the wide River Severn. On the far side of the bridge stood a gatehouse, guarded continuously and shut during the hours of darkness.

From his high vantage point, the Earl gazed down upon the river. The gates to the bridge were open and the guards stood to either side. The road leading away from the bridge was wide and straight, heading westwards towards the distant Welsh hills. Within the city, a cobbled road wound haphazardly around the buildings, then rose steeply to the castle. It was in the castle's courtyard that the two roads met.

Far below, a lone horse and a rider crossed the bridge. For several minutes the Earl had followed this rider's approach and was surprised to see the guards let the rider pass unchallenged. But as the rider moved across the bridge and into the city, the Earl recognised and understood. The rider was attired in a very distinctive claret and light-blue quartered tunic. These were the colours of the Council of the Marches, an assembly of overlords, earls and barons, gathered to protect and oversee justice in an area bounded between the River Severn and the border with Wales. This was the Marches.

The Earl sighed deeply and stroked his beard. This would be the council's herald, and at long last news was forthcoming. Briefly, he closed his eyes and prayed that the herald bore the long awaited news which both he and Lady Adela, his late cousin's wife, desperately wanted to hear.

He lowered his head to take one final look from the ramparts. Soon he would have to climb down from the tower to greet the herald's arrival. But for a while he reflected upon the Council of the Marches and what this meant to him. He was now a full member of the council, a position his cousin William once enjoyed. The thought invigorated him. At long last he held a position of power, a seat of authority where his voice could be heard. But for now he would accept their decisions. The herald came with word regarding the release of his cousin's wife, now that she was a widow, to be allowed to return to her native France.

The first thing he had done, following the death of William, was to write to the Council of the Marches asking that she should be permitted to go home. He hoped they agreed. But this was by no means a certainty. The Council of the Marches were responsible for choosing and bringing her here in the first place, and perhaps another marriage had already been arranged. If this was the case, the matter was out of his hands. There were too many on the council, and as yet, he held very little influence when it came to the making of decisions. The full council consisted of at least a dozen noble lords. To the south and west of Salopsbury lay the castles of Lodelowe, Powys, Montgomery and Cluntyne. Here, the de Clanceys, the de Mortimers, the Montgomerys and the d'Says ruled; all big and powerful families with much influence at the King's court. There were a few other minor lords and landowners that made up the full council, there were thirteen in all; but he was their equal now, and by status, the second most senior representative below that of Simon de Mortimer, the Earl of Powys.

Herbert Fitzgerald, the Earl of Salopsbury for just two short weeks, allowed himself a smile and a final look around. From his lofty position he could see for many a mile in all directions. Away in the distance, far to the south, a dense forest blanketed the hazy-blue hills of the Marches. It is here, and only here, that his eyes rested upon another lord's land. This distant forest he knew to be the Forest of Wyre, and hidden somewhere within this forest's midst stood the market town of Lodelowe. There the surrounding lands and titles belonged to the de Clancey family. But other than this far-flung, mist-shrouded forest, everything else he surveyed, belonged to him. To the north, east and west lay the full extent of the Earldom of Salopsbury. In accordance with his family's motto, this was his '*Floreat Salopia*'. His flourishing land, and everywhere he looked, all belonged to him.

The Earl reluctantly pushed himself away from the ramparts and stood erect. He managed a small nod of the head. He was thinking, perhaps things were not as bad as he first thought. He had waited a long time for this moment, and now he, Herbert Fitzgerald, son to the late Sir Rupert Fitzgerald, Knight of the Order of St. John of Jerusalem, was the new Fourth Earl of Salopsbury and master of all he surveyed.

However, there still remained one thorn in the new Earl's side. For only when Lady Adela, the young wife of his late departed cousin was well and truly gone from this castle, would he feel comfortable enough to accept his new inheritance. For as long as the French woman remained, he knew that he could not truly become the new lord and master of Salopsbury Castle. Lady Adela had, during her short stay, become aware of too many dark family secrets and she simply could not remain.

The Earl closed his eyes and offered a small prayer, praying the approaching herald bore the long awaited news, both he and Lady Adela were desperate to hear.

With a sigh, he pushed himself away from the ramparts and descended the tower. It was time to greet the herald.

Chapter Three

On the morning of the arrival of the herald, Lady Adela Fitzgerald, dowager to the late William Fitzgerald, Third Earl of Salopsbury, was to be found in the west wing of Salopsbury Castle. She was twenty-six years of age, exceedingly pretty, with a trim waist and jet-black hair that hung forward from her shoulders in two wide long plaits. She wore a full-length emerald-green gown with billowing sleeves, and on her head rested a small, square, ornately embroidered bonnet that matched the colour of her dress.

Alongside Lady Adela stood Mary, her trusted lady-in-waiting since the young French maiden's arrival in England some five years earlier. Mary was in her fifty-fifth year. She was short and fat, with greying hair and a chest that wheezed constantly. She wore a blue dress, not dissimilar to that of her mistress, but her bonnet was white with straps tied beneath the chin. This was the bonnet of a serving maid.

Lady Adela's chambers took up most of the second floor of the west wing of the castle. The main room through which one entered was the reception. This room lacked furniture, with just one tall, high-backed chair placed centrally on a high pedestal. Great hanging tapestries adorned the walls and light entered through four stained-glass, leaded windows displaying figures of saints alongside those of past members of the Fitzgerald family. It was here in the reception room that Lady Adela would hold an audience. Beyond this room lay further three rooms, all interconnected. These were Lady Adela's private quarters, off limits to men, whatever their rank or status, and this included the new Earl.

Lady Adela and Mary were occupied but not busy, both sorting and packing the last few remaining items needed for the long journey south. On the floor of the reception room, rested four plain wooden chests, each with their lids opens. After much trial and error a system of packing had been established, with separate chests for clothes, bonnets, shoes and undergarments. Lady Adela had requested more chests, insisting that four were nowhere near enough for all the dresses and shoes she owned. But she was told that the cart on which she was to travel would hold no more than four and this was to be her limit. Knowing this, however, she still demanded a fifth chest to hold expensive items such as jewellery, family heirlooms and silver. But the Earl had discouraged this, explaining the risk of robbery too great and such items best travel separately, under armed guard. So with four chests allocated and brought to the reception chamber, the two women had set about packing. Yet for all their effort, their mood remained sombre. Despite all their apparent activity, neither displayed much commitment to the task set before them. For it was still by no means certain that Lady Adela be allowed to return to her native France. News had not yet arrived from the Council of the Marches.

A repetitive loud rapping came upon the door of the chambers. Three loud strikes as if hit by a staff.

Lady Adela was folding a dress and about to place it in a chest when the raps came. She recognised the signal. It was the guard permanently assigned to her chambers that was knocking. She signalled to Mary to go to the door and find out what he wanted.

With the door slightly ajar, Mary held a small conversation. She then opened it wide for the guard to enter. He appeared attired in a pale blue tunic with three yellow snarling lion heads emblazoned upon his chest. This was the uniform of the Fitzgeralds. Beneath his tunic he wore a vest of chainmail, and on his head rested a shining, silver-domed helmet with a narrow nose-guard that reached down beyond the tip of his nose.

Lady Adela had not moved and stood close to the door, alongside the four chests. The guard took two steps forward and with a short pikestaff in hand, dropped to one knee. He bowed his head low and addressed Lady Adela.

Speaking down to the bare floorboards of the room, he said, "My Lady, the Earl begs you an audience."

Lady Adela showed no haste. She put away the dress, pushing it firmly down into the chest, before turning to the guard. He remained kneeling and with head bowed. She addressed him in the language of the Anglo-Saxons but with a strong Norman accent.

"Good, you may show him in," she told him.

Lady Adela glided her slender figure across the floor to take up position on the ornately carved chair, perched high upon the raised pedestal that faced the door. A woolsack rested upon the seat. She shuffled and settled, adjusting the cushion until she sat comfortably. At the same time, Mary hastily adjusted her flowing gown so that no part of her legs showed, then cast the long plaits of her jet-black hair to either side, and finally, content that all was in order, sidled away to a corner, where she would remain inconspicuous until the audience was over.

From her high position Lady Adela clapped her hands and waited with elbows resting lightly upon the arms of the chair.

From the dimly lit corridor beyond the open door, her late husband's cousin, Earl Herbert Fitzgerald, entered. Behind him, walking with head bowed, trailed a demure young kitchen maid. The Earl moved briskly to the raised pedestal and bowed his head as a mark of respect. But it was no more than a quick nod for the Earl's superior rank had to be observed and recognised.

Behind the Earl, about two paces back, the kitchen maid came to a halt. Here her low status in society immediately became evident. She curtsied, dropped to one knee and turned her gaze to the floor. She then held that position.

The Earl took Lady Adela's hand and kissed lightly upon her wedding ring.

As his head rose, he enquired, "And how does't my dearest and most cherished member of the family feel this fine morning?"

Lady Adela had long since grown wise to the Earl's silvered tongue. However, she had been raised a lady of noble birth and to act accordingly.

With poise and dignity she replied, "My health is good, and the weather is a delight since the deluges of the past few days."

The Earl looked to a narrow shaft of sunlight beaming in through a leaded window. He stroked his beard and for a while remained deep in thought. Lady Adela was right; the weather in recent days had been foul. The rivers were high and the flooding great, but now thankfully, the skies were clear and the thunderclouds gone.

He remained pensive for a little while longer before returning his thoughts to the reason for requesting this audience.

"My Lady," he said, releasing her hand. "I bring good news. The Council of the Marches hath ratified your departure. You are free, as the widow of your late departed husband, to return to your home in Normandy and with immediate effect. Your journey south has been heralded to all the Lords of the Marches and to those of Western Mercia and beyond. You are granted safe passage all the way to the Cinque Ports. Similar arrangements are also at hand over on the far side of the Channel, and news of your homecoming should be reaching your father, the Duke d'Honfleur, as we speak."

Lady Adela tried not to show her joy. However, this was everything she had hoped for. She was, at long last, free to return home to France. Her marriage to the late Earl had never been a great success. Not surprising, given that right from the start there existed the vast age difference. They had had sex together for the first two years; not often, but frequent enough to say that they had tried; yet the hoped-for child never materialised. After this, and for the past three years, the aged Earl's health had passed from bad to worse, and with this went all hopes of a successful consummation.

Lady Adela clasped her arms to her chest. She could no longer contain her joy.

"*Mon Dieu!* Then I am free to leave! I may return home?" she exclaimed with a hint of relief.

The Earl nodded and explained, "Final arrangements are being made as we speak, my Lady. A wagon is being prepared in the courtyard, and an escort of three of my most trustworthy men hath been assigned to accompany you all the way to the Cinque Ports. The men I have chosen for their knowledge of the road south. Reports of bandits abound and it is possibly safer to travel first to the town of Lodelowe. Its lands are well protected. Likewise, my sister Elizabeth resides as abbess over the nunnery at Wistanstow, just a few miles to the north of Lodelowe. Perhaps perchance you may stay there for the first night. But I will leave the chosen route to the men that escort you. Be guided by them, for they know the safest route."

Lady Adela smiled.

"Then I must thank you, my Lord, for all that you have done," she said.

The Earl turned to the wench that had trailed him into the room. She remained with one knee on the floor and with her head bowed.

He waved a hand in her direction and spoke, saying, "My Lady, I bring you a handmaiden to accompany you on your long journey south. This is Gwyneth. She is but a simple wench that fares from the castle's kitchens. She hath a kind heart and hath pledged to serve you well."

Mary, Lady Adela's lady-in-waiting and trusted friend, was in her fifty-fifth year, round and plump in stature, and with a chest that wheezed continuously from ill health. It was plain to see that to enforce upon her a trip to the Cinque Ports would be the ending of her. Her mistress had long foretold this, and even though the old lady did protest somewhat, it was agreed someone younger would replace her for the long journey south, and that all fond farewells be left in the castle's courtyard.

Lady Adela, from her high position, beckoned the wench to approach.

"Come my child, let me look at you," she said.

Gwyneth rose from the floor, hitched up the front of her kitchen maid's frock and stepped forward to curtsey before the raised pedestal. Even though both Lady Adela and the young kitchen maid had resided within these castle walls for the past five years, neither had set eyes upon each other before this day.

Lady Adela stepped down from her chair and eyed the kitchen maid up and down. She placed a finger beneath the girl's chin and raised her head. There were soot marks on her cheeks. Lady Adela looked into the girl's eyes. They were blue and radiated warmth and affection. Despite the kitchen grime, the wench had a pretty face with a fair complexion and a dimpled chin. Her hair were golden with long ringlets cascading down from beneath a white maid's bonnet. She was tall in stature, slender at the waist and large around the bosoms.

Lady Adela felt troubled by the kitchen maid's ragged and soiled clothes.

"Tell me my child, what clothes have you to wear?" she asked.

The kitchen maid looked up from her curtsied position.

"My Lady, I have this frock and a heavy coat to keep out the cold," she answered.

Lady Adela raised an eyebrow. It was evident that this girl was poor and owned nothing but the rags she wore.

"And shoes?" she asked. "Show me your feet."

The kitchen maid stood upright and hitched up the front of her dress as far as the ankles. Her feet were bare.

Lady Adela turned to the Earl.

"My Lord, when are we to depart?" she asked.

The Earl stroked his beard and gave the question much thought. He knew the answer he would like to give, the sooner the better as far as he was concerned. The truth was, he desperately wanted her away from his castle. However he did not want to sound too hasty. He looked towards the four chests and could see that they were almost packed.

He pointed to the chests and gave his reply, telling her, "My Lady, if you are packed and ready, then sunrise on the morrow, if that is convenient with you."

Lady Adela too, was keen to get away from the castle and sunrise on the morrow was fine by her. She turned to the kitchen maid.

"Then, Gwyneth, you must remain here with me," she said. "I will find you a new dress and provide you with stockings and shoes for the long journey south."

The kitchen maid lowered her soiled and ragged dress to the floor, then returned to her curtsy position with head bowed.

"Thank you, my Lady," she said softly as she held her lowered stance.

The Earl interrupted with a gentle cough. He had no desire to stand and listen to women's tittle-tattle, and besides, he had conveyed everything that needed to be said. He had brought news that both he and Lady Adela had hoped for. He took a light hold of Lady Adela's left hand, kissed her gently upon the same wedding ring as before and bid her farewell.

"Then I bid you fair journey south, my Lady, and may God give you most favourable winds with which to cross the English Channel," he said.

Lady Adela bowed her head.

"Thank you, my Lord," she replied. "You have been most kind and helpful. I am most grateful and I thank you for all that you have done."

The Earl took one step back and bowed gracefully. He then turned and without a second glance made quickly for the exit. As the door behind him closed, he lengthened his stride. He had people to meet and much work remained. Lady

Adela may well be leaving his castle on the morrow, but as everyone knew, the road to the Cinque Ports was long and arduous, and fraught with danger, especially from the marauding Welsh brigands across the border. There remained a distinct possibility that some great misfortune could befall her en route, and he needed to be certain that the escorts chosen knew exactly what was required of them. There was also an urgent letter to write and a rider to be despatched with haste to his sister, the abbess at Wistanstow Abbey.

His sister had to be made aware of Lady Adela's journey south and of the route he had advised for her first night's stay.

Chapter Four

Lady Adela traced a forefinger lightly down the soot marks upon the young kitchen maid's face. Rubbing lightly together the tips of her soot-covered fingers, she turned to her lady-in-waiting.

"Mary, prepare a hot bath and scent it with fine fragrances," she told her. "We must have Gwyneth scrubbed clean and smelling sweet for the long journey south."

Mary, upon hearing her mistress's request, hurried away to procure hot water from the castle's kitchen.

Lady Adela waited for her elderly lady-in-waiting to leave the reception chamber and the door to close before taking hold of the kitchen maid's hand.

"Come, come with me my child," she said. "Whilst we wait for a bath to be prepared, I will find you new clothes to wear."

Lady Adela led Gwyneth to a door leading off reception. As they reached the open doorway, the young girl hesitated and came to a halt, mindful not to step inside. From the doorway she looked into the room and stood in awe at all its splendour.

She had never stepped into a room this luxurious before and was afraid to do so now. This was Lady Adela's bedchamber and, up until now, forbidden territory for anyone of such lowly status to enter. She looked around the room. A great four-poster bed stood against one wall, the bedcovers and posters all braided in gold. Fine heavy tapestries draped the grey granite walls, and even though this was late summer and the weather outside quite warm, a log fire smouldered in an open fireplace.

Gwyneth was overcome with emotion, and tears welled up in her eyes. She snatched away from Lady Adela's grip and wrung her hands. She was thinking, surely nothing of this was real? Surely this was just a dream? Never before had the young kitchen maid come face to face with such luxury. She had lived in poverty since birth and knew no other way of life. Her father was a fletcher before his untimely death. But without war or conflict, demand on arrows was low and hunting was their only use.

She was an only child and her parents had desperately wanted a boy to work the fields to bring in a little extra income. But alas, this was not to be. Her father died of the plague when she was eleven years of age, and with no other family income she was sent to the castle's kitchens. Her mother, without a man to support her, fared little better. She became a whore and it is reported that she moved south to the neighbouring town of Lodelowe. Gwyneth no longer knew if her mother was alive, nor whether she still resided at Lodelowe. No contact had been made for the past five years.

Gwyneth was just sixteen years of age, lacked education and could neither read nor write. But more importantly, she lacked love, and now a fine lady of high and noble birth was showing her a warmth and affection she had never known.

"Come, come enter the chamber. You have nothing to fear," beckoned Lady Adela, reassuring the kitchen maid.

The young girl wiped away a tear with the back of a soot-stained hand and stepped hesitantly into the bedchamber.

Lady Adela moved to the centre of the room and with a comforting smile, waited patiently for the kitchen maid to join her. With open arms she beckoned her into the room.

"Gwyneth, come to me my child," she said. "Let me remove those ragged clothes. I will have them burned. I will find you new attire from my wardrobe."

The kitchen maid, with head bowed and eyes transfixed upon the floor, edged slowly into the chamber. She moved to stand before Lady Adela, then curtsied low and held that position.

With a slender outstretched finger Lady Adela raised the young girl's chin.

"Look to me, my child," she said. "Look into my eyes."

As the kitchen maid's head lifted, Lady Adela stared deeply into her big blue watery eyes and traced a forefinger lightly down the side of her soot-stained cheek.

"But first, we must remove all this kitchen grime," she said. "Mary goes for hot water. Soon she will have a bath prepared for you in the adjoining room. Now let's be having these clothes off."

Lady Adela removed the white bonnet from Gwyneth's head to reveal a tangle of golden locks. The ringlets were natural, but the hair were ruffled and unkempt. She ran her fingers through the tousled locks.

"We must wash this hair too my sweet Gwyneth, and give it a fine brushing afterwards," she said.

Her hands dropped to the dress she wore.

"Now, my child, let's have this frock away and in the fire," she added.

Gwyneth was not sorry to see the frock go. It was getting too small for her anyway. Of late, her bosoms had grown to maturity and the frock was tight about the chest. Bending, she grabbed hold of the hem and raised the skirt. As the skirt rose over her body, Lady Adela assisted by pulling the frock up and away from the head. The coarse woven fabric was heavy. It was also ragged around the hem and much soiled.

Lady Adela folded the frock in her arms. Then walking to the fireplace, she tossed it upon the large smouldering log fire. Immediately, the frock burst into flames. For a while she stared into what was suddenly a roaring fire. She smiled, relieved that these dirty rags were turning to ashes.

She turned to find a naked Gwyneth standing at the centre of the bedchamber. The kitchen maid, too, found herself staring into the flames, but she did so with a saddened heart. The frock, now well ablaze, was the only thing she owned, except for a well-worn heavy winter coat and a small wooden cross, held about her neck by a thin strand of leather hide.

Lady Adela turned to Gwyneth. Standing naked in the flickering light of the flames, she could see just how pure and radiant the kitchen maid really was. Her body was like an hourglass, with delicate white skin, plump rounded breasts and shapely hips that narrowed sharply at the waist.

She walked slowly towards Gwyneth and took grip of the thin leather strap that held a wooden cross about her neck. She moved to lift the strap over her head, and in doing so their cheeks momentarily touched. Lady Adela sensed the warmth of the young girl's skin against her own and retained the contact. As she withdrew she kissed Gwyneth lightly on the cheek before removing the strap from her head.

Lady Adela traced a forefinger down Gwyneth's right breast as far as the nipple. She pushed gently, flattening the nipple.

"My sweet little Gwyneth, I will bathe you personally," she said. "A body this pure, so pale and delicate, needs gentle caressing, and Mary can be far too abrasive."

Lady Adela moved to the bed and removed a linen sheet. She turned to Gwyneth and draped the sheet about her shoulders.

"Here, my child," she said. "This will keep you warm until you are ready for your bath. I will find you a new dress to wear as soon as you are bathed."

Gwyneth pulled the linen sheet about her shoulders and gripped it about the neck with one hand. She felt more at ease now that her body was covered.

Whilst waiting for the bath to be prepared, Lady Adela took the opportunity to enquire into her new servant's personal life. For other than being told that she worked within the castle's kitchens, she knew nothing else.

"Pray tell me my child, what of your parents?" she asked. "Are they alive and in good health?"

The kitchen maid grimaced. Her parents were something she rarely spoke about.

"My Lady, my father died of the plague when I was eleven years old, and my mother no longer resides here in Salopsbury," she replied. "She has long gone from here and now resides within the walls of Lodelowe."

Lady Adela turned pensive. But at least she now knew why this girl was so poor.

"Do you remain in touch with your mother?" she asked.

The kitchen maid shook her head.

"No, my Lady, I have not heard from my mother for the past five years," she said with a noticeable touch of sadness to her voice, and added, "Not since she went away from Salopsbury."

Lady Adela furrowed her brow.

"But you would like to see her again?" she enquired.

The young kitchen maid nodded her head. It was true she missed her mother.

"I would so dearly love to see my mother again, my Lady," she said with a sigh. "But alas, Lodelowe is many miles to the south and I have no means of transport."

Lady Adela recalled something the Earl had said earlier. The men chosen as escorts were specially selected for their knowledge of the road south, and because of reports of bandits in the area it was suggested they pass south through the town of Lodelowe. She was thinking, a small detour would take them directly through the walled town, and it would not add too many leagues to their journey. But all of this would have to wait till the morrow when she was with the escorts and setting off from the castle. But for now she had Gwyneth to bathe and dress.

"Sit down upon the bed my sweet Gwyneth," she said. "Whilst we wait for Mary to prepare your bath, let's see if we can find you some comfortable shoes to wear."

Gwyneth moved to the side of the big four-poster bed and perched uneasily upon the very edge. The mattress was soft and filled with the feathers of the eider duck. Apart from the softness, everything about the bed, the sheets, the blankets, the pillows, all smelled sweet and heavily scented. Tentatively, she drew her linen bed-sheet further about her body and waited.

Lady Adela crossed the room to rummage through a large oak chest. From deep inside, she selected a pair of shoes and held them to the light. Satisfied with her choice, she carried them to the bed and presented them to Gwyneth.

"I think these shoes will fit your slender feet," she said.

Gwyneth looked hesitantly at the shoes. They were French in design, with leather uppers and thick wooden heels. These shoes were clearly not English, for Saxons preferred flat soles and heels for comfort and walking. The bases of these shoes were carved of hard wood, probably oak. They were lacquered and stained dark brown, with metal studs on the heels and toes to prevent wear. The uppers were of soft, brown suede leather, laced above the ankles and riveted to the wooden base by a series of large brass studs that encircled the whole of the shoe. The newness of these shoes was all too apparent. It was likely they had never been worn. Gwyneth was moved to tears. No one had ever given her a present before, and items of such worth were way beyond her comprehension.

Gwyneth stretched out her right foot and waited whilst her mistress slipped on the shoe. Lady Adela did not lace it up, but held the sides closed about the ankle.

"How does this feel, my dear?" she asked. "Is this comfortable enough for you?"

Gwyneth nodded. It was all she could manage. Words choked her and it was difficult to speak. The only shoes she had ever worn were as a child, and for the past five years she had trodden barefoot about the castle.

"Then you shall have these shoes," Lady Adela told her. "These shoes are yours to keep."

A call from an adjoining chamber announced that Gwyneth's bath was prepared. Lady Adela cursed Mary for being too hasty. She had hoped for more time to be alone with Gwyneth. The water must have already been boiling for another cause. Removing the shoe and taking Gwyneth by the hand, she led her to the adjoining chamber. There was no bed in here, just chairs and carpet, and once more a fire blazed in an inglenook. To the centre of the room, several large earthen jugs of steaming hot water stood alongside a large square stone bath, not too dissimilar to the troughs that watered the horses. The female servants that had helped carry the water to the chamber were gone and amidst the steam Mary stood alone, her sleeves rolled up and waiting with a long-handled scrubbing brush in hand.

Lady Adela moved to the bath and tested the water with one hand. She nodded her approval. The temperature was just right, but the depth far too shallow for her liking.

"More hot water, Mary," she said. "We have many years of kitchen grime to scrub away."

Mary poured the last of the boiling water from the remaining jugs and added a little cold from a wooden bucket to bring the temperature down. Lady Adela tested the water once more and gave it a little stir with one hand. The water level was halfway up the bath. This was luxury, and not even she had ever had the bath filled this high before.

Satisfied with the temperature and water level, Lady Adela poured in a thick-syrupy liquid from a large stone jar that contained the crushed petals of roses and honeysuckle. With petal fragments of red, white and gold floating on the surface she stirred the water with a hand.

"These fragrances are from Normandy, made with herbs and flowers from my father's garden," she said.

With the bath prepared, Lady Adela beckoned Gwyneth to step inside. The kitchen maid released the linen sheet from about her shoulders and let it drop to the floor. She moved to the edge of the bath, raised a leg and dipped her toes in the water. She tested the temperature. Finding the water slightly on the warm side, but not unbearable, she placed her foot down and stepped inside. She lowered herself into the bath, stretched out her legs and placed her arms to the sides. Finally, she relaxed and leaned backwards to rest her shoulders against the rear of the bath.

The deeply scented water covered Gwyneth's body right up to her chin with only her head and breasts peaking above the waterline. The young kitchen maid held a secret. She had never had a hot bath before. Not one she remembered anyway. To wash, which was infrequent, she used a trough behind the castle's stables, and to bathe she used the river when the weather was warm and no one around. But to lie stretched out in a hot stone bath, heavily scented with the flowers of summer, was a new experience. She closed her eyes and eased herself further down in the warm water. This was bliss, this was heaven; the best moment of her life, and something that would live on in her memory forever.

Mary stepped forward with scrubbing brush in hand, her sleeves rolled up in earnest. Lady Adela raised a hand.

"I will do this myself, Mary," she said. "I will bathe Gwyneth. We need more water for the hair. Pray, return to the kitchen and get more hot water."

Mary did not argue. She rolled down her sleeves, picked up a large earthen ewer and set off for the kitchen. Mary was no fool and well aware of the reason for her mistress's intervention. Living every day for the past five years alongside Lady Adela had taught her much. The only sad part was that her mistress was leaving the castle in the morning, never to return. It was therefore, with a mixture of sadness and happiness that Mary set off for the kitchen; sad that five years of companionship were coming to an end, but happy that her mistress had found a new friend and companion for the long journey south. She also knew that it was wrong to hasten back. Lady Adela needed time to acquaint herself with her new servant. She would delay her return by talking to the cook.

With Mary gone, Lady Adela knelt beside the bath, rolled up her sleeves and began to soap her hands in sweet smelling oils and fragrances. When a fine lather was reached she brushed her hands lightly across the tops of Gwyneth's exposed breasts. Their eyes met but not a word was exchanged. There was no need.

Gwyneth knew what was expected. She sat more upright to expose all of her breasts above the waterline and closed her eyes. Her mistress's touch was something too wonderful to behold.

It is not long before gentle hands ventured beneath the water. Gwyneth opened her legs to accommodate her mistress's probing fingers. She did not mind. She did not have a care in the world. She simply smiled at her mistress with warmth and affection, and let her wash away at every small crevice of her body. No one had pampered her like this before, and her mistress was being so kind and gentle.

That night Lady Adela slept alongside Gwyneth in her bed, their naked bodies huddled closely together.

Gwyneth slept soundly. For the first time in her life she found herself sleeping with someone that exuded so much love and affection towards her.

For Lady Adela the experience also held a deep sense of satisfaction. For the first time in her life she too was sleeping with someone of her own choice and not someone forced upon her against her will.

For both young women, but for entirely different reasons, this was the happiest night of their lives.

Chapter Five

On the road south of Salopsbury Castle, a lone rider pulled his white horse to a halt before a swift running stream. A donkey tethered to the horse's saddle drew up alongside and sunk his nose deep into the murky waters. Snorts followed as water gushed upwards through the donkey's nostrils. The rider pulled on the reins. He was not planning to dismount.

Leaning forward in the saddle, he spoke in Latin.

"*Maneo Ventalbi*," he whispered in the horse's ear.

His words translated as, "Wait, Whitewind."

Upon hearing the command, the horse raised his head and settled.

The stream that lay before the horse and the rider was wide, but by all reports not very deep and could be forded easily. The centre of the stream ran straight and swift, but to either side, stood reeds and marshy ground. The road on which the lone rider travelled sloped gently down into the waters of the stream but rose steeply over on the far bank. The lone rider stood high in the saddle and looked to the far bank. Under normal circumstances the crossing before him would hold little danger. For this was a much used ford, on a much travelled road that linked the city of Salopsbury in the north to the market town of Lodelowe to the south. This was the ford at Marsh Brook and both horse and rider would, under normal circumstances, just keep on riding without giving the ford a second thought. But with all the recent thunderstorms, conditions on this particular day were very different and a possible danger threatened.

Bardolph of Wessex, Royal Falconer to King Henry III of England, had been travelling south since first light of day, and with dusk approaching, in need of a much welcomed rest. If information relayed to Bardolph at a wayside inn the previous evening was reliable, then the stream that now blocked his path had to be the ford at Marsh Brook. More importantly however, Bardolph was within one hour's ride of his objective for the night. His plan was to make Onneyditch before nightfall, a small hamlet that nestled on the very edge of the great Forest of Wyre. Here, he had been reliably informed, he would find a goodly resting place that went by the name of 'The Golden Lion'. The inn and the scattering of foresters' hovels that surrounded the hamlet being less than one hour's ride south beyond the crossing of the ford at Marsh Brook, and this was where Bardolph now found himself, sat high in his saddle, the front hooves of his white horse mingling with the murky waters of the swollen stream.

With a cloudless sky and sun sinking towards the western horizon, Bardolph dismounted and let his horse drink from the swift flowing waters. He then unhitched his donkey so that he too could continue to drink from the murky, muddy waters of the stream.

Standing with the waters of the stream lapping against the toes of his boots, Bardolph looked to the far bank and cocked an ear to the wind. For the last few miles he had ridden through open countryside, but here at the ford, a dense growth of trees flourished on either side, and even though his view to the front and behind was much impaired, he knew that he was not alone. To the far side of the stream he could hear horses moving fast, possibly up to half a dozen, and they were heading his way. He turned his attention to the road he had just travelled. A cart trundled a short distance behind, and had been for most of the afternoon. Bardolph shrugged his shoulders. There was not a lot he could do about the presence of fellow travellers, for this was a major road. Significantly, there were milestones by the side of the road, so this must be a major route. The last milestone passed indicated that he was some seventeen miles north of Lodelowe.

Bardolph returned his attention to the ford and his immediate dilemma. The distance between the two banks was not far, but the stream, swollen and muddied by recent thunderstorms, had made conditions such that it was impossible to judge the depth. He furrowed his brow and considered one further possibility. One hour's ride back there was a fork in the road that would take him further to the west. Here, the road traversed the tops of the hills of Welsh border country and would, in all probability, avoid the flooding in the valleys. But this alternative route offered one big drawback. It would add another couple of days to his journey, and besides, he was still not certain the route would avoid further flooding. He shrugged his shoulders. Whichever and whatever, there were bound to be other obstacles to his path, be it this one or the next, and with all the recent thunderstorms some streams would be even more formidable than the one that now stood before him.

Bardolph's concern, however, lay neither in his own safety, nor for that matter with the wellbeing of his animals, since both horse and donkey were quite capable of making the crossing. His anxieties lay elsewhere. He was far more concerned with the protection of his precious cargo. A cargo held in cages and strapped to the back of his donkey. For within the cages, there held a pair of extremely rare peregrine falcons. These were hunters of the air that flew and struck down prey with their great talons and huge powerful beaks. At present they were fledglings, but with adulthood and training they would eventually learn to follow the Royal Hunt and go for the kill at the King's sole command.

Bardolph was nearing the end of his long journey and now found himself in an area of England that bordered with the Kingdom of Wales. If he could keep up the same good rate of progress, then another ten days would see his journey through. When he had first set out from his lodge, at the edge of the King's New Forest in the ancient Kingdom of Wessex, snow was on the ground, now it was late summer. To begin with, his task appeared daunting, but he had managed to see it through. On the King's own command he had travelled north to the Kingdom of Scotland. Here he had stayed as a guest of King Alexander II at his palace at Scone. After this his journey took him further north and west, across the great glens to the Western Isles. At a point where the land met the endless ocean to the west, he had scaled the cliffs and taken the fledglings from their nests.

The fledglings were bigger now and were kept in two separate wooden cages, strapped to the sides of the donkey, and therefore, if the waters that now lay before him ran deep, then his fledglings were in danger of becoming submerged. What Bardolph needed was a sounding to establish the depth of the water at the centre, and this meant taking his horse in first. Wearily, he tethered his donkey to a nearby tree, remounted and rode slowly into the murky waters of the ford. The stream was flowing rapidly in the centre, but his horse remained calm and plodded slowly towards the far bank.

At the centre Bardolph pulled up his horse and looked down into the fast flowing waters of the stream. At the deepest point, the water lapped against the soles of his boots. But that was all. A feeling of relief came over him. His donkey was small, but the cages were strapped high and would be well above the waterline. The crossing was safe. He smiled and pulled on the reins, but this was as far as he got. His sharp hearing detected the imminent arrival of galloping horses approaching from the far bank. He patted his horse on the neck to keep him settled.

Immediately, the riders appeared there and issued a call from the far bank.

"Halt traveller! Stay right where you are!" the cry came.

Bardolph steadied his horse and waited.

Five soldiers on horseback came from between the trees. Within seconds they were splashing into the waters at the edge of the ford. Bardolph patted his horse's neck for assurance. The soldiers surrounded him on all sides. One took hold of his reins. He could see that four of the soldiers were men-at-arms, the fifth, his rank indicated by gold tassels on each shoulder, suggested a captain.

Bardolph manoeuvred his horse so as to confront the captain, then waited for him to settle his own horse before speaking.

The captain was a big man with a round, plump face and a large, sprawling, unkempt black beard. He was dressed in a dark blue and red halved tunic with three rampant white lions embroidered upon his chest. Bardolph did not recognise the uniform, but assumed this to be the crest of the de Clancey family whose home and castle lay at Lodelowe, some seventeen miles to the south. All five soldiers wore similar uniforms, and only the two gold-braided tassels upon his lapels set the captain apart from the rest of the men.

Before speaking the captain eyed the traveller up and down. He was curious as to who this smart young man, dressed in subtle greens of the forest, with a longbow and quiver over his shoulders and a sword on his saddle, might be. If an outlaw, then he was either brave or stupid. If not, then who was this dashing young man, with striking good looks and supporting a small, neatly trimmed beard and pencil thin moustache?

"Who dares venture onto the estates of Baron de Clancey, armed with longbow and sword?" the captain demanded, breaking the silence.

The captain's words were addressed in the tongue of the Anglo-Saxons. But whether it was Saxon or Norman, Bardolph was prepared, for he spoke many languages, including the many varied Gaelics of the Welsh and the Scots.

Bardolph gave his horse a pat on the neck to keep him settled, before replying. He spoke in the language addressed to him.

"My name is Bardolph and I venture south, returning to my home in the King's New Forest in the ancient Kingdom of Wessex," he explained.

The captain glared menacingly at Bardolph, then pointed to the bow strung about his shoulders.

"It is forbidden to hunt upon Baron de Clancey's lands," he told Bardolph. "The penalty is death."

Bardolph was ready with his reply, for this was not the first time he had been accosted in such a manner.

"Captain, can you read?" he enquired*.

"Yes, I can read," confirmed the captain.

Bardolph loosened the straps of his saddlebag and withdrew a folded parchment. He handed it to the captain.

"Then pray doth read this," he said. "I think this will answer all your questions."

The captain unfolded the parchment and stared at the contents. Even before reading he could see that the document was important, for it bore the great seal of King Henry III of England. He read the contents, which were written in three languages, Latin, those of the Anglo-Saxons and that of the Normans. He read it at least three times before re-folding and handing it back to its owner.

"Sire, it is indeed a great honour and privilege to have a Royal Falconer pass this way," he said, touching his forehead out of respect. "My name is Osbald, captain of the guard of Lodelowe and protector of the arms of the de Clancey's, and overseer for the duties of the high-sheriff of Lodelowe. If I or any of my men can be of any assistance, then pray do not hesitate to ask. We place ourselves at your service."

Bardolph stroked his small, neatly trimmed beard. Captain Osbald certainly held grand titles, but he knew this to be nothing more than professional soldier and tax collector when it came to overseeing the duties of the local sheriff. With regards the little matter of assistance, Bardolph gave the matter some thought before replying.

"Well, Captain, there is one thing you can do for me," he said. "You can help me get my donkey across safely to the other side."

Captain Osbald looked to the far bank and then towards the donkey tethered to a tree. He gave the matter some thought before addressing Bardolph.

"My men will do it," he said. "Leave it to them. Pray come with me sire, so that we may find a quiet place to talk without the rushing of waters about our feet."

This was not exactly what Bardolph had in mind, but upon seeing that the crossing held little danger, he reluctantly agreed. There were other things he needed, like fresh meat for his fledglings, and for this he needed permission to hunt.

Bardolph turned to the soldier that held his horse's reins.

"Re-tie those cages before crossing. Tie them high," he said. "Do not allow them to become submerged." He then turned towards the captain. "Those fledglings belong to the King of England," he said sternly. "In no way must they come to any harm."

Captain Osbald turned to his men.

"You heard what the Royal Falconer said," he barked. "Protect those fledglings with your lives. Now get that donkey across to the other side."

Bardolph followed Captain Osbald out of the water, up the steep bank on the other side and a little way down the rutted road in order to get away from the sound of the rushing stream. On a quiet, grassy verge some distance from the ford, but still within sight, the two men dismounted.

Historic Note: This was not a rude or insensitive question. Only about one in every hundred of the population could read during this period in history, and even those in more senior positions, such as this captain, did not necessarily fall into this category; thus the reason for the question.

As they tethered their horses to the branches of a tree, Captain Osbald turned to Bardolph and said, "Baron de Clancey does't decree that should anyone of noble birth, high rank or senior office pass this way, then they should be offered the hospitality of Lodelowe Castle. It is less than two hours ride south from here and just about reachable before sunset."

Bardolph stroked his pencil thin moustache.

"A kindly offer, captain," he replied, "but I was planning to rest at the inn at Onneyditch this very night, and this I believe is less than one hour's ride south. I am tired, and me thinks that a second hour would be just too much for a weary traveller that hath been on the road since the break of dawn."

Captain Osbald was well aware of the inn.

"Ah, a goodly inn and owned by decent gentlefolk," he exclaimed, nodding his head. "It is kept by four generations. They say that the old lady there is well passed her ninetieth birthday. But all the same, do consider Baron de Clancey's hospitality. He offers goodly fayre and a comfortable bed for the night, and we travel together for half the journey. So I beg of you not to make a final decision until we at least reach Onneyditch."

Bardolph considered Captain Osbald's offer. He had planned on spending the night at Onneyditch, then set off at first light in search of food for his peregrines. He had very little fresh meat left and his fledglings needed to be fed regularly. A night spent at Lodelowe Castle would ruin all this, especially if he were to be kept up late talking. He was already of a mind to decline, but decided now was not the right time to convey his thoughts, and besides, from the sound of it, he needed clearance to hunt. A subject he would broach upon his journey to the inn.

Bardolph began to explain, "A fine offer, captain. I will do as you ask and decide, like you say, only once we reach the ...'

But this was as far as he got before a distraction made him turn his head towards the ford.

The conversation ended abruptly as both Captain Osbald and Bardolph turned their heads towards the direction of the stream. Then, without another word being spoken, both were quickly away.

Bardolph's greatest fear had suddenly befallen him. He was desperate to know what had happened to his peregrines. What had they done to his fledglings? Were they safe? He set off at a run, with Captain Osbald matching his every stride. Bardolph, however, slowed when he saw that his donkey and fledglings were already safely across the ford and being led towards him by a soldier. He breathed a sigh of relief. His fledglings were safe and whatever the cause of the commotion, it had nothing to do with his peregrines. He ran on however, now two paces behind Captain Osbald. The problem it seemed, surrounded the arrival of a cart and a party of travellers. The cart was already mid-stream and there appeared to be an armed scuffle in the offing.

At the water's edge Bardolph stopped, removed his longbow from his shoulder, and with the ease of long practice strung it and withdrew an arrow from his quiver.

Captain Osbald, on the other hand, carried on running, plunging waist deep into the stream. Three of his men were engaged in hand-to-hand combat. All three were waist deep in the water, clashing swords with three other men. It was three against three. Three soldiers in the dark blue and red half-colours of the

Baron de Clancey, in pitch battle with three soldiers dressed in pale blue tunics with three yellow snarling lion heads emblazoned upon their chests.

One of Captain Osbald's men struck a decisive blow, running his sword through a vulnerable point between chainmail and helmet. With the luckless man's neck skewered to the hilt, the soldier set about holding him beneath the water until all signs of life had departed from his body. In the meantime, the waters ran red about the standing man's waist as he unflinchingly maintained his stance.

Bardolph turned his sight to the opposite side of the cart. Another of Captain Osbald's men was winning the day. This man had his opponent held below the water with his hands about his throat. He too, was holding his stance until all signs of resistance were gone from the man in his grip.

Suddenly, the horse pulling the cart shied and moved forward a pace. Captain Osbald stood alongside the cart, waist deep in the water, when it happened. Instinctively, he made a grab for the reins. One of his men had been swept beneath the cart, having caught a slashing blow to the thigh and lost his footing. After that, the fast flowing waters had washed him between the wheels, and as Captain Osbald arrived he was clinging to the spokes, trying desperately to stop himself from being washed downstream.

Whilst all this was going on, the soldier that had battled with the wounded man beneath the cart, had, in the melee, become parted with his sword and was bent down grovelling on the bed of the stream. Just as Captain Osbald was taking hold of the reins, the man's hand fell upon his sword. He took a firm grip, stood upright and looked around. Captain Osbald stood two paces away, fighting to control the horse that pulled the cart. With eyes ablaze and now sword in hand, the man lunged towards the captain.

Bardolph, realising what was about to happen, drew his longbow and released the arrow in one swift motion. The arrow grazed against the soldier's nose-guard and entered the eye. The man fell backwards and his sword dropped into the water with a splash alongside Captain Osbald.

No sooner had the arrow been released, Bardolph was ready to shoot again. In the short space of time it took for the first arrow to fly through the air, a second arrow was taken from its quiver, placed in the bow and the string drawn taut in readiness. But a second arrow was not required. The first, deadly aimed, had been enough to bring down the lunging attacker and effectively put an end to the conflict.

Bardolph lowered his longbow and reflected upon his shot. To be truthful, he was a little disappointed. For a man that could bring down a pigeon in full flight, and regularly practised on sparrows and other small birds, his arrow had fallen well wide of the mark. With the soldier wearing chain mail beneath his tunic and a helmet upon his head, there was little to aim for that would bring him down with a single arrow. The centre of the man's eyeball had therefore been his aim, and it was only the lucky glance off the edge of the nose-guard that had returned the arrow to its original intended target. Bardolph had been far too hasty with his shot and he knew it. He had snapped at the release when a gentle, smooth flowing action was needed. He knew where he had gone wrong and was angry with himself for not giving the shot his total concentration.

Captain Osbald settled the horse that pulled the cart, checked that the injured soldier beneath the cart was clear of the wheels, then set about leading the cart slowly out of the water. Bardolph stepped aside to let it pass. Whatever the reason for the skirmish, it was now well and truly over, and with the captain's men winning the day.

The cart was very ordinary, a simple flat bed with no sides, and with just a flat canvas cover supported by four upright poles to protect the occupants from the elements.

Seated near the centre, on four large wooden chests heavily roped down to prevent moving, sat two young women, one a young girl in her teens, the other in her mid-twenties. They were embracing each other for comfort. Both appeared to be dressed in fine attire. Yet all the same the more elderly woman appeared very much of a noble birth with a distinct air of authority, whilst the teenager had the obvious looks of a serving-wench. Each had their arms locked about each other. The younger girl was sobbing and the older woman comforting her in her arms.

Despite the adversary, the older woman sat poised with dignity. She had long, straight black hair knotted into two plaits that reached down to the waist. She was of medium to slight build and wearing a bright green dress with matching, ornately embroidered headdress. The younger girl, although seated, appeared taller and of a much bigger frame altogether. She had blonde, curly, shoulder-length locks, attired in a similar green dress of the same design, but wore a maid's white bonnet upon her head.

The soldier not involved in the action, but entrusted with the safekeeping of the peregrines had only enough time to tether Bardolph's donkey to a tree and return to find that the skirmish had ended. He came running with sword drawn. Captain Osbald handed him control of the reins and turned to Bardolph. He rested his hands upon the falconer's shoulders.

"Sire, we have known each other but for a short time, yet already I am indebted to you for the rest of my life," he said. "My good fellow, I thank you for saving my life. Although you journey far, I will make sure there remains always a welcome for you here at Lodelowe."

Bardolph shrugged his shoulders.

"I could do little else," he replied modestly and added, "A lucky shot at that."

Captain Osbald knew otherwise. This was no lucky shot. The way this traveller handled his bow told him so, but he kept his thoughts to himself. Instead, he gave Bardolph one final hug before turning to check on the rest of his men. He turned to see the soldier with a gash to his thigh being helped out of the water. Another of his men was struggling to drag a lifeless body onto the road.

"Is anyone still alive?" asked Captain Osbald, his question not addressed to anyone in particular.

The soldier nearest to him shook his head.

"No captain, all three escorts are dead," he said.

Bardolph was saddened. The skirmish, though minor, had left three men dead and another one badly wounded.

Captain Osbald helped the injured man down on the grass beside the road. He checked on the wound, then gave an order.

"Get this wound bandaged," he said. Then, upon seeing there was little else left to do, he turned to the soldier that had dragged him from the water and asked, "Egbert, what brought about this skirmish?"

The soldier removed his helmet and wrung water from his tunic before giving any reply. He was in two minds what to say. Somehow he had to get his story across in the most favourable way. Finally, he spoke.

"Captain, take a look about that woman's neck," he said and pointed towards the cart. "She wears the Baron's necklace if I am not very much mistaken. I asked that I may be permitted to gain a closer inspection, but she refused, and that's when the skirmish began. Her escorts were adamant that I get nowhere near the necklace and drew their swords. Sire, I had little choice but to take up arms. I swear to God that I am telling the truth."

Captain Osbald turned his gaze towards the cart now fully out of the water. Even before hearing Egbert's explanation, he knew that he and his men were in deep trouble. There was no way out of it. The three dead soldiers, all attired in pale blue tunics with yellow snarling lion heads upon their chests, belonged to the Fitzgeralds of Salopsbury. Worse still, this stream and this ford at Marsh Brook marked the boundary between the estates of Salopsbury and Lodelowe. The party had not even fully crossed into Lodelowe before they were assailed.

Another problem also loomed for the captain, and perhaps something far more serious. If the elder of the two women seated upon the cart turned out to be a certain lady of noble birth, then he was in deep, deep trouble. Since never having set eyes upon her, he could not be certain, but if this woman seated on the cart was Lady Adela Fitzgerald, then she was the very person he and his men had set out to meet. An order received from the Council of the Marches that very morning had decreed that Lady Adela Fitzgerald and her party be given safe passage throughout the whole of the Marches, and therefore, should she and her travelling companions ever venture onto the estates of the Baron de Clancey, then safe passage was to be ensured for all.

Captain Osbald strode towards the cart. He had to sort this matter out once and for all. He held up a hand towards the older of the two women.

"Hand me down that necklace!" he demanded.

The necklace was the only thing that would decide the fate of both himself and his men. If the necklace did in fact belong to Baron de Clancey, then perhaps the actions of his men could be justified.

Bardolph was close enough to get a good look at the item of jewellery hung about the woman's neck. It consisted of a large emerald stone set in a gold surround and suspended on an ornately woven, fine gold chain. With robbers about, he considered it unwise to display one's wealth so openly, but with soldiers as escort he guessed she must have felt safe enough to do so.

On hearing Captain Osbald's demand, the woman's servant drew her mistress to her chest.

"Go away you great fat oaf," she snarled angrily. "Leave her alone? Can't you see you've done enough harm already?"

Captain Osbald, enraged by the girl's effrontery, drew his sword and held it to her side.

"Silence, wench," he spat, "or you'll feel cold steel between your ribs."

The girl however remained defiant.

"My Lady has done nothing wrong," she bawled down from the cart. "So go away and leave us in peace."

Her mistress however, realising that the situation was getting out of hand, reacted quickly and broke away from the girl's embrace. She put a hand to her servant's mouth to silence her and covered the necklace in question with the other.

Speaking down to the captain, she said, "*Cette collier est mienne!*"

She had spoken in the language of the Normans, a tongue Captain Osbald obviously did not understand.

"The... necklace... pass... it... down..." he said, and speaking slowly and deliberately in an effort to get his message across.

"She says the necklace belongs to her," said Bardolph translating her words into the tongue of the Anglo-Saxons.

Captain Osbald turned to Bardolph.

"If she is who I think she is, then she can speak our tongue!" he snapped angrily.

"*Non!* This is my necklace!" said the woman, this time in Anglo-Saxon, and in order to save further embarrassment between the two gentlemen.

Captain Osbald stretched out a hand.

"I demand to see the necklace," he said. "Hand it down."

"*Non!* This necklace is mine!" she replied angrily and equally determined not to let the captain take it from her.

In a fit of rage, Captain Osbald swung his sword upwards and thrust it hard against the pit of her stomach. She winced. The sharpness of the blade and the force of the strike were such that the sword sliced through her dress and cut into her skin near the naval. The wound was not deep, nor life threatening, but all the same a small red patch appeared immediately about the spot where the point of the sword had pierced the flesh.

The woman looked deep into the captain's eyes and saw the rage that burned within. She could see that this was a person quite capable of killing, even a defenceless woman, and adjudged not to anger him further. Quickly, she removed the necklace from about her neck and dropped it down from the cart.

Captain Osbald caught it in one hand and withdrew his sword. Pensively, he turned his back to the cart in order to examine the necklace without interference. He had to be certain that this was the necklace in question. If Egbert was wrong and this necklace did not belong to Baron de Clancey, then he knew they were all in deep, deep trouble.

After a while Captain Osbald turned to confront the woman on the cart.

"I am of the belief that this necklace does not belong to you," he told her and with a look of much relief upon his face. "This necklace is the property of the Baron de Clancey. Consider yourself under arrest. You will come with me to Lodelowe."

On hearing this, the younger girl drew her mistress to her chest and glared down at the captain. She was angry and found nothing but contempt for this wicked man. From behind the seat she found an object that was loose amongst the travel items and hurled it down at the captain.

It was a hairbrush and it thudded against the side of the captain's head. The brush did no harm, but it incensed him. Stretching up an arm, he grabbed at the young girl's sleeve and yanked her down from the cart. She landed heavily next to his feet.

"Rope," he called to one of his men.

Within seconds a soldier appeared with two coils of rope. He handed one to his captain. The girl's sleeve was ripped and hanging from her shoulder by a thread. With a harsh kick from his boot he rolled her over to lie on her stomach. He placed a foot to the small of her back, then bent down and forced the girl's hands behind her back. The fall from the cart had winded her and she could find no strength to resist. With one end of what was a sizeable length of rope, the captain bound her hands behind her back. He then sat her up and wound what was left of the rope about her arms and body. To finish, he tied a tight knot close to the point where he had started.

"There, that should do it," he said with some satisfaction once he was done.

The soldier that retained the second coil of rope stepped forward.

"What about the woman on the cart?" he asked.

Captain Osbald looked upwards. The woman remained seated on a roped down chest. She sat erect and with the dignity expected of a lady of noble birth. He found himself in a dilemma and unsure of what to do next. If this woman was Lady Adela Fitzgerald then she had to be treated with respect. On the other hand, if she was not, then she could simply be construed as a common thief. He saw this second option as his way of escaping recrimination. He would say that he inspected the necklace, believed it to be the Baron's, then made the arrest. He was simply doing his duty and the identity of the woman he would leave for others to establish. As far as he was concerned these two women were no more than common thieves and therefore, to be treated accordingly. He turned to the soldier holding the rope.

"Yes, bind the one on the cart," he said. "However, she stays up there." Then kicking the girl at his feet in the ribs, he added, "But this one. Tether her to the back of the cart. She will walk to Onneyditch."

Captain Osbald stepped aside and watched pensively as the soldier set about binding the woman on the cart.

When he was done, the captain turned to Bardolph.

"My friend," he said, "with three bodies to bury, one man wounded and a heavy cart to pull over these rutted roads, we will be lucky to make the edge of the forest by nightfall. It seems perchance my friend that we will, after all, be spending the night together. For Onneyditch will be our resting place this very night."

Bardolph walked to his horse and donkey, and as he did so he reflected on what had just come to pass. In nearly eight months of travel he had managed to stay well clear of trouble. But now, as he neared the end of his journey, he found himself involved in a matter that was really none of his concern. He just hoped that the situation would remain that way. But somehow, he had his doubts. He held a niggling suspicion that repercussions from this small and somewhat pointless skirmish, were simply not going to go away.

Chapter Six

The bodies of those killed at the ford were laid to rest in one shallow grave over on the Salopsbury side of the stream. It seemed only right and proper that the fallen be laid to rest in land what was theirs. To mark the grave, three crosses cut from branches were placed on the mound and helmets placed on top. Captain Osbald explained that on his return to Lodelowe news of their deaths would be heralded to Salopsbury. What happened afterwards remained unclear, but the most likely outcome would be for the bodies to be exhumed and returned to Salopsbury.

Bardolph assisted in the burial and added dignity to the ceremony by saying a few words in Latin above the grave. It was the least he could do. After this, he felt under no obligation to ride with Captain Osbald and his men, but he did so at the start.

Under normal circumstances he would have remained with the party, but the cart trundled slowly over the rutted ground and, despite the incumbency of a trailing donkey, he could travel much faster. There was also something else, something more repugnant that brought about his early departure. From the outset he found it particularly distasteful to ride behind the cart and watch the young handmaiden being dragged along. With her arms tied behind her back and pulled along by a rope about her waist, she continuously tripped and stumbled on the uneven rutted ground, and when she fell, no one came to her assistance. She was simply left to regain her own footing, and for long periods bumped along behind the cart whilst struggling to regain her feet.

Having endured this unpleasantness for a short distance, Bardolph bade Captain Osbald and his party a fond farewell and set off at his own much faster pace. His excuse being he wanted to make Onneyditch before nightfall. He had looked to the west and the setting of the sun. At best, little more than one-hour's daylight remained, and Onneyditch was reportedly one goodly hour's ride south of the ford. Captain Osbald and his party, hindered by the presence of the cart and the badly rutted road, would in all probability take double this time, and it would be dark before they reached their destination.

The terrain between the ford and the northern edge of the great Forest of Wyre was flat and fertile. This was farming country with rich arable soil. To either side of the road, peasants worked the fields and being late summer, all were ripe for harvest. There were orchards too, all laden with apples for the making of cider. For this was Norman country. The invaders from across the Channel would have planted these cider-apple orchards more than a century ago, and now the trees were mature and bursting with fruit. Cider was always a Norman preference, since they considered Saxon ale most distasteful.

There were homesteads too. Bardolph passed many hovels of simple construction, mainly roofs of thatch and walls of wattle-work daubed with clay. Yet all had a sense of homeliness about them. Late summer flowers adorned the walls and smoke curled upwards from the chimneys. But all were small and dwellings of any reasonable size were few and far between.

One construction, however, did stand out. A building of considerable size, sited well away from the road and surrounded by a high wall, did catch Bardolph's eye. Much of the surrounding wall was engulfed by a dense growth of trees, yet above everything there protruded a square Norman tower. His immediate thoughts were this to be a religious establishment, but alternatives remained, perhaps a fortified manor house, or even a small, walled village.

Bardolph pulled up his horse and remaining in the saddle, looked to the building. It stood on a slope, about halfway up the rise and surrounded by open fields of golden dancing wheat. At the top of the rise there stood a small copse. He returned his gaze to the establishment that lay beyond the wall. There was a remote possibility this could be Onneyditch, for it was not unknown for even small hamlets to lie behind defensive walls, especially this close to the Welsh border. However, time was pressing, with the sun nearly set, and by his reckoning he had been travelling one goodly hour since departing the ford, he decided to ask. He turned in the saddle to face the side of the road opposite the building. A peasant hoeing between rows of cabbages worked a field a short distance away. He was just a boy, no more than eight or nine years old, but he seemed dedicated to his work and oblivious to the presence of horse and rider, pulled up on the road above.

Bardolph called down to the boy. He spoke in the tongue of the Saxons, for this seemed to be the language spoken in these parts.

He called, "Tell me young lad, what of yonder building? What is its purpose?"

The young lad looked up to see the rider on horseback pointing to the high wall over on the far side of the road.

Leaning on his hoe he called back; "That, good sire, is Wistanstow Abbey."

Bardolph's eyes settled upon the square Norman tower standing tall above the trees. He nodded his head in recognition. His initial assumption had been correct. This was a religious establishment and would be home to a community of monks and nuns. Probably of the Cluniac Benedictine Order, since its origins were obviously French.

Bardolph turned in the saddle to confront the lad who remained leaning on his hoe.

"Then what of Onneyditch?" he enquired. "How much further must I travel?"

The boy immediately pointed along the road, in the direction Bardolph was travelling.

"Onneyditch!" he called from the field, "It is not far, good sire. The village lies about two miles yonder in that direction."

Bardolph picked up the reins and kicked at his horse.

"Then I thank you for your service," he told the boy and set off.

He moved at a trot, but not that fast as to make the pace uncomfortable for his trailing donkey. His prime concern was always for his peregrines strapped high on the donkey's back. They were not his. They belonged to the King of England and were not to come to any harm. As if to indicate the late hour of the day and the need for urgency, from behind the high wall a lone church bell tolled. Bardolph counted eight. This would be the signal for the peasants to leave the fields and return to their homes.

The sun was setting and oil lamps and candles flickered in windows as Bardolph entered Onneyditch. The hamlet appeared a lot larger than expected.

Two rows of black and white timbered buildings, some with thickly thatched roofs, others with Welsh slate, faced each other across the banks of a small, yet swift flowing river. Two narrow cobbled streets followed the river to either side. This was the River Onney; a river that had started life far to the west, high in the distant Welsh Mountains, and now here at Onneyditch flowed west to east, to eventually join the southern flowing great River Severn. A single arched, humpbacked stone bridge spanned the river, and a weir a little further upstream held back the waters to provide a mill with power to grind the local flour.

Even though light was fading fast, distant objects remained visible to Bardolph's keen eyes. A little way beyond the mill and on a bend of the river, stood the remains of a motte and bailey. This, too, was past evidence of a once strong Norman presence in the area. The structure was in decay, and like most Norman defences had long since out-served its usefulness. The timber stockade that once protected the outer ditch, along with the old wooden fortification perched high atop the motte, had now fallen into disrepair. The whole site was overgrown with nettles and brambles.

He rode a little further on to confront a man walking towards him across the bridge. He stopped to ask directions.

"Tell me good sire?" he asked, "I seek the Golden Lion. Can'st you tell me of its whereabouts?"

The man pointed down the cobbled street that followed one side of the riverbank.

"It is not far. Keep to this side of the river and follow the road. You cannot miss it. There hangs a sign above the door."

Bardolph thanked the man and led his horse and donkey down the narrow cobbled street that ran alongside the north bank of the river. It was not long before that he came across the inn he was seeking. Above the door, swinging in the light wind, a weather-beaten sign displayed the heads of three snarling lions. There was no writing on the board and the colours were faded to a dirty yellow against a washed pale blue background. The sign, with three snarling lions' heads on a pale blue background, reminded Bardolph of the tunics of the three slain soldiers left buried at the ford. This was undoubtedly the coat of arms of the Fitzgeralds of Salopsbury. He pondered for a while, considering why this should be so? The hamlet of Onneyditch flourished deep within the estates of Lodelowe and he considered the arms of the de Clancey's a more appropriate display. However, he did not dwell long on the matter. His prime concern at this late hour lay with the welfare of his animals.

After passing down a narrow alleyway that ran between the inn and an adjoining dwelling, Bardolph came across a forge and stables. He dismounted and led his horse and donkey through two wide open doors.

Both stables and forge were contained within the one building. Like all constructions in Onneyditch, the walls were of timber frame and in-filled with wattle and daub. A high stone chimney towered above the slated roof, permitting the heat from the forge to pass safely into the air. If there were windows in the building then Bardolph could not see any. With night approaching, the only light within the stable came from the coals of a forge. Next to the forge a blacksmith hammered noisily on an anvil.

On sensing Bardolph's approach, the blacksmith stopped his hammering and looked up. He was a big muscular man in his mid-thirties. He spoke whilst holding a glowing horseshoe to the anvil.

"You'll be a wanting stalls for the night," he said then struck another blow with the hammer.

Bardolph nodded his head and replied, "Aye, good sire, and fresh hay and water. My animals have travelled far this day and are in much need of rest."

The blacksmith raised his head to the roof and called to the loft above.

"Ralph, come down here," he called, "Prepare two stalls for this traveller." He then set about further hammering before the shoe cooled and was in need of re-heating.

A young lad, aged no more than ten, appeared almost immediately, descending a ladder in a corner of the building. As the sound of hammer on anvil echoed about the forge, the boy led Bardolph to a row of stalls to the rear. There were about a dozen of them.

Whilst Bardolph unsaddled his horse and removed the burden from his donkey, the lad found fresh hay and filled the troughs with clean water.

When the animals were settled, Bardolph handed the boy a silver penny.

"If you watch over my horse and donkey this night, and see to it that they are not disturbed, then another silver penny awaits you in the morrow," he told him.

The boy's eyes lit up and touched his forelock in servitude.

He told Bardolph, "Aye, sire, for this I will stay awake all night. I will make sure your animals are not disturbed."

With his horse and donkey safely bedded, Bardolph crossed from the stables to the rear of the inn. He carried with him his saddlebag tossed over one shoulder and two cages, one in each hand. By now darkness had fallen. He entered the inn via a rear door and looked about him. The room was lit by lanterns hanging from beams that supported a low ceiling. The interior was clean and felt warm and cosy. Ale and cider barrels were stacked high against one wall and a large cauldron hung above the flames of an inglenook fire. A pottage bubbled above the flames and it smelt good. An old lady was seated next to the fire in a rocking chair. Other than this the room was deserted, the tables and chairs empty. Bardolph knew, however, that the inn would not remain this way for long. These were early hours and the place would soon fill once the peasants from the fields had returned home and partaken their evening meals.

The landlord appeared as Bardolph closed the door behind him. He was a man in his fifties with a round, plump, reddened face and bushy sideburns.

He enquired, "You'll be a wanting a room for the night?"

Bardolph nodded his head.

"Aye, good landlord," he replied and held up his cages. "A room that is clean and quiet for both me and my birds."

The landlord smiled and bowed low out of respect.

"All my rooms are clean and quiet," he replied. "If you'd like to follow me, good sire, I will show you to your room."

The landlord led Bardolph to the foot of the stairs. As they began to climb, Bardolph told the innkeeper, "You'd better prepare many rooms. Behind me travels the captain of the guard of Lodelowe along with four of his men and two ..." he was about to say, 'women prisoners', but changed it to "females in his charge."

The landlord stopped halfway up the stairs and turned to Bardolph.

"Ah! That would be Captain Osbald," he said. "But me thinks extra rooms will not be necessary. He and his men bed down on straw in the stables, but I can find a room for the females in his charge if that is what's required."

Bardolph said no more and followed the landlord to the top of the stairs. He considered perhaps, he had said too much. After all, Captain Osbald's problems were not of his concern.

The room was small but had a comfortable bed and clean linen. It also had a window that looked down upon the stables. The young lad Bardolph had handed the silver penny, was seated on a bale of straw by the door. A lighted lantern rested on the ground beside the boy. Bardolph was pleased to see that the lad was doing as promised.

As the landlord was leaving he addressed Bardolph.

"There is a pottage above the fire and ale or cider to drink when you are ready," he said. "Three rabbits and more vegetables were added to the pottage this very day, so it will provide a good and wholesome meal."

Bardolph nodded his head in recognition. This was how food was served to travellers. Inns invariably kept a large pot boiling over an open fire, ready for travellers to fill their bowls. These pots never emptied and usually had something added to them daily. Three rabbits would make the pottage particularly inviting.

"Yes, I will feed my birds then partake in your fine hospitality," he told the landlord. Then out of curiosity, he asked, "Three rabbits you say? Then rabbits must be plentiful in these parts?"

The landlord nodded his head.

"Aye, sire," he replied, "There is a copse riddled with warrens that overlooks an abbey just a few miles north of here. We never lack in rabbits. It is the hunting of wild boar and venison in the Forest of Wyre that is forbidden."

Bardolph stroked his small beard thoughtfully. He recalled passing the copse on his way to Onneyditch. Rabbit meat would do nicely, since wild boar and venison were not necessary for his birds. He nodded his head. He had a plan for the morrow. He would venture out at the break of dawn and travel to the copse. With his keen eye and longbow he could foresee no difficulty in bagging a rabbit or two.

The door was closing when Bardolph called, "Then landlord, I will enjoy your fine pottage and I will swill it down with some of your finest ale."

Chapter Seven

Bardolph descended the stairs of the inn. An hour had passed since his arrival and the place was filling with peasants from the fields. The room, silent when he first arrived, now buzzed with activity and conversation. As Bardolph descended the last stair, Captain Osbald and his men entered on the far side of the room.

The captain spotted Bardolph standing at the foot of the stairs and immediately set off across the room to join him. As he moved between tables he dismissed his men with a wave of the hand, sending them away to a vacant table.

All four soldiers under Captain Osbald's command were present, including the soldier wounded at the ford. He walked dragging a heavily bandaged leg, hobbling with two men supporting him to either side. His uniform was dishevelled, muddied from the ford and reddened with blood

Captain Osbald gave Bardolph a hearty hug, slapped him on the back and said, "My dear friend, it is time to repay you for what you did for me at the ford today. All hospitality, including your stay at this goodly inn, will be indebted to me. I will tell the landlord that this is to be so."

Bardolph felt embarrassed. He had done very little other than shoot a single arrow, and besides he had already paid for his room and had no intention of drinking more than one tankard of Saxon ale. However, one priority did remain. He needed to set out at sunrise for the copse behind Wistanstow Abbey in order to bag a few rabbits for his peregrines. Having learnt from the landlord that rabbits were plentiful around the abbey, he saw no reason to enter the forest. However, all the lands around Onneyditch belonged either to the church or Baron de Clancey, and he felt it only courteous to seek permission, regardless of where he should hunt.

Bardolph, being a Royal Falconer and in possession of a charter signed by the King of England, did not think he would have much trouble gaining this permission and was prepared to ask outright, but decided it more prudent to take up Captain Osbald's offer of a drink and broach the subject once seated at a table.

"A tankard of fine Saxon ale will do fine," he told the captain. "I will'st drink it whilst partaking in a bowl of the landlord's finest pottage."

The two men went separate ways, Captain Osbald to secure a table in a quiet corner and to order ale, and Bardolph to take up a bowl and move across the room to the inglenook fireplace.

An old lady rocked in a creaking chair alongside a blazing open fire. Bardolph recalled something the captain had said at the ford, something about the inn being run by four generations and an elderly lady that was well into her nineties. If this were true then this was a remarkable age. Men and women rarely made the 'three score years and ten' mentioned in the bible, and sixty was considered a ripe old age. Bardolph, therefore, felt it only courteous to speak to the old lady whilst he ladled pottage into his bowl.

More out of admiration than respect, he greeted her by saying, "Good evening ma'am, I pray that you remain hale and hearty, and in good health."

The old lady rocked the chair at an increased pace before replying.

"Aye, it is young man, and God willing I will outlive many of those that are here in this room this very night," she said.

Bardolph looked about the room and smiled. The life expectancy of the farming community was probably no more than fifty, fifty-five at most. All toiled hard and long without a break. They would attend church every Sunday, but this was about the only break they would get. He checked on the ages of all those present. There was no one in this room approaching anywhere near old age. The woman sat by the fire was probably three times the age of the next eldest person in the room.

As he ladled more pottage into his bowl, he said, "And I hope that you do outlive them all ma'am, for you are looking good for your ninety years."

The old lady smiled and showed one tooth at the front of what was otherwise a toothless mouth.

"Aye, I am ninety-three, ninety-four this coming autumn," she said. "I was born in the year eleven-hundred and forty-two when King Stephen was on the throne and the Normans were defending their mottes."

Bardolph nodded his head in recognition. He was well aware of England's turbulent history and the invasion of the Normans and there had been a noticeable touch of Anglo-Saxon venom to her voice.

He spoke politely in return, saying, "Then you will have witnessed a lot of changes ma'am."

The rocking chair moved at an even swifter pace.

"Changes! That I have! Aye, sire, that I have! A curse on all Normans!" the old lady muttered angrily and spat at the mention of the Normans.

It had never been Bardolph's intention to upset the old lady, but he could see that he had touched a raw nerve. He tried to calm her down.

"Then may we be thankful that the Norman influence wanes and the good King Henry and the House of Plantagenet does't speak our Saxon tongue," he said.

As the rocking chair continued to creak at a constant pace, Bardolph finished filling his bowl and bowed politely. He wished that he could spend more time with the old lady. She would surely have many a tale to tell, especially of the coming of the Normans, but at this hour he was a guest of Captain Osbald and could not ignore the hospitality afforded to him. He stepped away from the inglenook.

"Then I bid you a good evening ma'am, and may your remarkable health continue," he said.

Bardolph retraced his steps, placed his bowl upon the table and took a seat opposite Captain Osbald. A tankard of ale awaited him. To strike up a conversation he mentioned his encounter with the old lady.

"It is a remarkable old lady that does't sit by the fire," he said. "She informs me she is in her ninety-third year."

Captain Osbald took a swig from his tankard and wiped his mouth with the back of his sleeve.

"That's Agatha, a goodly old lady with a stout Saxon heart," he said. "She once served within the walls of Lodelowe Castle and is known and liked by many. She outlived her husband and children, and it is her grandson that is now landlord of this inn."

Bardolph spooned pottage from his bowl.

Between spoonfuls he enquired, "You mentioned at the ford did you not, that four generations does't run this goodly inn?"

Captain Osbald swigged more ale before explaining, "Aye, this inn and the stables belong to one family. The landlord's son is the blacksmith and he in turn has a young lad that tends the animals waiting to be shoed."

Bardolph reckoned the count would be five generations if you included the old lady's dead children, but he made no comment. It was four generations that lived and ran the premises.

The level of conversation remained light and cordial, and Bardolph preferred it this way. His thoughts at this late hour lay very much on retiring to his room and getting some well-deserved rest. But to keep the conversation going, he commented on the young lad in the stables, since he had given him a silver penny to stay alert throughout the night.

"I have perchance met both the blacksmith and his son," he said. "For the price of one silver penny I have entrusted the charge of my animals to the boy this night. So I hope he does't not fall asleep on the job."

Captain Osbald laughed heartily and downed more ale.

"And I too hope that he does't not sleep, for the lad makes a goodly profit out of us both this night," he replied, "For I too have given him a silver penny, though not to keep vigil over my animals, but to keep a watchful and alert eye on my prisoners."

Bardolph had been wondering about the two women, but had refrained from mentioning the fact, considering this to be none of his business. He had however, out of courtesy, expected them to be found rooms at the inn. He recalled commenting on the fact earlier to the landlord, but since then had not been aware of any activity in the upstairs' rooms. Furthermore, the four soldiers that accompanied Captain Osbald were all here in the room and seated at a table.

Out of curiosity Bardolph asked, "Pray tell me captain, what hath become of the prisoners?" Then looking about the room, he added, "I do not see them here! Does't you not offer them a bed for the night?"

Captain Osbald roared with laughter and thumped his tankard hard against the table.

He shook his head and explained, "A bed for the night you say? Nay sire, they'll get no fine bed from me. A bed of straw if they are lucky, but that's all they'll be getting from me this night."

Bardolph made no further comment. He considered the welfare of the prisoners none of his concern. He finished his pottage, downed the tankard of ale and rose from the table.

"Then captain, I will bid you a goodly night," he said. "I must arise at the break of dawn and hunt food for my peregrines. A point I hope that is acceptable to you, since I believe the lands around here doth belong to Baron de Clancey."

Captain Osbald was surprised to find Bardolph retiring so early, but understood. He too needed an early rise in order to continue on with his journey south to Lodelowe. As regards Bardolph's permission to hunt, he held no objections. He could not, anyway. As someone of lowly and common birth, he did not have the power or authority to prevent a Royal Falconer from hunting anywhere in the estates of Lodelowe, and besides, someone under Royal Charter from King Henry III of England probably held more sway than the Baron.

"My dear friend, you may hunt wherever the need does't take you," he replied. "The Baron's lands are yours to hunt and kill. I will'st convey this to him on the morrow."

"Then pray doth convey my gratitude to the baron," said Bardolph. "And tell him that I too will announce this grateful gesture to the king whence I see him next. But now I must retire to my room. I bid you goodnight my good captain. I thank you for your kind hospitality, and I wish you a sound and goodly night's sleep. It is now my desire to make one final check on my animals before retiring to my room."

Captain Osbald nodded in recognition.

"And a goodly night to you too, my dear friend," he said. "If perchance our lives does't never cross again, then I pray that your journey to the king's New Forest at Wessex does't go kindly for you, and may God and St. Christopher bide well with you on the long road south."

Bardolph bowed his head and took his leave. It was getting late. But one final visit to the stables was in order.

The young lad, Ralph, was seated upon a bale of straw outside the stable doors when Bardolph appeared. On seeing the Royal Falconer he stood up immediately. The interior was in darkness and a lantern burned on the ground alongside the door. Bardolph put an ear to the partially opened door. Inside all was quiet. The forge was out and the blacksmith gone. Only the snuffle of horses and the occasional rustle of straw could be heard.

"Does't all go well inside?" Bardolph enquired of the lad.

Ralph touched a forelock.

"Aye, sire, all goes well," he said. "Your animals will find goodly comfort this night."

Bardolph gave the lad a nod of approval. He was content with what he had heard. This was as far as he intended to go. To step inside the stable at this late hour would have a detrimental effect on his horse and donkey. He turned to walk away but stopped immediately and cocked an ear. Between the low snorts and shuffling of straw he perceived a noise that could only have issued from the mouth of a young girl. It was simply a faint murmur, drifting out through the partially opened door, but it was enough to suggest that from somewhere inside, all was not well.

Bardolph turned to Ralph, who had returned to sitting on the bale of straw. He pointed to the gap in the stable door.

"Tell me lad, what was that sound?" he enquired. "What goes on in there? Me thinks me heard the voice of a female in distress!"

Ralph nodded his head. He knew exactly what the noise would be even though he had heard nothing.

"Aye, sire, you did indeed," he told Bardolph. "The captain holds two female prisoners within these stables. He has left them in my charge until he returns from the inn. He assures me they are well tied down and cannot escape."

Bardolph bent down and picked up the lantern from the ground.

"Then I must seek out what disturbs them," he told Ralph. "Constant calls and murmuring throughout the night can only add distress to my animals, and this cannot be allowed."

With lantern held high, Bardolph entered the stables. Ralph stood up to follow, but Bardolph beckoned him to remain.

"Nay, lad, you stay here and keep a watchful eye on the doors," he said. "I enter the stable alone. Do not let anyone else enter. Tell Captain Osbald and his men to wait here until my return."

Ralph was a good lad and understood. He moved back to sit once more upon the bale of straw. He would guard the door and let no one pass.

Guided by light from the lantern, Bardolph crossed to the rear of the stable. Arranged in a long line there stood a row of small wooden compartments. His horse and donkey occupied the first two. He was aware of this. With lantern held high he leaned over the first partition and peered inside. His white stallion stood with head bowed. He whinnied in recognition and Bardolph patted his nose.

"Good boy, Whitewind, now relax," he whispered. "Get some rest."

Bardolph edged along to the next stall and leaned over the partition. His donkey was lying on his side with legs outstretched. He was spread out on a thick bed of straw and looked comfortable and relaxed. The donkey lifted his head, brayed briefly then settled down again.

Bardolph moved on down the row. In the adjoining box, he found Captain Osbald's horse. Moving on with lantern held high he recognised the other horses in turn. With just one more stall to investigate, he raised his lantern and peered over the partition. The two women prisoners were here; both bound with their hands behind their backs and with many a tight coil passed about their upper torso and arms. It was quite evident that nothing had been done to relieve them of their bonds since the ford. These were the ropes they were bound with when arrested. The elder of the two women, however, had been treated lightly. She was lying on a bed of straw with her ankles lashed together and secured to a post at her feet. On the appearance of the lantern she turned her head, then, on recognising that the holder was someone she had encountered at the ford, she quickly turned away not wanting to know.

On the other hand, the serving wench had been dealt with more harshly. She was stood to her feet in a far corner with her back to a post. She was lashed firmly to it. Coils of rope, in addition to those that already bound about her, had been wound about her body and around the upright pillar. She was bound from neck to foot, with very little movement afforded to her other than the motion of the head.

"Water! Please, water!" she croaked in a faint and much distressed voice.

Bardolph entered the stall and hung his lantern upon a hook. He found a ladle and filled it from a trough. He placed the ladle to the girl's lips and allowed her to drink. Her face was bruised and cut from the falls of the journey, and her dress torn and soiled. He ripped away a small portion of the dress from the hem and soaked it in the trough. He then wiped away the grime from her face. She winced as the cold water touched the many grazes to her cheeks.

Bardolph was saddened and shook his head. However, despite the sympathy on his part and the obvious suffering on hers, his thoughts at this late hour lay primarily with his horse and donkey. He, therefore, saw no option available other than to get this poor girl down upon the straw. Quickly, he set about unwinding the rope that bound her to the post.

As he did so he spelt out his concern, telling her, "I cannot allow you to remain like this. My animals will become much disturbed should your constant murmuring persist."

Bardolph did not untie the girl completely, retaining those bonds applied about her body at the ford. When she was free of the post he helped her down, laid her beside the other prisoner and bound her feet. He then offered the girl a final drink, and as she drank he spoke so that both women should hear.

He told them, "I will leave word with the captain that you are not to be further disturbed this night. Now rest and get some sleep."

As Bardolph walked away he heard the older woman whisper, "Thank you, kind sire, for all that you have done."

But he did not turn around or acknowledge that he had heard. He had done all he could and remained philosophical. There was nothing in his power that would alter their fate. Quite simply, they were none of his concern. By nightfall on the morrow he planned to be many miles south of Lodelowe and out of their lives.

The young lad Ralph stood up as Bardolph stepped out of the stables. He touched his forelock in servitude. Bardolph returned the lantern and took out a silver penny from his purse. He handed him the coin.

"This penny is for you, Ralph," he said. "You must tell the captain that I have re-tied one of his prisoners and laid her to rest upon the straw. Tell him, I have done so in order that my animals rest soundly this night. Tell him that the prisoners must not be allowed to make any further disturbance, and that I have given instructions that this must be so. Remind him that he will feel the wrath of the King of England if my instructions are ignored. Priority must rest with my horse and donkey. They must not be disturbed this night and that is by order of the king."

Ralph took the silver penny from Bardolph and touched his forelock.

"I will'st convey your message to the captain," he said. "Your animals will rest soundly this night. Pray rest assured that this be so."

Bardolph turned and walked from the stables, crossing the small alleyway and entering the inn via the rear door. Captain Osbald had joined his men and was sitting at a far table when he entered. They were laughing and joking and did not see him as he made for the stairs.

Back in his room, Bardolph settled down in his bed and pulled the covers over his body. It was his intent to sleep well that night and he tried to cast all thoughts of the prisoners from his mind. After all, they were none of his concern. But somehow, those thoughts would not go away.

Chapter Eight

Unlike the city of Salopsbury, protected by an area bounded by castle and a long horseshoe bend of the river, the market town of Lodelowe relied entirely on walls for defence. Outermost were the town walls, tall and wide with ramparts that could be walked by six men standing abreast. They formed an irregular circle that rose and fell, following the contours of the land. Within this outer circle lay the castle, and within the castle lay a third defence. This was the impregnable castle keep.

Though Salopsbury and Lodelowe were very different in both size and structure, there were however, many similarities. Like Salopsbury, there were two gates to Lodelowe, one to the east, the other to the west. The west gate stood before a fortified bridge that spanned the River Teme that ran alongside the western section of the outer walls. On the opposite side of the town, the east gate was high and wide, guarded by two towers, and a focal point for three merging roads from north, south and east. Both gates were constantly guarded and always closed during the hours of darkness.

The most notable differences lay in the position and construction of the castles. Salopsbury Castle, built entirely of red sandstone, stood on the outside of the city and in effect, completed a circle created by the vast loop in the River Severn. On the other hand, Lodelowe Castle was built of grey granite and stood completely within the town's defensive outer walls, and rested on a rise that towered above the town. Its walls, like the outer defences, were irregular in shape, with high ramparts and towers to the north, south, east and west.

At the very heart of the castle, standing impregnable and imposing, and perched atop a steep and rocky outcrop, stood the castle's keep. The walls were some twenty feet thick, and the windows, of which there were few, were nothing more than narrow archer-slits. It was rumoured that from the top of the tower, a clear and uninterrupted view of all the Baron's estates could be seen. But very few had ever been privileged to scale the heights and discover whether this be true or not.

Baron Richard de Clancey, overlord and supreme master of the estates of Lodelowe, Stanton and all of the Clees, was in his fiftieth year. He was an agile and sprightly man with nothing to suggest his advancing years other than a greying beard.

This particular day was a Tuesday, and normally on this day of the week the Baron would be seated astride his horse and leading his entourage, company of archers and hunting dogs out into the great Forest of Wyre. But this particular Tuesday was to be different. This day, the last Tuesday of August, in the year of our Lord 1235, had long been set aside to settle matters regarding taxes. This Tuesday, as was this day once a year, was the day when budgets were to be set and taxes agreed for both Lodelowe and the Crown.

Baron Richard de Clancey was seated with the high sheriff and his bailiffs in the south wing of Lodelowe castle when the captain of the guard burst in through the wide double doors at the far end of the great hall. Alongside the captain, raced the burly figure of Cuthred, the castle's sergeant-at-arms. Both were attired in the dark blue and red halved tunics of Lodelowe, the only difference in their attire being the tassels on their shoulders. One wore golden tassels, the other red.

About a dozen or so of the town's most senior clerics and officials, including the high sheriff of Lodelowe, were seated around a long table with the Baron at the head. As the doors flung open the hall fell silent and all eyes turned towards the two hurriedly approaching soldiers.

Without seeking pardon for his untimely interruption, Captain Osbald strode purposefully down the hall and placed a single item of jewellery upon the table before the Baron.

"I tried to stop him, my Liege!" protested Sergeant Cuthred, out of breath and apologising for his apparent lapse of security.

Anger flared within the Baron, for he had left implicit instructions that he should not be disturbed. However, he was well aware that his captain would never do such a thing unless it was extremely important, so he kept his council. Without reprimand to his sergeant for his inability to follow a simple instruction, he picked up the object laid before him and turned it over in his hands.

Despite the bright mid-morning sunshine that bathed the castle's ramparts, light entering the narrow, leaded windows of the great hall was poor and candles flickered along the full length of the table. In order to gain closer inspection the Baron drew the nearest candlestick and began to scrutinise the item placed before him. In his hand he held a large, green, dewdrop emerald embedded in a gold surround and suspended on an intricately woven fine gold chain. He recognised the item of jewellery. This necklace once belonged to his father and was part of a haul taken from the castle's strongroom some three weeks earlier.

The Baron raised his head and looked towards those seated at the table.

"Gentlemen, pray, leave the hall," he told them. "I have important matters to attend to."

There followed neither muttering nor dissent. It was obvious from the way the captain had approached the table that serious matters were afoot. So each in turn rose silently from his chair, bowed his head towards the Baron and made for the exit.

The Baron waited patiently as books and ledgers were gathered up and toted away. As the last man trundled towards the door, his arms laden with manuscripts, the Baron turned to his sergeant. With a dismissive wave of his hand he beckoned him to follow the others from the hall.

"Sergeant, you may leave us," he told him. "My business is with the captain alone."

Sergeant Cuthred beat his chest with clenched fist, clicked his heels, turned and marched purposefully from the hall.

The Baron waited for the doors to close before turning to his captain.

He raised the necklace in his hand and asked, "Tell me, Captain, how did'st you come by this?"

Captain Osbald moved forward a pace to stand against the corner of the long table. He, like Sergeant Cuthred, saluted with clenched fist against his chest. However he refrained from giving an immediate answer. Before replying there was something he needed to know. Naturally it was wrong and against protocol to speak out of turn, but nevertheless he still put his question to the Baron.

"My Liege, is this your father's necklace?" he asked and pointed to the item clutched in the Baron's hand. "If so, then pray doth tell me, was it amongst the items taken from your strongroom some three weeks past?"

The Baron frowned upon his captain's effrontery. It was not acceptable for any underling to question him. However, he kept his council and considered Captain Osbald's question. It was true, a midnight robbery had taken place within the walls of his castle some three weeks earlier, many items of value had been stolen and one of his men murdered. This necklace was one of those items. He therefore, answered his captain.

He told him, "Yes Captain, this is my father's necklace, and yes, it was taken from my strongroom." He then came directly to the point, saying, "Now, pray tell me Captain, how did'st you come by this?"

Confirmation that this truly was the stolen necklace made Captain Osbald breathe more easily. He could now relate events as they actually happened. But all the same, it remained his intent to tell the tale in a way that favoured both himself and his men. As far as he was concerned, the two women arrested at the ford were nothing more than common thieves. This was to be his story.

He explained, "My Liege, late yesterday at the setting of the sun my patrol came upon a cart and armed escort at the ford at Marsh Brook to the north of here. The ford runs unusually deep for this time of year and three of my men went to the aid of the party. Whilst assisting with the crossing, the keen eye of Egbert spotted this necklace about the neck of a lady seated upon the cart. He asked that it be handed down in order to gain closer inspection, but his request was refused, and after a long and bitter argument a fight ensued."

The Baron raised an eyebrow. This report was most unusual. Reports of skirmishes within his boundaries were uncommon. However his first concern was for his men.

"Were there any casualties?" he asked. "Were any of my men injured?"

Captain Osbald shook his head.

He answered, "My Liege, three soldiers escorted the cart. All three were slain. One of my men was wounded, though nothing serious, just a flesh wound to the thigh and he will survive." Then, as an afterthought he added, "The physician attends to his injuries as we speak."

The Baron stroked his beard, thankful that his men were safe. After a brief reflection, he moved on.

He asked, "So, Captain, what has transpired? You presumably made arrests? You say a lady was on the cart?"

Captain Osbald nodded his head.

He told the Baron, "Yes, my Liege, I made arrests. Those that remained upon the cart were arrested and brought here to Lodelowe."

The Baron gave a nod of approval and asked, "And what number might this be. How many remained upon the cart?"

Captain Osbald considered the time now right to mention the noblewoman.

He explained, "Two females remained upon the cart. I arrested both. They purport to be a noblewoman and her handmaiden, but I have my doubts. It is my belief they are no more than common thieves."

The Baron stroked his beard thoughtfully. The mention of a noblewoman and her handmaiden came as a surprise. He had assumed those arrested to be either his minions or Welsh raiders from across the border.

Concerned, he asked for clarification, saying, "This noblewoman you speak of? Is she of these parts? Do I know her?"

Captain Osbald replied with a hint of caution to his voice, saying, "It is possible my Liege, but I have my doubts. This noblewoman purports to be the Lady Adela Fitzgerald. But I have never laid eyes upon her, so I cannot say if this be true or not."

On hearing the name Fitzgerald, the Baron rose from his chair and thumped the table. Before him, candlesticks jumped and rocked under the impact. He turned his back on his captain and stared blankly up at the great tapestries of his ancestors, hung upon the wall behind his chair. And whilst he stared, he reflected upon a proclamation heralded to his castle just two days earlier. The Council of the Marches had issued instructions that Lady Adela Fitzgerald was free to journey south and return to her home in Normandy. The proclamation further decreed that should she venture onto the estates of Lodelowe, then she was to be offered safe escort and protection. Obviously if this woman on the cart proved to be Lady Adela Fitzgerald, then communications had gone badly wrong.

After much contemplation the Baron turned to face Captain Osbald.

"Captain, where is this person now?" he asked. "This woman you arrested, the one who purports to be Lady Adela Fitzgerald?"

Captain Osbald pointed to a window that looked down upon the courtyard.

He told the Baron, "She and her handmaiden are seated upon a cart in the courtyard and awaiting further instructions, my Liege."

The Baron moved to the window and from his lofty position looked down upon the courtyard. Two women were seated upon the rear of a cart, their legs trailing behind. Their upper bodies were coiled in rope and each had their hands secured behind their back. From his elevated position he could not see their faces, but the long black plaited hair of one of the prisoners made his heart sink. As if she felt his gaze, the woman looked up to the window and for a brief moment he saw her face. He shook his head slowly from side to side. There was no doubt about it; he recognised this woman; his captain had indeed arrested the Lady Adela Fitzgerald.

Thoughtfully, the Baron turned the necklace over in his hands and pondered upon the dilemma that now confronted him. His captain had indeed brought back with him a veritable hornet's nest of problems. The Fitzgeralds were masters of the neighbouring estates to the north of Lodelowe and Lady Adela Fitzgerald was well known and highly respected throughout the whole of the Marches. He collected his thoughts and tried to seek a solution. But for the time being, he could see no way out. To accuse this Fitzgerald woman of murder and robbery would turn all eyes towards Lodelowe, and this was something he could very well do without. He looked at the necklace in his hand and clutched it tightly. A deep anger flared and he shook a fist in rage. This was his father's necklace and this woman on the cart, be her of noble birth or not, had no right to wear it.

In time, the Baron's anger abated and he reverted to pondering upon the quandary that now confronted him. It was possible even as he spoke, that news of Lady Adela's arrest was spreading throughout the whole of the Marches. The peasants in the fields would almost certainly have seen her passing and since then, those that milled about the courtyard would have gained knowledge of her presence. He was therefore of the opinion that perhaps his best course of action was to simply let her continue on with her journey. The death of three escorts could, admittedly with some difficulty, be swept to one side and it would be no problem to replace them with his men and send them on their way. But somehow he could not see this as the solution. It simply rode in the face of justice. It was he that had been wronged, and as an upholder of the law it was his solemn duty to see criminals brought to justice.

The Baron, therefore, saw two possible solutions. One was to simply let the noblewoman go and in doing so, put an end to the matter. The other was to accuse her of murder and robbery, and in doing so have all eyes turn towards Lodelowe. He pondered long and hard before reaching his decision, in the end it was his heart that won the day. He simply had to do what he considered to be the right and proper thing to do. He made up his mind. The Norman noblewoman, Lady Adela Fitzgerald, would stand trial for theft and accessory to murder.

The Baron turned to his captain, his mind now made up.

"Well, Captain, it seems you have indeed arrested the Lady Adela Fitzgerald," the Baron told him. "But it makes little difference. You did the right and proper thing. This necklace belongs to me. She is a thief and she will stand trial for her crimes."

Captain Osbald bowed his head in recognition of the praise bestowed upon him.

"I thank you, my Liege, for the confidence you bestow on me," he replied.

The Baron took out a large silver coin from his purse and handed it to the captain.

"Give this silver crown to the man who spotted the necklace. Give it as a reward for his vigilance," he said and adding, "Also offer him promotion. A man with such a keen eye deserves to be at least a corporal in my army."

Captain Osbald took the coin.

"I will see to it that Egbert gets this silver crown and is promoted through the ranks, my Liege," he said and went on to ask, "But what pray must be done with the prisoners?"

The Baron stroked his beard thoughtfully. Speaking slowly and deliberately, he explained what actions were to be taken.

He told his captain, "Take the noblewoman to the north tower and take the handmaiden to my dungeon. You will personally oversee their confinement. Treat them both with respect. Neither must come to any harm. You may grant the handmaiden a blanket and a candle. The Norman you will treat as a lady of noble birth, and she will'st have a comfortable bed and wholesome food and fresh water. But she is to speak to no one and no one is to speak to her. Keep her isolated. Perhaps a bible will not go amiss. When you have done this, have the cart searched and search the prisoners too, just in case they conceal further stolen items about their person. But be not hasty. Give them time to reflect upon their crime. In the meantime, I will resume my meeting with the sheriff and his bailiffs. We have quite some hours left before our deliberations are through. Pray, summon them to return. Now Captain, you may go and perform your duties."

Captain Osbald saluted with clenched fist across his chest.

"Very good, my Liege," he said.

He turned to march away, but other than rocking on his heels he made no forward movement. With all talk of Lady Adela Fitzgerald and the stolen necklace, he had completely forgotten to mention the arrival of a King's falconer to Lodelowe. He turned to the Baron.

"My Liege, I have one more thing to report," he said. "My party also encountered another traveller at the ford and he did'st assist us greatly in the skirmish. A Royal Falconer no less, and under charter of the King of England. He passes this way, travelling south to the ancient Kingdom of Wessex."

The Baron raised an eyebrow. Royal visitors to Lodelowe were few and far between.

"Then I hope you did'st offer him my hospitality and a room for the night at my castle?" he said.

Captain Osbald nodded his head.

"Aye, I did'st so my Liege," he confirmed, "but the Royal Falconer insisted on going his own way. I bade him farewell at the inn at Onneyditch at break of dawn this very morning. He asked that he should be permitted to hunt should he come across hogs or venison on his journey south through the Forest of Wyre. I naturally gave him the permission he so desired."

As Captain Osbald spoke, the Baron's mind quite naturally rested heavily upon other matters. Giving some wayward traveller permission to hunt was neither here nor there. But then a thought occurred to him. This man, a Royal Falconer, was someone known to the King, and it gave him an idea. He mulled the thought over in his mind before speaking.

Eventually, he came to ask his captain, "Pray, doth tell me Captain, you mentioned did you not that this traveller assisted you in the fight? Then I take it, apart from being Royal Falconer to the King, he is also an able swordsman?"

Captain Osbald shook his head.

"Nay, my Liege," he explained, "his weapon was the longbow and an accompanying keen eye. And for that praise be, I owe this man a great debt, for he saved my life at the ford. He shot an arrow through the eye of a Fitzgerald soldier, just as he was about to strike me down. Without his timely intervention I would be dead now, my Liege. I must surely owe this man my life, of this there is no doubt."

The Baron tried not to show his delight, but this was exactly the sort of information he was looking for. Now he had a good excuse to waylay this Royal Falconer and bring him to his castle. But caution remained. It would be wrong to mention his plans at this early stage.

He put a simple question to his captain, asking him, "Tell me Captain, what is the name of this Royal Falconer? And where did'st you say he hails?"

Captain Osbald related what little he knew.

He told the Baron, "My Liege, his name is Bardolph and he hails from the south, from the King's New Forest in the ancient Kingdom of Wessex. He passes this way with a brace of young peregrines, presents from the King of Scotland no less."

If more delight was possible then it did not show in the Baron's eyes. But this was excellent news. For Lady Adela's trial to result in a successful conviction, then he needed to assemble a court that would look more favourably towards Lodelowe than Salopsbury. This would not be easy and a certain amount of guile and cunning was needed. He already had one or two people in mind to stand in judgement at the trial, but to make everything appear totally unbiased, what he needed was someone whose credentials could not be challenged; someone totally impartial and not connected with either the Baron's own lands, or those of the Fitzgerald's. A king's falconer from the ancient Kingdom of Wessex would be the ideal person for this purpose.

The Baron mulled this thought over in his mind and concluded the arrival of the Royal Falconer an opportunity too good to be missed. This man's chance arrival offered the ideal solution to the problem. He managed a smile. At last he could see a way out of his predicament. He would ask the Royal Falconer to stand in judgement against the accused. The Baron's knowledge of the law was not good, but enough to believe he was on safe ground. Under the terms of King John's great charter, the *Magna Carta,* some twenty years earlier, a proclamation issued by his court at Lodelowe and ratified by the Council of the Marches could not be refused. Not even if issued to a servant of the king. This much power had been passed to the barons by royal decree, and a new order existed in the land.

Not wanting to reveal his true plans at this stage, the Baron told his captain, "Then all the more reason to greet a man who keeps such distinguished company. I think a reception in his honour is in order, do you not agree?"

It was the turn of Captain Osbald to smile. Quite naturally, he was delighted that the man who had saved his life should stay as an honoured guest of the Baron.

"I will convey this to him, my Liege. But a fast horse is needed, for me thinks he will be many miles south of Lodelowe by now," he said.

The Baron looked to the sunlight beaming in through the windows. Already the sun was high in the sky and it was important he returned to matters of Lodelowe. He moved to the head of the table and resumed his seat.

"Right, Captain, I will summon this man myself. Just find me your fastest rider and send in the castle's scribe. He waits at the door. I will get him to draw up a proclamation to hand to this king's falconer, then send out your fastest rider to bring him back here to Lodelowe. In the meantime, carry out my orders. Attend to the prisoners," he said.

One worry, however, remained in the Baron's mind. He had not quite worked out how best to control the situation. Lady Adela's trail would be at least one week away and maybe two. Before this could happen, news had to be sent to Salopsbury and representation for the Lady despatched to Lodelowe. The nagging question therefore remained; what excuse could he use to keep the King's Royal Falconer at his castle? He decided the missive to the falconer had to be short and brief. It would simply summon him to stand in judgement at a trial without mention as to whom and when. He would inform him of his duties only once he was safely roomed within his castle.

Whilst contemplating these things, he waved the captain away. There was nothing more to be said and he had a lot of thinking to do.

Upon seeing the wave of the hand, Captain Osbald saluted, clicked his heels and turned for the door. As he marched away he did not look back. On leaving the hall he instructed the castle's scribe to enter and ordered Sergeant Cuthred to accompany him. Together they had some very important matters to deal with.

Chapter Nine

There existed a sense of urgency about Captain Osbald. He marched quickly from the Great hall, with Sergeant Cuthred one step behind and matching his stride.

Halfway down a long corridor the captain stopped and caught a pageboy by the collar. The pageboy, travelling in the opposite direction, was caught by surprise, but like any subordinate when confronted by a superior he adjusted his tunic and bowed low before the captain. The pageboy was probably not the best person for the job, the captain admitted this, but as far as he was concerned anyone would do. It was just unfortunate for the boy that he was the first person encountered.

The captain told the boy, "You, go to the North Tower and prepare a room. Do it right away. Find a room with a comfortable bed, a table and chair. Then light a fire and provide candles. Oh, and find a bible. Now go, and jump to it! I shall be along shortly to see that all is done."

No sooner had he finished speaking, Captain Osbald turned and sped away, heading for the courtyard. For a brief moment, the boy stood dumfounded. He then turned and set off in a rush. For the first time in his life he had been asked to do something important and he would do everything in his power to make sure his allotted task was carried out.

At the end of the corridor a door opened out into the courtyard. The captain burst through, then kept on walking. Out in the sunshine, he looked about him but did not stop. He knew exactly where he was heading, which was more than Sergeant Cuthred did.

Three soldiers, assigned to guard a cart, stood in the courtyard. On the back of the cart sat two women both heavily bound with rope.

Striding briskly towards the cart, Captain Osbald gave orders to Sergeant Cuthred, now racing by his side and matching his stride.

"Sergeant, I want you to conduct a thorough search of that cart," he said, pointing ahead he added, "Search for valuables. Leave nothing unturned. The Baron is looking for items of jewellery that may have been taken from his strongroom. But before that, alert Egbert and make ready a fast horse. The scribe prepares a missive for a traveller. Egbert knows him by sight and is a good rider. He is to ride out for this traveller and bring him back here to Lodelowe."

"Aye, Captain," the sergeant acknowledged as they marched along, "I will make ready a fast horse and alert Egbert. I will then set about searching the cart."

"Oh! And one more thing," said the captain taking a silver crown from his purse. "Give this silver crown to Egbert and promote him through the ranks. Make him a corporal. It is the Baron's wish that this be done.'

Sergeant Cuthred took the coin. He looked bemused, but did not question the command.

"I will do this too. Egbert will be promoted to corporal," he replied. Then, as if to show the same urgency as his captain, he saluted and veered away to the stables.

Captain Osbald carried on alone, striding purposefully across the courtyard. He approached two soldiers guarding the cart and stopped. The third soldier assigned the task, was stood to the far side.

"You two, get those prisoners down from the cart," he barked, then in the same breath called over the cart, "And you over there, go down to the dungeon. Tell the jailer I want a cell made clean and unfouled, and a candle and blanket provided. Tell him I shall be down shortly with a prisoner. Now go to it, and look lively."

The soldier, partially obscured by the cart, saluted and set off at a pace. At the same time, the two remaining soldiers set about their own allotted duty. The prisoners were lowered from the cart and made to stand on the uneven cobbles of the courtyard. Both remained bound with several coils of rope wound about their upper arms and body. They teetered unsteadily on the uneven ground, but each was held so they did not fall.

Once down and on their feet, Captain Osbald singled out one soldier.

Pointing to him first, then to Lady Adela, he told him; "You, escort this one to the North Tower. A room is being prepared as I speak. Take her to the room and release her from her bonds, then guard the door until I arrive. She is to speak to no one. Is that clear?"

The soldier saluted with clenched fist across his chest and clicked his heels.

"Yes, Captain," he replied and took hold of the ropes about Lady Adela's body. He gave a tug and they set off.

As they walked away, Lady Adela turned and called to her handmaiden, "Stay strong my sweet Gwyneth. Do not let your heart fall. My family will soon hear of this atrocity and come to our aid."

Gwyneth managed a smile. But tears filled her face and she said nothing, being too choked to speak.

Captain Osbald watched Lady Adela go. As she disappeared from the courtyard he turned to the one remaining soldier.

He told him, "You stay here, guard the cart and let no one approach until Sergeant Cuthred returns. You will then assist in whatever he commands." And as he spoke he took a grip of the ropes that surrounded the handmaiden. "And you, come with me," he told her and giving a sharp tug to the ropes.

The handmaiden stumbled forward, found her feet and then walked away with the captain pulling at the ropes.

A steep winding path led upwards from the courtyard to the castle's keep. With a hand gripped firmly around the handmaiden's ropes, the captain moved at a brisk pace. One step behind and at an arm's length, the handmaiden struggled to maintain the rapid pace set by the captain.

An arched gateway and portcullis defended the inner keep. This was the only entrance to the tall, square block tower that dominated the Lodelowe skyline. The portcullis was raised but the doors were closed. A guard came to attention and clicked his heels as Captain Osbald arrived. Without a word being spoken, he opened a small inner door inset within one of the larger double doors and let him and the prisoner step through.

Once inside, the small door closed and the captain moved on. Inside was dark and lit only by a few widely spread torches burning in brackets on the walls.

With the handmaiden in tow, the captain crossed the huge entrance hall and descended a flight of stone stairs. At the end of a long narrow corridor and on a level below the entrance hall, a lone soldier waited. Behind him stood a small, gated portal that came no higher than his shoulders. On seeing the captain he turned a key in a lock and opened out the small gate. Without stopping or a word being spoken, Captain Osbald stooped low and stepped through the portal. A tug on the handmaiden's bonds caused her to jerk forward. She ducked her head and stepped through to the other side.

The area beyond the gate was small and confined, and from here a narrow spiralling staircase descended deep into the hillside. Captain Osbald waited for the guard to lock the gate then tugged once more on the handmaiden's ropes. They set off down the long descent, the captain leading and both treading carefully for the steps were steep and the passageway badly lit.

It was one hundred steps down to the bottom. Here, a further gate blocked the way. A guard stood to the other side. He had heard their descent and was waiting, stooping low and peering through the bars. He recognised the captain and unlocked the low, iron-barred gate so that they may pass through to the other side.

After stooping low and passing through the final portal, the captain released his grip on the handmaiden's bonds. Stooping low, she followed through the portal, stood upright and looked about her. She was standing at one end of a long, low-arched corridor. The light was poor, lit only by a handful of blazing torches placed in brackets and spaced at irregular intervals down the long length of the wide corridor. The vaulted roof was black, stained by centuries of endless smoke. The damp and clammy air reeked of burning pitch. On both sides of the passageway stood rows of cells with at least a dozen solid oak doors to either side. All were closed and the wails of at least two prisoners could be heard from behind the doors.

Captain Osbald turned to the guard.

"Escort the prisoner. Follow me," he barked.

There remained a certain amount of haste to everything the captain did. He set off.

The soldier earlier despatched to herald the captain's arrival, was waiting halfway down the long corridor. Alongside him stood Cedric the jailer, a small balding man, his upper torso attired in a black leather waistcoat. His arms and chest were muscular, and strung to one side of a wide leather belt hung a number of keys. He pulled open a cell door and waited for Captain Osbald to arrive before speaking.

The captain stopped before the door and peered into the cell.

"The cell has been cleaned and a blanket and candle provided as instructed," said the jailer as he stood with one hand on the door.

Captain Osbald showed no emotion and continued to peer into the gloom. The cell was small, slightly longer than wide, with an arched roof and barely large enough for one person to lie down at full stretch. A coarsely woven blanket had been placed on the floor, and within a niche in the wall a candle burned. He sniffed the stale air. If the cell had been washed and the floor swept clean, then it had done nothing to remove the foul reeking stench.

The captain took one step back. The handmaiden had been brought to stand alongside. He placed both hands upon her shoulders and pushed her heavily into the cell. The push caught her unawares and sent her stumbling through the door. She landed on her knees with a thump and toppled forward onto her already bruised and battered face. She righted herself, but remained kneeling with her back to the door. She closed her eyes and began to pray.

Cedric removed a knife from his belt with the intension of cutting the handmaiden's bonds. Captain Osbald put out a hand.

"This I will do later," he said, "I will'st return within the hour. In the meantime, she remains bound. I have questions to put to this one."

Cedric's face showed no emotion. He put away his knife, pushed the cell door shut and turned a key in the lock.

"Is she to receive any special treatment?" he asked as he removed the key.

Captain Osbald shook his head.

"No," he replied curtly. "She is to have a blanket and a candle, but nothing more. She will eat and drink with the rest."

He knew this not to be strictly in accordance with the Baron's wishes, but he had come to despise this handmaiden. At the ford she had shown nothing but contempt for his authority and for this, she would be made to suffer.

Cedric shrugged his shoulders. The handmaiden's welfare was of little concern to him. He would, as always, follow his instructions to the letter. The prisoner would receive whatever food was sent down from the kitchens. This was usually mouldy old bread fit only for rats; and as for water, a barrel in a corner of the corridor collected a constant drip from the roof. This is what all the prisoners drank.

Captain Osbald took one last glance at the cell. As far as he was concerned he had carried out the Baron's orders. The handmaiden had been afforded a blanket and a candle, and he could not recollect the Baron wishing anything else. But he had little time to dwell on the matter. Much work remained. It was to the stables next, to issue final instructions to Egbert before sending him in pursuit of the King's Falconer.

Chapter Ten

Captain Osbald emerged from the castle's keep and shielded his eyes from the glare of the sun. Behind him, the door banged shut. He looked at the shortened shadows and concluded the hour to be somewhere near midday. For someone who had been on the go from way before sunrise, already his day seemed long and arduous. He reflected on his morning's work. It was still dark when he awoke in the stables at Onneyditch that very morning. Since then, he had roused his men; helped to saddle the horses; trundled his way to Lodelowe, following an unhelpful cart; got the physician to treat a wounded man; held council with the Baron; organised a search of the cart; confined two prisoners in accordance with the Baron's wishes and organised a rider to go out and bring back the King's Falconer. His stomach rumbled and he realised that he had not eaten at all that day. He put aside his discomfort and set off, striding briskly down the long, winding cobbled path that led to the courtyard far below. He would eat later. At present he was a very busy man with a lot more work to do before he could relax.

Once on level ground, Captain Osbald stopped briefly to take in some deep breaths of air. But no matter how hard he tried, nothing he did could get rid of the foul smelling stench of the dungeon. After about his tenth deep intake of breath he looked about him. His eyes were better adjusted now and he could see that things had changed since last visiting the courtyard. The cart remained, but the four chests, once heavily roped down, were now on the ground. All were open and their contents scattered about the cobblestones. Three soldiers worked alongside the cart, delving amongst the chests. From a distance Captain Osbald recognised all of the men. One was Sergeant Cuthred; the second was the soldier left to guard the cart and the third, the newcomer, was a corporal in his army and presumably ordered by Sergeant Cuthred to help in the search. His name was Guthrum.

A horse and a rider emerged from the stables away to the captain's right; the horse's hooves clattering over the cobbles.

He beckoned the rider to come to him, calling loudly, "Egbert, come here. I will'st speak to you before you go."

The rider pulled hard on his reins, turned and trotted across the courtyard to join the awaiting captain. He stopped and saluted from the saddle. He now wore the green tassels of a corporal on his shoulders.

"You have the scribe's missive?" asked the captain.

Corporal Egbert patted his saddlebag.

"Aye, Captain, it is here," he replied.

"Then you know where to ride? The King's Falconer heads for Worcester and could be many miles south by now," warned the captain.

Egbert understood but foresaw no problem.

"The Falconer trails a donkey and travels with a precious cargo. He will not have gotten far. I have a fast horse and can catch him," said Egbert and sounding optimistic.

"Then go, Egbert, make haste, and may God and St. Christopher go with you," said the captain and striking the rear of the horse with his hand.

Corporal Egbert set off, his horse's hooves clattering over the cobbles. With luck, he would catch up with the King's Falconer and bring him back to Lodelowe before nightfall.

Captain Osbald watched his newly promoted corporal disappear from the courtyard before moving on.

Striding briskly towards the cart he called, "Sergeant, how does't the search go?"

The search of the cart was nearing completion. The courtyard lay scattered with the contents of four large wooden chests; the items consisting mainly of clothes, coats, bonnets and shoes.

Sergeant Cuthred was bent forward and fumbling through a chest, not aware of his captain's approach until he heard his call. He looked up and shook his head.

"Nay, Captain," he replied, "there is nothing here that did'st once belong to the Baron." Then holding out a purse he added, "Ten gold sovereigns and some forty silver crowns. This is all they carried of any worth. Enough, I would say, to see them through to the Cinque Ports and hire a boat, but little more."

Captain Osbald joined the Sergeant and took the purse. For a while he pondered upon what he had just learned. To find only a small purse and nothing else of value he considered most odd. The robbers in the Baron's strongroom had taken quite a number of valuable items and he puzzled over where everything had gone, and why the necklace about the Norman woman's neck the only item to be recovered. He shook his head in despair before turning to more pressing matters.

"Then Sergeant, you'd best come with me," he said. "We still have much work to do. Both the handmaiden and Lady Adela are to be searched, and for this I will need your assistance."

He turned to Corporal Guthrum and pointed around the courtyard.

The captain told him, "Corporal, return all the items to the chests. Pack everything away. Make it neat, then store under lock and key. Nothing must go astray. Every item on the cart must be accounted for. It is possible everything will be returned to the Lady Adela."

Corporal Guthrum saluted.

"Yes, Captain, leave it to me," he replied.

But Captain Osbald was not waiting for a reply. As the corporal spoke, the captain spun around and set off, this time to return to the castle's keep. The handmaiden was first to be searched. A few paces behind raced the burly figure of Sergeant Cuthred. As ever Captain Osbald was a very busy man.

Chapter Eleven

Captain Osbald returned to the dungeon with Sergeant Cuthred trailing in his wake. On passing the final portal he collected a lantern from a hook and moved swiftly on down the corridor. He came to a halt before the cell that held the handmaiden. Cedric the jailer, aware of the captain's rapid return, moved to greet him. They arrived together to stand outside the cell door.

Captain Osbald slid open a small viewing hatch and peered inside. A candle flickered to one side of the cell and cast the shadow of the handmaiden against the wall opposite. She was kneeling and facing away from the door. He recalled this was the way he had left her, bound with her hands behind her back and arms pinned to her sides. On entry, she had collapsed to her knees and presumably remained in this position ever since.

He pointed to the lock on the door.

"Open up," he told Cedric. "I have business with this prisoner."

Cedric selected a large key from a ring containing twenty or more. He placed it in the lock and turned it slowly. There came a loud clunk as the barrels fell into place and the door sprang outwards by a fraction.

"Wait outside," Captain Osbald told Cedric, as the jailer pulled open the door. Then addressing Sergeant Cuthred he added, "Sergeant, you will enter with me. We will'st search the handmaiden together. Your witness is needed to show that nothing untoward is done."

Captain Osbald stepped inside the cell, with Sergeant Cuthred following closely behind. The conditions inside were cramped and there was barely enough space for two men to stand. The low roof too proved an obstacle, forcing them to stand at the centre of the arched roof, and even here, did so with heads bowed. Once inside, Cedric pushed the door shut, leaving it a few inches ajar.

The captain held the lantern high. The handmaiden remained kneeling with her back towards the door and showed no sign of recognition. A folded blanket rested beneath her knees, protecting her from the cold damp flagstones. Using one hand, Captain Osbald removed a dagger from his belt and cut away the bonds from her wrists. He then uncoiled what remained of the rope from about her body. Immediately on release, the handmaiden brought her hands to the front and set about massaging her wrists. She had been bound like this for almost twenty-four hours and her hands and wrists were numb.

Captain Osbald allowed time for the circulation to return.

Then, in a voice usually reserved for addressing his men, he bellowed, "Wench, stand up, turn and face me. I have questions to be answered."

On hearing the order the handmaiden rose to her feet, hitched up the hem of her full-length dress and turned to face the captain. With hands holding the hem of her skirt away from the floor, she stared back defiantly. She considered the time had come to have her say. She had been wronged at the ford and she knew it.

"Why are you keeping me here?" she demanded. "You cannot confine me in this place! I have done nothing wrong!"

The handmaiden's impudence angered the captain. Since their meeting at the ford a mutual hatred had grown, and now this serving wench had the audacity to ask questions of him.

"Silence wench!" he snapped. "You are here by order of Baron de Clancey and you will speak only when allowed to do so."

The handmaiden glared back at the captain and hatred burned within her eyes. She was fuming and made little effort to hide the fact.

Captain Osbald placed the lantern upon the floor to free his hands, the upward light casted dancing shadows upon the low arched roof. In this indifferent light he paused to take a good look at the handmaiden. Despite scratches and bruising to the face, she was young, fair and pretty. She stood gracefully tall, with a slender waist and a lithe body. Beneath her white handmaiden's bonnet, small ringlets of golden hair cascaded down about her shoulders. But time was pressing and he realised that he must move on. He still had a search of Lady Adela to conduct.

Captain Osbald removed a small blank parchment and a piece of charcoal from a pouch attached to his belt. This was paperwork and of all his duties, the thing he hated most.

"I need your name and other details," he told her, then went on to explain, "You are being held a prisoner here by order of Baron de Clancey. You are required by laws of the Council of the Marches and by the laws of the Crown of England to answer a few simple questions."

At this stage the handmaiden had little intention of co-operating. She remained firmly of the belief that she should never have been arrested.

She answered the captain bluntly, saying, "Before I answer anything, I demand to know why I've been brought here? I have my rights!"

Captain Osbald glowered at the young girl's insolence. He was not used to being addressed in such a manner. He shaped to slap her across the face with his heavy gauntleted hand, but refrained as he recalled the Baron's words.

He lowered his hand.

"I have little time for nonsense. Just answer the questions," he growled. "What is your name?"

Reacting quickly to the captain's raised arm, the handmaiden stepped away to stand against the back wall of the cell. From this position she answered grudgingly.

"Gwyneth, my name is Gwyneth," she said, spitting out the words as if venom in her mouth.

Captain Osbald wrote down the name *'Gwyneth'* on his parchment. But this was not enough. More was needed, for a single identity was no longer acceptable under Norman Law.

"Gwyneth, daughter of whom?" he asked. "What is your family name? I need a family name. Who is your father?"

Gwyneth bit hard on her bottom lip as memories of her father flooded back. She had loved her father dearly and recalled his constant smiling face, the way he used to bounce her on his knees in front of the open hearth, and the stories he told her in bed at night.

With a tear to her eye she told the captain, "Gwyneth, daughter of Thomas the Fletcher."

Captain Osbald nodded in response.

"Gwyneth Fletcher," he muttered whilst he wrote down the details. The handmaiden was now, on paper anyway, Gwyneth Fletcher, a name she had never been called before. In fact, no other name, other than Gwyneth, had ever been attached to her before this day. This insistence on a surname was of Norman doing and this too, she despised. She grimaced as she heard her given name spoken, but made no reply.

The captain moved on.

"And what is your age?" he asked and indicating some haste to the question. "How old are you?"

Gwyneth considered the question. The captain might be in a hurry but she certainly was not. She was going to take her time. And besides, her age was something she needed to think about. She had celebrated birthdays when her father was alive, but since joining the kitchen staff even the date was forgotten. She did her sums, but maths did not come easy. She had been eleven years old when her father died. This she knew, and since then she had worked five summers in the kitchens. This made her sixteen. But as for her exact date of birth, the month of April was all she remembered. However, it was something her mother would know. If only she could speak to her. Her mother was somewhere here in Lodelowe. If only she could get a message to her, she would know.

Gwyneth answered with some hesitancy.

"Sixteen, I am sixteen," she said. "I was born in the month of April. I was sixteen last April, but the day I do not recall."

Captain Osbald was surprised to hear such a young age. This mature and full bosomed girl looked much older and he would have put her at something nearer to eighteen or nineteen. However, her age was irrelevant and he pressed on with the questioning. He had much to get through before this day was out. He wrote down '16' then put his next question to her.

"And how long have you been in attendance to Lady Adela Fitzgerald?" he asked.

Gwyneth had little need to give this latest question much thought. She replied quickly, since she could answer with some accuracy.

"Some three days now, that is all," she replied. "I am in attendance to my Lady for the journey south. I travel with her to the Cinque Ports, then return to Salopsbury once she is safely aboard the ship. At least that is what I was meant to be doing until you ugly, murdering lot turned up."

Captain Osbald ignored her remarks. The skirmish at the ford was not of his making. The fight ensued because of the insistence of the Salopsbury soldiers to contest the right of Egbert to inspect the necklace. If they had not been so stubborn then all would be alive today. He put his final question to Gwyneth.

"Then tell me wench, what are your normal duties?" he asked.

Gwyneth thrust her hands to her hips, but at least this was a question she could answer.

"My duties lie within the kitchen," she said. "I tend the hearths and peel the vegetables. That's what I do. I am but a humble kitchen maid. So why are you keeping me here? I have done nothing wrong."

Captain Osbald ignored her insolence and because he wanted to get this over with quickly, he asked somewhat rhetorically, "The kitchens at the castle of Salopsbury?"

Gwyneth sneered.

"Where do you think?" she answered abruptly, "The king's palace?"

Captain Osbald jotted down '*kitchen maid*' along with the word '*Salopsbury*' then put the parchment and charcoal away. There was little more he could ask. These questions were just formalities demanded of him by the Baron's meddling scribe. He thought for a while to confirm he had not missed anything. Then, once satisfied that he had not forgotten anything, he addressed her again.

"Right, wench," he snapped, "Baron de Clancey hath decreed that you be searched, and that the search be complete and thorough. Nothing, no matter how small or insignificant must be left unturned. You are required, by order of the Baron, to take off all your clothes for inspection. You must take them off one at a time and pass them to me so that each item may in turn be inspected for stolen items. The Sergeant here will be your witness that all is in order and nothing is untoward, and that should anything be found, it can be recorded and verified accordingly."

Gwyneth thrust her hands hard against her slender hips and glared back at the captain. She made no move or uttered a single word to convey her disgust. She had no need to. The message on her face displayed clearly her feelings for this ignominy. In her mind there was no reason for this search. She possessed nothing of worth. She had been poor all her life and possessed nothing of value. Even the clothes upon her back belonged to the Lady Adela.

With nothing happening, Captain Osbald raised a hand with the intent to strike the handmaiden across the face. He had threatened this action before, and at the time it had produced the desired result. He hoped this act would do so again, even though he was well aware of the Baron's instructions to keep the prisoners from harm. Fortunately, his little rouse worked. On seeing the raised hand Gwyneth ducked low and cowered towards the back wall.

"Keep away!" she yelled. "Keep your filthy rotten hands off me you murdering pig!"

Captain Osbald's anger intensified. Orders or not, he would suffer no insolence.

"I am ordering you to strip," he said coldly. "I will not tell you again. Now take off your clothes, or I'll rip them off. You have to the count of ten to make up your mind."

He began to count.

Gwyneth glared back in defiance. As the count neared ten she turned her back on the captain. With one hand over a shoulder she pointed to the buttons down her back.

"Well, come on then!" she hissed. "I can't undo my dress by myself. It is fastened down the back. So if you want it, undo the buttons."

Gwyneth's dress had been selected from Lady Adela's extensive wardrobe. Like all her fine attire, this was a garment befitting someone of noble birth. The dress billowed outward from the waist. The skirt being multi-layered with the finest of satins and the bodice embossed in fine and elaborate gold-threaded needlework. A richly embroidered panel of floral design, holding a row of intricate small bone-carved buttons ran all the way down the spine. But all that was when the dress was new. Now a sleeve hung by the threads, the hem was ragged and torn and everywhere the bodice was caked in mud.

Captain Osbald checked on Sergeant Cuthred, confirming that he was in a position to receive items passed to him. He then turned back to concentrate on the handmaiden. He looked her up and down. He could see what was needed.

The wench wore a long flowing green dress covered in mud and with one billowing sleeve—the other had been torn to rags and hung loosely about the arm. The dress' waistline was pulled into the body by a wide, loosely tied sash. He set his mind on the task at hand.

"Right, let's be having the dress," he said. "What must I do with these buttons?"

Gwyneth did not turn round and remained facing the wall. On hearing the captain, she pulled the ringlets of her hair forward about her neck and waited with hands resting upon her shoulders.

"Work down from the top," she told him and touching with an extended finger the topmost button of her dress. "Start with this button here."

Captain Osbald removed his gauntlets, tucked them beneath his belt and stepped closer to the handmaiden. Working down from the position indicated by the tapping finger, he began to laboriously undo a long line of small round buttons. Slowly and with much difficulty, he fumbled his way down the spine. As the neck loosened Gwyneth assisted by firstly removing the sash about her waist, then by wriggling her arms free of the sleeves and allowing the dress to slide slowly down her slender body. When all the buttons were undone, she let the dress drop about her feet and stepped away.

The Captain gathered up the dress, folded it untidily about an arm and passed it to Sergeant Cuthred. Returning to Gwyneth, he looked her up and down. There was little else to remove. There were the shoes upon her feet, and just two items of clothing upon her body. These were a bonnet and a singlet vest. Both where white and made from the same fine, closely woven fabric. The bonnet was plain with no needlework of note, whilst the vest showed intricate embroidery about the neck and shoulders. He was not to know, but the bonnet had once belonged to Mary, Lady Adela's previous attendant, thus the plainness. The vest, however, had been taken from Lady Adela's wardrobe. About the waist was threaded a golden cord which passed through a series of neatly embroidered holes and tied to the front in a bow. The vest was also extremely short and from the telling appearance of just a hint of shining flesh-pink buttocks, the captain was in little doubt that this garment was all she wore about her person.

The ties of the white maid's bonnet hung loose about the shoulders. Captain Osbald took a grip from the rear, yanked it away and tossed it towards Sergeant Cuthred. There came a squeal of discomfort as he caught a handful of hair along with the bonnet. But the protests were short lived and Gwyneth said no more.

Once the bonnet was safely gathered in Sergeant Cuthred's hands, Captain Osbald looked down at Gwyneth's feet. He had already worked out the order of removal. To save unnecessary embarrassment the shoes would come first. The singlet vest he would leave till last.

"Let's be having the shoes," he told her. "Take them off and pass them back to me."

Keeping her back towards Captain Osbald, Gwyneth stooped to the floor and fumbled with the laces that strapped the shoes about the ankles. She removed each shoe in turn and pushed them backwards, beneath her body.

Whilst kneeling to unlace the shoes, and in the flickering half-light of the lantern, Captain Osbald saw clearly that the singlet vest was indeed the only item of clothing to remain upon the handmaiden. In different circumstances he would have without doubt become highly aroused at the sight that now greeted him.

But his hatred for this girl quelled all natural feelings. He therefore, felt no sexual tendencies. His mind totally focused upon carrying out his orders.

Having pushed the shoes behind her back, Gwyneth returned to an upright position. She did this with hands moving upwards against the rear wall for added support. Once erect she stood facing the wall and waiting for further orders.

After gathering up the shoes and handing them to Sergeant Cuthred, Captain Osbald returned his gaze to the kitchen maid. Only the singlet vest remained.

"Come wench, don't be shy!" he said, somewhat sarcastically. "Let's be having the vest."

Gwyneth loosened the golden cord about her waist and pulled the singlet up and over her head. Shaking her hair free so that the golden ringlets fell about her shoulders, she held out the vest for Captain Osbald to collect. He collected it and tossed it back to Sergeant Cuthred. As he did so he spotted something he had missed earlier. Gwyneth had a thin band of leather tied about her neck.

Curious to find out he told her, "Right, wench, turn round and face me. Come on! Move! Let's be having you! I want to see what you've got round your neck."

A naked Gwyneth turned to face Captain Osbald. Instinctively, she did what any decent girl would do under such circumstances. She cupped her left breast in her right hand, shielded the other the best she could with her forearm, then strategically placed her left hand between her legs to cover up her womanhood.

Captain Osbald stared back wildly at the sight that now greeted him. But for all the eroticism, the young girl's nakedness and vulnerability did nothing for him. His interests lay elsewhere. His mind totally focused upon a wooden cross about her neck. He held out a hand.

"The cross about your neck," he said. "Take it off. I want to see it."

Gwyneth hesitated. To do so would mean the removal of her hands from their strategically placed positions. However the delay was short lived, for she realised that to protest further would prove nothing other than to prolong this whole sordid affair. Raising her arms to the nape of her neck she unfastened the knot and tossed the cross to the captain. She then returned her hands to their original protective positions.

Captain Osbald inspected the cross. It was large and crudely constructed from two pieces of badly jointed wood. The strap too, was ordinary, just a thin strip of leather hide. He turned the cross over in his hands and considered what to do with this item. He had hoped to find some expensive jewellery about her neck, but there was nothing here to incriminate her. For a while he pondered upon the lack of valuables. If this cross was her only possession, then it had no obvious worth.

Whilst Captain Osbald pondered, a shout from behind broke his train of thought.

"Err, Captain, I think you'd better take a look at this," called Sergeant Cuthred.

The captain turned to see his sergeant holding up one of Gwyneth's shoes.

"What is it?" he snapped.

Sergeant Cuthred was quick to explain.

"Captain, I think you'd better take a look at this shoe," he said. "It's very similar to those found upon the cart. By perchance I discovered that they all hold secret compartments within the heels. These shoes are French, made by the same cobbler no doubt, and me thinks we could have something hidden inside this one. Listen!"

The sergeant shook the shoe from side to side. The captain listened and perceived a slight rattle coming from somewhere inside. Eager to locate the source of the rattle, he swapped the cross for the shoe. Now in possession of the shoe he shook it against his ear and perceived a slight rattle. He nodded his head. The sergeant was right. There was a strange sound and feel to the shoe. The heel was loose and something moved freely within the carved wooden base.

"There's a leather flap inside the shoe that rises up," Sergeant Cuthred informed his captain, and at the same time indicating exactly where he should look.

Captain Osbald followed Sergeant Cuthred's instructions. He placed his hand deep within the shoe and raised a leather flap about the heel. He then held the shoe close to the lantern in order to gain closer inspection. The heel had been hollowed from the inside and a small package, wrapped in parchment paper, rested inside. He knocked the package out and passed the shoe to his sergeant. With the package now resting in the palm of his hand he turned to confront the handmaiden.

"And what have we here?" he asked.

A look of bemusement crossed Gwyneth's face and she shook her head. Clearly she had no idea. She was not even aware of the secret compartment.

Captain Osbald unwrapped the parchment before her eyes so that together they would see the contents as they became revealed. Suddenly, his lungs burst.

"What the hell!" he bellowed. "No! Surely this cannot be!"

Colour drained from Gwyneth's cheeks. For a brief moment she forgot her embarrassment and put her hands to her face, but the action proved short-lived and her hands quickly returned to their original protective positions.

Captain Osbald raised the object high so that both Gwyneth and Sergeant Cuthred could see. He was holding a solid gold signet ring. On the face of the ring was a shield. Across the shield was etched a vertical line and three rampant lions, two above and one below. This was without doubt the crest of the de Clancey's, and the ring had no rights being in the shoe of a kitchen maid from Salopsbury, both Captain Osbald and Gwyneth knew this.

The captain retrieved the lantern from the floor and held the ring to the light so that Sergeant Cuthred could see.

"Tell me Sergeant, was this ring amongst the items taken from the Baron's strongroom?" he asked.

Sergeant Cuthred moved closer to the lantern in order to gain a better inspection. On seeing the crest of the de Clancey's he quickly confirmed what his captain already suspected.

"I do believe it was," he said. "This ring most definitely bears the crest of the late Edward de Clancey, and as far as I am aware this ring was being held within the castle's strongroom along with all the other items from the late Baron's legacy." He then went on to ask, "Then tell me Captain, what is this ring doing concealed within this shoe?"

Captain Osbald gave no reply. He had seen and heard enough. He swung around to confront Gwyneth and to hold the ring before her face.

"Tell me wench, where did you get this ring?" he demanded. "This is the signet ring of the late Baron. You, a mere serving wench of the Fitzgeralds, should not be in possession of such an item."

Gwyneth shook her head and tried to explain, or at least deny that she had ever set eyes upon the ring.

"I do not know!" she stuttered. "I have never seen this ring before. This is the truth. I swear before God that I have never seen this ring before!"

Captain Osbald raised a hand as if to strike, but despite his temper, he refrained.

"Do not lie to me wench!" he bellowed. "Answer me! Answer me! I must know how you came by this ring?"

Gwyneth was lost for words. The ring was within her shoe. But what could she say? How could she explain?

"I don't know where it came from!" she said, shaking her head. "I just don't know! I swear to God I just don't know! The ring's not mine! And neither are the shoes! They belong to Lady Adela!"

Captain Osbald's patience finally snapped.

"Answer me wench!" he screamed. "This ring is not yours and I want to know how you came by it."

Gwyneth became hysterical. She shrieked back in a wild panic.

"The ring isn't mine!" she shouted. "They're not my shoes! They were given to me by Lady Adela."

Captain Osbald shaped to slap the wench, his rage out of control. But Sergeant Cuthred grabbed at an arm.

"Sire, the Baron hath ordered that no harm should befall this prisoner," he said. "Please refrain!"

Captain Osbald shook himself free of the Sergeant's grasp and straightened out his tunic. He knew Sergeant Cuthred was right. However what he held in his hand would make the handmaiden pay dearly for her impudence. The ring would be her undoing. Clutching the ring tightly and collecting the offending shoe and scrap of parchment paper, he stormed out of the cell.

"Jailer," he snapped, "lock this door, I'm away to seek audience with the Baron. See to it that no one enters or speaks to this prisoner until my return."

Sergeant Cuthred emerged from the cell with his arms full of clothes and a lantern hooked about one finger. He shrugged his shoulders.

As Cedric slammed the door and turned the key, the sergeant told him pensively, "Cedric my friend, this wench hath turned our captain into a very angry man. She is pretty, the likes of which we have not seen here for a very long time. With her stubborn tongue we may have work to do in extracting the truth from her lips. Do you not agree?"

Cedric looked up and showed little emotion. He simply shrugged at his shoulders. If persuasion was necessary in order to gain a confession, then so be it. He would do whatever he was asked to do. But until he received different orders, then the handmaiden would be treated with respect.

"You could be right, Cuthred," Cedric answered thoughtfully as he withdrew the key from the lock. "You could very well be right!"

Chapter Twelve

Captain Osbald returned to the Great hall, but this time with a little more propriety. Having heralded his arrival, he stood before the closed doors to the hall awaiting a call from Baron de Clancey.

The meeting between the Baron and his bailiffs was nearing an end. As the bailiffs rose from their chairs and the guards opened the doors, Captain Osbald sped quickly through. He came to a halt at the end of the long table where the Baron remained seated. As on his previous visit, he had something to show the Baron. In his hands he held a single woman's shoe, a scrap of parchment paper and a solid gold signet ring.

Captain Osbald placed the ring on the table before the Baron.

"My Liege, pray tell me, can this ring be yet another item taken from your strongroom?" he enquired.

Baron de Clancy picked up the ring and examined it closely. He compared it with a ring upon the third finger of his left hand. Both rings were very similar. Both displayed a shield, its background half-divided by opposing etchings and to the fore, the three rampant lions of Lodelowe. He was quick to respond with a nod to his head. He had seen enough.

"This is indeed my father's signet ring," he said. "This ring did'st once belong to the late Baron Edward de Clancey, and until three weeks ago resided in my strongroom. Pray tell me Captain, how did'st you come by this ring?"

Captain Osbald placed the handmaiden's shoe upon the table along with the scrap of parchment paper. He pointed to the shoe and the inner flap within the heel.

"My Liege, this ring was found concealed within the heel of this shoe," he explained. "The shoe belongs to the handmaiden and I found it upon her person whilst conducting the bodily search you did'st so request."

The Baron collected the shoe and examined the heel. Beneath the inner flap of the lining he examined the small hollowed-out indentation. He frowned. This was all very well, but something was amiss, something not quite right. This shoe was French, of high quality and expert craftsmanship. This was not the shoe of a mere serving wench. He pondered deeply, always thinking ahead. There was much on his mind. When requesting the search, he was looking for evidence that would incriminate Lady Adela. Now he had the handmaiden to consider too. Prior to being presented with this ring he held no specific plans for the serving wench. He might even have granted her release at some future date. But the discovery of the ring had changed everything. He raised his head.

"Captain, you say this shoe was found upon the handmaiden?" he asked, speaking slowly and thoughtfully. "Pray tell me, could you not be mistaken? Could this not be the shoe of Lady Adela? Could it not have been switched, perhaps on the journey from the ford?"

Captain Osbald shook his head. There was no way the two women could have swapped shoes. He explained his reasoning.

"Nay, my Liege," he answered. "This shoe most definitely belongs to the handmaiden. This shoe was upon her foot when arrested at the ford. And it was there that both she and the Norman lady were bound, and those bonds were not removed until the search began."

The Baron reminded himself of the events. The necklace was first sighted at the ford, so both the ring and necklace could be tracked back to the time the party ventured onto his estates. He rubbed his chin thoughtfully. He was thinking ahead and concluded this find could be turned to his own advantage. Slowly, a revised strategy came to mind. He would conduct two trials, not one. This was indeed the answer he was seeking.

However the Baron was only too conscious that the trial of Lady Adela would take several more days to organise. Out of courtesy, Salopsbury had to be informed and representatives of the Fitzgerald family despatched to Lodelowe. But the trial of a serving wench was of little significance and would, in all probability, pass by unnoticed. He had the authority to try lowborn persons such as a handmaiden and mete out punishment as he saw fit. He smiled. He could now see a positive side to all this. A written confession from the handmaiden stating that both she and Lady Adela were implicated in the robbery would be a handy tool to present at the later and more formal trial of the Norman noblewoman.

The Baron looked up from the table. There was something else he needed to know.

"Captain, have all the searches been conducted?" he asked. "Have there been any more finds?"

Captain Osbald shook his head.

"Nay, my Liege," he replied. "The cart and handmaiden have been searched and nothing else found. But Lady Adela's search has not yet taken place. It is my intention to do so next."

The Baron remained pensive and turned his father's ring over and over in his hands. He had many plans and did not particularly want to reveal the true nature of his thoughts until such time as he was absolutely certain they would achieve his ends. Eventually, and after much thought, he gave his orders.

"This shoe must be kept as evidence," he told his captain. "Place the ring back in the heel exactly as it was found. Then store and guard everything. Nothing must be tampered with. This shoe must be presented exactly as it was found along with all the handmaiden's clothes and posessions. Is that understood?"

Captain Osbald nodded his head.

"Aye, my Liege, this will be done," he confirmed.

The Baron dismissed Captain Osbald with a wave of the hand. The meeting was over and he had much on his mind.

"Then go now, Captain," he said. "Finish off your work and conduct the search of the Lady Adela, then whence all is done, report back to me. Hopefully by then I will have completed arrangements for her forthcoming trial. Thank you, Captain. That will be all."

Captain Osbald saluted with clenched fist against his chest, collected the items from the table, then turned on his heels and made for the door.

As he walked away, the Baron called, "And recall my scribe. Tell him my need here is urgent."

The captain kept on walking and breathed a silent curse. The scribe had left the great hall when he had entered and could be anywhere by now. This looked like something else he had to do for himself. Why was everyone around him so useless?

Chapter Thirteen

Captain Osbald made his way to the North Tower. He had failed to locate the scribe and had despatched a servant to track him down. Sergeant Cuthred trailed the captain by a step. The two senior officers arrived to find a guard seated outside Lady Adela's door. The guard rose when he saw the men approaching.

Captain Osbald pointed to the lock and sharply snapped, "Open up, I will'st see the Lady now."

The guard placed a key in the lock, turned it noisily and pushed the door inwards. As the door swung open he stepped to one side to let the captain pass.

Inside the room, alerted by the activity at the door, Lady Adela rose to greet the visitors. Until this moment she had been seated on the edge of a bed with a heavy blanket wrapped about her body for warmth. She was noticeably shivering. There was a fireplace in the room stacked with kindled wood and logs, but it had only just been lit and the room remained cold and damp. What little light was present was coming from a narrow slit window and a single candle rested on the floor alongside the bed.

Unlike Gwyneth, Lady Adela's bonds had been cut before entering the room and, apart from light burn marks about the wrists, and possibly the noticeable coldness of the room, she felt no serious discomforts; however inwardly, she remained deeply concerned, not for herself but for her handmaiden. She should not have been parted from her servant. There was no reason for such action.

Captain Osbald entered the room, followed closely by Sergeant Cuthred. A lantern carried by the Sergeant added some welcome light to the room. Being the last man to enter, he pushed the door shut and placed the lantern on a small table next to the bed.

Captain Osbald waited for the lantern to be placed before addressing the prisoner. On this occasion he found it unnecessary to write down any details since her identity was known. This was Lady Adela Fitzgerald, the Norman bride of the late Edward Fitzgerald, Earl of Salopsbury, and youngest daughter of the Duke d'Honfleur. Also, unlike the search of the handmaiden, Captain Osbald recognised that Lady Adela needed to be treated with the utmost of respect. He cleared his throat and explained the purpose of his visit.

"My Lady, Baron de Clancey instructs that you be searched for jewellery," he explained. "I must inspect all that you wear, and this requires the removal of all that is about your person."

Lady Adela shook her head in despair. This was yet another affront to her dignity. She had not been told the reason for her arrest, her handmaiden had been taken from her and she was of the belief that her abductors were nothing more than common thieves. Furthermore, she remained convinced that the people that had assailed her at the ford were after her and not her jewellery, and in all probability now demanding a sizeable ransom for her release. After all, under advice from her brother-in-law, the Earl of Salopsbury, she had deliberately travelled light, so robbery could not have been the motive. She pondered for a while, not moving and saying nothing. Why did they need to check for jewellery? She had packed nothing of value other than what was about her person. Her most treasured possessions were to be sent to France separately and under guard, and the rest shared amongst her servants. Mary, her aged handmaid was to be the biggest recipient, an emerald brooch that matched the necklace taken from her at the ford being amongst the most valuable of her possessions.

Lady Adela raised her head towards the captain and answered in the tongue of the Anglo-Saxons, but with a strong Norman accent.

"There is no reason for such a search," she remarked. "I have nothing of value and my necklace is already gone! All I have of value is this ring about my finger." And she raised her hand to reveal a gold band about her marriage finger.

Captain Osbald examined the ring by lowering his head but not making contact. The three snarling lion heads of the Fitzgeralds was evident upon one side of the facet, whilst the other half bore the lymphad and escallop of the Norman port of Honfleur.

"You may keep the ring, my Lady," he told her. "But my orders are to search you bodily and this, I must do. I have explicit orders. I must ask you to remove your dress and all that is about your body so that all may be inspected. But hold little fear, my Lady, for all will be returned to you once I am satisfied that you conceal no further items of value."

Lady Adela frowned and looked to the captain with a steely glare. She had already suffered much ignominy, being bound at the ford, made to sleep the night on the floor of a stable and finally, being cast into this dingy room high in a tower without a servant. This was no way to treat a lady of such high and noble birth. She remained convinced that once her brother-in-law, the Earl of Salopsbury, or for that matter her father, the Duke d'Honfleur; if either were to hear of these atrocities, then those responsible for this outrage would be severely punished.

She stamped a foot.

"*Non!*" she snapped, "I will not do this! The Earl will have me freed as soon as he hears of this outrage."

Captain Osbald sighed. This search was not of his choosing or to his liking. He had been given orders and could in no way shirk his responsibilities. However to begin with, he decided to remain calm and apply reason.

He told her, "Please, my Lady, you must realise I have little choice in this matter. Baron de Clancey hath decreed that a bodily search of your person be conducted and it would be unfitting of me to do the deed forcibly. So I beg of you, my Lady, do pray reconsider your own position, and pray do not hinder me in my duties. For what must be done, will be done. Be it pleasant or unpleasant, neither you nor I have a choice in the matter."

Then to emphasise the point, he placed a hand upon his sword and withdrew it a short way from its scabbard.

Lady Adela glared hatred at Captain Osbald. The icy stare, then moved to confront Sergeant Cuthred who was stood one step behind. The partial withdrawal of the captain's sword had brought back bitter memories. Nervously, she fingered a small tear in the stomach of her dress. It was here that the captain's sword had penetrated the flesh. He had drawn blood and the caked remains still clung to her undergarments. She sighed as she came to realise the futility of her protests. She bowed her head and placed her hands together in prayer. Then, after a whispered verse in the Norman tongue, she returned her gaze towards the captain.

"Then let this foul deed be done," she said, "and let it be done quickly, and let's be over with it."

Captain Osbald returned his sword to the scabbard and pointed to Lady Adela's feet.

"My Lady, pray hand me your shoes," he said. "These, I will search first."

Lady Adela looked down to where the captain was pointing. The flagstones beneath her feet were wet from damp and shimmered under the lights of the candle and lantern. She bent down and spread the blanket she had held about her person upon the floor and stepped onto it. This was not the comfort she was used to, but the blanket offered some ease from the cold conditions underfoot. She would undress whilst standing upon the blanket. Bending down, she removed first one shoe and then the other and left them on the blanket for the captain to collect.

Captain Osbald picked up each shoe in turn and examined the heels. He knew now where to look and he examined each carefully. Noticeably, these shoes were identical to those worn by the handmaiden. He considered them to be of Norman origin since no English cobbler made shoes this way. The bases were of carved oak and the uppers crafted from the finest tanned leather. Brass studs hammered about the edges joined the leather to the bases, and large carved bone buckles provided the fastening. From within each shoe the captain raised the thick leather flap. Beneath each flap there was an indentation sunk in the heel, but on examination, each hollow held nothing. Both were empty. On concluding his inspection he passed the shoes to Sergeant Cuthred. It was his job to hold everything until the search was concluded.

When the arrests were made, both Lady Adela and Gwyneth, the handmaiden, wore similar attire, dresses with brightly coloured green bodices, ornate needlework and long white frilly sleeves. Even to an untrained eye it was obvious the same seamstress sewed both dresses. As the shoes were passed back to Sergeant Cuthred, Lady Adela turned to reveal a row of small, ornate bone-carved buttons running all the way down the middle of her back. Captain Osbald removed his gauntlets and placed them in his belt. He knew what was wanted. He had assisted in the removal of the handmaiden's dress, and now he must do the same for Lady Adela.

Starting at the neck, the captain slowly released each button in turn as far down as the waist. He then stepped away, leaving Lady Adela to do the rest. As the back of the dress loosened, she removed a sash from about her waist then wriggled her arms free of the sleeves. Finally, she let the dress slip gracefully down her slender body and drop onto the floor. As the dress gathered about her feet she stepped away, and keeping her back towards the captain, left it there for him to collect.

He picked up the dress and inspected it thoroughly. There were many layers and folds within the material, especially about the hips, but he could find nothing suspicious. Satisfied that no items of value were hidden within the folds, he passed the dress to his sergeant. He then returned to confront Lady Adela. She remained standing with her back to him. He looked to what items remained about her person, and reflect on what little remained. He recalled his earlier search and concluded that there was very little difference between the two prisoners. Both women wore basically the same items of clothing; their dresses, their shoes and now it seemed their undergarments were all identical. Draped about Lady Adela's upper body was a simple white singlet made from a fine, closely woven fabric and pulled tight about the waist by a golden cord threaded through holes in the material that tied at the front. This singlet, as did the handmaiden's previously, proved extremely short, and a hint of rosy pink flesh about the buttocks left the captain in very little doubt that this undergarment was the only item of clothing to remain upon her person.

Captain Osbald stood for a while waiting for Lady Adela to take the initiative and conclude the search. But on seeing no further action, he spoke quietly to her.

"I beg of you, my Lady," he said, "pray, do remove your last undergarment so that I may inspect it."

Lady Adela turned to the captain. She made no effort to conceal her womanhood and kept her arms to her sides. The steely glare of defiance was also gone, replaced by a warm, more sensual womanly glow. It was as if she was intending to tease. Slowly, she untied the golden cord about her slender waist. For a while she played with the open cord before moving her hands down to the hem and unhurriedly began to raise the undergarment upwards from her body.

For the first time since the search began, Captain Osbald found him aroused by the sensuality of the act. Chivalry told him to look away, but he found that he simply could not avert his eyes. Before him stood a beautiful young woman, in the prime of her life, as if drawn by magnets, his eyes moved upwards with the hands.

Lady Adela's hands began their ascent from what was the top of a pair of long and shapely legs. The hands continued upwards, exposing firstly the hips, then the waist and finally two most exquisite breasts.

Captain Osbald began to drool and wiped his mouth with the back of a hand. But all the time his eyes never strayed from the body of the young woman stood before him. As the undergarment gathered about her head, his sight moved up and down the slender naked body. For a while he stood in a dreamlike state, doing or saying nothing.

Lady Adela handed him the garment and he collected his senses. She was stood with one hand outstretched, waiting for him to take it from her. He took it, fingered the material and then squeezed it into a ball within his hands. It was obvious nothing was concealed. The material was too thin and delicate to hide anything. Quickly, he passed the singlet back to the sergeant.

From a pouch by his side Captain Osbald withdrew a bible. One of the Baron's commands was that Lady Adela should be afforded such a luxury. The bible was in Latin and handwritten by monks at the local monastery. He held it out and took Lady Adela's hand. He placed the hand on the bible.

"Pray, swear upon the Holy Bible," he said. "Swear before God that you conceal no further items and I will pry no deeper."

Lady Adela looked at Captain Osbald. Even in such a darkened room her face appeared radiant, so pure and innocent. With her other hand, she indicated to her body.

"Look me over," she said. "You see me as I am. I have nothing else to reveal but my womanhood. What else would you want of me? I am as naked and as pure as the day I was born, and I swear to God that this is so."

Captain Osbald turned the bible over so that it now rested upon Lady Adela's hand.

"This bible is yours for comfort, my Lady," he said. "It is the wish of Baron de Clancey. I will now leave you in peace. Your clothes will be returned now that they are examined."

He then turned and walked from the room. Behind him Sergeant Cuthred handed back the clothes and shoes to Lady Adela. He then followed the captain out of the room.

As the guard closed the door and turned the key, Captain Osbald shook his head in sorrow.

"It is such a pity," he said. "If the Baron had his way then she'll be swinging from the gallows come two markets from now. Such a pity. Such a waste of life!"

And with that he turned and walked briskly away.

The captain remained an extremely busy man with many more duties to perform. But first he had to report his findings to the Baron, and that was where he was heading next.

Chapter Fourteen

Baron de Clancy sat deep in thought at the head of the long table. Alongside him, in the great hall, sat the castle's scribe. Before the scribe on the table rested his escritoire, parchments, ink and quills. He was poised and ready to write down whatever the Baron dictated, but for some time nothing had been forthcoming.

The Baron stroked his beard. He sat pensive and considering his best options. He had a juggling act to do and two trials to organise. But one thing was for sure, whatever he decided his wording and involvement had to appear impartial. But what should he say? In his mind he went over the details once more. His plan was nearing fruition. However, the chance discovery of the ring found in the handmaiden's shoe had changed things somewhat. Ideally, what he wanted was a confession from an accomplice to the robbery; something that could be presented at the trial of the Lady Adela. This was his objective, but it had to be done with a certain amount of guile and cunning.

The date of Lady Adela's trial was now finalised. It was to be held in seven days' time. The delay necessary, because Salopsbury needed to be informed and legal representation despatched south to Lodelowe. So this was to be his first letter and simple enough. His difficulties arose over the letters that were to follow, and all these entailed the handmaiden.

The trial of the handmaiden did not depend on outside influences. As a representative of the Council of the Marches he had the authority to prosecute, and because of the urgency he would do this within the next twenty-four hours. But urgency was only one part of his strategy. Another was to appear impartial, and to do this he planned to assemble a court of local dignitaries, and if he chose right, then the verdict would go against the handmaiden.

There was also the problem of the Royal Falconer. Even now, as he sat deep in thought, a rider was on his way to intercept the falconer and bring him back to Lodelowe. One thing was certain, he did not want to be on the receiving end of the King's wrath. All this brought him to a decision that hopefully would suit everyone involved. He had already asked the falconer to reside in judgement over a trial, so why not stand in the trial of the handmaiden, and then as soon as it was over, let him go on his way. Hopefully, with a successful guilty verdict resulting from the trial, then this should be sufficient for his needs. As for the trial of the Fitzgerald woman, he could easily find another suitable candidate to stand in judgement at a later date.

He turned to the scribe seated alongside. His mind now made up and ready to dictate. However the thought of the handmaiden going to the gallows brought a smile to his lips. This would be the first hanging in many months and would give the people of Lodelowe something to cheer. He tried hard to conceal his pleasure at the thought.

With no time to lose, the Baron set about dictating his letters. If his plans were to succeed then speed was of the essence. He could delay news of Lady Adela's pending trial to Salopsbury for one more day, but that was all. However, the handmaiden's trial was to take place on the morrow. Her confession would add credence to his actions and defend his men against accusations of impropriety at the ford. It was therefore, imperative that the handmaiden be found guilty, and for this he would choose carefully the men to sit in judgement. The Royal Falconer was one. He was top of the list. Captain Osbald would be another, since he was the one that had found the ring, and more importantly a commoner, something certain to go well with the crowd. Now all that was needed was three more men of impeccable upstanding; three men that lived locally so as to be available on the morrow. Three names immediately sprung to mind. One was an earl, number two, an abbot and the third a squire. He smiled; he knew exactly who to choose.

"Right, Scribe, take this down," he said.

The Baron set about dictating the terms of the two trials to the castle's scribe.

As the scribe set to work, the Baron rose from his chair and began to pace back and forth upon the floor of the great hall. As soon as the scribe was done, he would organise riders to deliver the summonses to all concerned.

Chapter Fifteen

Bardolph's early morning hunting trip proved briefer than expected. Beside the road, one mile north of Onneyditch, his keen eyes spotted a brace of pheasants. Two swift arrows saw them in his sack. He had set out with the intention of hunting rabbits in the coppice that overlooked Wistanstow Abbey, but having bagged the pheasants he turned around and headed back to the stables.

Later that day, as mid-afternoon approached and with Lodelowe now several miles behind, Bardolph dismounted before a small stream. As his animals drank, there came the sound of distant galloping hooves. A rider was approaching fast. He primed an arrow in his longbow but relaxed as the rider came into sight. Bardolph's eagle eyes saw that this was Egbert, a soldier of Lodelowe and someone he had previously encountered at the ford.

Egbert pulled up but remained in the saddle. Bardolph noted that he now wore the green tassels of a corporal, but made no comment.

"You are to read this, sire," said the rider and handing down a scroll. "It is from the court of the Baron de Clancey. My orders are that you must read this missive and then return with me to Lodelowe."

Bardolph unfurled the scroll and read the contents. This was a court summons signed by Baron de Clancey and bearing two seals, one the House of Lodelowe and the other the Council of the Marches. The document was written in French, as most official documents were since the coming of the Normans. However this proved no difficulty for Bardolph since he was well-schooled in both the French and Latin languages, as well as his own Anglo-Saxon tongue. He read the court summons through. This was a proclamation from the court of Lodelowe demanding that Bardolph, Royal Falconer to King Henry III make himself available for a forthcoming trial and Bardolph was summoned to stand in judgement. The trial was to take place at Lodelowe Castle. However there was no indication as to who was on trial or when the date was set. He wondered if this could be the Lady from Salopsbury; the one on the cart at the ford, but decided the timing all wrong. When it came to trials of people of high or noble birth, then these things took time. At no point did he consider the fate of the lady's handmaiden. He concluded that the trial would be of someone totally unrelated to the incident at the ford. But this was not his main concern. His annoyance came at being selected in the first place.

Bardolph looked up to Egbert, still seated in the saddle.

"When is this trial to take place?" he asked.

For the falconer, time was of the essence and he could not afford to lose too many days on his journey south.

Egbert shook his head in response.

"I was asked to ride out and waylay you sire, and hand you the missive. I was told nothing else," he replied.

Bardolph understood. He was asking the wrong person. This was something he would only find out if he returned to Lodelowe, and as he stood there contemplating the summons he was not certain he would take up the offer. The King's birds took priority and he could still use this as an excuse.

"And what if I refuse?" he questioned, just to make clear the consequences should he refuse.

Corporal Egbert shook his head in response.

"Then alas, sire, my orders are to take you forcibly," he said. "It is not my wish, but a proclamation bearing the seal of the Council of the Marches cannot be ignored."

Bardolph cursed his misfortune. This was the last thing he wanted. But he understood the situation that now confronted him. After the signing of the *Magna Carta*, the great charter that gave power to the barons by King John some twenty years earlier, this was the new order in the land, and the barons ruled within their own domain. He shrugged his shoulders. There was little he could do other than return to Lodelowe with Corporal Egbert.

"Then I'd best come peacefully," suggested Bardolph, gathering the reins of his donkey and mounting his steed.

Some four hours later, Bardolph, escorted by Corporal Egbert, entered the courtyard of Lodelowe Castle. It was now late in the day and the sun was setting over the ramparts. Captain Osbald happened to be in the courtyard when the party arrived. Bardolph dismounted, walked to the captain and the two men embraced.

"It's good to see you again my friend," said Captain Osbald as he patted Bardolph on the back.

"And it's good to see you too," returned Bardolph as he broke away from the embrace.

Captain Osbald felt a need to explain the reason for bringing Bardolph to Lodelowe.

"Good sire," he said, "Baron de Clancey wishes me to speak for him. He offers you his finest hospitality whilst a guest at his castle. A comfortable room in the west wing has been provided and servants are at hand to cater for your every need. If there is anything you desire, anything at all, then pray do not hesitate to ask. Your every need will be catered for and comfort assured, and with it goes the freedom of Lodelowe."

Bardolph stroked his neatly trimmed beard. His immediate thoughts lay with his animals and more importantly, with his peregrines. Time away attending the forthcoming trial would leave his birds unattended. This was something he could not tolerate.

"There is one thing you can do for me, Captain," replied Bardolph thoughtfully, then pointing to the two cages strapped to the back of his donkey, he explained, "Good captain, I require a lad to tend to my peregrines. Those birds belong to the King of England and must not come to harm."

Captain Osbald understood the importance of the birds. This very fact had been pointed out to him once before at the ford. He nodded his head.

"I will find a boy that can be of service," he said.

But Bardolph already had a boy in mind.

"I know of a lad that hath already served me well," he told Captain Osbald. "Someone I can trust. If you have no objections then I ask that the lad Ralph, from the stables at Onneyditch, be called upon to serve my needs."

Captain Osbald considered the request then nodded his head. He had no reason to object. The boy mentioned could be trusted. He could vouch for this.

He turned to Corporal Egbert who remained seated upon his horse.

"Corporal," he said looking up, "I have another task for you. Ride forthwith to Onneyditch and return with the lad Ralph. Let it be known to his father that the falconer's every need must be met and that Baron de Clancey hath decreed this to be so."

Corporal Egbert saluted, turned his horse and set off from the courtyard with a clatter of hooves upon the cobbles. Onneyditch was one hour's ride north of Lodelowe. It would be at least two hours before his return and by then it would be dark.

As the horse disappeared from the courtyard, Bardolph turned to Captain Osbald.

"I thank you good captain," he said. "God willing, I may now be allowed to perform my courtly duties safe in the knowledge that the King's birds does't remain in safe hands."

Captain Osbald nodded in agreement.

"Is there anything else you so desire?" he asked.

There were two things Bardolph still wanted to know. When and where was this trial to be held? And who was on trial?

"Tell me Captain, why I was asked to return to Lodelowe? What of this pending trial? And who stands in judgement?" he questioned.

The captain looked a little surprised, but he had not read the Baron's missive to the falconer and therefore, did not know the contents of what was said.

"You does't not know then?" he replied. "It is to be the trial of the handmaiden we encountered at the ford. A signet ring that once belonged to the Baron's late father was found upon her person. The ring was taken from the Baron's strongroom some three weeks past. It was I and Sergeant Cuthred that did'st conduct the search and came across the ring. The handmaiden now stands accused of robbery and murder, since a guard was slain during the robbery."

It was Bardolph's turn to look surprised. But there was something else he needed to know.

"And when is trial to take place?" he asked.

As they spoke, a young stable lad approached leading a saddled horse. Captain Osbald wanted to stay a little longer, but was a busy man. By sunrise on the morrow he was charged with having the Baron's court assembled. He placed a hand upon Bardolph's shoulder.

"The trial is on the morrow in the castle's keep," replied the captain, responding hastily to the falconer's question, and explained, "the Baron doth assemble his court as we speak. In fact, I must be away. There is my horse now. I go to meet a fellow member of the court and escort him back to Lodelowe. Bardolph, my dear friend, alas I must bid you fond farewell. Pray, go now to your room and make yourself comfortable. Perchance if all goes well, I will call upon your room when my duties are through."

The two men embraced one final time then went their separate ways; Bardolph was led by a servant to a room in the west wing, whilst Captain Osbald mounted his horse and rode swiftly away from the castle's courtyard.

Bardolph had wanted to find out more about the forthcoming trail but decided this could wait. It was obvious that Captain Osbald was a very busy man and did not want to detain him any longer. And besides, he had more important matters to deal with. For the next two hours, until the boy Ralph arrived, he had two valuable peregrine falcons to care for.

Chapter Sixteen

Bardolph was in his room feeding pheasant's intestines to his peregrines when a rap came upon the door. At first he considered this to be the arrival of the lad Ralph, but quickly changed his mind. To visit Onneyditch and return was a good two hours' journey and barely an hour had passed. This had to be the serving maid with the jug of water he had ordered.

"You may enter," he called.

Bardolph had his back to the door when the rap came and saw no reason to look around. However when the door swung open noisily, he immediately moved a hand to his dagger. His keen senses told him this was not the entrance of a serving maid. Quickly, he turned to confront the visitor.

A burly soldier with a ruddy face, an unruly shock of unkempt red hair and a large bulbous nose took one pace into his room and banged the door shut behind him. All the man's actions appeared heavy and clumsy. There was no helmet to his head and his chain-mail hood was down about his shoulders, but he was attired in the distinctive dark blue and red halved tunic of the de Clancey's along with the three rampant white lions of Lodelowe emblazoned upon his chest. Two twisted bright red tassels, one to each lapel, indicated this to be a man of senior rank, and most likely the castle's sergeant-at-arms, a position that ranked one below that of Captain Osbald. Slowly, Bardolph's hand relaxed from his dagger and moved to his side.

The sergeant stood rigidly in attention. He cleared his throat before speaking.

"Sire, my name is Cuthred," he told the falconer, "Sergeant-at-Arms to Lodelowe and the Baron de Clancey. Captain Osbald regrets that he cannot join you at this hour. He has other duties to perform. He therefore sends me to ask if there is anything you so desire? I have instructions to ensure that your every need is met."

Bardolph was well aware of Captain Osbald's duties and why he could not attend in person. However, he gave the question of need some thought. He concluded there was not a great deal he wanted. His birds were well fed and the lad Ralph, even though he had not yet arrived, was in all probability well on his way to the castle. Furthermore, his horse and donkey were stabled and being well looked after. He looked about the chamber. He had clean linen on his bed and the room was warm and well aired. He could think of nothing he so desired. Then a thought occurred to him. The name Sergeant Cuthred triggered something in his mind. He recalled something Captain Osbald had said about how he and Sergeant Cuthred being present at the search of the handmaiden. At the time he had not had time to question Captain Osbald further, so he was thinking perhaps the Captain's second-in-command might enlighten him with details of what actually happened. He addressed the Sergeant.

"There is something you can do, Sergeant," he told the sergeant. "Tell me what you know about the forthcoming trial of the handmaiden? Tell me about the search and the signet ring, and what part you did'st play in finding it?"

Sergeant Cuthred looked a little surprised, but had no objections and was fully prepared to reveal what little he knew.

"Sire, both the Captain and my good self did'st conduct the search of the handmaiden in her cell. The ring was found concealed upon her person. It was hidden within the heel of one of her shoes," he explained.

Bardolph rubbed his chin thoughtfully. Curiosity was getting the better of him. He recalled the handmaiden's shoes that she had been wearing that day at the ford. If he was not mistaken, they were of Norman origin and very similar to those worn by the Lady Adela.

"What else can you tell me, Sergeant?" he asked. "Was anything else found? What of the trial? Who stands in judgement alongside me?"

The sergeant shook his head and attempted to answer the questions in the order they came.

"Sire, only the ring was found upon the handmaiden," he replied, answering the falconer's first question. This he could do, but as regards the rest, these were subjects he knew nothing about. He therefore continued by saying, "There is nothing else I can add, sire. That is all I know. Other than being present at the search, I have no other involvement. I know nothing of the forthcoming trial or who stands in judgement, other than that it is scheduled for the morrow. Such things are organised by the Baron."

Bardolph turned pensive. The sergeant was just a minnow of the Baron and he did not expect any more from him. However, he remained curious and he had an idea.

After giving the subject much thought, he asked, "Sergeant, you say you have been given instructions to ensure that my every need is met?"

"Those were my instructions, sire," he confirmed.

"Everything?" added Bardolph.

"Everything, sire," assured the Sergeant.

Bardolph smiled. His curiosity was now greater than ever and he wanted to learn more. But obviously, this would not come from this man. He decided on a change of voice and addressed the Sergeant speaking as a superior; the tone of his voice suggesting that of a man in charge.

"Sergeant, there is one thing you can do for me," he said. "You will'st take me to see the prisoner whose trial I attend on the morrow."

Sergeant Cuthred hesitated even though it appeared to be a direct order. The Falconer's request was irregular and had come as a complete surprise. However, the Sergeant's orders were implicit. He had been despatched with instructions to ensure that this man's every need be met. He turned towards the door. He was a soldier and obeying orders was what he understood best.

"Pray accompany me, sire," he said. "I will'st escort you to the dungeon."

Bardolph slung a cape about his shoulders.

"I am ready," he said. "Lead the way, Sergeant."

Walking side-by-side, Sergeant Cuthred and Bardolph traversed the main courtyard, their destination the castle's keep. On arrival at the keep and with the doors closed behind them, the two men waited for their eyes to acclimatise. What little light existed came from two narrow slits positioned high and to either side of the big entrance doors.

Bardolph peered into the gloom and as his eyes adjusted he found himself standing in a vast empty hall. Nothing existed, no refineries and no decorations. There was a long table, almost the width of the hall, but this was pushed back against the far wall. To the right stood a large inglenook fireplace and on the hearth there rested a brazier and bellows. It was not lit. Other than these items, all that existed were plain walls and a damp flagstone floor.

After a short pause, Sergeant Cuthred moved off through a door to the left, leading the way along a series of long, dark passages before descending many steps before coming to an abrupt halt before a small arched and gated iron portal. A lone soldier stood guard. The soldier, with one large key attached to a chain that was anchored to his belt, turned the lock and allowed the two men to step through to the other side.

Immediately, beyond lay a stone staircase that spiralled down into the blackness of the castle's dungeon. Sergeant Cuthred took three steps down, then turned to check that Bardolph accompanied him. Bardolph nodded and the two men began their perilous descent. There was a burning torch about halfway down, but for most of the descent the stairs remained in total darkness. It was only the even pacing of the steps and the presence of the endlessly curving outer wall that kept Bardolph dropping at a steady, mechanical pace.

A second gate placed before the final step blocked the stairwell at the bottom. A guard on the other side unlocked the gate and stood rigidly in attention as the two men stepped through onto the uneven flagstones beyond. For a while they tarried whilst Sergeant Cuthred talked briefly about security to the guard. Bardolph took the opportunity to look about him. He had arrived at one end of a long, low arched corridor, dimly lit by a scattering of blazing torches placed in brackets and spaced at irregular intervals down the distant length of the passageway.

They set off again with Sergeant Cuthred leading the way. In the middle of the passageway there stood a table. On it rested a pile of clothes. Bardolph moved to view the items. On display was a long, green frock with one sleeve hanging loose, a white singlet undergarment, a plain white bonnet, a small wooden cross on a short leather thong and a pair of ladies' shoes. He recognised the items; these were the clothes of the handmaiden, torn and stained by the journey from the ford.

A small, balding man came to join them. Sergeant Cuthred introduced him to Bardolph.

"Sire, this is Cedric the castle's jailer," he said. "He keeps a goodly dungeon here and applies his trade with diligence." Then turning to Cedric, he explained, "And this is Bardolph, Royal Falconer to the King of England. He sits in judgement on the morrow at the trial of the handmaiden."

Bardolph gave a slight nod of recognition and pointed to the pile of clothes on the table.

"These items are those of the handmaiden, are they not?" he queried, even though the question was rhetorical, for he was well aware of their ownership.

Cedric nodded his head.

"Aye sire, they are," he replied. "They are the clothes of the handmaiden. They are to be presented as evidence at her trial."

Bardolph turned to Sergeant Cuthred.

"May I take a look?" he asked. "May I be permitted to examine the evidence in advance of the trial?"

Sergeant Cuthred saw no reason to oppose the request. The Falconer would be presented with them on the morrow anyway.

"Aye sire, pray carry on," he said.

Bardolph fingered the material of the dress then moved on to pick up the shoes. He looked them over. The shoes were of Norman origin, most certainly cobbled in France and of the finest quality. The bases were of carved oak, the uppers shaped from soft tanned leather and the edges surrounded by big brass studs, hammered home to seal and waterproof the uppers to the base. The heels suggested little wear, despite the mud. Bardolph concluded that these shoes had hardly been worn.

Sensing something loose, Bardolph raised the shoes to an ear and shook them vigorously. One shoe rattled and he decided to investigate. He placed a finger within the heel and raised the thick leather inner lining. The wooden base beneath had been hollowed to create a small secret compartment. Inside was a small object wrapped untidily in a torn piece of yellowed and stained parchment paper. Bardolph knocked out the contents and returned the shoe to the table. He then carefully unravelled the parchment. Upon opening, he discovered a solid-gold signet ring, the face engraved with a vertical stripe and the three rampant lions of Lodelowe set within a shield.

Bardolph turned to Sergeant Cuthred and showed him the face of the ring.

"Is this the seal of the House of Lodelowe?" he asked.

Sergeant Cuthred nodded his head.

"Aye, sire, it is the signet ring of the late Baron Edward de Clancey. His legacy was locked within the castle's strongroom. This ring was stolen from there some three weeks past."

Bardolph remained curious and furrowed his brow.

"Is this how the ring was found?" he asked. "Wrapped and concealed within the heel of this shoe, just as I see it now?"

Sergeant Cuthred nodded his head.

"Aye, sire, it was," he responded, "and no evidence has been tampered with. Those were my strict instructions. You see the ring exactly as it was found."

Bardolph continued with his questioning.

"Who conducted the search? Was it just you and Captain Osbald?" he asked.

Sergeant Cuthred answered immediately, since he had nothing to hide.

"It was, sire," he revealed, "I did'st assist in the search, along with Captain Osbald. No one else was there. Together we did'st search the handmaiden, and it was I that pointed out the secret compartment to the captain."

Bardolph's face turned quizzical.

"So you knew beforehand of these secret compartments?" he said. "Pray tell me Sergeant, just how might this be?"

Sergeant Cuthred was quick to answer.

"Sire, I had earlier searched the contents of the cart," he explained. "There were many shoes amongst the luggage and all had heels shaped in the same fashion. So when the turn came to search the handmaiden, I was well aware of the cobbler's craft."

Bardolph stroked his beard.

"I see," he said thoughtfully. "So, pray tell me Sergeant, was anything else found upon the cart?"

Sergeant Cuthred shook his head.

"Nay, nothing else, sire," he said, "nothing more was found, neither within the shoes nor amongst the rest of the luggage. Both the cart and Lady Adela's person were clean. Only the handmaiden was found to be concealing anything that did'st not belong to her."

Bardolph held the offending ring high and pointed to the shoe on the table.

"Then only this ring was found and discovered by both you and Captain Osbald?"

Sergeant Cuthred nodded his head.

"That is correct, sire," he confirmed, "nothing else was found."

Bardolph considered the matter before continuing with his questioning.

"Then, pray tell me, Sergeant," he asked next, "what did the handmaiden say when the ring was presented to her?"

Sergeant Cuthred shrugged his shoulders and thought back to the time when Captain Osbald presented the ring to the handmaiden.

"The handmaiden denied all knowledge of it," he said coldly.

Bardolph frowned and gave a look that suggested incredulity, for the rattle within the heel was most evident.

"And she offered you no explanation?" he quizzed.

Sergeant Cuthred shook his head.

"Nothing that held credence, sire, just feeble excuses," he said. "She spoke of the shoes being handed to her by Lady Adela for the journey, and if prior to this any objects had been placed within the heels, then she bore no knowledge of them."

Bardolph frowned.

"And you do not believe her story?" he suggested. "Could the handmaiden not be speaking the truth?"

"I think not, sire," answered Sergeant Cuthred scornfully. "When challenged, the handmaiden did'st merely repeated what she had been told to say. It is my opinion that she was always aware of the ring's presence."

Bardolph looked to the shoes and scratched his head.

"But, Sergeant," he said, sounding sceptical, "I remain puzzled! Surely if the handmaiden knew of the ring's presence, then why did she not try to get rid of the evidence long before the search took place? This ring is small, it could be hidden anywhere, even in her cell there would be cracks in the walls where such damning evidence could be concealed and never traced."

Sergeant Cuthred laughed a hearty roar for he was now on much safer ground.

"Sire, the handmaiden remained with her hands bound from the time of her arrest to the time of the search. A fortunate happening no doubt, for what you hypothesise could very well have happened and we would not now be gathered here to debate upon such matters."

Bardolph gave a wry smile. This was not the answer he was expecting, but he could see it all now. The only logical conclusion was that the girl was lying for her mistress. However, he made no comment, instead he turned his attentions to the wrapping. Someone had torn away a corner of a manuscript for the purpose. There were traces of writing, faded but very distinctive light blue ink, but it had become rubbed and smudged and too blurred to decipher. He turned the ring over in his hand before re-wrapping it carefully, using the same folds and placed it back in the heel of the shoe. He then shook the shoe vigorously so that the sergeant should once again be reminded of the rattle.

"Was there no other packing inside?" he asked. "Is this exactly how the shoe was found?"

Sergeant Cuthred nodded his head. "This is exactly how the shoe was found, sire," he confirmed.

Bardolph did not speak. It seemed hard to believe that the handmaiden had worn these shoes for at least two days and not sensed something loose within the heel. He had noticed it straightaway. After pondering for a little while longer, he decided to put no further questions. He would save them for the morrow at the trial of the handmaiden.

As Bardolph pondered and stroked his beard, he turned to leave. His birds had been left unattended and as yet, the lad Ralph had not arrived. He said no more and headed for the portal at the foot of the spiral stairs.

He felt sorry for the young handmaiden. It seemed that her guilt had already been decided. However, if he could help he would. Perhaps at her trial on the morrow he would get a little closer to learning the truth.

Chapter Seventeen

The trial of the handmaiden was to be held in the castle's keep. This was not unusual, as most trials for the peasantry were held here. The official line being that it was for the convenience of transporting prisoners from the dungeon below.

Bardolph was last to arrive, escorted by Sergeant Cuthred. Bardolph refused to be rushed. The lad Ralph, who had arrived the night before, needed to be instructed in the ways of caring for two very precious peregrine falcons. Only when Bardolph was totally satisfied that his birds could be left in safe hands did he venture from his room and make his way to the keep.

A large crowd had gathered outside. Normally those waiting would be the privileged few, either by invitation or those that could afford entry, but on this occasion, no fee was asked. Baron de Clancey had been deliberate in his choosing and left nothing to chance. He wanted as many people as possible to attend. It was important that rumours spread quickly throughout the entire length and breadth of the Marches. This way, by granting free admission, the outcome of the trial would become common knowledge long before the arrival of anyone from Salopsbury.

Bardolph entered the castle's keep and looked about the vast entrance hall. The sight that greeted him was certainly not as expected. He had passed this way the day before and had encountered very little but a vast empty space. But now, all had changed. The long table that rested against the back wall had been brought forward and now stood behind a row of ornately carved high-backed chairs. There were seven in total. The hall itself was brightly lit. Hundreds of candles blazed upon the table and torches flared in brackets about the walls.

Six men stood behind the long table and chairs. Five were debating in a group, a sixth stood remote and at several paces' distance. The group of five were busy pawing over items of clothing laid out upon the surface of the table. All appeared oblivious to the arrival of Bardolph. Only the man standing remote noted his coming, but said nothing and simply stared blankly at his approach.

Of the six men to the rear of the table, only one was known to Bardolph. This was Captain Osbald. Of the remaining five, however, it was not difficult to place any of them, if not by rank then by standing amongst the community. A man at the very centre of the group, aged about fifty, with well-trimmed beard and cape about his shoulders had to be Baron de Clancey. His actions and demeanour exhumed complete authority.

Of the others, Bardolph began to categorise them accordingly. He started with the man standing away from the group. He was most certainly a scribe. He stood with escritoire, a great number of scrolls, an inkwell and several quills before him. He was tall, thin and of almost skeletal appearance, with pale, drawn yellow skin and dark sunken sockets for his eyes. He was dressed in a white robe and a black bonnet, with ties hanging down before him.

With the Baron, the scribe and Captain Osbald identified, Bardolph turned his attention to the identifying of the remaining three. Most obvious of the three was a man of the cloth, an abbot by all accounts, for he wore a white habit with a black hood and in his hands he clutched a bible and a crucifix. This man was excessively overweight, with a great protruding belly and sagging jowls. His hood was down and from the top of his head shone a brightly cropped tonsure of almost pure white. On every finger he wore a ring, some of plain gold, others studded with emeralds and rubies.

With two more men to categorise, Bardolph moved his attention to what appeared to be the youngest member of the group. By his demeanour and attire he could only assume this youth to be of minor nobility, possibly the son of an earl or a baron. He was young, in his early teens and not yet shaven. But for all his tender years he exhumed an air of authority. He was dressed in the finest silk robes and about his shoulders, draped a heavy cloak hemmed in pean.

The final dignitary of the group proved the most difficult to categorise. He was undoubtedly a man of wealth, for he was dressed in the finest attire, all highly decorated and in matching royal blue. He was rotund, though nowhere near the size of the abbot. He sported a finely trimmed greying beard, a flat cloth hat and in one hand held a long staff topped with a silver orb. He was a man of ageing years, probably in his mid-sixties and most definitely the oldest person amongst this gathering of Lodelowe's elite.

Baron de Clancey stood with his back to Bardolph as he entered. But the instant he heard footsteps, he turned.

"Ah, at last, my court is complete!" he remarked. "Come, join us good sire, for we are eager to begin."

Bardolph walked around the table to join those gathered to the rear of the hall. The Baron held out his hand in greeting. The two men shook hands.

"Welcome to my court," said the Baron. "It is indeed a great privilege and honour to have a servant of the King grace us with their presence this day."

Bardolph acknowledged the greeting with a polite bow.

"Likewise, my Liege," he said, "it is indeed an honour and a privilege for me to be here today."

The time for introductions had come. The Baron moved firstly to the man of the cloth.

"May I introduce you to the Father Monticelli, the Abbot of Wistanstow," he said. "He heads a religious order that does't lie to the north of Onneyditch and a place you must have passed on your journey south. The Abbot's presence at my court is two-fold. One, I ask him to judge, for his opinions and knowledge of the law are held in high esteem. And two, I ask him to oversee the spiritual side of the proceedings, for it is imperative that we get a written confession from the wench today. She must be made to disclose all she knows concerning the robbery. But if she is not forthcoming and proves non co-operative, then I am sure his blessings will come as welcome relief."

Bardolph dropped to one knee. The Abbot placed a hand upon his head and recited a little prayer in Latin, and on conclusion all those present voiced, "Amen."

As Bardolph rose, the Baron turned to the youngest member of the group.

"Next, may I introduce you to Edwin," he said, "son of Earl de Mortimer, Lord of Powys, High Sheriff of Salopia and Overlord to the Council of the Marches."

Bardolph took the young man's hand and bent low in respect.

"Greetings, Edwin, son of Earl de Mortimer," he said sounding humble.

Edwin acknowledged with a nod to the head.

"It is indeed a great pleasure and privilege to sit in judgement alongside a member of the King's court," he said sounding equally humble.

The Baron moved on. Time was pressing. He was aware that Bardolph had already met Captain Osbald so he passed him by simply uttering, "Captain Osbald you already know."

Only one man remained to be introduced. This was the man of wealth.

"Finally, may I introduce you to Squire Henry Stokes," said the Baron, "once servant to a knight of the Order of St. John of Jerusalem. Squire Henry graces my court with his presence as a fine and upstanding gentleman, not only here in Lodelowe, but across the entire length and breadth of the Marches."

Bardolph offered the squire his hand and bowed his head. With the squire's cloak partially opened, Bardolph noted the cross of St. John of Jerusalem upon his left breast. The two gentlemen shook hands.

"It is a privilege to be by your side," said the squire.

"And me by yours," said Bardolph returning the complement.

With all formalities over, Baron de Clancey clapped his hands to gain attention.

"Gentlemen, let us begin," he said. "God willing, we will see justice done this day."

"Praise be to God that He gives us strength," chanted the Abbot in response.

The Baron knelt and clasped his hands in prayer.

"Let us pray to God for strength," he said. "Let us pray for guidance. Come, let us all kneel in prayer."

Bardolph knelt, as did the others. The Abbot added his own blessings to the ceremony by reciting several verses in Latin that culminating in the Lord's Prayer. When he was done, the Baron rose and straightened his tunic.

"Gentlemen, we have much work to do," he said. "The trial must begin forthwith. So, may I ask of you all to take your seats."

He then turned to Sergeant Cuthred and added, "Sergeant, bring forth the accused and open the doors to the hall so that the good people of Lodelowe may enter."

The Baron took his place behind the table, sitting in the middle chair of the row of seven, the table being so arranged that it faced directly towards the doors through which the awaiting crowd would enter.

To the Baron's right, the scribe had already arranged his escritoire and waited alongside his chair. Moving quickly, the young nobleman took the vacant chair to the Baron's left. It seemed rank was important and a seat next to the Baron was an effective way of displaying his status.

With the three central positions taken, the Abbot settled his huge bulk down on the side of the scribe and Squire Henry Stokes moved to sit next to the young Edwin de Mortimer.

The two men left standing, Bardolph and Captain Osbald, looked to each other then moved to sit at opposite ends of the long table. Bardolph positioning himself next to the Abbot and Captain Osbald alongside Squire Henry Stokes. Bardolph found himself seated behind a pile of clothing.

Whilst the seating arrangement was underway, the doors to the hall were opened and those waiting outside entered. They were to stand to the rear, held back by a row of guards. For a while there was shuffling and murmuring, but soon silence fell and the court waited patiently for the accused to appear.

The creaking open of a door saw the appearance of the handmaiden. From the side door she shuffled slowly into the hall, a heavy blanket draped about her shoulders. On entering she hesitated briefly and looked about the room. She had not expected to see people. Not this many, anyway.

Sergeant Cuthred urged her forward with the flat palm of an open gauntlet. She stumbled, caught her balance and moved on. To be truthful, she was at a loss as to exactly what was expected of her. She had been told nothing of her trial, or of what to do or say, since no one was prepared to defend her. Sergeant Cuthred continued to push her forward, guiding her towards the centre the floor, then called a halt. Here he turned her around to face the table, directly in front of the Baron.

A hushed silence befell the hall. The Baron, on sensing the earnestness, added further solemnity to the occasion by pausing several seconds longer than necessary before raising a silent finger and signalling to the Abbot to begin proceedings with a blessing and a prayer.

The man of the cloth rose awkwardly from his chair, propped his paunch over the edge of the table and addressed Gwyneth across the wide surface.

"Prisoner, kneel down before us," he told her at a chant, "so that we may all pray together and ask God to give us strength."

Still clutching doggedly to her blanket, Gwyneth sank slowly to her knees and lowered her head. The Abbot, biding his time, recited several long verses in Latin before finally making the sign of the cross before his body and retaking his seat. At a loss as to what to do next, Gwyneth remained on her knees, her head bowed.

The Baron's voice broke the silence.

"Will the accused please rise and stand before this court?" he said loudly so that those at the back could hear.

Gwyneth looked up to see the Baron's steely eyes glaring across the table towards her. She rose awkwardly, but determined not to release the blanket. Turning her head from side to side she looked along the row at seven stern faces seated behind the great table. She recognised two of the seven. They were sitting at opposite ends. One was the captain she loathed and despised. The other was the man that had shot an arrow and killed one of her escorts. He had been kind to her at the stables when he cut her down and allowed her to rest upon the straw. But this did not make up for his evil deed at the ford and she concluded that she despised him too.

A hush settled upon the court. The Baron's stentorian voice cut the silence.

"Scribe, hand me the charges," he said holding out a hand.

The thin skeleton framed man, forever silent, handed over a scroll. The Baron unfurled it and holding it out before him, proceeded to read the contents. It was written in the Saxon tongue.

"Gwyneth, daughter of Thomas the Fletcher of Salopsbury," he started and then continued, "serving wench and handmaiden to the Lady Adela Fitzgerald, you stand before this court this day accused of robbery and murder, in so much that on the fifth day of August, in the year of our Lord twelve hundred and thirty-five, you did aid and abet in the theft of property from his lordship the Baron de Clancey and also did aid and abet in the murder of Richard, son of Frederick, guard to the Baron de Clancey's strongroom, and thereafter did wilfully partake in the concealment of stolen property from their rightful owner."

Then, looking up and addressing the accused, he asked directly, "Gwyneth, daughter of Thomas the Fletcher of Salopsbury, how does't you plead to these charges, guilty or not guilty?"

Gwyneth was lost for words. Surely they did not mean her? She had done nothing wrong. With furrowed brow she stood staring numbly back at the Baron whilst she gathered her wits. These charges were all new to her. She had not been told anything beforehand, either of the accusations or what to reply. Since the search in her cell, she had neither seen nor spoken to anyone.

Gwyneth took a deep breath and gave her response.

"Not guilty, sire!" she replied in a clear and loud voice.

The Baron frowned and drummed his fingers upon the table.

"Then you do not confess to the charges laid before you?" he asked and holding up the unfurled scroll for her to see.

Even if from this distance she could see what was written on the parchment, it would have done the court no good, for she could neither read nor write. However, the gesture was simple enough for her to understand and she knew exactly how to respond, for although illiterate, she was no fool. Knowing only too well that to admit to robbery and murder meant certain death.

"No sire, I cannot confess. For I am innocent of all crimes," she replied in a clear and purposeful voice.

The Baron drummed his fingers hard upon the table.

"Record her words, scribe," he growled. "The accused denies the charges in the first instance,"

Then returning his attention towards the handmaiden he spelled out clearly the consequences of her denial.

"By the laws of Lodelowe," he began to explain, "and of the Council of the Marches, this court can allow you but two more chances to freely admit your guilt. Plead guilty now and reveal to us your knowledge surrounding the robbery and you may depart from this court unharmed. This much, I promise. But continue to refuse and I warn you, that before this day is out this court will have the truth extracted from your lips, so help me God. So I ask you for a second time; Gwyneth, daughter of Thomas the Fletcher, how do you plead to these charges; guilty or not guilty?'

Gwyneth stood her ground, determined not to give in.

"Not guilty, sire," she replied in an equally loud and purposeful voice.

The Baron thumped the table.

"Scribe," he growled, "record this wench's second denial. This court's patience grows thin and me thinks she be reminded that more forceful measures may be needed in order to gain the confession we so desire. Sergeant, move the accused closer to the table and relieve her of her blanket."

Sergeant Cuthred stepped forward, placed his hands upon Gwyneth's shoulders and tugged at the blanket. Doggedly she clung on, fighting for possession, but the sergeant's superior strength proved too much and the blanket slipped from her shoulders. Standing naked, she was pushed forward two paces.

As Sergeant Cuthred stepped back a pace, the Baron gestured to the Abbot. The man of the cloth rose from his seat and set off slowly and solemnly around the long table. Those that remained bowed their heads as the Abbot moved to stand before the handmaiden. He offered her his blessings. Speaking in Latin and with his broad back to the table shielding his actions, he traced the sign of a cross before her body, passing the edge of his flattened palm firstly in a line directly down between her breasts, then secondly in a crosswise direction, and in doing so, brushing lightly but deliberately against the tips of her nipples.

Gwyneth spoke quietly to the Abbot.

"Holy Father, I am innocent of all crimes, please tell them I am innocent," she whispered. "I beg of you Holy Father, tell them I am innocent."

The Abbot placed a hand upon a breast to cover her heart.

"Then you have nothing to fear my child," he replied. "God will be your witness and your strength."

The handmaiden tried to move away but the hand followed.

"Then pray for me Holy Father. Please, pray for me," she begged.

The Abbot chanted another little prayer and shuffled even closer. Once more he traced the sign of the cross before her breasts, but on this occasion with the edge of his hand remaining in contact with her body on both the downward stroke between her cleavage and on the lateral movement across her breasts.

He concluded in Anglo-Saxon with the words, "Put all your trust in God, my child. May He remain with you, and protect you from evil, forever and ever. Amen."

The Baron waited patiently for the Abbot to conclude his blessing and return to his chair before speaking.

"Amen," he repeated loudly as the Abbot resumed his seat.

The Baron then addressed those seated at the table.

"Since the accused does not readily admit to her guilt, then gentlemen we must work hard for that confession," he told them.

After a brief pause he turned to the accused.

"Gwyneth Fletcher, you have now denied this court on two separate occasions and our patience grows thin," he warned her. "Under the laws of Lodelowe, and of the Council of the Marches, deny this court a third time and we will have no option but to resort to other, more brutal ways of extracting the truth from your lips. You will be returned to the dungeon where we have means of making you speak the truth. Do you understand what I am saying?"

Gwyneth understood only too clearly. This was no idle threat from the Baron. Having lived and worked within the walls of a castle for the past five years, she was fully aware of the threat and danger that lay coded within the Baron's words. By the kitchen fires at night, she had been told many a gruesome tale of what went on down in the castle's dungeon, and had seen with her own eyes the crippled wrecks of bodies forced to hobble and crawl their way to the gallows. She closed her eyes and said a little prayer before nodding her head in response.

But a nod was not good enough.

"Speak up, wench, so that your response can be recorded accordingly," stated the Baron. "Tell this court you understand."

The handmaiden swallowed a dry mouth.

"Yes, sire, I understand," she replied.

The Baron motioned for the shoe that contained the ring to be passed along the line. Bardolph, being seated at the far end of the table, passed it along. On receiving the shoe, the Baron held it high for Gwyneth to see.

"Wench, is this your shoe?" he demanded.

Gwyneth stared blankly at the shoe but give no reply.

"Answer me wench, so that it may be recorded," snapped the Baron, sounding more impatient than ever.

Gwyneth nodded her head, but remained unsure of how to answer. For this was not her shoe. It belonged to the Lady Adela.

"Sire, the shoe was given me by Lady Adela so that I may have something to wear on the journey south," she replied and trying to put things into their proper context.

The Baron scowled. Not getting the answer he desired, he rephrased the question.

"Gwyneth Fletcher, I demand a straight answer. Were you wearing this shoe at the time of your arrest at the ford? Just answer this court, yes or no?" he said.

With the question rephrased Gwyneth had little option but to reply honestly.

"Yes, sire, it is the shoe I was wearing at the ford," she admitted quietly.

Satisfied, the Baron continued.

"And is this the same shoe you wore in the cell when searched?" he enquired.

Even more quietly and with head bowed she whispered her response.

"Yes, sire, it is," she said.

The Baron waited for the scribe to take everything down. Keeping the shoe held high, he raised the flap in the heel and removed the signet ring wrapped in parchment. He placed the shoe upon the table, removed the wrapping and held the ring aloft.

"So if you do not deny this shoe is yours, then pray explain to this court how this ring came to be found inside?" he demanded, with a hint of incredulity to his voice.

Gwyneth shook her head and answered back in a raised voice that held a touch of contempt for what was being implied.

"Sire, you are wrong," she answered. "I swear before God that I know nothing of the ring."

The Baron thumped the table hard and tried to contain his temper. The handmaiden not only blasphemed and took the name of the Lord thy God in vain, but also issued an insult to his person. As upholder of the law, no one had the right to accuse him of being wrong.

"What!" he exclaimed, shocked by the tone in which she had addressed his court. "With all this damning evidence, you have the audacity to say that I am wrong? I must warn you, we who sit in judgement are no fools and not to be trifled with."

Gwyneth looked firstly to the Baron and then to all the other faces seated at the table. She pulled herself together and answered even more loudly and clearly so that all those assembled would understand the message she was trying to get across.

"Sire, and my noble lords," she said, "on my solemn oath, I do swear before you and before God that I know nothing of the ring found within my shoe."

The Abbot audibly tutted and began to shake his head.

"Sire, this wench continues to take the name of the Lord thy God in vain," he said. "This amount of blasphemy cannot be allowed to go unpunished."

The Baron held up a hand to silence the Abbot. For a while he stood rocking backwards and forwards in his chair, for anger raged within him also. The handmaiden had raised her voice and shown nothing but contempt for his court. Eventually, he calmed down enough to speak.

"Me thinks gentlemen, this wench has uttered her third and final denial and the time has come for us to put a stop to this nonsense. Is this not the verdict of you all?"

Captain Osbald took no time in replying.

"Aye, my Liege, you are right as ever," he said. "This court cannot remain lenient with her a moment longer. It is like you say; the time for nonsense is over. Let the jailer extract the truth from her lips."

Squire Henry Stokes was similarly quick to voice his opinion.

"I see no other course of action left open to us, my Liege," he said. "The wench procrastinates. She has denied this court on three separate occasions, and the situation can no longer be tolerated. I agree with the good captain, her tongue must be loosened. Let the jailer do his work."

Next was the turn of the young Edwin de Mortimer. All eyes turned his way.

"I can only agree with Squire Henry and the captain, my Liege," he said. "This court must take what steps are necessary to ensure that justice is done. We are left with no other option."

One side of the table had now passed its verdict and all eyes turned towards the Abbot and Bardolph sitting to the right of the Baron, beyond the scribe. It was the Abbot that spoke next. He sat in prayer, his podgy hands together before his face. He lowered them to the table before speaking.

"I must agree with everything that has been said, my Liege. Three denials and three impious lies have been issued from this young maiden's lips. One so blasphemous that it cannot be allowed to go unpunished. Lucifer is within her. I say the jailer must expunge the devil from her loins."

The Baron nodded his head. He was in total agreement with the Abbot's sentiments. However, he could progress no further until receiving one last verdict. He waited patiently for the man seated at the end of the table to give his response. But when it was not readily forthcoming, he spoke along the table.

"Bardolph, good sire, this court needs to record a statement from all those that sit in judgement," he said.

Bardolph stared back long and hard and then at the handmaiden, now sobbing gently. A lock of hair was cast down over one eye, and wet dishevelled strands clung to the side of her face. He wished that it was within his power to save her from certain torment, but already the verdict was four to none, and he was well aware that nothing he could add would alter the final outcome. The handmaiden's fate was already decided and the Baron's justice would run its full and brutal course. In the end he prayed that once taken away, she should break quickly, for there was nothing in his power to save her.

Bardolph spoke his thoughts, apologising for his reticence.

"Pray forgive me, my Liege, for not giving an immediate answer," he said, "for I remain ignorant of the laws of Lodelowe and of the Marches. My knowledge is only of Wessex and the laws that prevail at the King's court at Winchester. But if the law requires three denials before sentence of persuasion be passed, then I can confirm I have heard this young maiden deny the charges laid out before her on no less than three separate occasions. You may mark my words on that, for that which remains a fact cannot be denied. But as for what is to follow, then I am neither for nor against what is proposed. For it is my belief that this court will glean very little from her, save that she remains loyal to her mistress and that her soul holds nothing more than youthful naivety."

Murmuring from the crowd filled the hall, and the Abbot seated next to Bardolph glared silently back at him. Bardolph could see that his words had not found favour in certain quarters. However, the Baron was more conciliatory, recognising that if to succeed, then this trial needed the full blessing of the King's Falconer.

"Fine words and well spoken, sire," uttered the Baron, breaking the silence, "and I must echo your sentiments, for it is clear this wench says what she does in order to protect others, and as yet cannot foresee what dire consequences this action holds for her. However, I must remind you that it remains the duty of this court to establish the truth in this matter, and we must apply the full force of the law with unrelenting pressure until those ends are met. So, do you not agree that the jailer offers the only means left to us?"

Bardolph regretted that it should come to this. However, this was not his home and not his problem. The road south beckoned and with autumn approaching, he had much to do in the training of his young fledglings. He nodded his head.

"I remain guided by your judgement in such matters, my Liege," he said sadly. "If the only way left open to this court in seeking the truth is by alternative means, then so be it. I offer no objections."

The Baron waited for the scribe to stop writing before turning to the handmaiden. Tears trickled down her cheeks. She had listened to their verdicts and could find not one ally amongst them. Every one of them thought her guilty. In desperation, she made one last plea for mercy.

"Please, I beg of you, do not do this to me," she called. "I am innocent of all crimes. Pray do me no harm."

Affronted by the outburst, the Baron called upon Sergeant Cuthred who was standing one pace behind.

"Sergeant, silence this wench," he said. "She remains as impudent as ever. In future she must only be allowed to speak when this court requests her to do so."

Sergeant Cuthred stepped to the front. Turning to face Gwyneth he removed a gauntlet and raised a hand as if to strike. On seeing the threat she shut her eyes and turned her head away. The strike however, did not materialise and the sergeant lowered his hand, but all the same she remained with her head to one side whilst she listened to the Baron pronounce sentence upon her.

The Baron placed his hands together and spoke.

"Gwyneth, daughter of Thomas the Fletcher of Salopsbury," he said, "this court has, in accordance with the laws of Lodelowe and under the jurisdiction of the Council of the Marches, allowed you ample opportunity in which to confess your crimes. You have been presented with the evidence and on three occasions this court has offered you the chance to openly and freely admit your guilt. But alas, you have failed to comply on every occasion and this court simply cannot continue in this vain. There comes a limit to our generosity and a time when the truth must be out. That time for you, alas, has now come. We tire of your stubbornness, and you therefore, leave us with no alternative. This court decrees that your tongue be loosened by whatever means we deem fit, and so, Gwyneth, daughter of Thomas the Fletcher of Salopsbury, this court returns you to the dungeon where by whatever means are available, we will have the truth from your lips. So help you God!"

"Amen!" voiced the Abbot upon hearing the Baron's stern words.

"Amen," added the young Edwin de Mortimer and Squire Henry Stokes in unison.

The Baron looked around the room.

"Where is the jailer?" he asked. "I want him here, now."

"My Leige, Cedric the jailer is down in the dungeon," answered a soldier holding back the crowd.

"Then summon him here immediately," ordered the Baron. "And be quick about it."

The soldier who had previously spoken, moved quickly and disappeared through an adjoining door.

Whilst the court waited for the jailer to appear, the Baron turned to address his distinguished guests.

"Gentlemen, it seems we have a slight delay," he told them. "Come, let us partake of a goblet of wine whilst we wait. I have some goodly Norman wine from the vineyards of Anjou."

The Baron snapped a finger and a young boy appeared. He carried a silver tray, a flagon of wine and seven silver goblets. He poured the wine into the goblets.

When all goblets were filled, the Baron spoke to his guests.

"Gentlemen be standing and pray do quench your thirst," he said. "We have a long day before us and are in need of much sustenance."

The Abbot was first to the tray. He blessed the wine and took a goblet. The others rose and moved to collect theirs in turn.

Bardolph was last to rise. Taking up the last goblet, he moved to stand beside the Baron.

"Pray tell me, my Liege," he said, "surely one ring and one necklace do not constitute a great deal towards the recovery of all that was taken from your strongroom? Pray tell me, just what was taken? Not as a list but in physical size?"

The Baron pondered upon Bardolph's question, but clearly had no answer. He had seen an inventory of the missing items, but had never visualised the actual size of the haul.

"In sacks, maybe? One sack? Two sacks? Several sacks?" suggested Bardolph, trying to be helpful.

Captain Osbald, standing alongside and overhearing the conversation, came to the Baron's aid.

"At least three sacks, my Liege, maybe four," he interrupted. "The robbers must have taken at least three, possibly four sacks of treasure, for there were silver plates and goblets in the haul as well as many gold coins."

Bardolph pondered for a while before speaking.

"Ah!" he exclaimed. "So this begs a second question. If one necklace and one ring are all that have been recovered then where is the rest?"

The Baron held out a hand towards the scribe who was standing some distance away.

"Hand me the map, scribe," he called.

The scribe collected a scroll from alongside his escritoire and passed it down the table. The Baron spread the map out upon the surface and held the corners down with the tray and the wine jug. It was a map of West Mercia and of the Marches, and included the town of Lodelowe and the city of Salopsbury.

"Pray look here," said the Baron, indicating with one finger the various points on the map, "to the north lies Salopia, and here to the centre lies Salopsbury and the castle of the Fitzgeralds. Whilst down here to the bottom is Lodelowe. This is where we are now," he said, tapping a finger on the spot. "Reportedly, Lady Adela's party was travelling to the Cinque Ports to board a boat for France. The ports are down here, to the south and east and off the map. This line here, this is the road they should have been taking. This is Watling Street, an old Roman road that leads to London and the Cinque Ports, and as you can see this road does not pass through Lodelowe. But all the same, they chose a different route. I therefore, beg the question? Why go out of their way when it is not necessary? Could it be that my treasure is buried somewhere in my forest, and their intention was to collect it on their way? I think this to be the reason, does't you not agree?"

Bardolph rubbed his chin thoughtfully and studied the map. In time, he replied.

"Your reasoning is sound and logical, my Liege. I find no fault," he agreed.

The Baron placed a hand upon Bardolph's shoulder.

"If my treasure is buried somewhere in my forest and this wench knows of its whereabouts, then I will have it from her lips. I swear before God that this will be so," he said with a hint of bitterness to his voice.

As the Baron spoke there came the sound of a door opening.

"You call for me, my Liege," called Cedric as he entered the room.

The Baron looked to those assembled about the table.

"Pray gentlemen, retake your seats," he told them. "My court is back in session."

Stood to the centre of the hall, the handmaiden could only ponder upon her fate. She shook with fear. As the Abbot took his seat, she called out to him.

"Holy Father, pray give me your blessing," she called.

The Abbot, on hearing, turned to the Baron. He had not expected this intervention and looked a little surprised.

The Baron raised a finger and pointed to the handmaiden.

"You may proceed," he told the Abbot. "The accused may receive a final blessing before she is returned to the dungeon."

The Abbot rose awkwardly and walked around the long table. As he approached the handmaiden he recited a verse in Latin.

"*Qui nos rodunt confundantur et cum iustis non scribantur,*" he chanted.

Bardolph translated the words. The Abbot was saying; "May those who slander us be cursed and may their names not be written in the book of the righteous."

Bardolph felt sorry for the handmaiden. She had asked for the Abbot's blessing and these were not the words he should have spoken. Bardolph looked down the long table. There was no reaction from those seated, save that of the scribe who was gently nodding his head. It was apparent to Bardolph that, other than himself and the scribe, no one seated at the table had any understanding of Latin.

The Abbot came to stand before Gwyneth, his rather large and rotund figure shielding her from the table. With the edge of his hand in constant contact with her body, he traced the sign of the cross, firstly down between her breasts, then horizontally to brush across the tips of her nipples.

As he did so he chanted once more in Latin, "*Pulchra tibi facies, capillorum series, a quam clara species.*"

The Abbot's words were low and whispered, but Bardolph, with his keen sense of hearing, heard every word. The Abbot had chanted, "Beautiful is your face, your braided hair; what a glorious creature!"

Bardolph seethed. The Abbot was taking gratification from her nakedness and this was no way for a man of the cloth to behave.

Bardolph's instinct was to protect Gwyneth. She needed someone to stand up for her. He was aware, however, that this trial was just a charade, a face-saver for the Baron, and everyone concerned were just pawns in his game. Inwardly he wanted to speak out and defend the handmaiden, but his loyalty to the King overrode such action. His priority lay with his peregrines, and he realised this court would pronounce its verdict regardless of anything he said or did. He took comfort from the fact that this trial would be soon over and he would be on his way.

As the Abbot returned to his chair, the Baron, with voice raised so that all those assembled in the hall could hear, called Cedric to the table.

"Jailer, escort the prisoner to the dungeon. Do your best work and loosen her tongue. The scribe will accompany you and prepare a confession in readiness for her mark," he said.

Gwyneth turned to face the table and began to recite a small prayer, asking God to give her strength and the will to survive.

The Baron waited for Gwyneth to conclude her prayers. He then spoke loudly so that everyone in the hall should hear.

"Gwyneth Fletcher," he began, "are you now ready to confess your guilt? This is your last opportunity to speak openly before the jailer does his work. Even at this late hour this court is willing to withdraw the threat. So we ask you for one last time. Are you prepared to relent your stubborn ways and confess to this court the true nature of your crimes?"

Through clenched teeth Gwyneth gave her reply.

"My Liege," she told the Baron, "I am innocent. I know nothing of the ring. I can tell you no more. Please, I beg of you, do not do this to me."

The Baron issued a loud tut and shook his head from side to side.

"You can tell this court no more because you do not choose to tell us. Is this not the truth?" he snapped angrily.

Gwyneth shook her head and tried to justify her words.

"No, my Liege," she said, "I swear to you all, I know nothing of the ring, and this is the solemn truth. I swear this before God."

The Abbot protested immediately, for once more this wench did blaspheme in the name of the Lord thy God. But the Baron was quick to hold up a hand and silence him. He placed his hands thoughtfully together as if in prayer. After a long pause he spoke through his hands.

"Jailer," he said, "this court can no longer hold back its leniency. Proceed with your work. This court needs an answer this very day. So be quick about it. Take her away."

Taking his cue, Cedric moved to stand before the accused. At the same time Sergeant Cuthred, from behind, took a firm grip of Gwyneth's arms. She struggled to break free.

"Wait!" a call from the table came.

All eyes turned to Bardolph. He rose and addressed the Baron.

"My Liege, may I be permitted to put one last question to the handmaiden before she is taken away?" he enquired.

The Baron clasped his hands before his face and considered the request. After much deliberation, he replied.

"Pray tell me good sire, what question needs to be put to the wench at this late hour?" he said.

Bardolph remained standing while addressing all those seated at the table.

"Gentlemen, this court demands answers as to why the Baron's ring was found within the heel of the handmaiden's shoe," he reasoned. "I agree, she must surely be hiding the truth. But as yet I have not heard the reason asked why Lady Adela and her party should venture this way. Of this, I am most curious." Then addressing the Baron directly, he added, "My Liege, did you not speak earlier saying that the road the party was taking not to be the direct route between Salopsbury and the Cinque Ports? Surely, this court demands an explanation as to why this should be so?"

The Baron nodded in agreement. He too was curious but held his own theories on the matter. He was convinced his treasure to be buried somewhere within the Forest of Wyre, and that it was the intention of these people to collect it on their way through. However, he was also very much aware of his ultimate objective. For his plan to succeed, a verdict of guilt upon the handmaiden needed the full blessing of this court, and that included Bardolph.

"You may proceed," the Baron told him. "You may put your question to the accused."

Bardolph beckoned Cedric to step away. He then addressed the handmaiden.

For comfort, he spoke her name, saying, "Gwyneth, pray tell this court why you did'st so come this way? And tell us this, why did'st you and your party find it necessary to venture south to Lodelowe when the Cinque Ports are to the south and east?"

Gwyneth swallowed deeply and considered the question. Slowly and hesitantly, she began to relate what little she knew. It probably had nothing to do with the ring found within her shoe, but it did explain her party's detour to Lodelowe.

"Good sire," she explained, "on the night before our departure from Salopsbury I spoke with the Lady Adela and she enquired of my parents. I told her that my father was dead and my mother no longer resided at Salopsbury, and that she does't now live somewhere within the walls of Lodelowe. Lady Adela was most kind to me and promised that I should see my mother on our way to the Cinque Ports, since the detour was small and would add very little to our journey. We were to spend our first night with the company of the Abbess at Wistanstow, then travel to Lodelowe the following day. But we never reached the abbey. We were waylaid at the ford and there our escorts were slain. Good sire, I know nothing more. Please believe me. I know nothing more."

With the mention of the abbey all eyes turned to the Abbot. All those seated were waiting for confirmation. The Abbot shrugged his shoulders before speaking.

"I know nothing of the affairs of the Abbess," he told the court. "However, she is a Fitzgerald. She is the sister of Herbert, the new Earl of Salopsbury, so some arrangement for stay may have been made."

Bardolph stroked his beard thoughtfully. Gwyneth's tale was all very well, but the Baron and his court needed a whole lot more if he was to save her from torment. Her tale still did not account for the ring in her shoe.

He raised the question of her mother, saying, "Your mother, what is her name?"

Gwyneth was quick to reply.

"Madeline," she answered. "My mother's name is Madeline."

The Baron raised a hand to interrupt Bardolph and put a hold on any further questioning. Having heard what Gwyneth had to say, he was curious as to the identity and whereabouts of her mother. He turned to Captain Osbald seated at the far end of the table.

"Captain, do you know of this woman?" he asked. "This Madeline the wench speaks of?"

Captain Osbald nodded his head.

"I believe so, my Liege," he said thoughtfully. "If I am not mistaken, she is a whore at the local tavern."

The Baron put his hands together in thought. He was now seeing things in a very different light. He was aware that several whores operated from the tavern within the town and also knew of the relationship they formed with many of his men. He could therefore, foresee a possible link between Gwyneth's mother and the robbery. He reasoned that if anyone needed inside information, then what better way was there than to get it from the comfort of a bed?

Slowly, a picture began to form and the Baron spoke his thoughts aloud.

"This woman?" he queried. "This Madeline the accused speaks of? She would have no doubt slept with many of my men? And if this were to be true, then would it not be easy for such a person to obtain intimate knowledge of my strongroom and my security and the watch and the changing of the guard? And this information in the hands of someone with a mind to robbery could prove most invaluable, could it not? Does't I not speak the truth?"

Captain Osbald agreed most heartily with the Baron.

"It could very well indeed, my Liege," he replied. "This wench may well be telling us the truth when she speaks of this Madeline. This whore is very popular with my men, and could well have been responsible for the passing of information."

All those seated listened with interest. There came mutterings from the Abbot, Squire Henry Stokes and the young Edwin de Mortimer. It seemed they too were very much in accord with the Baron's thoughts.

Turning to confront the handmaiden, the Baron addressed her in a loud and authoritarian voice.

"Tell this court more, wench," he said. "Tell us more about your mother. Was she involved in this conspiracy too? Tell us! And tell us whom it was that did the robbery? Could it possibly have been the soldiers that escorted you? Was it they who raided my strongroom? And was it they who distributed my stolen jewels, perhaps my ring to you, my necklace to the Lady Adela, possibly as a favour for your loyalty, or more likely as a reward for your involvement? Is this not the truth? You were given the ring and Lady Adela the necklace, as a reward for your silence? You are just as much guilty of this crime as they, are you not? Now confess. Admit to this court your obvious guilt."

The handmaiden turned pale and fraught. The Baron had put so many questions that she could think of no reply. Nothing of which the Baron had spoken was true. She froze and closed her eyes. She could no longer think. Her mind had gone blank. All she wanted to do was curl up and die.

"Answer me, wench!" bellowed the Baron. "It is true, isn't it? You knew that the ring was stolen? Stolen by the men that brought you here! So you concealed it within your shoe? Confess, wench, confess and put an end this ridiculous charade."

Gwyneth remained confused and did not reply. She was thinking perhaps, there was some truth to the Baron's words. Perhaps, this is how the ring did get into her shoe. Perhaps, the soldiers that escorted her party did commit the crime. Perhaps, they gave the necklace to the Lady Adela and it was she who concealed the ring within her shoe. But with all this said, to implicate her was a lie, a total and utter fabrication of the truth. She was innocent. So why did they not believe her?

Impatient for an answer, the Baron called Cedric, saying, "Jailer, take her away, do your best work. Bestow upon this wench the pain that does't accompany such blind stubbornness."

The handmaiden gave a sideways glance and caught sight of the little man stepping forward to grab her by an arm. She closed her eyes and began to pray.

"Confess, wench!" yelled the Baron from behind the table.

She struggled to break free, but the jailer's hand remained firm. Suddenly, she snapped. With a quivering bottom lip she called for mercy.

"Stop! Please, stop! Don't let him take me away! I confess," she cried. "I confess. I confess to everything. Lady Adela put the ring in my shoe and the men that accompanied us did the robbery. Just don't let him hurt me! Please, please don't let him hurt me!"

Cedric released the handmaiden's arm and she dropped to her knees. Here she remained, her body shaking and heaving with sobs.

The Baron slumped back on his chair. With hands placed before him as if in prayer, he gave orders to his scribe.

"Scribe, prepare a fresh confession," he said.

On hearing the Baron's words the scribe sorted out a brand new scroll. He had a fresh confession to write, one that included the three soldiers that escorted Lady Adela's party, and also included a mention of the whore Madeline.

Turning to his sergeant, the Baron issued further orders.

"Sergeant, arrest this Madeline and take her to my dungeon," he told him. "Then conduct a thorough search of the tavern in the town. Look for anything that may have come from my strongroom. Leave nothing upturned. Ransack the place if necessary, strip it of its floorboards if need be. But be sure to leave nothing upturned. Is this clear? If my treasure is not within the tavern but hidden in the forest, then this Madeline will be sure to know of its whereabouts."

Finally, the Baron addressed all those seated at the table.

"Gentlemen, at last we have it!" he pronounced. "Not only does't we have the confession we does't so desire, but me thinks we have found someone who knows the secret to my treasure's whereabouts."

On conclusion, the Abbot chanted a few words in Latin, and both Edwin de Mortimer and Squire Henry Stokes clapped a small ripple of applause.

After a short silence, the Baron spoke again.

"Gentlemen, you have all done my court proud this day," he told everyone. "May I congratulate you all on the fine work done? Now I suggest we partake of some much-needed refreshment? Let us drink more of the goodly Norman wine that warms the heart. Then perhaps afterwards, once the accused hath made her mark, we shall return to the table and complete what we have started here today. Once again, gentlemen, my hearty thanks to you all."

Bardolph felt despondent at not being allowed to question the handmaiden further.

He called to the Baron.

"Pray tell me my Liege, what fate now awaits the handmaiden?" he asked as chairs began to shuffle away from the table.

The Baron rose from his chair and turned to Bardolph.

"She will be asked to make her mark upon her confession," he explained. "When this is done, this court will reconvene and agree her guilt. Sentence will then be passed. As is tradition here at Lodelowe, on the day of the market she will be taken to the gibbet outside the town walls where she will be hanged. No doubt there will be a goodly crowd present to partake in the spectacle. However, we may make it a double hanging, with this whore from the tavern accompanying the handmaiden to the gallows. But we will see, there is no rush and justice will run its course."

Bardolph felt sorry for the handmaiden but said no more. Slowly, he followed the court from the hall to an adjoining room where wine and refreshment awaited them. Only the scribe remained to conclude matters, and with the handmaiden down on her knees and sobbing deeply on the floor at the centre of the hall.

There was, however, one small item Bardolph carried with him. The scrap of parchment folded about the ring was now safely tucked away in his purse. He did not know why he had taken it. There seemed little point now that the handmaiden had confessed and pointed an accusing finger towards her mother. Yet somehow, a doubt remained and this scrap of parchment he considered to be the only true clue into solving this mystery. His heart was telling him to remain at Lodelowe and seek out the truth. But his loyalties lay with the King of England, and this remained paramount. The peregrines in his charge simply had to be trained, and this had to be done whilst they were still young.

For the King's Royal Falconer today was a very sad day indeed.

Chapter Eighteen

A banquet fit for a king awaited the Baron's court. Those that stood in judgement, along with their servants and entourage, were all invited. The castle's keep emptied slowly, each leaving in their own time and at their own pace; their destination being the great hall in the west wing of Lodelowe Castle.

It was a day to saunter and enjoy the sunshine. Blue skies and a scattering of white fluffy clouds filled the air. The walk from the castle's keep to the courtyard was pleasant, and because the path was downhill, the exercise troubled no one, not even the Abbot who trundled slowly with the aid of a servant at each arm.

Whilst walking the steep and winding downhill path, Bardolph found chance to speak to the Baron. It was not a conjured meeting, the two men coming side by side inadvertently, the Baron moving backwards through the rank in order to converse with the Abbot who brought up the rear. But this was a chance meeting Bardolph could not let pass and he took full advantage. As the two men's stride brought them together, Bardolph slowed his pace to match that of the Baron.

With a courteous nod to the head, he asked, "My Liege, now that the trial of the handmaiden hath ended, I pray that I may be permitted to be on my way? For the King does't eagerly await his birds and I must tarry in these parts no longer."

The Baron stopped in his stride and placed a firm hand upon Bardolph's shoulder. It had always been his intention to let Bardolph go once the trial was over. He had achieved all he wanted. The handmaiden had been found guilty and the sentence had been passed, and the Royal Falconer's signature upon the document was good enough to make the verdict look totally impartial.

"Good sire," he replied, "I hereby absolved you from partaking in anymore responsibilities regarding the affairs of Lodelowe. You are free to continue with your journey south. But I ask of you, pray do not leave my castle in haste and pray do not depart until you have at least partaken in a little refreshment. For I have organised a goodly feast for this distinguished company. You, in particular, did'st serve my court well and I must thank you for all that thou did'st do and say. So please, good sire, I beg of you, before you depart, allow me one last wish and dine with me. And besides, me thinks it would cast an ill-favoured shadow over Lodelowe should the good King Henry get word that I did'st not bestow a just and deserving reward upon one of his most trusted and faithful servants."

Bardolph ignored the Baron's silver tongue and considered his invitation to the feast. He had eaten early that morning and then nothing more than a meagre bowl of oats and goat's milk. He looked to the sun. Noon had passed and the summer nights were drawing in. At best he would have no more than three hours ride before darkness descended. But at least this would see him three hours nearer home. The road south from Lodelowe would take him through the Forest of Wyre, and earlier enquiries suggested the forest's southern edge to be a good six hours ride from here. So there would be no wayside inn awaiting him, no village or hamlet as his aim, and no comfortable bed to signal journey's end. He would simply have to bed down the night at the edge of the forest's road and continue on next morning.

Eventually, and after giving the matter much thought, Bardolph replied to the Baron. He too could master the silver tongue.

"My Liege," he said. "I must thank you for the great honour thou does't bestow upon me. To sit alongside such distinguished company is indeed a great privilege. Therefore, if it pleases you, my Liege, I will'st do as you suggest and partake of your hospitality and dine with you and your honoured guests. But then, my Liege, I must be away. The King eagerly awaits his birds."

The Baron accepted both Bardolph's adulation and his excuse. He patted Bardolph on the shoulder.

"Then it is settled," he said. "Eat well my friend, eat well."

After this brief encounter nothing more was said. The Baron bowed his head and took his leave of Bardolph to walk alongside the Abbot, who in the intervening period had caught up with the stationary pair. The Baron was a busy man and had many matters to discuss, including final arrangements for the following week's more important trial, that of Lady Adela Fitzgerald.

On reaching the courtyard, Bardolph found himself striding alongside Squire Henry Stokes. Once again, a chance encounter, since it was Bardolph's overriding wish to stay well clear of nobility and keep himself to himself. However, Bardolph had in the course of his duty met with several squires, most of whom were resident in the ancient Kingdom of Wessex and attendant at the King's court at Winchester. The title squire being an honour bestowed upon a man that did once pay attendance to a knight and bore his shield in battle.

Out of politeness, Bardolph turned to the squire.

"Good squire," he asked, "did'st you not say that you were in service to a knight of the Order of St. John of Jerusalem, whom did himself serve in the Great Third Crusade alongside the good King Richard?"

Squire Henry Stokes was a modest man. Walking with staff in hand, he turned to Bardolph.

"I did'st my good fellow," he replied. "I bore the arms of Sir Rupert Fitzgerald in battle, and it was indeed the Great Third Crusade."

Bardolph did a quick calculation. The year was now 1235. The Great Third Crusade of the Holy Land in which King Richard led his troops into battle, occurred in 1192. Forty-three years had passed since this date. Therefore, if Squire Henry was sixty now, and he was only guessing his age from his appearance, then the squire would have been just seventeen at the time. As for Sir Rupert Fitzgerald, the knight he served in battle, Bardolph tried to place in his mind this knight's relationship with the present family of Fitzgeralds that ruled from Salopsbury. He had gained a little knowledge from the trial of the handmaiden, but remained unsure. Herbert Fitzgerald was the current Earl of Salopsbury and the Lady Adela's late departed husband was William Fitzgerald. So just who was this Sir Rupert Fitzgerald?

Out of curiosity, and considering the time scale of forty-three years, he asked, "Sir Rupert Fitzgerald, the knight upon whom you served. Would he be the brother of the late departed William Fitzgerald?"

The Squire stopped briefly before walking on. The family history of the Fitzgeralds' was never easy to explain and required some thought. He turned to Bardolph as they walked slowly across the courtyard and towards the doors to the west wing.

He explained, "Nay, sire, Sir Rupert was the brother of the late Earl's father Geoffrey Fitzgerald, the second Earl of Salopsbury. The bloodline of Sir Rupert should have ended many years ago, but by an odd twist of fate it prevails once more. For Sir Rupert was the father of Herbert the current Fourth Earl of Salopsbury. William Fitzgerald, the third Earl of Salopsbury who hath just passed away, departed this world leaving no heirs to the title, so the inheritance passed back up the line to Sir Rupert, then down again to Herbert."

Bardolph tried to take it all in, but like the squire, he too realised the relationship complicated. He wanted to ask for clarification, but by now they were entering the west wing of the castle.

"Then one day I must learn more of the Fitzgeralds and the bravery of Sir Rupert in battle," he commented and left it at that.

Candles burned aplenty within the great hall of Lodelowe Castle, casting lively dancing shadows upon the walls, tapestries and high-beamed rafters. Yet it remained mid-afternoon and further bright lights beamed in through the many leaded windows. A band of drums, tambourines and trumpets played high in the minstrel gallery and the lavish feast laid out by the Baron was soon in full swing. Bardolph, however, felt a need to be on his way. He had dined alone, choosing cooked venison and fresh fruit for his plate and shunned most conversation, and to all those that approached he issued nothing more than a courteous greeting in return.

Bardolph moved to the far end of the hall in order to seek a private audience with the party's host. The Baron, with goblet in hand, was standing gazing up at a great tapestry hanging on the wall when Bardolph moved to stand by his side. The huge tapestry depicted two young boys, a Norman motte and bailey, and a fast flowing river and mill. At the top of the tapestry flew a raven looking down upon the scene. The boys could have been the same person since one half of the tapestry was a mirror image of the other, each standing to either side of the riverbank.

"Greetings, my Liege. Are these ancestors of the de Clanceys?" enquired Bardolph whilst gazing up at the tapestry.

The Baron turned to Bardolph.

"Aye, good sire they were," he answered. "They were twins, brothers Edmund and Edward. Edward is on the right. He was my father. Whilst on the left, is Edmund. Whilst still a child he was reportedly drowned after fleeing an incursion by Welsh marauders. The raven is that of the Lord Rhys, the leader of the Welsh rebels at the time. But alas, Edmund's exact demise will never be known. His body was never recovered."

Bardolph said nothing and for a while the Baron remained pensive before returning to matters more immediate. Finally, the Baron spoke.

"Then you are ready to take your leave of Lodelowe?" he enquired. "Is this not why you join me?"

Bardolph nodded his head.

"Aye, my Liege," he replied, "with your permission, I now beg of your leave, for the hour grows late and the long road south beckons to my call."

The Baron placed a hand upon Bardolph's shoulder.

"Then pray go with God, good sire, and go with a proud heart," he said. "You did justice to my court today. The handmaiden goes to the gallows on the day of the market. It will be a goodly spectacle and a lesson to my subjects not to cross the house of Lodelowe, for justice will always prevail. But more importantly, and why I offer you my humble gratitude, the handmaiden's written confession can now be presented before the trial of the Lady Adela. So there is little more I could have asked of you my friend. Therefore, I bid you fond farewell and a safe journey south, and pray give'th my kind regards to the good King Henry whence thou does't see him next. Remind him of Lodelowe's faithfulness and dedication to the crown of England."

Bardolph read sincerity in the Baron's words.

"I will do what you ask of me most gladly, my Liege," he replied. "I will'st convey your allegiance to the King whence I am next in his presence."

He then bowed gracefully, turned and retreated from the hall. At no point did he look back or catch the eye of anyone in the hall, least he be detained further. His destination was the courtyard and the saddling of his horse.

As he stepped out from the hall, he breathed a sigh of relief. He was at long last free to continue on with his journey south.

Chapter Nineteen

Whilst minstrels played and dignitaries feasted, in another part of the town Sergeant Cuthred had his own duties to perform.

The Baron had given orders, telling the sergeant, "Go to the tavern in the town, arrest this Madeline and take her to my dungeon. I must have this mother of the handmaiden." And the sergeant, ever dutiful, was determined to carry out the Baron's orders to the letter.

The tavern lay at the very heart of the walled town of Lodelowe and overlooked the market square. It was a big imposing timber building with a rambling thatched roof that rose and fell like hills and dales above the small protruding windows of the upper floor. Over the main door there hung a sign that swung freely in the wind. The sign was in the shape of a shield, its background painted half dark blue, half red, and in the foreground stood the three white rampant lions of Lodelowe. This was the 'The de Clancey Arms'. But to those who most frequented this establishment, the tavern was known by another name. To these people this was 'The Craven Arms' (or more meaningfully; 'the coat of arms of the fainthearted'.)

Sergeant Cuthred stormed into the tavern through the main entrance, followed closely by a dozen soldiers of Lodelowe. The landlord was busy moving barrels. This was the hour before noon and the tavern held few customers. He looked up as the soldiers clattered in.

"Where is Madeline?" demanded Sergeant Cuthred, shouting across the floor.

The landlord, a look of surprise upon his face, pointed to the stairs.

He told the sergeant, "Madeline's room is at the top of the stairs; the door at the far end of the corridor."

He was about to add that she was not here today and that the room was being used by someone else, but Sergeant Cuthred was away, heading for the stairs.

"Get everybody out of here. Only the landlord is to remain," bellowed the Sergeant as he scaled the stairs, two steps at a time.

Six soldiers, their swords drawn, followed him up the stairs. Six more remained to clear the rooms below. On reaching the top, Sergeant Cuthred turned to the men that followed.

"I want every room searched," he told them. "Put everyone you find out on the streets."

The landlord had said Madeline's room was at the far end of the corridor. Sergeant Cuthred strode purposefully towards the door and kicked it open. A man jumped out of bed and pulled on his breeches. A woman in bed sat upright and held the bedclothes to her breasts. She was allowed no time to protest.

Sergeant Cuthred called two of his men forward. One of them held rope in readiness.

"You," he bellowed, "Arrest this woman. Tie her hands and take her to the dungeon."

Then turning to the man getting hurriedly dressed, he placed a boot to his backside and pushed him towards the door.

"And you, get out!" he yelled.

The man grabbed the rest of his clothes and scurried off, leaving his boots behind.

Sergeant Cuthred pulled away the bedclothes. The woman in the bed was naked. She was in her early thirties, with long light brown hair and a fine, youthful figure that suggested an age some five years younger. She screamed loudly as two soldiers grabbed her arms and yanked her out of bed. There followed a mouthful of abuse as her hands were tied behind her back.

"Get her out of here," snapped Cuthred, "take her to the dungeon."

The woman, with hands tied, was pushed towards the door. Shouting and protesting, she raised a foot to the jamb. For a moment she wrestled to remain in the room, but she lacked strength. With the intervention of a second soldier she was controlled. With one on either side, she was lifted bodily from the floor and carried out of the room.

As the soldiers and the protesting woman disappeared down the corridor, Sergeant Cuthred called, "Be quick about it, then return here immediately. There is still much work to do."

One soldier remained in the room with Sergeant Cuthred, the rest either milling about the building, evicting both men and women, or bursting into unchecked rooms. As chaos ensued, the sergeant turned to the one remaining soldier.

"Right, start searching," he roared. "We're looking for jewellery and valuable items. Anything you find I want to see."

They set to work. The drawers and cupboards were first, followed by the slicing up of the mattress and the dismantling of the bed. Downy feathers filled the air and choked the throats. Sergeant Cuthred spat them out and cursed.

He recalled the Baron's words, 'Leave nothing unturned, ransack the place if necessary, strip it of its floorboards if need be, but be sure to leave nothing unturned.'

And this is exactly what he was going to do, starting with this room, then the next and the one after that, until the whole building had been thoroughly searched.

With only the floorboards to pull up, Sergeant Cuthred turned his attention to a dress draped over the back of a chair. He assumed this to be the dress of the woman found in bed. He inspected the dress then turned to the soldier aiding with the search.

"Come here, take a look at this!" he called.

The soldier crossed the room and the sergeant held the dress high for him to see. There was a brooch pinned to the chest. It was dewdrop in shape with a large emerald stone inset on an ornate gold surround.

"Me thinks we have another piece of the Baron's stolen treasure," he told the soldier.

The soldier nodded. The brooch certainly looked valuable and not the sort of item a whore would wear, especially on her working clothes.

Sergeant Cuthred folded the dress over one arm and moved quickly to the door. This was an important find and had to be reported immediately.

"Carry on searching. Search every room in the building. I'm away to seek an audience with the Baron. Me thinks he will want to see this straightaway," Sergeant Cuthred told the soldier, then hurried away.

Chapter Twenty

Whilst music played, dignitaries dined and mayhem ensued in the town, away in the castle's keep, one member of the Baron's court felt obliged to stay behind. As ever, Captain Osbald was a very busy man. The return of the handmaiden to her cell would normally fall to Sergeant Cuthred, but the sergeant and all available men-at-arms were gone, sent by order of the Baron to the tavern in the town.

Having overseen the return of the handmaiden in her cell, Captain Osbald returned to the hall above. He was in the process of moving chairs when a female prisoner, her hands tied behind her back and escorted by two soldiers, entered the hall. He said nothing and watched them cross the floor. Quite naturally he assumed the prisoner to be the whore Madeline. But somehow the image that greeted him seemed wrong. This woman would be no more than ten years older than the handmaiden.

However he was a very busy man and finished moving the chairs and, with the aid of servants, having the table moved back against the far wall before returning to the dungeon.

On arrival, Captain Osbald moved to confront Cedric.

"Where is the new prisoner?" he enquired.

Captain Osbald was a man in a hurry and had no time for pleasantries. He wanted to have a final word with Bardolph. The King's Falconer was soon to leave and he felt obliged to say a final farewell.

Cedric pointed to a cell door a short distance down the corridor.

"She is in that cell there," he told the captain.

Captain Osbald moved briskly to the door. His interest lay in confirming the prisoner to be the handmaiden's mother; a woman that reportedly worked at the local tavern. Other than this he cared little. He pointed to the door.

"I'm looking for the whore Madeline," he said. "Is she in here?"

Cedric shrugged his shoulders.

"I was told to lock this woman up, that is all. I do not enquire of names. I leave such details to the scribe," he said.

Captain Osbald opened up the small viewing hatch and peered inside. He was disappointed. There was nothing to see other than blackness. Neither candle nor lantern burned inside. But the presence of an occupant was obvious. On opening the hatch, a female voice began to call for her release.

He pointed to the lock.

"Get her out here," he bellowed. "I want to see her in the light."

Cedric unlocked the door, entered and bundled out the occupant. The woman was naked and had her hands bound behind her back.

Captain Osbald looked the woman up and down. He was seeking the mother of Gwyneth Fletcher and did not see any likeness. The handmaiden had a head of golden locks and he assumed her mother to be the same. This woman had dark hair. He rubbed his chin thoughtfully. The mother of the handmaiden would be in her late thirties, maybe even forty or more. This was a younger woman; twenty-eight, maybe twenty-nine at the most. Suddenly, he had his doubts.

"Are you Madeline?" he asked.

The woman shook her head. She looked scared and had no idea what the raid on the tavern was all about.

"Nay, sire, my name is Margaret," she replied. "Madeline was not at the tavern when the soldiers arrived. I was using her room."

Captain Osbald beckoned the guard at the portal to join him. He knew this man to be a frequent visitor to the tavern in the town.

The guard arrived and saluted with clenched fist across his chest.

"We are seeking a woman called Madeline, do you know of her?" he asked.

The guard stood to attention and nodded his head.

"Yes, sire, I do," he replied. "I know of this Madeline."

Captain Osbald pointed to the naked prisoner.

"Is this her?" he asked.

The guard shook his head.

"Nay, sire, it is not," he replied.

"Then who might this be?" he enquired and pointing once more to the naked woman.

"This is Margaret," replied the guard. "She also frequents the tavern."

Captain Osbald seethed. Sergeant Cuthred had failed to find the one person he had been sent to arrest, and Madeline must have slipped the net.

Captain Osbald turned to Cedric.

"Return her to the cell," he snarled. "The Baron will soon be here. He will tell you what must be done with her."

Having given his orders, Captain Osbald turned and sped away. He had much work to do, and now it seemed a visit to the local tavern had been added to his ever-growing list. As ever, he had to do everything himself.

What troubled him most however, was the call for Madeline's arrest being commonplace by now.

In all probability she had already fled the town.

Chapter Twenty-One

Whitewind was saddled and awaiting Bardolph's arrival in the courtyard. Following a message sent hastily from the great hall, the lad Ralph was busily organising the Royal Falconer's departure. This efficiency pleased Bardolph. Ralph was a good lad and knew horses well. He also rode his own pony and as Bardolph arrived, three animals awaited him in the courtyard, a white stallion, a donkey and a pony. Two cages, one on either side, were strapped to the back of the donkey. Inside each cage perched a half-grown peregrine falcon.

Captain Osbald, running and holding his sword to his belt, arrived to say farewell. He had received news of the Royal Falconer's imminent departure and sped all the way from the dungeon. Needless to say, he was out of breath.

The two men embraced.

"I'm so glad I have caught you before you left," said Captain Osbald panting, "I have raced all the way from the dungeon. Sergeant Cuthred has arrested a whore, and as we speak he is having the tavern in the town stripped of its floorboards. I must haste away and see what is happening before the people rise up in anger. The Baron's name does't not go down well with the people that frequent the tavern, and me thinks I must intervene to prevent an uprising."

Bardolph held Captain Osbald close to his chest in a final embrace and patted him on the back. Breaking his grip, he passed the horse's reins over his head and placed one foot in the stirrup.

"Then haste away to the tavern my dear friend," he told the captain. "Perhaps one day I will'st return to Lodelowe, and perchance we will meet again, and no doubt under happier circumstances. For the sentence of death upon the handmaiden, even though she hath admitted her guilt, still grieves me greatly."

Captain Osbald held the bridle to steady the horse whilst Bardolph mounted the saddle.

"Think not of the handmaiden, she is a convicted thief. Go with God speed my friend, and a safe journey south," he said patting the stallion on the neck.

As they spoke, Sergeant Cuthred appeared in the courtyard. He was moving fast across the open cobbled square towards the west wing of the castle. In his arms he carried a woman's dress. Captain Osbald held out an arm to halt the sergeant's progress as he approached.

"Sergeant, how does't the search go?" he said.

Sergeant Cuthred stopped in his tracks to stand before his captain. He held up the dress in his arms. Visible was a brooch pinned to the front.

"Captain, this dress was found at the tavern. On it is pinned this brooch. I believe it to be part of the Baron's treasure. I head to the great hall to seek audience with the Baron and present this brooch to him."

Captain Osbald looked at the brooch. Bardolph, now seated in the saddle and looking down, saw it too. The brooch was large, dewdrop in shape, with an emerald mounted on a gold surround. In shape and appearance it was very similar to the medallion necklace found upon the Lady Adela.

"Me thinks you could be right," mused Captain Osbald. "This brooch could very well have been taken from the Baron's strongroom."

Sergeant Cuthred refolded the dress in his arms.

"Then, Captain, may I have your permission to proceed and enquire of the Baron?" he asked.

Captain Osbald nodded his head. He saw no reason to object. He considered whether to accompany Sergeant Cuthred, but decided against it. His immediate priority lay in quelling a riot at the tavern.

"Yes, Sergeant, go seek an audience with the Baron," he said. "He hath informed me that he wishes to visit the dungeon once the feast has ended. So pray doth accompany him when the time comes, and in the meantime I will'st pay a visit to the tavern and see what disturbances my men have caused."

Sergeant Cuthred sped away with dress in his arms and leaving Captain Osbald standing next to Bardolph and his horse.

"My friend, it seems I never have the time for the courtesy our friendship allows," he said. "Pray beg my pardon and for the interruption of my sergeant."

Bardolph however found Sergeant Cuthred's intervention most fascinating and had watched from the saddle with interest. One more stolen item had been recovered, and this time locally, and presumably at the tavern where the whore Madeline worked.

"Presumably that dress belongs to the handmaiden's mother and that she is now held in the Baron's dungeon?" queried Bardolph.

Captain Osbald shook his head, for he had recently established this not to be the case.

"Alas, my friend," he told Bardolph, "the whore Madeline was not the woman arrested at the tavern. News will be rife. The whole town will know by now that we are looking for her. It is therefore my belief that she hath already fled the town. But this is my problem, not yours my friend. Pray go whilst there is still some daylight, ride south and may God and St. Christopher remain with you."

Bardolph pulled on the reins and turned to the lad Ralph seated alongside on his pony.

"Then Ralph it is time for us to depart," he said. "I will'st accompany you to the parting of the ways, then as you turn north to Onneyditch, I will'st head south and take the road that leads to the King's New Forest in the ancient Kingdom of Wessex."

Captain Osbald watched Bardolph and the lad Ralph pass beneath the portcullis, then turned and sped away, his destination on this occasion being the tavern in the town. Somehow he had to quell the mayhem caused by his sergeant before it got out of hand.

Hopefully he would be able to calm the people down.

Chapter Twenty-Two

The great hall echoed to the sound of merriment. The feast was all but over and the Baron's guests thronged in groups, some sitting, some standing, some talking and some laughing. But whatever they were doing, a goblet of wine was always at hand. And if that goblet should ever be close to empty, then there was always a serving wench stood in readiness to replenish the stock.

The Baron was deep in conversation with the Abbot when a servant came up to him. The Baron frowned.

"What is it?" he snarled. "Can't it wait?"

The servant dropped to one knee.

"My Liege," he replied nervously, "Sergeant Cuthred awaits you at the door. He says it is most urgent and seeks an immediate audience."

The Baron looked towards the double doors at one end of the great hall. They were open and the sergeant was standing in the opening. He turned to the Abbot.

"Pray forgive me Holy Father, but I have some urgent business to attend," he said.

The Abbot made the sign of a cross and gave a slight nod of the head.

"God be with you," he said and followed by a chant in Latin.

The Baron strode briskly to the door, and taking Sergeant Cuthred by the arm he moved on further to a quiet spot in the corridor beyond.

"What is it Sergeant?" he asked. "Have you arrested the handmaiden's mother?"

Sergeant Cuthred signalled with a nod to his head. He was not aware that had arrested the wrong woman.

"Yes, my Liege," he said. "Madeline has been arrested and taken to the dungeon."

He held up the dress in his arms.

"And I have found this, my Liege," he said. "This is her dress, and on it is pinned this brooch."

The Baron looked to the brooch and recognised it immediately. This brooch was part of his father's treasure taken from his strongroom. He took the dress from Sergeant Cuthred and turned the brooch over to view the rear without undoing the pin. This was the confirmation he needed. There was a groove beneath the pin that once held a feather. This was not a brooch to grace a female's dress. This was a hatpin that once held a feather to the side of his father's hat.

The Baron looked at Sergeant Cuthred.

"This hatpin most definitely belonged to my father and was taken from my strongroom some three weeks past," he said, and adding as an afterthought, "Sergeant, you have done well."

Sergeant Cuthred acknowledged with a nod of his head.

"Thank you, my Liege," he replied.

The Baron wanted to know more.

"Tell me, Sergeant," he asked, "did'st the handmaiden's mother say where she did'st get this brooch. Has she spoken of the robbery?"

Sergeant Cuthred shook his head.

"Nay, my Liege," he replied, "the whore proved stubborn and did'st protest her arrest. I had her escorted to the dungeon."

The Baron handed back the dress.

"Then sergeant take back this dress," he said. "Keep the brooch safe. Do not let it out of your sight and remain here, next to the doors. As soon as I am finished, you will accompany me to the dungeon. I will'st speak with this Madeline personally, and if she does't remain stubborn then I'm sure we can find a way to loosen her tongue."

Sergeant Cuthred folded the dress about one arm.

"I will'st remain here at the door, my Liege, until I am called," he said, "and the dress and brooch will remain safe with me."

The Baron placed a hand upon Sergeant Cuthred's shoulder.

"Sergeant you have done me proud," he told him. "I will'st try to get away shortly. But with all the distinguished company I keep, my duty is to remain. But do not lose heart. I will'st see what I can do to get away."

And with that the Baron turned and marched quickly back into the hall. He remained a busy man, but also a pleased man now that the whore Madeline was safely locked away in his dungeon.

Chapter Twenty-Three

The sun was low over the ramparts when Baron de Clancey, accompanied by Sergeant Cuthred, set out for the dungeon. They marched briskly, with the Baron always one step ahead. Sergeant Cuthred carried a brown dress, on it was pinned a large emerald brooch with a gold surround. On arrival, both Corporal Guthrum and Cedric the jailer were present to greet them. The Baron gave immediate orders to Corporal Guthrum.

"Go and find the castle's scribe and bring him here without delay," he said and added, "And do make haste. Tell him to bring with him parchment, quills and ink."

Corporal Guthrum saluted with a clenched fist across his chest, bowed his head, clicked his heels and moved swiftly away.

The Baron turned to Cedric the jailer.

"Bring the whore Madeline to me," he told him. "I will'st see her now."

Cedric returned a look of bemusement. From his earlier encounter with Captain Osbald he had established no one by the name Madeline had not been brought to him. He stepped towards the nearest cell, for it was here the whore, whatever her name, was being held.

He told the Baron, "My Liege, I am sorry but no one by the name of Madeline hath been brought to me. Just one woman was handed to my charge, and she does't not go by the name of Madeline."

Baron de Clancey gave a look of bewilderment and pointed to the dress in sergeant Cuthred's arms.

"Then pray tell me to whom this garment doth belong?" he asked.

Cedric shook his head. He did not know. Still shaking his head he unlocked the cell door.

As he pulled the door open, he told the Baron, "My Liege, you had best ask for yourself, for I know not the answer to your question."

As the door creaked open, the occupant of the cell began to beg for her release.

"Silence!" snapped the Baron peering in through the open door.

No light burned within and all he could see was a dark shadow moving within the gloom. He beckoned Sergeant Cuthred to his side and together they stared into the cell.

The Baron addressed the dark shape.

"Are you the one that doth go by the name of Madeline?" he asked.

A quiet woman's voice from inside answered, "My name is not Madeline, my Liege. The one you speak of was not at the tavern when your men-at-arms entered the building."

The Baron looked to Sergeant Cuthred. He was naturally confused, but eyeing the dress in the sergeant's arms he had other ideas.

"Sergeant, you say you arrested the owner of this dress," he said. "Pray identify her so that I may speak with her."

Sergeant Cuthred strained his eyes. As if to help, the prisoner stepped forward in the light in the doorway. She was naked with hands tied behind her back. The sergeant had no problem recognising this woman. How could he forget that face and body? This was the whore in bed when he burst into her room. He pointed to the woman standing in the doorway.

"This is the whore I arrested at the tavern, my Liege," he said. "She was in bed with this dress resting upon a chair by the side. I assumed her to be Madeline. I was informed it was her room."

The Baron's face retained the look of puzzlement.

"So this woman is not the Madeline I seek?" he uttered.

Sergeant Cuthred shook his head.

"My Liege," he answered nervously and repeated his excuse. "I was told the room belonged to Madeline. I assumed this woman to be the one you sought."

The Baron collected his thoughts. This Madeline had to be arrested and on his return to the courtyard he would organise a party to go in search of her, but for the time being, he had another problem. His sergeant had discovered an item of his father's jewellery in this woman's possession, and this was the most important thing right now. The raid on the tavern may well have been bungled and the wrong woman arrested, but perhaps some good fortune had come of it. He indicated to Cedric with a flick of the finger.

"Get her out," he told him. "Bring her to the light so that I may'st see more clearly."

Cedric dragged the woman by the arm and slammed the door shut with a kick of his boot. The woman had little time to find her feet and rocked unsteadily. Cedric grabbed a handful of hair at the back of her head and turned her face towards the Baron. The Baron was already pointing to the dress in Sergeant Cuthred's arms.

He demanded of the woman, "Is this yours? Does this dress belong to you?"

The woman steadied herself, and as the grip to the back of her head relaxed, she looked to the dress. As she did so, Sergeant Cuthred held the dress high in order that she could see it clearly, but at the same time remaining careful not to reveal the brooch. After a while the woman responded. She bit hard on her bottom lip and nodded her head.

"Yes, my Liege, this is my dress," she said.

The Baron grimaced.

"Then tell me wench, if you are not Madeline, what is your name?" he asked.

The woman bowed her head before replying.

"My Liege, my name is Margaret," she told him.

The Baron placed a hand beneath the woman's chin and raised her head in order to see her face clearly.

"Then pray tell me, where is this Madeline? The woman I seek?" he asked.

Margaret looked to the Baron's eyes.

She explained, "My Liege, today is Madeline's day off. I use her room whilst she is out."

The Baron considered the woman's reply. At least it made some sort of sense. But there was still a question that remained unanswered. He collected the dress from Sergeant Cuthred and turned it over so that the brooch became visible.

"Where did you get this?" he asked and pointing to the brooch.

Margaret gasped and was lost for words. She had not seen this brooch before. She shook her head from side to side in an attempt to signal her complete surprise.

The Baron fought hard to control his temper. This brooch was the property of his late father, taken from his strongroom some three weeks earlier, and now here it was pinned to this woman's dress. Receiving no immediate answer, his anger flared.

"Where did you get this brooch?" he snarled. "Tell me! And tell me quickly!"

Margaret shook her head wildly from side to side and tried to explain.

"My Liege," she said, "I have not seen this brooch before! This should not be on my dress!"

The Baron clenched his fists in rage. This woman was making a fool of him. His reaction was to strike her across the face, but he controlled his temper and turned to Sergeant Cuthred.

Pointing to the low portal at the end of the corridor, he told his sergeant, "I have little time for such nonsense. I demand an answer now. Take her to the far chamber. Let's see if we can loosen her tongue by other means."

Sergeant Cuthred grabbed Margaret by the arm. She screamed in protest but was powerless to resist the strength of a man much bigger and stronger than herself. Reluctantly, she found herself being marched towards the far chamber.

Cedric set off at a run in order to arrive at the portal ahead of Sergeant Cuthred.

The Baron waited a while, watching them go.

Eventually, he called, "Pray do your best and let's have some goodly results this night," he said. "Alas, it is my duty to be elsewhere. It must be seen that I dwelt here no longer than the need be. And pray let it be recorded that I was not present when this woman did'st make their mark. It is important I be seen as a true upholder of the law, even though it is I that has been much aggrieved. So I bid of you both a fond farewell, and may God give you the strength to stay the night."

Then with the woman's dress slung over one arm he turned and walked away. He would return to his rooms and, with the scribe on his way, he would wait for a written confession to be forthcoming from the whore.

Chapter Twenty-Four

The streets of Lodelowe were awash with rumours. At first it was word of a possible hanging. A young girl from Salopsbury had been caught stealing it was said. If this was true, then it was most likely she would be flogged through the streets on the next market day, then hanged on the gibbet tree outside the town walls. This was always something to look forward to.

But the question on everyone's lips was who would this girl be? To be truthful, nobody knew. Then came news of a raid on the tavern and yet more rumours ensued.

Now the people were asking, 'Why the raid?', 'What were the Baron's men looking for?', 'And who were they after?' and 'Had anyone been arrested?'

Then a most extraordinary event happened, a sight not seen for many a year materialised on the hillside above the town. A plume of black smoke appeared, wafting upwards from a short square-bricked opening on the grassy bank next to the castle's keep. Darkness was falling, but still a large crowd gathered in the market square, all looking upwards, their eyes focused upon a plume of black swirling smoke.

The forge in the dungeon had been lit. This was all too obvious, but more importantly they were aware of its significance. The rising black plume of smoke was issuing from the torture chamber and someone was about to be put to the test.

In time curiosity turned to speculation and a new question arose. Now the inhabitants of Lodelowe wanted to know who was down below, and who was being put to the test?

"Could it be the girl soon to be hanged?" one person was heard asking.

"No, that's ridiculous," replied another. "It couldn't possibly be her, she has already confessed. It must be someone else."

So just who was being held down there? This was the new question on everyone's lips. Inevitably, speculation returned to the raid on the tavern. It was rumoured a whore had been arrested. So perhaps, this was the answer. Perhaps, it was the whore.

Then yet another rumour spread, and reportedly from a most reliable source. The Baron was looking for one whore in particular. Her name was Madeline and she was not the whore arrested at the tavern. She was last seen fleeing the town with two men. The guards on the gate had reported this. The two men with Madeline were strangers to Lodelowe and had passed through the gates before news of the whore's arrest had reached them.

So what was going on? Who exactly was down there? What had she done and why the smoke?

The people required an answer. They demanded to know. They confronted the town crier, but he simply shook his head, for he too awaited news.

Baron de Clancey found it difficult to sleep. He also required an answer, but alas, with nothing forthcoming from the dungeon, he too awaited news.

As he lay on his large four-poster bed staring upwards at the drapes, a rap came upon the door. A lone candle burned in the room.

"What is it?" he snarled, sounding much displeased by the interruption.

The door opened wide enough for a head to appear.

"My Liege," said a male servant, bending low in the doorway, "Sergeant Cuthred awaits you in the great hall. I am to tell you that the whore hath confessed and that Lady Adela hath been implicated."

The Baron leapt out of bed. Suddenly, he was wide awake.

"Come," he called, "assist me. I must get dressed."

The servant had come prepared and entered the room carrying freshly washed clothes and clean boots.

It was not long before he was dressed and making haste for the great hall.

The vast open space of the hall shimmered to the light of many candles as the Baron entered via a rear door. He moved to take his seat at the end of the long table. Before him, on the surface, rested two scrolls, both waxed and sealed with red ribbons. One scroll bore news of the Lady Adela's impending trial. The other contained the confessions of the handmaiden, Gwyneth Fletcher.

The main doors to the great hall were already open, and it was here that Sergeant Cuthred and the castle's scribe stood awaiting their call. The Baron signalled for them to approach. Sergeant Cuthred marched to the head of the table, clicked his heals and saluted with a clenched fist across his chest. The scribe, less formal in his attitude and travelling in the sergeant's wake, moved to the opposite side of the table and placed a scroll before the Baron. The scroll was similar to those already on the table, but bore no ribbon or seal.

The Baron's eyes sparkled in the candlelight as the new scroll was placed before him.

"Then that stubborn whore ... that, err ... what was her name? ... Margaret ... she did'st finally confess then?" he said and sounding much relieved. "So what did she have to say? Something good, I hope."

And with that the Baron unfurled the scroll and began to read the contents. It was in French but he translated into Saxon as he read aloud.

He began, "I, Margaret daughter of William the Cook of the town of Lodelowe, does't readily confesses to the handling of stolen property that did once belong to the late Baron Edward de Clancy, and that the crime had been instigated by the Lady Adela Fitzgerald of the city of Salopsbury. Let it be known that I, Margaret, along with two men whose names were unknown to me, were hired by the Lady Adela to break into the Baron's strongroom and take certain items of gold, silver and jewellery. Money for our services was shared between us three. I was given the brooch as payment for my services."

At the bottom of the scroll lay Margaret's mark; a simple scrawled and straggly cross.

The Baron re-rolled the scroll and looked at Sergeant Cuthred and then at the scribe. He tapped the scroll with a finger.

"So, at last I have it!" he commented. "This is damning evidence against the Norman noblewoman. Her trial will now go well. You have done well."

Sergeant Cuthred clicked his heals.

"Thank you, my Liege," he said.

The scribe said nothing and acknowledged with a simple nod to the head. The truth was that the wording on the confessions was not his. He had merely written what Sergeant Cuthred had dictated and waited for the prisoner to make her mark. But he cared little that procedure had not been followed. The night had been long and he could hardly keep his eyes open. All he wanted to do at this moment in time was retire to his bed and sleep.

The Baron tapped the confession with a finger.

"These two men that assisted Madeline?" he asked. "Who might they be?"

On this account Sergeant Cuthred was prepared. With the lavish feast that followed the trial, the Baron had been too preoccupied to receive news from the gate.

"My Liege," he explained, "Madeline has flown the town. She was seen leaving with two men before news of her arrest did'st reach the gate."

The Baron sighed. This was not good news. He collected his thoughts. Madeline and these two men were to be caught. At first light he would send out a party. But for the time being he had more important duties to perform. A herald was to be despatched to Salopsbury. The documents on the table had to be in the hands of the Fitzgeralds before the setting of the sun.

The Baron looked to Sergeant Cuthred and then to the scribe. He could see that both were very tired.

"I thank you for a job well done," he told them. "You have done me proud this night. This confession will accompany those of the handmaiden to Salopsbury. You may go now. Retire to your beds and sleep well. Send Captain Osbald to me. I will'st speak to him next."

Sergeant Cuthred saluted, spun around and marched quickly from the hall. The scribe moved off too, following on a few paces behind. Both were pleased their ordeal was over and were now free to go to their beds.

Captain Osbald was sleeping when his wake-up call came. Naturally he hurried, but it still took time to put on his uniform, and his sleeping quarters were a good distance from the great hall.

The Baron, alone in the hall, grew impatient and fingered the three scrolls laid out before him. He picked each scroll up in turn and placed them down again, then arranged all three into a neat row. He did this several times until in frustration he drummed his fingers on the table and looked to the door.

"Where is the Captain?" he muttered.

He rose from the table and turned his gaze upon the great tapestry hanging against the back wall. The tapestry was of the twins, Edmund and Edward. They were standing on either side of a fast flowing river that ran centrally down the full length of the tapestry. There was a water mill and a motte and bailey in the background and above their heads flew a large black raven. The boy on the right was Edward, the Baron's father. The other boy, the one on the left, was Edmund. Edward's twin brother had died whilst a baby, reportedly drowned in the river at Onneyditch whilst being abducted by a band of Welsh marauders. His body was never recovered.

The Baron looked to the feathered hat worn by his father Edward. The hat was turban in style, and to the side was pinned a brooch that held a large feathered plume. He recognised the brooch as the one found upon the dress of the whore. He cursed the whore and vowed she would hang. His anger did not stop there. All the others involved in this conspiracy would hang too. He decided upon his next course of action. He would convene a trial for the whore that very morning. It meant waking up his scribe, and possibly his sergeant, but the trial would not take long, not with a confession already signed, so half an hour at the most, and afterwards they could return to their beds. He would judge the whore alone. He had the authority to do so and other dignitaries were not necessary in this case since she was just a common whore. He would find her guilty and sentence her to join the handmaiden at the gallows.

This thought pleased the Baron and he looked forward to a double execution. Both women would be strung up together on the gibbet tree outside the town walls. He smiled at the thought. The streets would be packed and people from miles around would flock to the town to witness the spectacle. He tried to recall a time when two women were hanged on the same time, but could not. Perhaps there never was such a day.

The Baron's thoughts moved to Lady Adela Fitzgerald and her forthcoming trial. Here, he had to tread more warily. Whatever action he took had to remain within the law. But at the back of his mind he had an idea. Now that the whore had implicated the Lady Adela, then surely it was within his rights to interrogate the Norman noblewoman? A written confession from her would certainly make things a whole lot easier. He pondered over the possibility. The trouble was his knowledge of the law was limited when it came to judging his fellow peers. There remained a strong possibility that approval from the Council of the Marches was needed before he could embark on any form of physical interrogation.

The Baron was in two minds and considered where best to turn for help. Then a thought came to him. There was one man that knew the law well, one man that would undoubtedly give clarification. The Abbot of Wistanstow was the council's authority on the law. The Abbot would certainly pass a ruling.

Captain Osbald arrived to find the Baron deep in thought. Unlike Sergeant Cuthred and the scribe before him, he had entered the hall unannounced. The Baron was looking at the tapestry hanging against the rear wall of the hall at the time. Captain Osbald coughed lightly so that his presence should be heard.

The Baron turned, saw Captain Osbald and returned to sit at the head of the table.

"Ah, Captain!" he remarked, "I've been waiting for you. There are things I want you to do."

Captain Osbald clicked his heals and stood to attention. The Baron added ribbons to the new scroll, sealed them with a candle, and used his signet ring to impress the crest of the de Clanceys upon the wax. When he was done he turned to Captain Osbald.

"These three scrolls are to be despatched to Salopsbury forthwith," he told the Captain. "It is a task for my most experienced horseman and he must leave at first light. It is important these despatches reach Salopsbury before the setting of the sun."

Captain Osbald knew the very man.

"I will'st send Corporal Egbert," he said. "He is a fine horseman and capable of reaching Salopsbury within the day."

The Baron handed over the scrolls.

"Then make sure the task is done," he said. "These despatches must get through to Salopsbury and be in possession of the Earl before nightfall."

Captain Osbald took the scrolls, saluted and turned to leave.

"Wait, Captain, there is one thing more," said the Baron.

The captain swung around to face the Baron and clicked his heels. The Baron placed his hands together as if in prayer and spoke thoughtfully between his fingers.

"Captain, I have received reports that the whore Madeline hath escaped Lodelowe and that she is accompanied by two men," he said. "I will'st have them found. They must be arrested. Use every man available. You may include my archers in the search, for I will'st not be hunting until after the trial of the Lady Adela. Their knowledge of the Forest of Wyre should prove useful in the search."

The Baron's archers were a select group of eight soldiers that accompanied him on the hunt. In normal times, they would take orders directly from the Baron and not the captain.

"I will'st lead the search personally," said Captain Osbald. "I will'st use every man available, including your archers, to scour the countryside."

The Baron shook his head. There was something else he wanted from the captain.

"No Captain, you will'st organise the search but take no part," he told him. "I have a separate mission for you. One that is for you alone and no one else must know."

Captain Osbald clicked his heels for a third time and waited. The Baron's secret mission involved the Lady Adela. His thoughts lay very much in clarification of the law. But first, a letter to the Abbot of Wistanstow was needed.

"Captain, return here once your duties are done," he told him. "You are to take a missive to the Abbey at Wistanstow. This task is for you alone. The missive will be for the Abbot and must not fall into the wrong hands. So go now, perform your duties, organise the search parties and return quickly. I will'st have a letter ready on your return."

Captain Osbald saluted, turned and marched purposefully from the hall. In his hands, he carried three scrolls. He would entrust these to Corporal Egbert. But first, the corporal had to be woken, his horse saddled and food for the journey provided. After this he had to organise a search party and when all this was done he was to ride to Wistanstow with a letter for the Abbot.

On leaving the hall Captain Osbald sighed deeply. He had another busy day ahead, and he wondered when he would be allowed to get a full night's sleep.

Chapter Twenty-Five

At first light, Corporal Egbert set off for Salopsbury. Shortly afterwards, three dozen soldiers on horseback left the castle; out searching for the whore Madeline and the two men that accompanied her. Finally, it was the turn of Captain Osbald. He rode alone, and no one knew of his mission or which direction he was to take.

Baron de Clancey, from a window, watched them all go in turn. As soon as the last rider departed beneath the portcullis he moved away. He had much work to do. The trial of the whore Margaret awaited his presence.

Shortly afterwards, the Baron sat central at the long table within the entrance hall to the castle's keep. The venue being the same as that used for the trial of Gwyneth the handmaiden. The great table as it always was, had been pulled away from the wall and seven chairs placed behind. The scribe, bleary-eyed and yawning, sat to the Baron's right. The remaining chairs were unoccupied. On the table before the scribe lay his escritoire, quill and ink along with several rolls of parchment. At different stations within the hall stood Sergeant Cuthred, Cedric the jailer and a guard transferred from the gate, since available soldiers were now in short supply.

The Baron struck the table with the hilt of his dagger.

"Bring forth the prisoner," he called. "This trial is now in session."

Margaret was being held in an adjoining chamber. She had been dragged up from the dungeon since she was incapable of walking. On hearing the Baron's command, Sergeant Cuthred saluted and moved to the door. Cedric and the guard joined him and all three disappeared from the hall.

Cedric was first to reappear, stepping backwards and dragging Margaret by the legs. She was naked, her body blackened with the marks of the branding iron. The jailer dragged her across the floor to the centre of the hall, then raised her to her feet. She was barely conscious and incapable of standing without support. The jailer gripped her about the waist and standing to the rear, turned her to face the table. He then tugged at her hair to raise her head and held that position.

The Baron, seeing the prisoner now standing facing him, albeit with assistance from the jailer, read from a parchment prepared by the scribe. The charges were identical to those levelled at Gwyneth the handmaiden the previous day. As with Gwyneth the language was in Anglo-Saxon so that the woman would understand.

"Margaret daughter of William the Cook of the town of Lodelowe, you stand before this court this day accused of robbery and murder, in so much that on the fifth day of August, in the year of our Lord twelve hundred and thirty-five, you did'st aid and abet in the theft of property from his Lordship, the Baron de Clancey, and also did aid and abet in the murder of Richard, son of Frederick, guard to the Baron de Clancey's strongroom, and thereafter did wilfully partake in the concealment of stolen property from their rightful owner."

Looking up he added, "How does't you plead to these charges, guilty or not guilty?"

Margaret gave no response. She was to all intent unconscious. Cedric lifted her head higher and put his mouth to her ear.

"Speak quickly, the Baron awaits your plea," he hissed into her ear.

He then squeezed her tightly about the midriff, expelling air from the lungs. Initially she groaned, but as Cedric's arms continued to squeeze hard against her blistered and peeling skin, the groans turned to words of protest. They were probably to the effect of a curse, or possibly a plea to let her go, but her words were jumbled and undecipherable.

The Baron leaned forward across the table and cocked an ear.

"What did she say?" he asked. "I did'st not hear."

"She said she is guilty, my Liege," Cedric answered.

The Baron turned to the scribe.

"Record her plea. The prisoner readily admits her guilt," he said.

As the scribe scratched quill to parchment, the Baron proceeded to pass sentence. The trial had taken but a few minutes, and this is the way he liked it.

"Margaret daughter of William the Cook of the town of Lodelowe, this court finds you guilty of the charges laid before you. I hereby sentence that you be hanged by the neck until dead. The execution is to take place on the next day of the market."

Margaret never heard the Baron's pronouncement, or realised what a dreadful fate awaited her.

The Baron stood and addressed the few men in the hall.

"Return the prisoner to the cell," he said. "This trial is over and I thank you for you cooperation."

Immediately, on pronouncing an end to the trial, the Baron made for the exit. He was a very busy man and had many things to do. Lady Adela Fitzgerald's trial was less than a week away and there was a feast to organise, a band of minstrels to assemble, extra rooms to prepare, additional servants to employ, not to mention all the logs needed for the fires and the dozens of candles required for the evenings. His list went on and on.

The Baron was indeed a very busy man. The trial of the whore had come as a great inconvenience, but at least it was now out of the way and his objective achieved.

Chapter Twenty-Six

Bardolph pulled his horse to a halt. Ralph, astride his pony, drew up alongside. Man and boy were at a crossroad. Lodelowe was two miles behind. The road ahead continued east to scale the hills of the Clees, and ultimately to Lichfield and the heart of Mercia. But straight ahead was not the way for either traveller. From this point on they would go their separate ways, with one traveller turning left, the other going right. To the left the road headed north, skirting the eastern edge of the Forest of Wyre, whilst to the south it passed through the very heart of the forest. This junction at the very edge of the forest was to be the parting of the ways for both man and boy; Ralph to head north to Onneyditch, whilst for Bardolph the road south beckoned.

Bardolph turned in the saddle. He took out a silver crown from his purse.

"This is for you, Ralph," he said, handing over the coin. "Ride home to Onneyditch and go with a proud heart. Go tell your family that you did'st serve the King of England. For the birds that you did'st tend so well does't belong to him, not I."

Ralph took the silver crown and stared at it with open eyes. This was more than he had ever earned in his entire lifetime.

"I thank you good sire," he said humbly.

Bardolph kicked at his horse to move away, but immediately cocked an ear and pulled on the reins. He turned to Ralph.

"Did'st you hear that sound?" he said. "It was a scream coming from the forest."

Ralph shook his head. He had heard nothing.

Bardolph dismounted.

"Come Ralph, follow me. Lead your animal to the bushes. Remain out of sight whilst I investigate," he said.

Amongst a thicket of trees and well away from the road, Bardolph left Ralph in charge of the animals. Taking his longbow and quiver he set off on foot into the forest.

Ralph looked to see the path Bardolph had taken, but within seconds he was gone. Ralph strained his ears, perhaps to hear the crack of a small branch, or the rustle of leaves, but other than the gentle breeze in the branches above, he could hear nothing. Bardolph had, in the course of a few paces, simply vanished from sight, ghosting effortlessly through the forest like a spirit of the night.

Ralph was not to know, but this was Bardolph's environment. Bardolph was at home and with nature now—away from the castles and dungeons he did so much despise. He moved swiftly yet silently. Not even the creatures of the forest were aware of his passing.

Bardolph came to a clearing. Smoke rose from a small campfire and to the far side, two saddled horses grazed the forests ferns. From the cover of a large oak, he looked on with concern at the goings on.

Two men, both of whom Bardolph recognised, were molesting a woman. He had seen these men earlier this day, stood to the back of the hall at the trial of Gwyneth the handmaiden. The woman, however, he had not seen before. She had blonde hair and if to guess her age, he would put her in her late thirties, maybe early forties.

The woman was being held to the ground by one of the men and beaten with a stick by the other. The man doing the beating held a thin supple rod cut from the branch of a willow. As Bardolph looked on, the man holding the woman to the floor tore away the top half of her dress. The standing man, now having a target of naked flesh to aim at, slaked the woman with a whip-like action across her breasts. She screamed and kicked out in protest. His response was to kick her hard against the thigh before beating her again with the stick.

It seemed the men were trying to gain information from the woman, but as yet had not achieved any success.

"We're getting nowhere like this," bemoaned the man that pinned her to the ground. "Let's tie her to a tree and burn the truth out of her."

A look of delight spread across the face of the standing man.

"Me thinks she'll start squealing the moment her flesh starts to sizzle!" he remarked.

Together they dragged woman to a tree over on the far side of the clearing. She did not make things easy for them and the physical strength of both men was needed to lift her bodily against the tree. With one man pressing her hard against the tree and the other working from the rear, her hands were finally drawn around the trunk and lashed together by a thick course rope.

Whilst this was happening Bardolph moved a little nearer to the action. From a much closer position he watched as one man returned to the fire, whilst the other remained at the tree.

The one that remained quickly returned to questioning the woman, repeating over and over and at the same time beating her with his stick, "Where is the Baron's treasure? Where is it buried?"

But the woman was no longer responding either to his torments or the beating. Her body had fallen limp; her head slumped to her chest.

Bardolph edged a little closer, choosing carefully his cover at every move. He considered it time for action and moved to the rear of the tree. The trunk was wide and the rope that bound the woman's hands passed from wrist to wrist. With his dagger he sliced through the rope.

To the front of the tree the man was taken by surprise when the woman slumped and toppled towards him, but he reacted quickly and sidestepped the fall. As she hit the ground his immediate reaction was to return her to the tree. His assumption being that the rope that bound her wrists had come apart, and he cursed his comrade for not tying the rope properly in the first place.

As the man leant forward, Bardolph struck with a fallen branch. It broke over the man's head and he collapsed to the ground.

The crack of the branch alerted the second man, knelt kindling the fire. He looked around to see two bodies lying on the ground next to the tree.

"What's the hell's happening over there?" he called as he rose and sped across the clearing.

As he bent down and reached out to touch the shoulder of his fellow comrade, Bardolph struck again. A second branch shattered across the man's head and he too collapsed to the ground.

After this, Bardolph moved quickly and dragged the unconscious woman out from beneath the bodies of the two collapsed men. In one quick movement, he slung her over his shoulder and set off at a run. Within seconds he was gone, moving swiftly through the forest.

Back at the thicket, Bardolph laid the woman down upon a grassy mound so that she should sit more upright. He looked to Ralph.

"Quickly, get me a flagon of water," he called.

Ralph moved to his pony and returned with a leather flagon. Bardolph tore cloth from the woman's dress and poured water upon it. He then set about washing away the blood from her face and breasts. When he was done he placed the rag to her forehead and poured out more water. Slowly, the woman came round and opened her eyes. Immediately on seeing Bardolph she began to tremble and tried to speak, but nothing more than a feeble whisper passed her lips.

Bardolph untied the loose ends of rope from about her wrists.

"Relax dear lady, you are in safe hands," he told her and held the flagon to her lips. "Come, drink. Drink deeply. This will help wash away the pain."

The woman sipped a few mouthfuls, enough to wet her lips then looked nervously about the thicket. Her vision was becoming less blurred. A man and a boy knelt by her side and beyond, three animals champed the grasses. However, she remained confused. These were different men, not the two that had brought her to the forest.

"Those two men?" she uttered. "Where are they? I must hide. They must not find me here."

Bardolph tried to reassure the woman.

"Relax fair lady, the men you speak of will no longer harm you," he told her. "You are in safe hands. Now drink a little more water. You have taken a beating and these wounds need washing and dressing."

Bardolph offered more water, which the woman took and drank more readily. When she was finished he removed the rag from about her forehead, soaked it once more and placed it gently upon her breasts. She gasped a sharp intake of breath as the cold water came in contact with her lacerated skin, but as the initial sting eased, she took the rag and began to wash away the blood for herself.

"Fair lady, pray tell me your name?" asked Bardolph once the woman had gained enough strength to respond to gentle questioning.

"Madeline," she replied. "My name is Madeline."

Bardolph on hearing the name Madeline gave a little knowing smile. It was what he had expected and everything now made sense. The two men he had seen at the trial would have heard of the involvement of the handmaiden's mother and somehow managed to get to her before the Baron's men. He put his next question to her. He was pretty sure he already knew the answer, but he asked it anyway.

"And where do you work?" he enquired.

"I work in the town of Lodelowe, at the Craven Arms," she said, "the tavern within the walls of Lodelowe."

Noticeably she had called the tavern the 'Craven Arms' and not the 'De Clancey Arms', but this did not matter, this was the confirmation Bardolph needed. This woman was indeed the mother of the handmaiden and the one being sought by the Baron's men. However her reply still puzzled him. He had not heard the words 'Craven Arms' mentioned in connection with Lodelowe. As far as he was aware, there was only one tavern in the town and this was the 'De Clancey Arms'. However, he recalled something Captain Osbald had said; something about the Baron's name not going down too well with the people at the tavern. Could it be that the de Clancey family failed to support King Richard in his crusade of the Holy Land? Could the family be classed as cowards in the name of the people?

"Pray tell me Madeline, why the Craven Arms?" he asked. "Surely you mean the De Clancey Arms? For this is the only tavern within the walls of Lodelowe."

Madeline shook her head.

"Pray forgive me good sire, I meant no offence," she said. "The tavern does indeed hold the arms of the de Clancey's above the door. But to all those that does't drink within its walls, these arms are considered to be those of the fainthearted, since no de Clancey did'st support the good King Richard in his crusade against the infidels."

Bardolph understood. This was not the only Craven Arms or Craven family encountered on his many journeys. It was a natural reaction of the people to cast disdain upon those that refused to fight alongside the good King Richard in the Holy Land. However, he too considered King Richard to be a bad king. Richard had ruled this land for almost ten years and in all that time, spent only six months upon its soil. But Bardolph had always kept his council. Even now, some thirty-five years after the death of King Richard, it was foolhardy to speak openly of such matters.

After a short pause Bardolph put another question to Madeline. One more thing still puzzled him and it concerned the two men in the forest.

"The two men in the forest, who are they? Where do they come from?" he asked.

The mention of the men filled Madeline with apprehension. She looked anxiously about the thicket.

"They're not here are they?" she asked. "Those men, they're not here?"

Bardolph shook his head.

"Those men will no longer harm you, Madeline," he assured her. "You are in safe hands now." He then put his question to her again. "Those men, who were they?"

She looked nervously around before answering.

"Sire, I do not know!" she said. "I had not seen them before last night. They visited the tavern last evening and we drank together. Then today, they came upon me whilst I was at the market. Today is my day off and I was shopping for fresh food. They put a dagger to my back and said I was to go with them. They brought me here to the forest. This is all I know. I swear this to be the truth."

Bardolph understood. Things were becoming a little clearer now. He had seen the two men at the trial. They were standing at the back. They would have heard the handmaiden's talk about her mother. Having met her the night before they would know of her identity, and it was probably a chance meeting in the market. The abduction would have been spontaneous, and they would have left the town way before the alarm was raised.

"This treasure the men were seeking," he asked. "You know nothing of what they were taking about, is this not the truth?"

Madeline nodded her head.

"You are correct, sire," she replied. "The question the men kept asking was unknown to me. I know nothing of the Baron's treasure. You must believe me sire!"

Bardolph took Madeline's hand and squeezed it. He wanted to tell her about the arrival of her daughter Gwyneth to Lodelowe, but chose not to disclose this information. News of her daughter's conviction and execution, he would leave to others, and at a time when she was stronger.

"Yes Madeline, I does't believe you," he said, "but my problem now is what must be done with you? I cannot leave you here in the forest, and I cannot permit you to return to the tavern, for both venues can no longer offer refuge. I must get you to a safe place of shelter, for methinks it will not only be the men in the forest that wish you harm, but also the Baron's men. So you are certainly not safe to return to Lodelowe."

Bardolph was at a loss. What must he do? A safe haven was needed. But where could he find such a place? The trouble was; he was a stranger to these parts. Salopsbury came to mind. This was Madeline's birthplace and she would be safer there, at least safe from the Baron's men. He could pay someone to take her there, but whom could he trust? Who could he ask to undertake such an enormous risk? And besides; Madeline was not fit to travel. Not yet anyway. She was in need of rest and time for her wounds to heal.

With a look of anguish Bardolph turned to Ralph.

"Ralph, what can I do?" he asked. "I cannot leave Madeline here, and neither can she return to Lodelowe. I must get her to Salopsbury, but who will'st do this bidding? Is there anyone here I can trust?"

Ralph was quick to respond.

"My father," he said without giving the matter any more thought. "My father will do it."

Bardolph furrowed his brow.

"Your father!" he said, "The blacksmith at Onneyditch?"

Ralph nodded his head.

"My father is loyal to the King. You are his servant and he will do your bidding," he said. "He will do anything for you and the King. He also distrusts the Baron's craven family. He will do your bidding; of this I am certain. He will shelter this woman and make her well again, for he has knowledge of medicine. And I will take her to Salopsbury once she is strong again. This, I will do personally."

Bardolph was filled with admiration for Ralph. These were words that could easily have been spoken by someone much older and wiser than a lad of ten. Ralph was indeed much mature for his age.

Bardolph pondered long and hard. Did he really want to get someone else involved, especially when it spelt danger?

After much thought, Bardolph sighed and shook his head.

"Ralph, it seems fate hath once more taken a hand to discourage me from my journey south," he said. "Perhaps it is God's will that we must suffer each other's company for a little while longer. I will'st do as you suggest and consult with your father. For I see the stables at Onneyditch to be the refuge Madeline needs.'

With the sun setting and about one hour of daylight remaining, Bardolph set off from the thicket and to take the road north to Onneyditch. With him travelled Madeline and Ralph. They moved swiftly and in line, with Madeline seated to the fore of Bardolph. Behind them rode Ralph upon his pony, and to the rear there trailed the donkey.

Bardolph took the lead in order to keep an alert eye on the road ahead. If they were to be met they would take cover. From now on, danger lurked at every turn and no chances could be taken. And whilst they rode, Bardolph considered his own future. His immediate priority was to find a safe haven for Madeline, but once this task was done his duties towards her must end.

This night he would stay at the Golden Lion Inn at Onneyditch, but come sunrise he would be away. The King's birds were his priority and he could tarry here no longer.

Deep in the forest two men stirred, each holding their blood-caked heads. With water from leather flagons they bathed away the blood and dressed their head-wounds.

As they mounted their horses, one man spoke.

"We must ride to Salopsbury and do so through the night despite what dangers this may hold," he said, "for the Earl must be made aware of all that has happened. News must reach Salopsbury ahead of the herald. Informants within Lodelowe tell me that the rider leaves at sunrise on the morrow and with good speed should reach Salopsbury before sunset. We must beat him to it and arrive whilst the sun is still high."

As the two men rode from the clearing, the topcoat of one of the riders opened to reveal the pale blue uniform with the three yellow snarling lion heads of Salopsbury. He quickly closed the topcoat. It was dangerous to display these colours this far south of Salopsbury.

Chapter Twenty-Seven

One hour's ride north of Lodelowe stood the village of Onneyditch. However, one hour was all the daylight that remained as the party set out from the thicket of trees. Bardolph took the lead. Drooped before him in the saddle, sat Madeline. He held her by the waist whilst she bounced up and down with head bowed. Behind, followed Ralph and pony, and to the rear trailed a donkey laden with sacks and cages.

Darkness was falling as the small party approached the high, humped-back bridge that straddled the River Onney. Bardolph saw a need for caution and moved slowly into Onneyditch. As luck would have it, the streets were empty. The bell at Wistanstow Abbey had not long sounded, tolling eight times. This was the signal for workers in the fields to return to their homes.

Despite this late hour however, much caution remained. Bardolph was well aware of the risks involved with bringing Madeline to Onneyditch. The land from Wistanstow to Lodelowe was very much under the control of the Baron, and his spies were everywhere. But Bardolph recalled his previous visit to Onneyditch just two nights earlier. Dusk was falling and lanterns burned in the windows, but more significantly, the streets were empty. On this occasion he could perceive nothing different. As he crossed the high, humped-back bridge that linked the two halves of the hamlet, the Golden Lion Inn greeted him with a welcoming glow from its downstairs windows.

Bardolph led the way, following the north bank of the river then turning down the narrow alleyway that ran alongside the inn. To the rear of the old black and white timber-framed building he dismounted and handed his reins to Ralph. With Ralph seated upon his pony and steadying his white horse, Bardolph helped Madeline down from the saddle. All movement was painful, but Bardolph bided his time and let her alight at her own pace. He could see no need to rush now that they were at the inn.

The stables and smithy stood to the rear of the inn. The doors were open and the forge inside glowed brightly in the gathering gloom. Through the open doors the sound of hammering upon an anvil could be heard.

Bardolph turned to Ralph.

"Ralph, lead the animals to the stalls," he told him. "Give them fresh hay and water. I will'st speak to your father alone."

Ralph's father was a big man, well over six feet tall, with a thickset neck and powerful muscles. Yet inwardly, he remained a gentle giant. He hated to see suffering of any kind and had many cures for animal sicknesses. He would pick herbs from the forest and collect bark from trees to make up his special remedies, and people for miles around would bring their sick animals to him.

Bardolph had met with John Smith on two occasions, the first being on the evening of his arrival to Onneyditch, the second on his departure the following morning when he collected his animals. So the two men knew of each other, if only on business terms. However, local gossip had since reached the blacksmith.

Hearsay told of Bardolph's close proximity to the King. This man from Wessex was a Royal Falconer, a position considered to be one of great esteem. Also and probably more importantly, another incident had occurred. A Baron's soldier had arrived with a proclamation ordering that his son Ralph return with them to Lodelowe. The soldier had said that Ralph was being commandeered by Bardolph to tend the King's birds whilst he was away on the Baron's business.

So this much was known, but as Bardolph approached the anvil, there also things the blacksmith did not know, things such as the recent trial of Gwyneth the handmaiden, or the search for her mother.

Bardolph approached the anvil with caution, for he knew little of Ralph's father other than what Ralph had told him. Somehow, by whatever means at his disposal, he needed to gain John's allegiance. But with a sizeable reward upon Madeline's head, and most of the population of Lodelowe out looking for her, he knew this not to be an easy task. Somehow, he had to talk John into sheltering a fugitive from justice, and to find somewhere safe for her to rest until she was fit enough to travel.

Bardolph held the stumbling Madeline steady in his arms as they walked side by side towards the anvil. She moved painfully and at a stoop, with head bowed and holding the two halves of her tattered dress together before her breasts. The birching in the woods had sapped her strength and she was very weak. At the hands of her captors, the beating had been indiscriminate, catching her face as well as her breasts, and thin trickles of blood still oozed from the deepest welts. There was a further injury too. A boot to the thigh had caused severe bruising and she walked with a limp.

John looked up as Bardolph and Madeline approached the anvil. Immediately on recognition, he laid down his hammer and touched his forelock in servitude. He recognised Ralph too in the background so he guessed the reason for this visit. His son had returned and the King's Falconer with him.

Bardolph stopped before the anvil with Madeline supported on his arm.

"A goodly evening," he said. "Pray do tell me, have you time to talk? For I see you have a hot shoe upon the anvil."

John nodded his head.

"A goodly evening to you too, sire," he said. "The shoe is not important. It can be reheated. There is no hurry. I have time to talk."

Bardolph had long worked out a strategy. He would affirm John's loyalty to the King before any mention of Madeline.

"John, where does't your loyalties lie?" he asked. "Does't thou support the King of England."

John looked bemused. It was a question not to be asked lightly, not this close to the Welsh border anyway. But he answered honestly and truthfully. He nodded his head.

"Aye sire, I does't support the King of England," he said. "It is where my allegiance lies. In me, he will find a true and loyal servant."

Bardolph knew it to be wrong, but saw the use of the King's name as the best way forward. His authority needed to exceed that of the Baron's.

"Then John, there is something I want you to do for the King," he said. "Something most important and does't require your solemn oath that nothing that is said between us shall pass beyond this forge."

John looked further bemused. But he was an honest man and would never break a trust upon oath.

"Sire, you have my solemn oath. Nothing that is spoken here will pass beyond these four walls. I swear before God and as a true and loyal servant of the King that this be so." And with this he brought the hammer down upon the anvil.

Bardolph nodded in recognition of the oath sealed by the strike of a hammer on the anvil.

John was a good man and would not go back on his word, and he knew this in his heart. He raised Madeline's hand to show about whom he was about to speak. The time had come for an explanation.

"Then good servant of the King," he began. "I must tell you that this lady is a fugitive from justice. The Baron hath put a reward upon her head, and as I speak, his men are out scouring the countryside for her. I'm looking for a place to hide her, a place where she can remain until she is recovered fully from her wounds. I therefore, ask of you, good servant of the King, pray do see it within your heart to find shelter for this good lady until she is well again. And when this is done I want her to be taken north to Salopsbury where I know she will be safe, for it is the place of her birth. Your lad Ralph has said that he will do this for me, and I will pay in advance for this service; but until the time is right, Madeline needs to be well hidden and her presence remain unknown to all those outside these stable walls."

John considered what was being asked of him and all the implications thus entailed, for these were dangerous proposals and he knew the Baron to be a ruthless man. After giving the matter much thought, he nodded his head. He would do Bardolph's bidding. He disliked the Baron anyway, as did most of the residents of Onneyditch, and for this reason alone he would do it. The de Clancey family had failed to support the good King Richard in his crusade to free the Holy Lands from the infidels, and even though some forty-three years had since passed, bitter memories of the family's refusal to fight still lingered.

John nodded his head.

"Good sire, this lady's secret remains safe with me," he said. "There is only my son and I that does't reside here at these stables. It is our home since my good wife did pass away at childbirth. The lady that you bring to me will be safe here, and no one shall get to hear of her presence. And when the time comes I personally will take her to Salopsbury. It is not a task I would beset upon a boy. So these deeds will be done. Of this I do swear my solemn oath to both you and the King."

Once more he brought his hammer down hard upon the anvil.

Bardolph stretched his free arm across the anvil and took John by the hand.

"Then John, I thank you greatly for the loyalty and trust you put upon both me and the King," he said. Then indicating to Madeline supported on his other arm, he added, "this, good sire, is Madeline. She is a fugitive from justice and right now is in need of hot water and bandages, for she hath taken a severe beating and is in much need of care and rest."

Madeline raised her head as Bardolph spoke, and for the first time John saw the full extent of her injuries. He was appalled by the injuries to her face. He stepped around the anvil to take a closer look. Parting her torn dress slowly and delicately so as not to cause unnecessary suffering, he inspected the full extent of her injuries. He shook his head slowly from side to side. He was horrified at what had been done. However he did not ask of the people that had perpetrated this evil act, he merely assumed it to be the Baron's men.

John shook a fist in anger.

"This is no way to treat a lady!" he said. Then turning to Bardolph he added, "Pray, leave Madeline with me good sire. She will be safe here. I will tend to her injuries. I have clean linen and will apply a poultice to soothe away the pain."

Bardolph handed Madeline over to John by releasing her arm. John picked her up in his strong arms and carried her across the floor to rest upon a sheaf of hay. He turned to Bardolph.

"The hour is getting late good sire," he said. "You best go to the inn and find yourself a bed for the night. And pray good sire, fear not, for Madeline will be safe with me. I will make her a bed above the stables where she can rest from prying eyes."

It was never Bardolph's intention to leave Madeline, not so soon anyway, but on seeing that she was now in capable hands he decided to take up John's offer. He bowed gracefully.

"Then John, good servant of the King," he said. "I bid you a goodly night, for I will do as thou does't suggest and retire to the comfort of the inn. I leave Madeline in your care, and Ralph with my birds and animals. For I know you both capable of serving the King's needs, and for this I must thank you greatly."

Leaving Madeline lying on the hay and with John kneeling over her, Bardolph collected up his saddlebag, placed it over an arm and set off for the inn. It was dark by now, and after a bowl of pottage an early night was called for.

He already had plans for the morrow. He would rise before dawn and make his way to Wistanstow. This would be a good place to hunt having been told of rabbits on the coppice above the abbey. A brace would suffice to feed his birds. This was all that was needed. He had tarried far too long in Lodelowe and the time had come to move on.

Chapter Twenty-Eight

John Smith took Madeline up in his strong arms and carried her to the loft above the stables. As he did so he called down to his son.

"Ralph, put hot water on the forge then bring it to me when it is boiled," he told him.

Once in the loft, he laid Madeline down on a bed of straw then set about pulling away the tattered remnants of her dress.

"It is best I remove these torn and blood-stained clothes," he told her. "I will'st prepare a poultice to soothe away the pain. Soon you will be well again. My poultices never fail to work, albeit on a horse's fetlock bruised from a fall."

Madeline did not protest, since nakedness meant nothing to her; as a whore by trade, lying naked on a bed in the presence of a man held no embarrassment.

"Pray do whatever thou think'est best," she told the blacksmith. "For I does't know that I have been left in the charge of a good and honest man."

Slowly and with great care John removed Madeline's tattered clothes. To be truthful it was John, not Madeline, who felt uncomfortable with the act. But one look at her injuries reminded the blacksmith of the harm that had been done. This sweet lady, now entrusted into his care by a servant of the King, needed healing, and it was well within his power to do so.

Kneeling alongside the bed of straw, John examined the full extent of Madeline's injuries. He traced the tips of his fingers lightly across her welts; everywhere wept with blood. There were other injuries too. One side of her of body was blue from bruising.

John shook his head in disbelief.

"What kind of a man would do this to a woman?" he uttered. "If God ever gives me a chance to come upon this person, then I will tear his throat apart with my bare hands."

Madeline held out a hand and gripped John by the wrist. Their hands moved to hold and comfort each other.

Madeline squeezed John's hand and said, "John, you are a good man. Good and God fearing. But pray, anger not for my aggressors. If it is God's will then the Almighty will punish them."

John nodded his head. He was a big man with powerful muscles and bulging chest, but beneath laid the mind of a gentle giant.

"You are right good lady," he said. "Anger is the mark of the devil, and it was unjust of me to utter such words. My task is to make you whole again, not condemn those that perpetrated this evil deed. It is a poultice that is needed here, and for this your dress must go. But fear not good lady, for whence you are well again, I will re-clothe you. I keep dresses of my late wife. She was of the same size and the dresses have been well stored."

Madeline felt deeply touched by John's caring words. She recalled something he said at the anvil and she gripped John's hand tightly.

"Did you not say you had lost your good wife at childbirth?" she asked.

John nodded his head.

"Aye, nigh on ten years now, at the birth of Ralph," he said with much sadness. "Alas, I have brought him up alone and he has never known a mother."

John paused briefly as memories of his wife flooded back to him.

"But what about you my sweet Madeline?" he continued. "Have you no man of your own?"

Tears welled up in Madeline's eyes. How could she explain to such a sweet and God-fearing man that she was nothing more than a common whore, a lowlife who plied her trade at a tavern in Lodelowe? She shook her head and explained the best she could. But it was not within her heart to reveal her true profession. Not yet, anyway. She squeezed John's hand tightly.

"I lost my husband too, John," she replied. "He died of the plague that struck my village some six years back. I have a daughter, but I have not seen her these last five years. She will be sixteen now and works in the kitchens at Salopsbury Castle. As for me, I have no man to look after me. I earn my keep at the tavern."

John returned a loving smile.

"Then Madeline, we have much in common," he said and returned the squeeze to her hand.

A hint of a loving smile appeared on Madeline lips. She was about to speak again when John stopped her.

"We waste time with this idle talk," he told her. "This dress must go and a poultice applied. And it must be done quickly, before any badness seeps in."

Their hands parted and John set to work. Slowly and carefully he removed what remained of the dress. For a while Madeline lay naked upon the bed with John holding her hand for comfort. Nothing was spoken and Madeline closed her eyes. They were waiting for Ralph. But the wait was not long. Soon, the boy arrived with a kettle of boiling water to break the tenderness of the moment.

John took the kettle.

"Have you stabled the falconer's horse and donkey for the night?" he asked his son.

Ralph nodded his head.

"Yes father, they are comfortable and will rest well this night," he confirmed.

John nodded his own head in response.

"Then pray go now, Ralph, and tend to the falconer's birds," he said. "Remember you are in the service of the King and those birds must remain in good health. I too have much work to do this night. This sweet lady is to be made well again. I must mix a poultice and treat her wounds. She hath endured much this day and it will be several days more before she is fit to walk again."

As Ralph descended from the loft, John set about mixing his poultice in a stone jar. The base consisted mainly of oats and boiling water, but the further crushing of herbs and barks turned what was no more than a meal fit for a horse into something that would cure Madeline's injuries.

With a rag soaked in hot water then cooled to a bearable temperature, John washed away the blood from Madeline's body, and when he was done he applied his special mixture of oats and herbs.

The hot poultice stung and brought tears to Madeline's eyes, but she remained calm throughout, for she knew in her heart the cure to be good. When the application was done, John placed a sheet of linen soaked in warm water across her breasts and pressed firmly down onto the poultice.

John's attention now turned to Madeline's bruised thigh. A second poultice with a different mixture of herbs was applied and held in place by a linen bandage wound about the leg.

When he was done, John took Madeline's hand.

"There, my good lady," he said. "The deed is done. Pray, now lie still until such times as the poultice cools. By the morrow the soreness will have gone and you will be fit to move more freely. Of this I have no doubt."

Madeline squeezed John's hand.

"John, you are a good and God fearing man," she told him. "Whence I am whole again I can only pay you for your kindness, for I have but a little money saved. But what I have is all yours."

John squeezed Madeline's hand in return. He did not want money. The things he had done, he had done with the goodness of his heart.

"My dear sweet Madeline," he told her. "I does't not want your money. I do this from my heart and for the oath I have sworn to the King. You are a good woman and I would do what I have just done to anyone beaten this badly."

For a while nothing was said. Their eyes met and a smile passed between them.

"Now Madeline, my dear sweet Madeline," continued John. "Pray close your eyes and rest. For sleep is needed for my poultice to do its work."

Madeline squeezed John's hand. The hour was late and apart from one solitary lantern that burned nearby, the loft lay in darkness. She closed her eyes but found sleep impossible. Since the death of her late husband she had not felt this way about any man. Was this love she felt in her heart, or simply the pain of her wounds? She had no way of telling.

With thoughts of being carried in the strong arms of a gentle giant, she finally found rest.

As she did so she gripped tightly the hand of the man that sat beside her.

Chapter Twenty-Nine

As darkness had already fallen, Bardolph had little choice other than to stay the night at the inn at Onneyditch. He was given the same accommodation as before, a small room to the rear of the inn that overlooked the stables. An hour after settling in, he descended the stairs and crossed the downstairs room to the inglenook. A cauldron filled with meats and vegetables simmered above the fire. In a rocking chair alongside the fire sat Agatha, an ageing crone now in her ninety-third year. As Bardolph moved to ladle pottage into his bowl, he turned to Agatha and out of respect touched his forelock.

"A goodly evening ma'am," he said in greeting.

Agatha set the chair rocking and strained her eyes towards Bardolph.

"I've seen you somewhere before, haven't I?" she asked quizzically.

Bardolph nodded a response.

"You have indeed ma'am," he replied. "It was here but two nights past we did last meet. For then, I did'st take a room for the night at this goodly inn and partake of your most agreeable pottage."

Agatha raised an eyebrow and studied the face of the handsome young man stood between her and the fire. She managed a toothless smile as memories of this man's visit came flooding back.

"Yes, I remember you!" she said. "I don't forget faces! You asked of my age and health."

Bardolph stopped ladling the pottage into his bowl and turned to the rocking chair.

"That I did, ma'am," he answered, "and what a remarkable age you are. You told me you were in your ninety-third year, and I think you must hold many a fond memory of Lodelowe and of the family that rules there. For I am led to believe that you did'st once serve within the castle walls."

Agatha smiled as memories of her younger days came flooding back. She had been a servant to the de Clanceys in her youth.

"Yes, I was at the birth of the present Baron," she told Bardolph, "and I was also there when the twins Edmund and Edward were born. Edward was the present Baron's father. But that was a long, long time ago."

Bardolph recalled the tapestry hanging in the great hall of Lodelowe Castle. He had stood next to the Baron looking up at the tapestry when saying farewell. The twins Edmund and Edward were depicted on that tapestry standing to either side of a river with a motte and bailey in the background. A thought came to him. Could the scene on the tapestry be that of Onneyditch? And could the river that flowed alongside this inn be the one in which the twin Edmund drowned? There were a lot of similarities.

"Ah!" remarked Bardolph, "The twins, Edmund and Edward! Yes, I have this very day gazed upon the Baron's tapestry in the great hall of Lodelowe Castle. Pray tell me, was it here in Onneyditch that the tragedy of Edmund's death did'st so take place? I recall seeing a river and a motte and bailey on the tapestry, and the raven of the Lord Rhys hovering above the scene."

Agatha rocked in her chair, swaying vigorously forwards and backwards.

"I too have seen the tapestry you speak of," she told him. "It was sewn by the nuns of Wistanstow many years after the event, and mostly on hearsay. The twins were never that grown up. They were just babies. Edmund had not reached his first birthday when the Lord Rhys's men cast him in the river. But good sire, you are right, it was here at Onneyditch that the tragedy occurred, a raid by the men of the Lord Rhys did'st send mayhem amongst the people of this village. Edmund and Edward became parted in the confusion. Edward was saved and whisked away to Lodelowe, but Edmund was seized and cast into the river."

Bardolph found the family history of the de Clanceys' most fascinating and wanted to know more. But the dates confused him.

"Tell me dear lady, what year would the twins be born?" He asked.

He doubted whether he would get a true answer. Not an accurate one anyway, but in his mind he was trying to piece together all of the facts.

Remarkably, however, Agatha could pinpoint the year, for the birth of the twins coincided with a very important date in the English calendar. The actual year was unknown to her, but she was able to explain.

"The twins were born some three to four days following the death of King Stephen," she told him. "I know this because the news of the King's death came along with the crier's announcement of the birth of the twins."

Bardolph was well aware of the year of King Stephen's death. The King had died in 1154 and King Henry II had succeeded him to the throne. He did a quick calculation. Agatha, at the age of ninety-three would have been born in the year 1142, and would, therefore, have been just twelve years old at the time.

Now Bardolph had the year, there was something else he could fit into place, for he was aware of other events that occurred about this time. The Lord Rhys, the Welsh overlord who's symbol the raven was depicted upon the tapestry, succeeded to the throne as the King of Deheubarth in 1155, and this just six months into the new King Henry's reign. Therefore, if the twins were just under one year old at the time, then this would have been one of Lord Rhys's first raids into England; a time when he was trying to establish his Welsh supremacy and state his independence from the new King of England.

Bardolph mused upon what he had just heard, then changed the subject, for there was one more thing that puzzled him. The name of this inn, the Golden Lion, seemed inappropriate for Lodelowe, for it bore the coat of arms of the Fitzgerald family.

"Tell me my dear lady," he asked, "the name of this goodly inn, the Golden Lion. Is it not the sign of the Fitzgeralds of Salopsbury that hangs above this door?"

Agatha rocked in her chair.

"The name of this inn goes back to a time when this side of the river did'st belong to the estates of Salopsbury," she explained. "The River Onney was once the boundary between Lodelowe and Salopsbury. There were many skirmishes and disagreements between the de Clanceys and the Fitzgeralds until a settlement was finally reached. It was agreed that the ford at Marsh Brook, to the north of here, should be the new boundary. It was the Abbey at Wistanstow that had the final say, as most of these lands belong to the church. And to keep the peace, it was agreed that the abbot be appointed by Lodelowe and the abbess by Salopsbury. And that is how the arms of the Fitzgeralds came to hang above this door. This inn once resided in the estates of the Fitzgeralds and its name has never changed since those early days, and besides anything is better than the *'Craven Arms'* of the de Clanceys."

Bardolph could detect bitterness in Agatha's voice and decided to press the matter no further. Instead, he ladled more pottage into his bowl.

"And about what year would this be?" he asked, "The year when the boundary was moved northwards from here?"

Agatha gave Bardolph's question some thought. She held many memories of Onneyditch and of Lodelowe, but to fit them all together and in a particular order that made sense, proved most difficult. She answered Bardolph with a touch of uncertainty to her voice.

"I think it all happened at about the same time; the year Edmund was cast into the river," she told him. "It was the reason the twins were here in Onneyditch. That much I do know. They were here to celebrate the signing of the treaty between Lodelowe and Salopsbury that resolved the border issue. It was the church that arbitrated in the final agreement and the twins were here to receive a gift of gratitude from the Abbot of Wistanstow."

Bardolph turned pensive. This happened just over eighty years ago and it would have been a different abbot then. As would everybody else that took part in this agreement.

"You talk of a gift. What would that be?" he asked.

Agatha shook her head.

"Kind sire, I cannot recall. My mind is not what it used to be," she said after much deliberation and leaning back in her chair in exhaustion.

Bardolph could see that he was over-taxing Agatha and decided to bring their conversation to an end. He finished filling his bowl with pottage and turned to walk away.

"Then I bid you a goodly night, dear lady," he said. "May you sleep well, and may your many fond memories fill you with pleasant dreams this night."

Agatha cackled.

"And a goodly night to you too young man," she said. "For my dreams this night will be sweeter since reminding me of days long past."

Bardolph moved to a vacant table. As he spooned his pottage he mused upon the things he had just learned. What he had heard would probably bear little or no significance upon his life, but all the same he felt better for knowing a little piece of Lodelowe history.

Chapter Thirty

The nuns of Wistanstow were in a state of deep shock. Sister Anne had sinned and brought disgrace upon the Holy Order.

The novice had been assigned to the orchards and with summer giving way to autumn, the apples on the trees were almost ripe. Sister Anne's instructions were implicit. Those apples that had fallen in the recent storms were to be collected, placed in baskets and taken to the kitchen.

But one large rosy apple never reached the kitchen. Instead, the apple found its way beneath the habit of Sister Anne to be consumed in her cell that evening. But Sister Maud, much wiser and more devout, spotted the misdemeanour and informed the head of the order. Now, with matins concluded and the sun about to rise, it was time for Sister Anne to confess her sins and suffer whatever punishment the Abbess thought merited such a wicked crime.

The office of the Abbess was austere. Just a heavy wooden table cut from oak yet unstained. On it burned a single candle, a strip of sealing wax, a feathered quill and an inkwell filled with distinctive light blue ink. Beyond the table stood a chair, it was simple in design with straight back and unpolished wood. The candle cast a flickering light about the room. On one wall hung a huge wooden cross with the gilded body of Christ nailed upon it. Against a second wall stood wooden shelves stacked with books, manuscripts and scrolls. These were the records and communications between the abbey and families of the sisters at the nunnery. At the centre of the table rested a solitary rosy-red apple.

On the chair sat Lady Elizabeth Fitzgerald, sister of the Earl of Salopsbury, but here at the nunnery she went by another title. Here she was the Abbess of Wistanstow, or to use her more accepted title, the nunnery's Mother Superior. The Abbess was seated at the table, her back straight, fingers drumming on the surface. To the front of her knelt a young novice, her head bowed and her young freckled face hidden beneath her wimple.

The Abbess collected the apple from the table and held it aloft. With a voice deep with despair, she addressed the young novice.

"Sister Anne you have sinned and brought wicked shame upon this Holy Order," she told the novice. "So just what am I going to do with you?"

Sister Anne knew that she must not answer. The Abbess was only thinking aloud. Kneeling before the table and running a rosary through her fingers, the young novice could tell from the tone of the Abbess's voice that whatever punishment she meted out, it would be harsh. There would almost certainly be tasks of scrubbing and cleaning that would wear away the nails from the fingers. There was also the threat of flagellation. She dreaded the thought, but was ready to accept this punishment, should the Abbess think it a fit chastisement for her sins. But there was something far worse; something far more dreadful a fate that could befall her, and she hoped it would not come to this. Far worse would be her transfer to the other side of the abbey for correction. Only the most dreadful of sins warranted correction, but deep down she knew that what she had done ranked up there with one of the worst.

The Abbess, deep in shock, shook her head from side to side.

"Sister Anne, you have sinned greatly," she told the novice. "It has been a long time since a sister of this order hath committed a crime that doth warrant such severe punishment. I can administer punishment of my own choosing, and this I will do. But I must also consult with the Abbot and hear his thoughts on the matter. Correction over on the other side may well be in order."

The Abbess continued to shake her head from side to side. This hurt her as much as it did the young novice. However, she could think of no other course of action other than to refer Sister Anne's misdemeanour to a higher authority. The situation was not ideal, and not what she wanted, but what other option did she have?

With some reluctance, she made her decision.

"Sister Anne," she told the novice after a period of deep thought, "as punishment you will chastise yourself by administering twenty-four lashes of the scouge, one for every hour of the day. You will return to your cell immediately, remove your novice's attire and wait there until you are called. I am informed that the Abbot hath returned from his tiresome journey to Lodelowe and attends matins as we speak. But as soon as his morning worship is over, I will seek an audience. I will send a message across to the other side that I wish to speak with him. I must be guided by his knowledge of the law and by what he has to say on the matters of theft. There is no place in this order for thieves. So go now, Sister Anne, return to your cell, prepare yourself for chastisement and pray. Pray forgiveness and pray to God that He gives you strength."

Sister Anne rose, and bending low and walking backwards, made her way to the door. The punishment of the scouge was inevitable, she accepted this, and already she was praying for strength and forgiveness. However, she had no wish to be handed over to the other side for the second part of her punishment. This would be the worst punishment of all. She had heard other nuns of the order; nuns much older and wiser, tell tales of sisters being taken across to the other side of the abbey for correction. And what they did to young nuns filled her with both horror and dread.

Surely any punishment meted out by the Abbot was not for her? Surely the Abbess would not take council from the Abbot and agree to send her across to the other side? She was nothing but a mere novice and as yet unschooled in the teachings of this abbey's religious order.

As daylight began to break, and facing each other through the high iron-latticed partition that divided the Abbey's church, the Abbot and Abbess met.

After their formal greetings and prayers in Latin, the conversation turned to Sister Anne and her misdemeanour.

Having explained the problem and what punishment the wayward sister was already due to expect, the Abbess queried of the Abbot.

"Then what more, if any, must be done with our wayward novice?" she asked.

The Abbot turned pensive. For a while he closed his eyes and put his chubby hands together in prayer. Eventually, he came to a conclusion.

"You have put to her that she may be handed over to this side for correction?" he queried.

"I have told her so," confirmed the Abbess.

"And she agrees?" returned the Abbot. "She gives no objection?"

"I have told her so and she holds no objection," assured the Abbess. "She is fully aware of the error of her ways and is deeply repentant."

The Abbot turned pensive once more. Putting his hands together and bringing to his face in prayer. After a long pause he spoke again.

"Then correction it must be. God's will must be done," he said eventually. "It has been a long time since we had a thief amongst our sacred order. Bring her to the gate and I will have her collected."

"I will organise it," returned the Abbess. "Sister Anne will be waiting at the gate after matins on the morrow. Today I will administer my own punishment on Sister Anne."

"Praise be to God," responded the Abbot. "Send her prepared and I will see to it personally that the devil is purged from her soul, and that she be returned to the Sisterhood a more devout and god-fearing Christian."

"Praise be to God," echoed the Abbess.

"Praise be to God," repeated the Abbot.

And with that the two moved away to kneel before the altar and pray. Both remained close together with only the iron grating that divided the church keeping them apart.

There was nothing more to be said. Sister Anne's fate was decided. It would start within the hour, when twenty-four lashes would be administered, and conclude the following day with correction over on the other side of the Abbey.

A little later that day, behind the abbey walls, a ceremony was about to take place. Sister Anne was to receive the first of her two punishments. A high-latticed fence ran down the middle of the garden to the rear of the church. Against the fence, on the nunnery side of the abbey stood a small grassy mound.

Stood around the area in a semi-circle gathered the nuns of the order. All were assembled, for the Abbess had bid that all should attend the nunnery's punishment of Sister Anne. Over on the other side of the fence there stood a small line of monks. The Abbot was amongst them. Unlike the nuns, the monks were not obliged to attend and some had moved to the church to pray.

When all were assembled, the Abbess called Sister Anne to the garden. The novice was already stripped of her habit and entered the garden wearing nothing more than a sleeveless coarsely woven woollen vest. Her back remained bear and the front covered her breasts with straps tied around the back of her neck. Her head was shaven with only a covering of ginger stubble showing. With head bowed, Sister Anne knelt on the grassy mound before the gathering and, clutching at her rosary and a crucifix, began to pray for forgiveness.

A senior sister of the order moved forward. In her hands she carried a chalice of holy water and a scouge.

"Sister Anne, the time has come," informed the Abbess.

Remaining on her knees, Sister Anne laid down her rosary and crucifix. She rose to her feet and signalled to the Abbess that she was ready.

The Abbess, in a final act of preparation, called for the chalice of holy water. She was told the waters came from the Holy Land, from the river of Jordan. This, she believed to be true, but others had their doubts. She dipped two fingers into the vessel and splashed droplets upon the novice's freckled back. She repeated this several times and concluded with a little prayer. Now they were ready, she handed back the chalice and in return collected the scouge. It consisted of a stout leather bound handle and several lengths of plaited hide. The Abbess had a choice of three scourges. One just had plain leather straps. A second had small metal nodules attached to the end, and the third had the same nodules, but each having one sharp point protruding to the side. In this instance, for a first time punishment, the Abbess selected the first. It would naturally hurt, but cause little damage to the skin.

"Sister Anne," said the Abbess, speaking aloud so all should hear, "it is by order of the authority invested in me, and by this most holy and religious order that you are sentenced to chastise yourself with twenty-four lashes of the scouge, one for every hour of the day. You do this in order to amend your ways. Afterwards, it has been decreed that you receive further correction from the Abbot personally, and for this you are to be taken to the other side so that your evil ways may once and for all be purged from your body, and that you be returned to the nunnery a more devout and believing Christian."

Having explained the sentence, the Abbess handed the selected scouge over to Sister Anne then turned to the sisters of the order.

"Come sisters, let us all kneel and pray for Sister Anne," she said. "Pray that the evil that is within her be cast away, and that the devil's presence be driven from this holy place for ever."

All knelt in prayer, and from the other side of the lattice fence, the Abbot began to recite a verse in Latin. The service was long and solemn, and ended with a chant from the handful of monks that elected to attend the ceremony.

A silence descended over both sides of the lattice fence as the novice raised the scouge and held it high.

"Are you ready, Sister Anne?" enquired the Abbess.

Sister Anne nodded her head.

"I am ready, Holy Mother," she said and biting her bottom lip.

"Then pray Sister Anne. Pray for God's forgiveness, and pray loudly so that we all can hear," said the Abbess.

Sister Anne took a deep breath, held the scouge out before her, braced herself then swung her arm backwards over one shoulder.

She grimaced as the scouge slaked down her bare back. She prayed loudly through gritted teeth so that all those gathered should hear her call for forgiveness.

Whilst she prayed, the monks observing through the lattice fence began their intonations.

"*Uno pro Christianis cunctis,*" they chanted. [One for all the Christians].

To conclude, the Abbot recited a special little prayer to accompany the chant.

For a while silence descended upon the garden, the only noise coming from Sister Anne as she gulped for air in an effort to regain her breath. However, she knew what was wanted of her and was determined to play her part. She had been instructed to keep on praying. But to do this she needed to breathe. As the pain eased, but still gasping loudly, she recited a little prayer for forgiveness.

Only when her prayers were concluded did she strike for the second time. As the scouge cracked loudly and echoed about the garden, the monks chanted for a second time.

This time they sang, "*Duo pro sororibus vanis.*" [Two for the loose sister].

And so the ceremony went on, a sequence of scouge, incantations and blessings.

"*Tres pro penitentibus,*" [Three for the penitent] chanted the monks after the third chatisement.

"*Quatro pro fratribus perversis,*" [Four for the errant brethren] for the fourth.

"*Quinquies pro vivis.*" [Five for the living].

"*Sexies pro fidelibus defunctis.*" [Six for the faithful dead].

And so it went on until all twenty-four strokes had been administered.

On conclusion, and with final prayers said, the Abbess led the nuns away, leaving Sister Anne alone in the garden in order to regain her breath and the pain to ease.

As the door to the nunnery closed, the Abbot handed two keys to a senior monk. Only the Abbot and Abbess held such keys. These were the keys that would gain access to the nunnery, and the only way through was via the church. A route always barred and locked by two gates.

As the senior monk collected the keys, the Abbot spoke his intentions.

"On the morrow, on conclusion of morning prayers, go to the other side and collect Sister Anne. She will be waiting at the gate," he said. "Take her to my chamber in the crypt. I will attend to her later in the day and personally administer the second of her corrections."

Chapter Thirty-One

Bardolph kicked at his horse and set off from the stables. Dawn was breaking as he emerged from the alleyway that ran alongside the Golden Lion Inn. He was aiming for the coppice that overlooked the abbey at Wistanstow. For here, he knew to be a good place to find rabbits, and before he set off home he intended to travel with a plentiful supply of food for his birds.

From the inn it was but a short distance to the high humped-back bridge that spanned the River Onney. As Bardolph reached the bridge he cocked an ear. A horse at a gallop was approaching from the south. As the horse crested the high point of the bridge Bardolph recognised the rider. It was Corporal Egbert. He pulled up his own horse and waited for the rider to arrive.

The Corporal on seeing Bardolph, pulled up his horse too and strained hard on the reins.

"A goodly morning, sire," he said and greeting the falconer. "Me thought you would be many miles south of Lodelowe by now."

Bardolph collected his thoughts. This was a meeting of ill chance and something he could not have foreseen. He thought quickly. He did not want his presence at Onneyditch to be of concern and a simple explanation was required. There should be no mention of Madeline, but he saw no problem in explaining his presence on the road this early in the morning. Most was the truth, anyway.

"Last night I did'st return with the lad Ralph to Onneyditch," he told Corporal Egbert. "For one good favour deserves another. Now, having refreshed myself with a goodly night's sleep at the inn, I does't intend to continue on with my journey south. But before I go I must bag myself some rabbits, for my birds are short of fresh meat."

Egbert readily accepted Bardolph's explanation.

"Then I pray, sire, that thou does't hunt well," he said, "but I must tarry no longer, for my mission is to make Salopsbury before the setting of the sun. I have here in my saddlebag despatches that announce the forthcoming trial of the Lady Adela. It is in my charge to herald these despatches to Salopsbury and to present them to the Earl in person."

Bardolph was well aware that the journey to Salopsbury was a good twelve hours ride at a steady canter, and twelve hours was about all the daylight available with the month of September now upon them.

"Then go, pray make the haste you require my friend, and may God and St. Christopher go with you," he said, wishing Egbert a safe journey.

Egbert saluted with clenched fist across the chest, then dug his spurs into the horse and set off at a gallop. Bardolph waited until the rider was well out of sight, then at a more leisurely pace, pursued him north along the same road.

The road to Wistanstow was nothing but a track, badly maintained and well rutted, and Bardolph saw the danger in galloping. He hoped that Egbert recognised the danger too and would ride warily over the ruts.

With Wistanstow Abbey in sight, Bardolph pulled up from a canter. A horse and cart stood in the middle of the road barring his way. Next to the cart there stood two peasants. They were looking down upon ditch. As Bardolph drew close he saw the cause of their concern. A horse and rider lay in the ditch. The rider looked badly hurt, and his horse writhed in agony.

Bardolph dismounted and climbed down into the ditch.

"Egbert, you have fallen badly!" he exclaimed. "Pray tell me, what damage hath been done?"

Corporal Egbert lay clutching his shin. He grimaced before speaking.

"It is my lower leg, sire. It is broken below the knee, and my horse, me thinks that he too hath broken a fetlock," he told Bardolph.

One of the peasants, calling down, tried to explain.

"Sire, the soldier did'st come upon us fast," he said. "To pass us by he rode upon the ditch and his horse did'st stumble. Sire, he gave us no warning. No chance to get out of the way."

Bardolph stood upright in the ditch and looked about him. The abbey was not far away. The white painted walls could be seen clearly beyond a field of wheat.

Bardolph looked up from the ditch and addressed the peasants.

"I need your cart," he told them. "I will'st set a splint against his leg, then he must be taken to the abbey. The monks will tend his injuries."

Bardolph looked about him. To either side of the rutted track, the fields danced to a sway of golden wheat. The nearest trees lay some distance away and the only timber suitable enough to make a splint lay upon the cart. Bardolph climbed from the ditch, ripped a plank from the cart and broke it in two with a foot. This would do for a splint.

As Corporal Egbert bit hard on a piece of leather, Bardolph set the broken bone and strapped the planks tightly to either side.

"There!" he said as he tied the final knot. "This splint will hold the bones in place. I will'st get you to the abbey. The monks will know what to do. But fear not my friend. This break is clean and will heal. Your leg will be straight and fit to walk again within weeks."

Bardolph moved to inspect the fallen horse. Once more, he felt saddened; Corporal Egbert was right, a fetlock was broken. Drawing his longbow he directed an arrow through the eye of the horse and into the brain. As the horse trembled in its death throes, Bardolph collect the saddle and bag and cast them over the back of his own horse.

Bardolph returned to Corporal Egbert and cast an arm about his shoulder. Hopping on one leg and supported by Bardolph, he got to his feet and climbed slowly from the ditch.

"I will'st get you to the abbey," Bardolph told the injured man.

But the Corporal had others ideas.

"Good sire, pray lend me your horse, for I must get to Salopsbury this day," he said. "My despatches must be placed in the hands of the Earl of Salopsbury this very day and before the setting of the sun. I have sworn an oath that this will be done."

Bardolph shook his head. The Corporal was courageous, but it was obvious he could go no further. For a while Bardolph considered how best to help, and he saw two possibilities. One, he could return to Lodelowe and call for help; and two, he could deliver the despatches himself. Neither option appealed. To return to Lodelowe would alert the Baron's men about Madeline, and to travel to

Salopsbury would delay his journey south by another three, possibly four days. He also had his birds to consider. But thankfully on this score he had Ralph. His birds would remain in safe hands if he were to take the journey north.

Bardolph came to a decision. Of the two options, he felt it best not to return to Lodelowe. The two men in the forest, though dressed in civilian clothes, talked and acted like soldiers. And if they were, then news of Madeline's capture and escape could very well have reached the ears of the Baron by now. And what if his horse or Ralph had been seen at the forest's edge whilst he was away? Suspicion of his continuing presence may lead them to the stables at Onneyditch. No, all things considered, it was best he did not return to Lodelowe. This option was far too risky. He therefore, saw only one choice open to him. He personally would take the Baron's despatches to Salopsbury.

Bardolph conveyed his intentions to Corporal Egbert.

"No Egbert, I must take you to the abbey," he insisted. "The monks will care for you. But do not despair, your despatches will get through, for I personally will take them to Salopsbury, this I does't solemnly swear."

Egbert gripped Bardolph's hand.

"Then I must thank you good sire, for I have failed in my duty," he said. "Look at me, a cripple with a broken leg. News of this accident must reach Captain Osbald. It was he that did'st entrusted me with such an important mission. He must be informed."

Bardolph squeezed Egbert's hand in return.

"On my return from Salopsbury, I will revisit the abbey," he said. "God willing, you may ride with me to Lodelowe and tell the good captain for yourself. For I have treated this break before. With the aid of splints and a goodly few days rest you will be fit to ride again, of this I am certain."

Chapter Thirty-Two

Two soldiers pulled up from the gallop. Heavy topcoats concealed their uniforms. They were at the top of a rise and Salopsbury was in sight.

Unlike Lodelowe with its outer town walls, inner castle and defensive keep, Salopsbury Castle stood aloft and isolated above what was a sprawling shamble of hovels and houses. There was no outer defence to the city other than the river. Here the great sweeping bow of the River Severn protected all that dwelt within, and apart from the castle's gate to the rear, the only other access to the city was via a bridge that spanned the river to the west. This bridge was fortified, with two square block towers and gates that were always locked during the hours of darkness.

Morning was breaking and a thin line of red sky to the east glowed dimly above the ramparts of the castle as the riders moved down from the rise. They had ridden hard through the night and now moved at a gentler pace. After arousing the slumbering overnight guard at the gates, they crossed the bridge and passed on through the narrow streets of the town. Eventually, they reached the rise in the ground that led to the castle. At the top of the winding road they passed beneath the castle's portcullis and into the courtyard beyond.

In the cold morning air, the pale blue banners bearing the three snarling lion heads of the Fitzgeralds's hung limply above the ramparts. The flags flew to celebrate the inauguration of the new Earl. With horses still steaming from their overnight run, the two soldiers dismounted, cast their reins towards an awaiting stable lad and sped hurriedly towards the reception hall of the castle.

The Earl was an early riser and normally at this time of day he would be enjoying his first meal. But on hearing news of his men's arrival he moved quickly to his chambers.

With the Earl seated upon his high chair, he dismissed his attendants and summonsed the two soldiers to enter the room. They strode briskly though the doorway, their swords and armour rattling as they moved. Their topcoats were gone and both displayed the blue tunic and three snarling lion heads of the Fitzgeralds. Gold tassels upon the shoulders of one of the soldiers signified a captain. The other soldier bore the red tassels of a sergeant. There was also something else. Both wore chain-mail hoods upon their heads to conceal deep gashes in their scalps.

"Greetings Captain Clarence and Sergeant Godfred," the Earl called across the chamber. "Come and join me, for I am eager to hear what news thou does't bring of my late cousin's pretty little Norman wife."

Both men dropped to one knee and bowed their heads. The captain's message was brief and well-rehearsed, but hopefully conveyed all.

"The news is not good, my Liege," he said. "Lady Adela remains alive. She is a prisoner of Baron de Clancey and is to stand trial for robbery and murder."

The Earl gripped the arms of his chair. This was not the news he was expecting and he fought hard to control his anger.

"What!" he exclaimed; "Lady Adela still alive! And a prisoner of Baron de Clancey! Surely this cannot be! What has happened to our plan?"

Captain Clarence was prepared for the Earl's outburst. Keeping his head lowered so as not to make eye contact, he began to explain the best he could, for he was not fully aware of all the facts.

"Lady Adela and her companions were waylaid by soldiers of Lodelowe some miles north of the Abbey at Wistanstow. A fight ensued and the men that escorted her were slain. Lady Adela and her handmaiden were then taken under guard to Lodelowe. We did'st rendezvous with the Welsh brigands and had our ambush prepared, but our wait was in vain since they never appeared."

The Earl thumped the arm of his chair. All his careful planning had come to nothing. He shook his head in disbelief.

"So Captain, are you telling me that Lady Adela and her party never reached the Abbey at Wistanstow?" he enquired.

Captain Clarence shook his head.

"My Liege, our plan was to waylay the party on the morning of their departure from the abbey," he explained. "The journey south from the abbey passes through the Forest of Wyre, and it was there we lay in wait. We had, like you arranged my Liege, met with the men of Lord Llywelyn, and all lay in wait in the forest, but by then and unbeknown to us, Lady Adela was already taken prisoner."

The Earl sighed and shook his head. This was not the news he had expected. His plan had been foolproof, or so he thought. Lady Adela was to be ambushed by Welsh brigands from across the border. He had dealt directly with the Welsh Lord, Llywelyn ap Iorwerth, and negotiated a heavy price for his services.

The Earl, for a while, sat dumbfounded and gripping hard at the arms of his chair. He could not bring himself to believe that Lady Adela remained alive and was now being held captive at Lodelowe. Furthermore, if what his captain had said was true then she also stood accused of robbery and murder. The Earl shook his head in disbelief. Surely this could not be so? There had to be some mistake? Lady Adela's party had clearance from the Council of the Marches. There was no way she could have been arrested, and Baron de Clancey would not be so foolhardy as to do such a thing, since safe passage for all had been decreed throughout all of the Marches.

The Earl shook his head. He wanted to know more.

"Captain, tell me the rest of the story," he said, "You said Lady Adela was now a prisoner of the de Clancey's and that she stands trial for robbery and murder. How can this be? Surely you have heard this wrong?"

Captain Clarence answered the best he could.

"It appears, my Liege, that some three weeks back Baron de Clancey's strongroom was raided, a guard killed and a considerable amount of treasure taken," he explained. "An item of jewellery found upon Lady Adela was from the strongroom, a necklace that did'st once belonged to the Baron's father. Then there was another item found, this time in the possession of Lady Adela's handmaiden. The handmaiden, the kitchen maid chosen by you to accompany Lady Adela, hath already been brought to trial. We were present at the trial. The handmaiden was found guilty of robbery and murder and she is to be hanged."

The Earl pondered long and hard, and slowly came to the conclusion that perhaps this was not bad news after all. If Lady Adela were to be found guilty, then she too would be hanged. But he remained troubled.

"Then the trial of Lady Adela hath not yet taken place?" he enquired.

Captain Clarence shook his head.

"Nay, my Liege," he said. "We rode through the night. A herald follows with the news. Lady Adela's trial takes place in six days' time."

The Earl stroked his beard and a hint of a smile touched his lips. If Lady Adela were to be found guilty then her secrets would die with her, and Baron de Clancey would have done his dirty work for him. After the hanging, her body would be returned with due pomp and ceremony to Salopsbury and laid to rest in the family chapel.

Feeling a little better after seeing things in a different light, the Earl's thoughts turned to the Lord Llywelyn and the services of his men from across the border, for a little matter of payment remained unresolved.

"Where are the Welsh brigands now?" he asked. "Have they returned across the border?"

Clarence shook his head.

"Nay, my Liege," he replied, "on our departure they were insistent on payment. They argued that the money was agreed regardless of the outcome. We have ridden one day ahead of them. On leaving it was agreed we meet again this very night at the twentieth milestone marker set alongside the road deep within the woods at Longnor."

The Earl recalled his own clandestine meeting with the Lord Llywelyn. They had met at midnight at his hunting lodge at Longnor. They had agreed a price of one hundred gold sovereigns for his services. But nothing had been put down in writing and as far as he could recall, failure had not been considered. Both were confident of the outcome.

"How many brigands did the Lord Llywelyn send to do this deed?" he asked.

"Five, my Liege," answered Clarence. "They considered five enough to overpower three escorts."

The Earl pondered for a while.

"Five you say?" he said. "And they will be rendezvousing with you in the woods at Longnor this very night?"

Clarence nodded his head.

"Aye, my Liege, tonight at midnight, at the twentieth milestone marker," he confirmed.

The Earl sighed. Even though he hated parting with the money, he considered it best to pay up. He had no wish to suffer Lord Llywelyn's wrath, which would almost certainly be the case if he reneged on the deal.

"Then you must meet with these brigands and pay them what is owed. It grieves me that this must be done. But at present, Salopsbury enjoys peace with our Gaelic speaking neighbours from across the border and it is best it remains this way. I will order one hundred gold sovereigns to be taken from my strongroom. That is all Captain, you may go."

Clarence bowed his head and took one step backwards.

"I will see to it personally that the brigands are paid, my Liege," he said. "I will'st also insist that they return with much haste across the border."

As the Earl waved a hand of departure, Captain Clarence saluted with clenched fist across his chest. He then turned and walked briskly from the hall, with Sergeant Godfred following in his wake.

However, Captain Clarence had a different plan. If five brigands were to disappear and never be seen or heard from again, then who was to know whether they had been paid or not?

Chapter Thirty-Three

The cart carrying Corporal Egbert rumbled to a stop before the abbey gates. Bardolph rode alongside. Brambles of wild roses encased the high outer walls. The gates were closed, but not locked. Bardolph dismounted and opened the gates. The path inside led directly to the church. To the left stood the monastery, to the right the nunnery. A strict order of internal walls and partitions divided the abbey. Entry to either the monastery or the nunnery was only possible via a locked gate within the church.

Bardolph tethered his horse and climbed the steps to the church and entered. The interior was dark and lit only by a few candles. Before the altar there knelt several monks in prayer.

An iron lattice partition ran down the centre of the church, segregating the monks from the nuns, and immediately inside the door there stood another iron partition. To enter the church you had to pass through one of two gates; one leading to the monastery the other to the nunnery. Both gates were locked and behind the entrance door hung a bell. Bardolph rang the bell and waited.

On the monastery side of the church, several monks were knelt in prayer. On the nunnery side, there knelt but one sister. She was facing the altar but at a distance, kneeling to the back of the church and close to the gate where Bardolph stood.

On hearing the ringing of the bell, Brother Dominic rose and walked to the back of the church. Through the bars of the locked gate he addressed the tall and elegant stranger stood to the other side.

"Good day, sire," he said. "Pray what brings you to our humble place of worship?"

Bardolph acknowledged with a courteous bow.

"I am no stranger to the Abbot of Wistanstow," he replied, "For he knows me both by sight and name. But this is not my plight and not the reason for my coming. There is a man outside with a broken leg and his injury needs attending."

As Bardolph was speaking, two monks entered the church via a door near the altar. Brother Dominic looked around, saw who was coming and nodded his head.

"Ah!" he exclaimed. "It seems we have the key by which you may enter. Pray bring in the injured man so that we may tend to his leg."

Bardolph moved to the church door and from the top of the steps signalled down to Corporal Egbert and the peasants to join him. Behind Bardolph, the two approaching monks unlocked firstly the gate to the monastery; then on passing, unlocked the gate to the nunnery.

As the two monks passed through the second gate Bardolph questioned what was going on, for he thought this to be wrong.

"Brother, does't not my eyes deceive me?" he said, "Two of your holy order entering the nunnery! Can this be right?"

Brother Dominic nodded his head.

"A young novice of our order has sinned and is being passed to the Holy Father for correction," he explained. "She is there now and awaiting their presence."

Bardolph had little time to ponder upon the explanation. The peasants were already aiding Corporal Egbert up the steps and into the church. With the corporal's arms about their shoulders and hopping on his one good leg, he made their task easy.

Bardolph ushered Corporal Egbert through to the awaiting Brother Dominic. Like all monks of the order, protocol forbade Brother Dominic from passing out through the gate and into the outside world without the permission of the Abbot.

Not wanting strangers to encroach any further, Brother Dominic held up a hand.

"Pray, leave the injured man here," he said. "The brethren of this order will tend to his injuries."

The peasants laid Corporal Egbert down by the gate, for the luxury of chairs did not exist in either half of the church.

Bardolph knelt down by the corporal's side and gripped his hand.

"I must bid you a fond farewell my friend," he said. "I go now to Salopsbury. For that which you were entrusted to do will be done. I personally will deliver your despatches to the Earl. Of this I give you my oath. In this holy house and before God as witness, I swear that this shall be so."

Corporal Egbert squeezed Bardolph's hand.

"Then God speed my friend," he said. "And pray do have better luck than I. Ride north to Salopsbury and do what I have failed to do."

As Bardolph spoke the creaking of an iron gate made him turn and look up. The two monks were returning. Between them they escorted the sister that had been praying on the other side of the gate. She looked in pain and was crying.

As the party passed by, the sister recognised Corporal Egbert. For a moment she stopped and looked down upon the soldier lying on the floor.

"Egbert!" she croaked, her voice strained.

At first Corporal Egbert did not recognise the young novice in her nun's attire.

"Anne?" he questioned.

Sister Anne smiled but could say no more. It was wrong to speak other than in prayer in God's house. Even to stop momentarily was wrong. Quickly, she turned and moved on with her escorts.

Corporal Egbert returned the smile, but like Anne, said no more.

Both he and Bardolph felt concern for the young novice, but knew it to be wrong to question the ways of this Holy Order. The regime in a place such as this was fully dependent on a strict code of conduct. Both sides of the abbey were dedicated to a life of celibacy and religious seclusion, and any young novice would have been made aware of this strict regime before taking her vows.

As Sister Anne and the monks escorting her disappeared from the church, Bardolph queried what he had just witnessed.

"Pray tell me Egbert, who was that novice?" he asked. "She spoke your name if I am not mistaken."

The corporal waited for the door to close before replying.

"That, my dear friend, is the daughter of Sergeant Cuthred," he said. "That is Anne, his one and only child from a marriage that is sadly ended. His wife passed away some two years back, and it was always his daughter's wish to take up Holy Vows. I did not know that it had been done. But it seems that her wish hath come true. I am pleased for her." Then with a deep sigh and sounding much concerned, he added, "but pray what is happening to her? Surely to enter this side of the abbey cannot be right?"

Bardolph squeezed Egbert's hand.

"I believe that she hath sinned and is to be taken before the Abbot for correction," he said. "But I know little else. Perhaps with you at the abbey you may be permitted to enquire as to her health and conduct."

Egbert nodded his head.

"I will do just that good sire," he said. "I have known Anne since she was a child and she hath brought me much pleasure watching her grow up into a fine young lady."

Brother Dominic intervened, for it was not fitting to have this many intruders within his church. There remained monks in prayer, and their devotion to God was paramount.

"Good sires, pray leave us now," he said. "The soldier is in good hands. This Holy Order will look after him and tend to his injury."

Bardolph rose to his feet. Already, the peasants had moved to the exit. Bardolph turned to step through the gate.

"Then Egbert, I leave you in safe and caring hands," he said. "I will return in two days' time to enquire of your progress. Perchance, we may ride together to Lodelowe. Let us wait and see how quickly thou does't heal."

Egbert smiled. The splint was tight and the bones held straight. The injury would mend, and quickly he hoped. Egbert called to Bardolph as he passed out through the gate.

"Good speed to Salopsbury my friend," he said, "and may God and St. Christopher go with you."

Brother Dominic pushed the gate shut and enquired of Bardolph.

"You did'st mention that you were known to the Abbot of this order," he said. "Then pray whom shall I say delivered this soldier to us?"

Bardolph turned to Brother Dominic.

"When you see the Abbot, tell him it was Bardolph of Wessex, Royal Falconer to the King of England that did'st call upon your Holy Order. The good Abbot and I did'st serve together at the Court of Baron de Clancey only yesterday. He will know of whom you speak."

Brother Dominic bowed his head in respect.

"It is indeed an honour and a privilege to do service to a servant of the King," he said.

As Bardolph spoke the Abbess of Wistanstow arrived. She carried a large key and was about to lock the gate to the nunnery, for it had been left ajar. Bardolph turned and greeted her with a touch to his forelock.

The Abbess acknowledged Bardolph's greeting by holding up an open hand. She had only heard the end of the conversation, but what she had heard aroused her curiosity.

"Did'st I not hear you say you are a servant of the King?" she asked through the bars of the gate.

Bardolph bowed.

"Holy Mother, I am indeed a servant of the King," he told her. "My title is Royal Falconer, and my home is in the King's New Forest in the ancient Kingdom of Wessex. My name is Bardolph, and you Holy Mother, you must be the Abbess of Wistanstow?"

The Abbess responded with a nod to the head.

"Pray forgive me good sire, for not introducing myself with the dignity this order requires," she said. "I spoke out of turn and will do penitence for my sins. But you are right good sire, I am indeed the Abbess of Wistanstow. That is my title here. This and Mother Superior, for I am indeed the head of this most devout and Holy Order."

Bardolph raised a hand.

"A penitence is not required Holy Mother, for no offence was taken," he said. Then seeing a signet ring upon her finger, and picking up on something he had heard the Abbot mention at the trial of the handmaiden.

He enquired, "But when not here at the nunnery, then pray tell me Holy Mother, are you not a Fitzgerald by birth?"

The Abbess furrowed her brow. It had been a long time since she was called a Fitzgerald. She became guarded.

"Yes, I am indeed a Fitzgerald by birth," she replied. "But I am married to God now and that name no longer applies. But pray tell me good sire, how did'st you come by this information? And by what importance do you bear upon this fact?"

Bardolph stroked his small beard. He had not intended his remark to cause upset. He pointed to the ring.

"Is this not the crest of the Fitzgeralds?" he asked. "These three lion heads I have seen before on the soldiers of the Fitzgeralds's, and it's just that I go there now, to Salopsbury to seek audience with the Earl. I must do what this poor soldier, lying on the ground, can no longer do. I am now entrusted with this soldier's despatches, and I did'st swear upon oath that I would deliver them safely to Salopsbury."

The Abbess looked through the bars at Egbert lying on the floor. She saw his leg in splints and understood. Her gaze returned to her finger and the ring.

"You are most observant good sire," she said. "This ring does indeed bare the crest of the Fitzgeralds. Pray send my good wishes to the Earl. Tell him that you have received these words from the Abbess of Wistanstow. He will understand, for I am the Earl's sister. I am Elizabeth Fitzgerald."

Bardolph bowed his head in respect.

"Then Holy Mother, I will'st do just that," he said. "I will'st inform the Earl that his sister sends her good wishes from the abbey at Wistanstow."

The Abbess turned the key in the lock.

"Then God speed to Salopsbury, good servant of the King," she said, "and St. Christopher go with you."

Bardolph bowed and stepped towards the door.

"Then farewell Holy Mother," he said, "and God remain with you always."

He then turned and marched quickly out of the building.

Back in daylight Bardolph stood for a while atop the steps. He sniffed the air and cocked an ear towards the coppice on the hill that overlooked the abbey. It was here he had intended to hunt rabbits, but now horses were there, at least half a dozen. Men could stay silent and out of sight, but horses could not. He wondered what this was all about. Could they be soldiers of Lodelowe out looking for Madeline? Could they be following him in the hope he would lead them to her? On reflection he doubted this, and besides if they were he would be leading them away from Onneyditch. He considered the possibility of Welsh raiders, but dismissed this idea too. The monks and nuns here led a frugal existence and the abbey held little of value.

Bardolph decided to carry on. If the men in the coppice were to follow, then he would soon know. He looked to the sun. Much time had been lost and noon had come and gone. Furthermore, he had no intention of making haste and falling into the same trap as Corporal Egbert. The best he could hope was to get within three to four hours' journey of Salopsbury.

He descended the steps and called a peasant to his side. He handed him two silver crowns.

"One of these silver crowns is for you and your friend," he said. "The other I want you to give to the boy Ralph that tends the stables at Onneyditch. Tell him that I had a change of plans and that I now go to Salopsbury, and that he is to tend to my birds until I return. Tell him I will return to Onneyditch in two days' time. That is all. He will know what to do. He is a capable lad."

The peasant touched his forelock. His share of the silver crown would feed him and his family for a month.

"I will do that, sire. I know of the boy Ralph and he will be told," he assured the falconer.

Bardolph transferred the contents of Egbert's saddlebag to his own and deposited the soldier's saddle on the steps to the church. There were provisions in the saddlebag as well as despatches. These would see him through the journey to Salopsbury.

After taking stock, and with one final look around, Bardolph mounted his white horse and set off. His plan was to ride until nightfall and see how far this would get him.

Chapter Thirty-Four

On a hillside overlooking the abbey at Wistanstow, the leader of a band of Welsh brigands looked out from the cover of a small coppice. Idwal, their leader, stood alongside Maredudd, his second in command. He spoke to Maredudd. His language was that of the Welsh Gaels.

He told him, "The visitors to the abbey are leaving. It is time for us to act. Come, let us descend the hill."

Five men armed with swords and daggers, but wearing no armour, mounted their horses and set off down the hill towards the abbey. Their attire was that of faded Welsh tartan and their hair was long and plaited. They rode in a line with a tethered riderless horse bringing up the rear.

Idwal was a good leader and was no fool, being wary of his midnight tryst with the Captain of Salopsbury. To ride into the woods at Longnor after dark would be fraught with danger. He knew this. However, what else could he do? What other choice did he have? To return to Lord Llywelyn's castle at Dolwyddelan without payment by Salopsbury would prove just as dangerous. Lord Llywelyn was no lover of failure. Idwal therefore, needed a safeguard and he had a plan. It was simple in the making and he could foresee no flaws. He planned to kidnap the Abbess of Wistanstow and take her with him to Longnor. He considered it to be fair exchange; the Earl's sister for one hundred gold sovereigns.

The abbey walls were high, but for Idwal and his band this proved no obstacle. They had scouted earlier and knew that the walls could be scaled easily at many points due to the abundance of trees. Those that grew within the grounds had branches that stretched out beyond the walls, and those on the outside, sprouted branches that extended well within the perimeter of the abbey. At one convenient point branches from trees both within the grounds and outside the wall met to form a bridge. It was here, beneath the branches of a large oak, the riders dismounted and looked about them. Hopefully, they had not been seen. But at least here on the side furthest away from the road they were out of sight.

Four men scaled the oak using the saddles of their horses to reach the lower branches. A fifth man stayed behind to tend the horses. With Idwal leading, they moved along the branches and dropped down into the gardens of the nunnery. A sister, hoeing between rows of vegetables, squealed loudly as four men dropped down from the branches of a tree. She was grabbed immediately and a dagger held to her throat.

"Take us to the Abbess," Idwal demanded as the point his dagger pressed hard against her throat.

The sister had little choice but to obey and set off for the nunnery with the dagger held firmly to her throat.

Other sisters in the garden stood rooted in the spot, mostly in shock and too terrified to move. Some dropped to the knees and began to pray, but no one argued or mounted any protest. This was not done in a house of God.

The men were taken into the building and once inside, led along several corridors. The sister came to a halt before a door and pointed. She was terrified.

"This is the Abbess's room," she said trembling.

The men tossed the nun to one side and she crashed against the opposite wall. She was hurt badly, but survival instincts told her to get up and get out of there fast. She made straight for her cell and bolted the door.

The Abbess was seated at her desk when the door burst open. She was about to put quill to paper. She remained calm as four men entered.

She reminded them, "This is a house of God. Men are forbidden here. What do you want?"

Idwal grinned.

"Not what, but who; we want you," he said as he rounded the desk, produced a dagger and held it before her face.

"This is a place of worship and we hold nothing of value here. You will not get a ransom," she told the man, sounding calm despite the obvious danger.

The quill and paper spread before the Abbess gave Idwal an idea. He pressed the dagger firmly to her throat.

"I want you to write a letter for me," he told her, "a letter to your brother, the Earl of Salopsbury. I want you to tell him that you are being held prisoner, and unless he hands over the money promised to the Lord Llywelyn, you will die."

Idwal thrust the quill in the Abbess's hand into the pot of ink.

"Write," he told her.

The Abbess put quill to paper.

'Frater veni ne me mori facias,' she wrote in Latin. [Brother, come, do not let me die].

Idwal saw what was written and pressed his dagger to the Abbess's throat. A trickle of blood appeared.

"Write in a language I understand," he told her. "Write in the language of the Saxons."

The Abbess, with hand visibly shaking, moved the pen a little further down the page and began to write once more.

This time the message read in the Anglo-Saxon tongue; *'Brother, I am being held prisoner. Pray do as they ask.'* She then finished with the single word, *'Elifabeth'*.

When she was done, Idwal grabbed the Abbess's hand. A gold signet ring bearing the three snarling lion heads of the Fitzgeralds's rested upon a finger. He tore it away and the Abbess squealed.

"A little token to prove it is indeed the Earl's sister, the Abbess of Wistanstow we hold," he told her.

The Abbess rubbed at her bruised finger.

Idwal withdrew his dagger and stepped aside.

"Bind her," he instructed, and as he spoke he crossed the floor to inspect a large wooden cross with the body of Christ nailed upon it.

The crucifix was of polished and stained wood and of little value, but the body of Christ was gilded in gold.

He pointed to the crucifix and instructed one of his men.

"Take down the cross," he told him. "We will take it with us. If we take nothing else, then we will return to Dolwyddelan with at least one item of value."

Maredudd stepped forward with rope and bound the Abbess's hands behind her back.

Idwal, on seeing they were now ready, collected the parchment from the table and turned to the rest of his men.

"Come, let us go," he told them. "We must now make haste to the woods at Longnor. We have a meeting there this very night, and we can't let the captain of Salopsbury down."

The brigands departed the nunnery in a more civilised manner. With the use of the Abbess's keys they left via the church doors where their horses awaited. They mounted quickly, and with the Abbess placed upon the spare horse, they set off at a canter, for they had a long ride ahead. With them went the gilded crucifix, strung to the back of one of the men.

Chapter Thirty-Five

Bardolph pulled up from a canter and looked to the skies. The position of the sun told him that midday had come and gone. He turned his gaze to the ground and the stream that stood before him. He was back at the ford at Marsh Brook where his misfortunes began. He moved on into the water. Caution was no longer needed. The water level had dropped significantly over the past few days and now barely covered his horse's hooves.

On the opposite bank, Bardolph stopped briefly to look at the grave of the three slain soldiers. From the saddle he said a little prayer for lost souls.

Before moving on, Bardolph turned to the road he had just travelled and cocked an ear to the wind. A light breeze rustled the leaves and high above a buzzard circled the air, but there was nothing amiss. No one was following, or at least not within three to four miles of the ford. He kicked at his horse and set off at a gentle pace. He considered there to be no point in going any faster. Salopsbury was no longer within reach before nightfall. There was also another reason for not rushing. The gates of Salopsbury closed with the setting of the sun and would not reopen until first light on the morrow. Bardolph had therefore, long decided that he would ride as far as he could that day, and as darkness descended, make camp for the night. He calculated that it would be mid-morning on the morrow before he reached Salopsbury.

From the ford that marked the boundary between the estates of Salopsbury and Lodelowe, Bardolph rode northward without pause until the setting of sun. As daylight faded he found himself on the edge of dense woodland. A milestone indicated that he was some twenty-two miles from Salopsbury. He had no maps and knew not the name, but had passed this way on his journey south. The road through the woods was some five miles long. He looked to the setting sun. It would be dark before he reached the other side. He kicked at his horse and moved on into the woods. He would find a secluded spot amongst the trees and make camp for the night.

There was a specific reason for moving off road. For the last two hours a band of riders had been slowly catching up on him. He thought back to the coppice that overlooked the abbey. It could very well be the same horses, but he had no way of telling. However, it was more likely they were just travellers heading for Salopsbury, and as for several horses, well there was safety in numbers. After all, this was bandit country, with the Welsh border not far away.

Deep in the woods and at a good distance from the road, Bardolph stopped and cocked an ear. The horses that followed had not yet reached the woods, but all the same they were not far away. He turned in the saddle and listened to what the trees had to say for they spoke a language he could understand. Drifting on the wind, high amongst the branches and issuing from a point much deeper into the woods, he detected the faint sound of horses whinnying, and these were not just several horses, but many times that number. There could be a hundred or more.

With very little daylight remaining Bardolph decided to press on, and it was not long before he came upon the source of all the reverberations. In a clearing about two miles from the road and set deep in a steep sided valley, stood a number of wooden buildings. These were stables, with the sound of many horses in their stalls now clearly audible even to the most untrained ears.

One large stone building was also present in the valley. This was a small square fortified Norman tower that stood remote from all the other buildings and was sited upon a small knoll above a stream. A branch of the stream had been channelled to flow through gardens that held beds of flowers, winding paths, bridges, pavilions and a network of pergolas, all overgrown with masses of climbing roses. There was even a swing suspended from the branch of a large ash tree. Bardolph had come upon a hunting lodge, and since he was now deep into the estates of Salopsbury, he concluded that this place, with all its buildings and associated stables, belonged to the Fitzgeralds.

From his high vantage point Bardolph looked down on the stables far below. It was getting quite dark and lights flickered from within the many buildings whilst others moved to-and-fro, suggesting lanterns being carried. He could also hear many voices, people calling, and possibly orders being given. He kicked at his horse with the intention of setting off down the slope, but pulled up immediately. More horses were approaching, and this time from the opposite direction. These were horses at the gallop, and he estimated the number to be at least a dozen.

With riders closing in on him, Bardolph moved deeper into the trees and dismounted. This was his environment. They would never find him here, and perhaps for a while it was best he kept out of sight, at least until he had seen these people and found out what they were doing this deep in the woods.

Leaving his horse behind, Bardolph made his way on foot towards the edge of a well-worn track. Here he found himself back at the top of the rise, looking down into the valley below. In one direction, the track wound its way down the hillside to the lodge, and on the other, trailed back into the woods and most probably issuing from a branch in the road. With the sound of approaching hooves almost upon him, Bardolph moved into the trees and waited.

At the top of the rise where the long descent into the valley began, two riders pulled up their horses whilst the others continued on down into the valley below. The two were soon deep in conversation. Concealed behind bushes, Bardolph listened to what was being said, and the more he heard the more interested he became. But it was not the content of the speech that aroused his attention, but the voices of the men doing the talking. He had heard these two voices before, and fairly recently too. These were the voices of the men that had tormented Madeline in the Forest of Wyre.

Bardolph edged a little closer. From his new position he could see and hear things more clearly. For a start he could identify the riders. These were soldiers, both wearing the light blue uniforms with three snarling lion heads of the Fitzgeralds's. Bardolph gave a wry smile. He now understood. He had been correct when thinking these men to be soldiers, but wrong in assuming them to be soldiers of Lodelowe. But nevertheless, these were the very same men that had tormented Madeline, and the tassels on their shoulders told Bardolph they were a captain and a sergeant.

Bardolph listened intently to what was being said.

The captain was doing most of the talking and he heard him say, "We alone will rendezvous with the Welsh brigands at midnight this night. They will be waiting in the woods as agreed at the twentieth milestone marker. We will convince them that the gold is here at Longnor and ready to collect. We will arrange for them to visit the lodge at first light. It is then we must lie in wait. There are five of them and all must die."

As the men set off down the hill, Bardolph returned to his horse. He smiled as he walked. His mind was made up and he knew what must be done. Come midnight, he would be back at the road and hiding somewhere close to the twentieth milestone marker.

Chapter Thirty-Six

Six riders slowed in pace as they entered the woods at Longnor. They had set their sights on reaching the woods by nightfall and by riding hard, their objective had been met.

The party consisted of five men and one woman. As they entered the woods, the five men talked of moving well away from the road and making camp for the night. They spoke in a language not of the Anglo-Saxons, or of the Normans, but in an ancient Gaelic tongue unique to the people of Wales.

The one woman in their midst wore the habit and headdress of a mother superior. This was the Abbess of Wistanstow and she knew nothing of what was being said, for the Welsh language was unknown to her. She rode exhausted, bouncing in the saddle with head bowed and arms tied behind her back. Yet, she was familiar with her surroundings. These were the woods at Longnor, and her brother the Earl of Salopsbury kept a hunting lodge not far from here. As a young girl she had resided at the lodge during the summer months, and by day had ventured and played in these woods. By the time she had reached her teens there was not a tree, gulley or stream she could not identify.

The leader of her abductors, apparently the only one amongst them that could speak her tongue, had hinted at the purpose of their incursion into England. It was to meet with the Earl's representatives. The Abbess had not been told the timing or reason for this meeting, but the venue would most certainly have been pre-arranged. It therefore, seemed reasonable for the woods at Longnor to be the rendezvous point. But wherever and whatever, she prayed to God that the negotiations went well and that she would be delivered safely into the hands of her brother.

The lead rider moved from the road and set off into the woods. The others followed. They chose the opposite side of the road to the hunting lodge and kept moving until coming upon a rocky sandstone outcrop. Beneath an overhang of dark red sandstone stood a cave. The cave was large in both width and height, but shallow in depth, and the area outside displayed evidence of previous use. A circle of stones held remains of a fire, and bones from both a wild boar and a deer lay scattered where they had been tossed aside.

The riders dismounted and set about preparing camp. Dry branches were collected and a fire started. The men were well organised and each to their separate task, and it was not long before a brace of pheasants turned on a spit above the fire.

At the rear of the cave, seated with her back to the rock face, squatted the Abbess of Wistanstow. Her hands remained tied behind her back. Alongside her, resting against the rock face, stood the crucifix taken from the abbey.

As darkness descended and with light from the flames of the fire dancing upon the roof of the overhang, the men began to relax. Seated around the fire, and with bedrolls laid out on the ground beneath the overhang, the men began to laugh and joke amongst themselves.

If there was any fear of being detected, then it did not show.

Idwal, leader of the brigands, moved to kneel alongside the Abbess. He held a knife in his hand. Skewered to the blade was the meat of a pheasant.

"Here, eat some meat," he said, holding the knife to her mouth.

The Abbess wretched and turned her head away in disgust. Whatever meat was being offered, it smelt rancid and revolting. At this time of night she would normally be partaking of a little bread and a cup of water.

"Come, it is pheasant, hung for a week so that the meat does't mature and hold in the flavour," Idwal told the Abbess and pushed the knife closer to her mouth.

Meat was never served at the nunnery and the smell had turned the Abbess's stomach. Bread and cake was the nunnery's mainstay, with homegrown vegetables from the gardens, and fruits from the bushes and trees as supplements to their meagre diet.

The Abbess shook her head.

"Take it away," she said. "Your meat disgusts me."

Idwal rose to his feet and put the knife to his mouth. Chewing on the pheasant he tutted and shook his head.

"I hope your brother does't not prove so stubborn," he told her, "for if perchance this is a family trait, then alas, all does't not bode well for you on the morrow."

Chapter Thirty-Seven

News of the Abbess's abduction spread quickly. There had been monks in prayer when the brigands passed out through the church. It is doubtful whether the handful of monks present had the courage to prevent the abduction, since these were men of peace, not violence. But with the gates to the abbey's side of the church locked, they were powerless to do so anyway. All they could do was stand and stare through the bars as the Abbess, with hands tied behind her back, got bundled out of the building.

It was not long before the abduction reached the ears of Corporal Egbert. He was in a cell having fresh splints tied about his leg when the door flew open and a brother rushed in.

"The Abbess has been abducted; taken by marauders from across the border," he said, speaking quickly and in earnest.

Having spoken, he moved on immediately to the next cell to deliver the same message before continuing on down the row.

The corporal rose from his pallet and with the aid of a staff made his way to the Abbot's office. With total disregard for protocol he burst into the office only to find the room empty.

Brother Dominic, the monk that had greeted him on arrival, was hurrying along the corridor. News of the Abbess's abduction seemed to have sent everyone scurrying to-and-fro like headless chickens.

Corporal Egbert blocked Brother Dominic's path with his staff.

"Where is the Abbot?" he demanded, speaking with much urgency. "I must speak with him. He must be informed of the Abbess's abduction."

Brother Dominic also spoke with a sense of urgency.

"The Abbot is down in the lower chambers," he explained, trying to remove the staff that blocked his path. "I go there now to see if I can seek an audience and inform him of this evil deed."

Corporal Egbert removed the staff.

"Then go brother, lead the way and I will'st follow the best I can," he said. "I need a horse. I must ride to Lodelowe. The Baron must be informed straightaway."

Brother Dominic pointed to a large arched doorway to the far end of the corridor.

"The lower chambers are through that door," he said. "There are steps down that lead to the crypt. You will find the Abbot in a chamber that lies beyond the crypt and to the left. I will'st go on ahead for I am quicker. But first I must find a brother to help you down, for the steps are narrow, steep and winding."

Corporal Egbert did not want help.

"Don't worry about me," he told the brother. "Just go quickly and I will'st follow. My leg is fine. It is strapped tightly. I can walk."

Brother Dominic sped away, leaving the door to the crypt open. Within seconds he was gone.

With the aid of his staff and with splinted leg dragging the ground, Corporal Egbert reached the door a few seconds later. At the top he halted and looked down. The steps were dangerously steep and spiralled away into blackness. He looked for a torch or lighted candle, but there were nothing. Brother Dominic must have taken what was at hand. He considered waiting. The Abbot would surely return the moment he heard of the Abbess's abduction. But then again, what if he remained and only sent orders?

Corporal Egbert needed to confront the Abbot in person. To do differently, would only delay his departure. He wanted a horse and only the Abbot could give permission. He therefore, could see no alternative other than to move on. He took one last look down into the darkness and set off.

By the time the corporal reached the bottom his leg throbbed with pain. He gritted his teeth and carried on. He found himself in a long narrow aisle that stretched away into the distance in both directions. The roof was arched and to either side stone caskets rested in alcoves. This was the abbey's crypt, the resting place of monks that had passed away over the last two centuries. A smell of dampness filled the air, but at least here there were candles burning in niches in the walls.

He moved off to the left as instructed. At the far end of the aisle Egbert came upon another arched doorway. Brother Dominic had left this open too. Dragging his splinted leg, he moved on. As he passed through the door he stopped briefly to look left and right. He was in a new aisle that passed at right angles to the one he had just traversed. The proportions were much same as before, long and narrow and tunnel-like, and each side was lined with caskets, all placed in rows against the walls. There was one big difference, however. This aisle was far more ornately decorated. All caskets were brightly painted with Latin inscriptions gilded on the sides. The corporal understood. This was the final resting place of the more senior dignitaries at the abbey.

Egbert looked to his left and in the distance saw Brother Dominic waiting at a door. He moved to join him, hobbling with aid of his staff.

"What is it brother?" he asked on arrival. "Is the Abbot beyond this door? Have you spoken?"

Brother Dominic gave a look of resignation.

"I have spoken to the Abbot and he will be out shortly," he said and shaking his head.

"Is the door locked?" asked Corporal Egbert, moving a hand towards a large iron ring that turned the latch.

Brother Dominic raised a hand and gripped at the corporal's wrist.

"The door is locked from the inside," he said. "We must wait for the Abbot to come to us."

Some minutes later, from the other side of the door, a key turned in the lock. The iron ring moved and the door opened just enough for the face of the Abbot to appear.

A look of puzzlement crossed the Abbot's face.

"Brother Dominic, can't you see I am busy doing the Lord's work," he said. "What is so important that it cannot wait?"

Brother Dominic was quick to explain.

"Holy Father, the Abbess has been abducted," he said. "Welsh brigands have broken into the nunnery and taken her away."

Egbert spoke immediately, adding his own urgent message.

"And Lodelowe must be informed," he said. "I must have a horse."

The Abbot's lower jaw dropped.

"What!" He exclaimed and stepping out of the chamber. "When did this happen? Tell me more," he added as he closed the door behind him.

As the Abbot stepped out of the chamber Egbert caught a brief glimpse inside. It was just a fleeting glance, but long enough to arouse his curiosity. If his eyes were not deceiving him, then surely he had caught sight of a young girl kneeling inside the chamber.

However, as the door closed it was not Egbert's wish to pry into matters of the church. His thoughts lay elsewhere and with matters far more important. He needed a horse and to ride with much haste to Lodelowe. The Baron had to be informed and his soldiers mustered quickly.

The Abbot moved away from the door and set off down the aisle.

"Come, come quickly," he said. "To my office, we must get things done."

The obese Abbot moved swiftly despite his size, but at a pace easily manageable by Brother Dominic, and the monk followed just one pace behind.

Egbert moved quickly too, but his own pace was never enough to keep up. He was worried about the ascent of the spiralling stairs. It was awkward coming down, and returning to the top would be twice as difficult.

However, as Egbert turned to enter the first crypt he pulled up immediately. The Abbot and Brother Dominic were standing in wait, and two other men were racing down the aisle towards them. The two men in question were a monk and a soldier. The soldier was wearing the dark blue and red halved uniform of Lodelowe, with its three rampant white lions. But this was no ordinary soldier. This man bore gold tassels upon his lapels. This was a high-ranking officer racing down the aisle. This was the Captain of the Guard of Lodelowe. This was Captain Osbald.

Egbert was surprised to see his captain approaching.

"Captain, what are you doing here?" he called.

Dragging his leg he moved to stand alongside the Abbot.

Egbert was not the only person surprised by this chance encounter. Captain Osbald, too, was taken a little aback. His corporal was meant to be on his way to Salopsbury with important despatches concerning the trial of the Lady Adela. So why was he here? And why was his leg in a splint? And more importantly, where were the despatches? These and many more questions flashed through Captain Osbald's mind. But protocol demanded that he first address the Abbot.

Captain Osbald arrived and bowed his head before the Abbot.

"Holy Father, I come here with a missive from Baron de Clancey," he said. "But I arrive to find more devious work afoot. The Abbess has been taken by marauders from across the border."

The Abbot was quick to respond.

"Yes Captain, I am aware of this dreadful act and I am on my way to my office," he said. "I must draft a letter. Lodelowe must be informed without delay."

The Abbot began to move away but Captain Osbald stopped him.

"This, I have already done," he said. "As we speak a messenger rides to Onneyditch. There are soldiers there and the message will be relayed to Lodelowe with much urgency. The Baron will be informed within the hour, and I have asked for all available men to assemble here at Wistanstow. We must act quickly if we are to intercept these brigands before they reach the border with Wales."

The Abbot gave a look of relief.

"Then we can only pray that the Abbess is safe and that God protects her from the evils of these men," he said.

Captain Osbald gave thanks, saying, "Amen to that Holy Father," then turning to Corporal Egbert he questioned, "Corporal what brings you here? Where are Salopsbury's despatches? They were meant to be on their way."

His corporal was quick to explain.

"I did'st fall from my horse and my leg is broken, but the King's falconer did'st come my way and rescue me. He brought me here to the abbey and placed me under the care of the monks, and he now rides to Salopsbury with the despatches. They are safe and on their way."

Captain Osbald remained confused. Corporal Egbert had mentioned a King's falconer, so could this be Bardolph? And if so, what was he doing here some several miles north of Lodelowe when he was meant to be heading south? Nothing made sense. But on the other hand, he could think of no better person to continue on with the mission. Barring a complete disaster, the Baron's despatches would reach Salopsbury as intended.

"This King's falconer?" asked Captain Osbald. "Perchance, could this be Bardolph of Wessex? And is it he that hath taken the Baron's despatches to Salopsbury?"

Corporal Egbert nodded his head.

"Yes Captain," he replied, "the King's falconer is indeed Bardolph of Wessex, and it is he that now rides to Salopsbury with the Baron's despatches."

Captain Osbald, though not completely satisfied with his corporal's explanation, had no time to dwell further upon the matter. If the Baron's despatches were heading for Salopsbury, then regardless of who the herald might be, then all was well. He turned to the Abbot, for there was a far more pressing matter to deal with.

"Holy Father," he said, "I need quill and ink and parchment on which to write. It is my intention to go on ahead and track down these brigands. They cannot have gotten far. Last reports say they are heading north to the ford at Marsh Brook. I will'st pursue them, but I must leave instructions for my men when they arrive. Can you do this for me?'

The Abbot nodded his head.

"Yes, Captain," he replied, "come, come to my office. Everything you need is there."

They set off at pace with Egbert travelling in their wake, but by the time he reached the steps they were gone. He started the long climb but did not get far. Some half a dozen steps later he turned and sat down. He dropped his head in his hands. He could go no further. He was a cripple and of no use to anyone. His mind filled with despair. He had failed in his mission to Salopsbury. He had failed to find a horse, and now he could not even climb a set of steps.

He began to sob.

Captain Osbald was now in charge and any assistance from him, no longer required.

Chapter Thirty-Eight

Egbert shuffled his way down to the bottom step and put his head in his hands. He had waited a long time, squatted uncomfortably on the sixth step up, with splinted leg stuck out before him. His mind was full of questions. Where was everybody? How much longer did he have to wait? Surely they would not leave him alone down here? Somebody was bound to remember and come to his aid. Now he found himself at the bottom and the same questions filled his head. But then he recalled that he was not alone and he raised his head. There was at least one other person down here. He had seen her in the far chamber. So surely someone would arrive if only to see her?

Egbert, supported by his staff, rose to his feet and set off down the long aisle, his splinted leg dragging on the flagstones. His movements were laboured and progress slow, but he was a man with a purpose.

He reached the door from which the Abbot had emerged and tested the latch. It was not locked. He knew this. The Abbot, in his haste, had forgotten to turn the key. As the door opened inwards he strained his eyes and peered into the gloom. The light inside was poor and only illuminated by a few candles spread around the walls. He waited for his eyes to adjust then looked around. Next to the door rested a nun's habit and wimple. At the centre of the chamber stood a huge wooden cross, and before the cross there kneeled a young girl. She was naked, deep in prayer and with her back to the corporal.

With the aid of his staff and dragging his splinted leg, Egbert hobbled to the centre of the chamber. The young girl remained kneeling, deep in prayer and looking up at the cross. He looked to her back and was horrified for it looked red and raw.

Sister Anne had heard someone enter, but had assumed it to be the return of the Abbot. She had been told to pray for forgiveness whilst the Abbot was away, and she was doing this with all her heart.

"Anne?" questioned Egbert at a whisper, for he was uncertain.

He had only ever seen Sergeant Cuthred's daughter with long flowing ginger locks, and this girl's head was shaven, so he could not be sure. But he had seen Sister Anne come this way, and that bundle of clothing next to the door was that of a nun.

Asking a little more loudly, he said, "Anne! Is that you?"

Egbert's raised voice caused the girl to stir. She turned to look over one shoulder and on recognising the corporal a hint of a smile appeared.

"Egbert! Is it you?" she asked, then with a look of horror she told him, "You should not be here! The Abbot must not find you here!"

Egbert shook his head.

"Anne, my dear sweet Anne, what are you doing?" he said. "Are those your clothes on the floor? And what has happened to your back? It is red and raw. This is no state for a young girl. You must have your back treated and clothes to cover your modesty. I will'st get your clothes."

And with that he turned to hobble back to the door to collect her habit.

Anne shook her head when she saw what Corporal Egbert was about to do, and she called out to stop him.

"No, Egbert! No! Please no! Stop!" she called in earnest. "You must not interfere in the Abbot's work! It is by my own will that I am here, and my back shows the scars of my first of two punishments. I am here to receive the second and I come of my own free will. When the Abbot returns I am to be tied to the cross and to suffer as Jesus did. And only when my penitence is served can I return to the sisterhood."

Egbert shook his head.

"You have agreed to all this?" he asked. "Agreed to suffer so on the cross, because it is your will?"

Anne managed a distorted smile.

"It is God's will, not mine that I am here," she told him and added, "Egbert, you are a good man. Good and God fearing. But go and leave me to my penitence. I am well, and the Abbot will be returning soon. There is no need to worry. I have sinned against this most Holy Order, and this is to be my final correction."

Egbert shook his head.

"Then can I get you something?" he asked, "Water, perhaps?"

Anne shook her head.

"No, Egbert," she told him. "I want nothing but to be left alone with my prayers. The Abbot must not find you here. So, please go and close the door. And Egbert, worry not about me. I am fine and will endure this ordeal."

Egbert's head dropped. He did not agree, but understood. Anne had committed a sin and this was her punishment. He looked to her face and shook his head.

"Anne, you are indeed a brave young girl," he told her. "May God remain with you and help you through your dreadful ordeal."

Anne managed a smile.

"Yes, God is here. He is here with me," she said. "So fear not. I will survive the ordeal and come out of this a better and more devout Christian."

Egbert bit hard on his bottom lip. He was moved to tears.

"Then farewell my dear sweet Anne," he told her. "Be brave and my thoughts will always be with you."

Using his staff for support, Egbert turned and hobbled from the chamber. At the door he turned to take one last look. Anne was indeed a brave young girl, but like she said, the Abbot must not find him here.

He closed the door and set off down the aisle. When the Abbot returned he would find him waiting at the foot of the steps.

Chapter Thirty-Nine

The band of Welsh brigands set up camp for the night in the woods at Longnor, some distance from the Earl of Salopsbury's hunting lodge. A campfire burned within a circle of stones a short distance from a cave that was to be their resting place that night.

As midnight approached, Idwal called Ifor to his side. His language was that of the Welsh Gaels.

"I go now with Maredudd to our midnight rendezvous at the twentieth milestone marker," he said. "If, perchance we do not return, then kill the Earl's sister and return with haste to Dolwyddelan. News of such treachery must reach the Lord Llywelyn."

Ifor nodded his head. He fully understood. The possibility of betrayal had always been present, but they had little choice in the matter. The Lord Llywelyn had negotiated his services for one hundred golden sovereigns, and to return to his castle in Wales empty handed was unthinkable.

"Let us pray that it does't not come to such treachery," he said thoughtfully, then after a short pause agreed, "The deed will be done. If indeed such foul circumstances arise, the Earl's sister will die. I will do it personally."

Idwal placed a comforting hand upon Ifor's shoulder and sighed.

"Then let us hope for all our sakes that Salopsbury remains true to its word and that one hundred gold sovereigns are forthcoming," he said. "But if not, we hold insurance. We hold the Earl's sister, and I take with me her letter and signet ring as proof. So I doubt there will be much treachery afoot this night."

On this point Ifor agreed.

"It would be foolhardy to think otherwise," he said. "Captain Clarence, the man you are to meet, would not risk the life of the Earl's sister. You and Maredudd are safe and will return to camp with the one hundred golden sovereigns. Mark my words."

Idwal remained pensive. He was not as confident as Ifor. There was something about Captain Clarence that filled him with deep mistrust.

"I hope you are right, Ifor," he said, "I hope you are right."

Idwal tested the blade of his sword with a thumb. It was sharp and ready to kill if the need be. He placed the sword back in his belt and called to Maredudd. It was time for the two to leave. They would travel on foot through the woods to the road and the twentieth milestone marker, a distance of some two miles.

Ifor waited for Idwal and Maredudd to be well clear of the camp before collecting a large flask from his bedroll. He offered the flask to Daffyd.

"It is calvados," he told him. "A drink of distilled cider and much favoured by the Normans."

Daffyd took the flask, held it to his mouth and sipped cautiously. He lowered the flask and gasped at the strength of the alcohol. He regained his breath and nodded his approval.

"It's good," he said, licking his lips and passing the flask to Dewi.

Dewi tested the contents and gave the same choking gasp, followed by a nod of approval. Ifor recovered the flask and moved to the campfire.

"Come, let us sit around the fire and drink," he said.

It was not long before all three were in high spirits, and bawdy camp songs echoed about the campsite.

As the men drank and sang, to the rear of the campfire, tucked away beneath the cavernous overhang, squatted the Abbess of Wistanstow. By her side, propped against the rear cave wall, rested the gilded crucifix taken from the nunnery.

The Abbess, with hands tied behind her back, was not too uncomfortable in her seated position. Mostly she spent the time in prayer and only occasionally would she look up to see what the men were doing. Uttering mostly in Latin, she prayed forgiveness for those that had wronged her, and prayed for the Angel Gabriel to come and deliver her from the hands of her abductors.

With the leaders gone, the Abbess came to realise that those remaining were taking little heed of her, and she began to put together a plan of escape. Firstly, she could run. Only her hands were tied behind her back. Secondly, she knew these woods well. She had spent most of her childhood here. The woods of Longnor had been her playground. So knew of this cave, and if ever she could get away, then she knew exactly what paths to take and where to hide. She made up her mind. She would attempt an escape.

Slowly, she rose to her feet. From the rear of the cave she looked to the campfire. The men were seated with their backs towards her. They were laughing and joking. Her escape plan was simple. She would edge along the rear wall of the cave until she reached a point where a clear path stretched out in front of her. She would then take off, running as fast as she could past the campfire and out into the blackness beyond. After this, she knew what direction to take and places to hide.

Creeping along the rear wall, and keeping one eye on the campfire, she moved off. Her plan was going well for a while, but then disaster struck. Her elbow caught the crucifix and sent it crashing to the ground.

A loud crash came echoing out of the cave and the men seated about the campfire all turned their heads.

The Abbess, realising she had to act quickly, set off running from the cave. Providing she was quick, she still had a chance of escape. The men had consumed a lot of alcohol and were unsteady on their feet. All she had to do was get clear of the campfire and keep on running into the blackness beyond. If she managed this they would never find her.

Dewi however, saw her coming, and as the Abbess sped past the campfire, he put out a hand and caught an ankle. The contact was just a glance and did not stop the Abbess in her flight. For a few paces beyond the campfire she managed to keep her feet, but at each stride she began to lurch more and more forward.

The Abbess's full-length and billowing habit proved to be the main hindrance; this coupled with the fact that her hands were tied behind her back, meant she had no way of righting her balance. In the end, and some six paces beyond the campfire, she crashed to the ground. Within seconds, Dewi was upon her and holding her down. She turned under his weight and tried to kick him away with her feet, but with little success. Dewi was just too heavy for her.

Ifor arrived on the scene. He was staggering and unsure of his feet, but he still had his senses about him. He was well aware of his duties and under no circumstances was the Abbess to escape.

"Leave her to me," he said, his voice slurred and speaking in the tongue of the Welsh.

Taking hold of the Abbess's ankles he dragged her feet first back beneath the overhang and dumped her against the rear wall. Then to show his anger he gave a kick to her thigh and issued a stream of verbal abuse. But Ifor's words meant nothing to the Abbess for they were in a language she did not understand.

She was badly bruised, her face grazed from the fall, and all she wanted to do was put her hands together and pray. But this, she could not do with her hands tied firmly behind her back.

Cowering against the back wall, and as a second kick struck hard against her pelvis, she dropped her head and prayed; prayed for the Angel Gabriel to swoop down and carry her away.

Chapter Forty

Well before midnight, Bardolph returned to the road that passed through the woods at Longnor. He travelled on foot, leading his horse. A full moon and keen eyesight combined to make easy passage through the trees. From the ridge above the lodge to the twentieth milestone marker was a distance of a little under two miles. There was a wide track that led from the lodge to road, but Bardolph chose to stay well clear and remain within the cover of the trees.

Captain Clarence and Sergeant Godfred had a little further to travel; their starting point being the stables at Longnor Lodge. Even though darkness had fallen, they chose to wear full armour and ride upon their horses. The track from the stables to the road was navigable with care by the light of the moon, but to assist their passage they carried a lantern held on a long pole that stretched out before the leading horse.

First to reach the road was Bardolph, but not until he had left his horse at a safe distance. The milestone marker lay at a point alongside the road and at the junction with the track from the lodge, here the clearing was wide and stars twinkled in the heavens. The road through the woods took many turns and at this point ran roughly east-west, with the moon casting shadows upon the southern side and throwing light against the northern edge of a line of trees. Bardolph chose the darkened southern side and settled down behind a thicket of low bushes and young trees.

It was not long before two men arrived on foot from the south. Bardolph heard them coming and ducked low and out of sight as they moved to stand alongside the rendezvous point. They passed within a few paces of him, but at no time did they sense the presence of a stranger hiding in the bushes. Their conversation was light and nervous, with only the occasional word spoken. Bardolph, however, found this interesting, for the men conversed in the language of the Welsh Gaels. He listened to what they had to say, for he spoke many tongues including this one. It appeared they were on edge and apprehensive about their forthcoming tryst. Midnight, it seemed, was not a good time and neither was the venue. The meeting should have been held out in the open, and in daylight. But they waited all the same.

Either one party was early or the other late, for the wait was considerable. But eventually, from the woods to the far side of the road came the sound of horses' hooves. Two soldiers on horseback emerged from the darkness and out onto the road. The lead rider held before him a lantern on a pole. They were protected by chainmail and wore the light-blue tunics and three yellow snarling lion heads of the House of Salopsbury.

Captain Clarence and Sergeant Godfred dismounted and beckoned Idwal and Maredudd to join them. The two Welsh brigands moved to the centre of the road but retained a reasonable gap between the two parties.

"You're late," hissed Idwal, speaking now in the language of the Anglo-Saxons.

"We came as quickly as we could," Captain Clarence answered curtly. "The track from the lodge is hazardous and in the dark, must be ridden with care. But we are here now. So let us talk."

Idwal looked bemused and shook his head.

"What is there to talk about?" he said, "We're here to collect one hundred golden sovereigns. Hand us the money and we go."

Captain Clarence shook his head.

"But the deed was not done," he reminded Idwal. "Lady Adela still lives. Surely you cannot expect to be paid without fulfilling your part of the bargain?"

Idwal clenched his fists.

"That was not the deal," he snapped angrily. "We were hired to do your bidding. It was not our fault Lady Adela was arrested and taken to Lodelowe. We fulfilled our part of the bargain. We did what Lord Llywelyn sent us to do."

Captain Clarence shook his head once more.

"No action, no golden sovereigns," he stated flatly. "The deal is off. Go back to Dolwyddelan and explain that to your Lord Llywelyn."

Idwal put a hand to a pouch attached to his belt. Immediately, Captain Clarence withdrew his sword from its scabbard and Sergeant Godfred did likewise.

"Relax," Idwal told them, "I've something here that might interest you. Let me show you." Then slowly and making no sudden movement, else it be misinterpreted, he withdrew a folded piece of yellow-stained parchment from his pouch and handed it to Captain Clarence.

"Read this. It will make you change your mind," he said.

Captain Clarence stepped to the centre of the road and took the parchment. He unfolded it and moved to the lantern. He began to read. The first few words were in Latin, which he did not understand, but beneath and written in his own Anglo-Saxon tongue was the message; *'Brother, I am being held prisoner. Please do as they ask.'* It was signed, *'Elifabeth'*.

The captain read the message several times before showing it to Sergeant Godfred.

Eventually, he turned to Idwal stood to the centre of the road.

"This note is for the Earl?" he queried. "And this is his sister's hand in writing?"

Idwal nodded his head.

"The letter is for the Earl," he confirmed, "and the note is in his sister's hand."

Captain Clarence mused for a while before asking, "What proof have I that you hold the Earl's sister?"

Idwal delved once more into his pouch and took out the Abbess's signet ring. He held it at an arm's length.

"This is her ring," he said, "It bears the crest of the Fitzgeralds's. Take it. The Earl will confirm that this ring belongs to her."

Captain Clarence moved to Idwal and took the ring. He turned it over and over in his hand. In the moonlight he could see the three lion heads of the Fitzgeralds. This was a turn of events he was not expecting. These Welsh brigands had been too cunning by half. His plan was to slay all five of them, including their horses, either now or on the morrow, and to bury everything deep in the woods. He would say that they had met as arranged and that the one hundred golden sovereigns were handed over, and that his sergeant was with him to verify the act. Afterwards, when they could not be found, he would suggest they had absconded with the money instead of returning to Dolwyddelan?

"And what will happen to the Earl's sister should we not comply," asked Captain Clarence after considering the situation further.

Idwal was quick to respond for this was something he wanted to be known.

"Then the Earl's sister will be put to the sword," he told Captain Clarence. "I have left instructions for this to be done if perchance we do not return. So, I think it best you hand over the gold sovereigns and we will be on our way. The Earl's sister we will leave here by the roadside for you to collect at the break of dawn."

Captain Clarence considered the demand.

"I must consult alone with my sergeant," he said. "You put unfair demands upon us which were not part of the deal, and we must discuss this between ourselves."

Idwal was now of the belief that he held the upper hand. Captain Clarence would not risk the life of the Earl's sister and would hand over the gold.

"Then be quick about it," he snapped, and taking hold of Maredudd he moved away to the edge of the road.

Captain Clarence, however, had other ideas. With Idwal and Maredudd both out of earshot, he moved to Sergeant Godfred.

"We must kill them both now," he whispered. "I will bring the leader to my saddlebag. I will tell him the gold is there. When he goes for the saddlebag, I will strike with my sword, and you must do the same to the other brigand. Make sure you are close and ready to strike."

"But what about the Earl's sister?" quizzed Godfred apprehensively, "If these brigands do not return to their camp she will be put to the sword? You heard what he said."

Clarence leered in the dark. He cared little for the life of the Earl's sister.

"Her death, we will blame upon the brigands," he replied coldly. "Their camp will be somewhere in these woods. We ride out with the men at first light. We will find them and slay them. And if perchance, we discover the body of the Earl's sister, then we say it came as a shock, for we did not know. And if perchance, she is found alive then we will gain praise for her rescue. Either way, we cannot lose."

Sergeant Godfred did not relish his captain's words, but nonetheless agreed, for he had little choice in the matter. His share of the brigand's payment was twenty golden sovereigns, and once having agreed, found himself having no alternative other than to go along with his captain. He gripped the hilt of his sword tightly and nodded his head.

"Then, so be it. I will strike down the other brigand the moment you make your move," he said.

Captain Clarence placed a hand upon Sergeant Godfred's shoulder.

"Then strike swiftly and surely, and on my signal. Death must come quickly," he said. "We will conceal their bodies in the bushes and return to bury them at first light. We will say we met at midnight as arranged and handed over the golden sovereigns. Other than this, we know nothing. We suggest they must have absconded with the money."

With a final pat on Sergeant Godfred's shoulder, Captain Clarence beckoned Idwal to come to his horse.

"Come, my friend; we agree," he called. "The one hundred golden sovereigns are in my saddlebag. Come and collect."

Idwal moved cautiously towards the horses. At the first sign of trouble they were ready to draw their swords and fight. Whilst stood to one side, the two men had worked out a plan of campaign and were prepared for action should anything untoward occur.

Captain Clarence loosened a strap on his saddlebag.

"Come, the golden sovereigns are here," he called.

Idwal, however, remained suspicious. Something was not quite right. For one thing, Sergeant Godfred was sidling towards them with his sword drawn. Idwal withdrew his dagger and held it to his side. If any treachery was afoot, then he was ready.

He whispered to Maredudd, since he had not moved far, to do the same, saying, "I will go to the saddlebag, but be ready with your dagger, for treachery may be afoot here."

Maredudd withdrew his dagger and held it by his side. He stood watching as Idwal moved cautiously towards Captain Clarence's horse.

The captain threw open his saddlebag.

"The money is in here," he said. "Come, it is yours, take it."

Idwal edged closer to the saddlebag but remained wary and moved with caution. Captain Clarence had drawn his sword when he had made a move for the Abbess's letter and the sword was never replaced. He, now, held it before him with the point to the ground.

Idwal gripped his dagger tightly with one hand whilst raising the other to the saddlebag.

Captain Clarence was an experienced soldier and knew exactly when to strike. As Idwal's eyes turned to the saddlebag, he struck. In one swift action he raised his sword and lunged forward with the blade. The thrust penetrated Idwal's chest and struck at the heart. He died on the spot.

Captain Clarence's strike was the signal for Sergeant Godfred to do likewise. But Maredudd was prepared, and as the sergeant swung his sword, he sidestepped and parried with his dagger. Maredudd was a seasoned fighter too and knew that to strike against the body of someone wearing chainmail to be foolhardy and ineffective. As the sergeant swung his sword for a second time, Maredudd ducked. Then, stooping low and with a stabbing action, he aimed his dagger to a point below the hem of the chainmail. As the blade sunk deep into Godfred's thigh, the soldier yelped with pain and dropped his sword.

As Sergeant Godfred fell to his knees, clutching his leg, Maredudd seized the opportunity. He righted himself, turned and fled, leaving his dagger sunk deep within the sergeant's leg. He knew that once he reached the trees he would be safe. Men weighted down with armour were no match for fleet of foot.

Captain Clarence, having disposed of Idwal, put a boot to his chest and withdrew his sword. As he wiped away the blood on the clothes of his victim, a piercing shriek echoed about the woods. He swung around. He was expecting to see Maredudd lying in the road and Sergeant Godfred standing over him. However, the sight that greeted him was very different. Instead, it was Sergeant Godfred lying on the ground, and Maredudd rapidly disappearing into the dark.

Captain Clarence ran to Sergeant Godfred, to kneel by his side. A dagger was sunk deep into his thigh and blood oozed between clutching fingers. Captain Clarence knew best not to remove the dagger. The leg would only bleed worse.

"I must get you to the lodge," he said. "This wound needs a physician to staunch the bleeding."

Captain Clarence helped Sergeant Godfred to his horse, then dragged Idwal's body to the bushes. He was about to mount his horse when he remembered the Abbess's letter and ring. These items would only incriminate him if found in his possession. He crumpled the letter about the ring and tossed it into the bushes. His only problem now was the remaining Welsh brigands. Their leader was dead, but four remained. He vowed that at first light he would send out his men with instructions to slay them all.

As the two horses moved from the road, Bardolph stretched out a hand and picked up a tightly screwed-up ball of paper. He had listened with interest, and even though he had not heard all that was whispered, he had learnt enough to distrust the captain. As a result of this man's treachery, one man lay dead and the Earl's sister stood in mortal danger.

Bardolph unfolded the screwed-up paper. Inside, he found a gold signet ring, and by the light of the full moon he could just about make out on the dexter side, the three snarling lion heads of the Fitzgeralds. He recalled his encounter with the Abbess as she stood behind the bars of the church and locking the gate to the nunnery. This ring was upon her finger and he recalled commenting on it at the time. He grimaced. So it was true, the brigands held the Abbess captive and the leader was not bluffing.

He turned his attention to the letter. With the lantern gone, it was too dark to read, but all the same he found it fascinating. The ink on the paper he could see, and it was a very distinctive pale blue. This set him thinking. He had seen this colour ink before and under very similar circumstances. The ring found within the handmaiden's shoe had been wrapped in a similar manner, and in the very same yellow parchment, and written in the same distinctive blue ink. He furrowed his brow. Surely this was more than coincidence? And what was equally puzzling, the handmaiden had never visited the abbey, nor had cause to receive any form of communication. Most odd, he was thinking. Most odd!

He pondered for a while then pocketed the ring and the letter. He would come back to these later when he had time to think. But now, he had far more pressing matters to deal with. He cupped his hands to his face and gave the hoot of an owl. From amongst the trees, and at some distance along the road, out trotted a white stallion.

Bardolph climbed upon the saddle and whispered quietly in the horse's ear, "Come Ventalbi, we have a camp to find and a Holy Mother to rescue. Let's hope we are not too late."

Chapter Forty-One

High in the treetops, a lone owl hooted, but this was the only sound to be heard. Ifor, Daffyd and Dewi were seated around the campfire. Gone were the bawdy campfire songs and jokes about the English, and gone too was any talk of returning home to the lush green valleys of Dolwyddelan. All three were subdued and keeping their thoughts to themselves. The fire too was dying, but no one was concerned even though there was a chill to the air.

Dewi sat cross-legged before the dying embers, a flagon on his lap. Ifor, seated next to him, held out a hand and Dewi passed the flagon to him. Swaying unsteadily, Ifor placed the flagon to his mouth and tossed his head back. A few drops of Norman cider spirit trickled out. Vigorously, he shook the flagon, but could extract no more. In a fit of rage he tossed the flagon away, wiped his mouth with the back of his sleeve and burped loudly. He decided it was time for sleep and rose to his feet, but his legs buckled and he fell back to his knees. Not bothering to stand, he crawled towards his bedroll beneath the overhang.

The flagon struck Daffyd on the shoulder before bouncing harmlessly away. Daffyd stretched out an arm, retrieved the flagon and held it to his mouth. A single drop of spirit touched his lips. He cursed and tossed the flagon away into the darkness. He rose to his feet and swaying from side to side, tottered unsteadily to his bedroll; soon both Ifor and Daffyd were sound asleep.

Seated by the campfire, Dewi watched them go. For him, sleep was impossible. He felt sick and moved closer to the fire. His head throbbed. He placed a few broken branches upon the dying embers and slowly the flames returned. Feeling a little warmer, he returned to sitting cross-legged before the fire, placed his head in his hands and vomited into the flames. He had never felt this bad before and vowed never again to drink the cider spirit of the Normans.

Dewi's problems were nothing compared with those of Maredudd. Idwal, their leader, was slain, and come sunrise Longnor Woods would be swarming with soldiers.

Maredudd ran all the way back to camp. He did not stop even though he knew pursuit to be impossible; Captain Clarence and Sergeant Godfred were too heavily armoured and on horseback. To ride through the woods at night would be dangerous, and besides, Sergeant Godfred was wounded. He had sunk his dagger deep into the sergeant's thigh. If anything, he would be returning to the lodge for treatment.

But this did not mean they would not come looking. It only gave Maredudd and the rest of the brigands a short breathing space. By dawn soldiers would be crawling all over these woods, and their only hope of survival was to head immediately for the Welsh border and safety.

Maredudd entered the camp to find both Ifor and Daffyd asleep on their bedrolls. Dewi was awake. He sat before the fire, but looked worse for wear. Maredudd looked around. With the only light coming from the flickering flames of the fire it was difficult to see into the cave. He strained his eyes, peered deep into the darkened recess and breathed a sigh of relief. The Abbess was still there, sitting with her back to the far wall. She had not been put to the sword. This was good. He was now the leader and his plans for her had changed. She would accompany him to Dolwyddelan. He would leave the decision of what best to do with her to the Lord Llywelyn.

Maredudd moved towards Dewi and the fire, and in the darkness tripped upon an empty flagon. He picked it up and sniffed the contents. The smell of alcohol was all too obvious.

"What's this stuff you've been drinking?" he snarled angrily at Dewi.

Dewi looked up and grinned childishly. With head rocking loosely upon his shoulders he tried to speak, but nothing more than a few slurred and incomprehensible words issued from his lips.

Maredudd tossed the flagon into the trees and rushed into the cave. He knelt down alongside Ifor and shook him vigorously.

"Ifor, wake up," he shouted. "We've got to get out of here."

Ifor grunted and rolled over. Maredudd grabbed him by the collar and dragged him to his feet. He shook him again.

"Get the horses saddled," he bellowed. "Idwal is dead and soldiers are coming. We have to get out of here."

The seriousness of the situation brought fresh life to Ifor. He shook his head in an effort to clear away the mist and staggered towards the horses.

Daffyd, lying on the adjoining bedroll, remained snoring throughout. Maredudd gave him a kick.

"Daffyd, get up," he bellowed. "We've got to get out of here. Go and help Ifor saddle the horses."

Daffyd pulled the bedroll over his head.

"Go away!" he moaned.

Maredudd kicked again, this time and with the point of his boot.

Daffyd yelped, sat upright and cursed.

Maredudd dragged Daffyd to his feet and shook him vigorously.

"Go and help Ifor saddle the horses," he told him. "Soldiers are coming. We have to get out of here. I'll get the Abbess. She's coming with us. We are returning to Dolwyddelan."

Dewi had remained sitting by the campfire when the first of the arrows flew through the air. Bardolph was standing atop the overhang and looking down upon the campsite when he released the string to his bow. The arrow, aimed straight and true, struck Dewi with a dull thud just beneath the shoulder blade and carried on through his chest to pierce the heart. Dewi slumped forward, his face landing in the campfire, and there it stayed, unmoving with hair on fire and flames dancing about his head. Dewi had died even before his face hit the embers.

A few paces beyond the fire, Ifor heard the thud of an arrow. His progress towards the horses had been slow and erratic. Unsteady on his feet, he stopped and turned around. With the sudden burst of flame from the fire as Dewi's hair burned, the figure of Ifor stood out in the darkness. It was at this point the second arrow struck home, once again piercing the heart, and Ifor dropped to his knees then toppled sideways.

Daffyd, too, faired little better. Assisted by a shove from Maredudd, he was staggering out of the cave when the first arrow struck. Instinctively, Daffyd stuck out a foot to arrest his forward motion. But this proved too little, and far too late.

Swaying unsteadily, his forward momentum took him one step too far, and this was all that was needed for Bardolph to release his third arrow. The arrow travelled vertically downwards and entered the top of Daffyd's scull. The arrow sunk deep into his brain. He dropped to his knees, maintained that position for short while and then toppled face forward to the ground. He too died almost instantaneously.

The Abbess had no idea of what was happening. Sitting to the rear of the cave she bore witness to a frenzy of activity, but was at loss to its meaning. The heated discussions between Maredudd and Ifor, then Maredudd and Daffyd, had all been in a language she did not understand.

Then there came the dull thud of an arrow striking its target. She raised her head and looked outside the cave. A few sparks jumped from the fire and quickly followed by a sudden burst of flames. For a few seconds the figure of a man standing a few paces beyond came into view. There came a second dull thud and this man too, fell to the ground. It was difficult to see in the half light, but it looked like he was clutching an arrow to his chest as he fell.

Her eyes turned to the two brigands that remained in the cave. For some time now they had been shouting and arguing and as she turned her gaze, one man was being pushed towards the entrance. This time she saw the arrow strike. She screamed as the man dropped to his knees then toppled forward to the ground.

Maredudd was quick to realise the danger. The moment the third arrow struck, he retreated to the back of the cave. Knowing the camp to be under attack, he moved swiftly towards the Abbess. He struck her across the face to stop her from screaming and dragged her to her feet. Having lost his own dagger, sunk deep into the sergeant's thigh, he drew his sword and pressed it hard against her throat. Taking a firm hold of the Abbess he cast her to the front, and using her as a shield, moved cautiously towards the cave's entrance.

"I have the Abbess," he called into the darkness. "She dies if you enter the cave."

Maredudd's words were in the tongue of the Welsh Gaels, but Bardolph understood. The languages of the Gaels and Celts, be they spoken in Scotland, Wales or across the sea in Hibernia, all were known to him.

A voice from somewhere out in the darkness answered Maredudd in his own native tongue.

"Brother, I did'st not realise you were from Wales. You are safe now. I mean you no harm. I am not a soldier."

Maredudd, however, remained cautious, knowing this could very well be a trap. Whoever was out there had just killed three of his men, and that spelt danger no matter what language was being spoken.

With the Abbess as his shield, Maredudd pushed her towards the entrance.

"Come out of hiding. Show your face. Let me see you," he called.

From somewhere beyond the sparks that danced about Dewi's head, a voice called, "But I am out brother. I am out of hiding. I am here, standing by the fire. Can't you see me? Come brother, let us talk. I told you I'm not a soldier. I mean you no harm."

Maredudd pushed the Abbess closer to the mouth of the cave and peered into the blackness of the night. The only visible light was coming from the dying flames and there was little else to see.

"I can't see you," he called. "Step to one side. Let me see who you are, or the Abbess dies."

The voice returned once more.

"But I am here," it said. "Here, out in the open for you to see. Can't you see me?"

Immediately, Maredudd looked to his right, for the voice was now coming from his side.

"Who are you? What do you want?" he called, the tone of his voice audibly strained.

"I want you. Don't move. Drop the dagger and release the Abbess," said a voice from behind as the point of a sword pressed hard against Maredudd's back.

Maredudd froze but continued to hold his sword to the Abbess's throat. The voice had moved again and was now coming from behind his back.

The point of the sword gave a little reminder of its presence, and the voice said, "Drop your sword and release the Abbess. Make one sudden move and you die."

Maredudd withdrew the sword, held it out at an arm's length and let it drop. He then released his hold on the Abbess and pushed her away.

She collapsed to her knees, her arms tied behind her back. Bending forward and with her forehead resting on the ground, she began to pray. She feared for her life and her prayers were for the Angel Gabriel to come and carry her away. Whatever was happening behind her back, and whatever these men were talking about, she did not understand. Once more the language spoken was that of the Welsh Gaels and unknown to her.

Maredudd shaped to turn, but the sword to his back gave another sharp reminder of its presence.

"Do not turn around," said the voice. "Just answer my questions and I will let you go."

"How did you get behind me, in the cave?" asked a puzzled Maredudd.

"You were busy staring into the darkness. It was easy to pass by your side," answered the voice. "Now you answer me this. What were you doing at the twentieth milestone marker? What is so important that a brigand from across the border should be meeting with soldiers of Salopsbury, and at the midnight hour too? This intrigues me greatly and I want to know the reason."

Maredudd did not answer the question.

Instead, he asked, "Who are you? Where do you come from?"

The sword prodded once more and the voice said, "It is I doing the asking. Now pray do answer my question. What were you doing at the road? Tell me or you too, will join your friends on the ground."

Maredudd, his body trembling, began to explain.

"We were sent by the Lord Llywelyn," he said. "Sent to ambush and kill a party of travellers. We came here to collect our money, but we were betrayed. There was never any money."

"Ambush and kill who?" asked the voice.

Maredudd shook his head.

"I do not know. The travelling party was to be identified to us by soldiers of Salopsbury. But the party never appeared. The money should have been ours and we were here to collect at midnight. But we were betrayed. They killed our leader."

"Then why the Abbess, why did you bring her here?"

"She was our insurance. She is the sister of the Earl of Salopsbury. We took her from the abbey and brought her with us."

"So this agreement to ambush and kill a travelling party; this agreement was between the Lord Llywelyn and the Earl of Salopsbury, was it not?"

Maredudd nodded.

"They met some weeks back, here at the lodge in the woods, and it was all arranged," he explained.

"But you were betrayed and there was no money?"

Maredudd nodded his head once more.

"Yes, we were betrayed. There was never any money, and as for insurance, it seems the Captain of Salopsbury bears little regard for the life of the Earl's sister."

"You were going to kill her too, if you were betrayed, were you not?"

Maredudd shook his head.

"No, I was going to take her to the Lord Llywelyn. Her fate is for him to decide. A ransom could still be asked," he said.

"Is this all you can tell me?'

Maredudd nodded.

"This is all I know, except that come the dawn, these woods will be crawling with soldiers. They will be out looking for me. If they find you, they will kill you too. They are ruthless and have no honour."

"Then you'd best go quickly. I release you. You are free to go. Saddle up your horse and return to the Lord Llywelyn. Explain to him the treachery, but advise him not to cross the border and meddle in the affairs of the Marches. This land belongs to the King of England and best left alone. He decrees that any man of Wales that doth cross into England be slaughtered. So think yourself lucky that I let you go. I do this so that the Lord Llywelyn will hear of this night's treachery, and for no other reason."

"You let me go? I'm free to return to Dolwyddelan?" asked a suspicious Maredudd.

"I release you. You are free to go. Walk to your horse. Do not look back. Saddle up and ride away. With speed you can be well clear of these woods before the sun rises. Now go, else I have change of mind and do the King's command."

Maredudd knew better than look back. As the point of the sword dropped from his back he heard the sound of an arrow being placed in a bow and the string drawing tight. He walked slowly from the cave, stepping over the body of Daffyd in the entrance. He would do as the voice ordered. He would saddle up his horse and go.

Back in the cave, the Abbess remained kneeling in prayer. Whatever the men were talking about, she did not know. Perhaps they were discussing killing her. Then she heard one man walk away, and this followed a little later by the sound of horse's hooves riding off into the distance. But even now, with one man gone, she still feared for her life. One man remained in the cave. But no matter how hard she strained her ears, she could not detect his presence.

A knife sliced through the ropes that bound the Abbess's hands and gentle arms enfolded her and turned her around. And whilst she remained seated upon the ground, those same strong arms comforted her about the shoulders.

She opened her eyes and looked up. There was little light save that which came from the dying embers of the campfire. All she could see were feathers held within a quiver upon her saviour's back. The light was poor and her vision blurred and she thought these to be wings.

She thanked God for answering her prayers. She was safe and in the arms of the Angel Gabriel. She had wished death upon those that had wronged her, and God had answered by sending his messenger to cast them down.

"Holy Mother, you are safe from danger now," the angel told her.

The Abbess of Wistanstow fainted.

Chapter Forty-Two

When the Abbess awoke, she found herself resting between two large outstretched roots of an old oak tree. All about her the woods echoed to the sound of the dawn chorus.

For a while she simply lay there, unmoving in an attempt to collect her thoughts. She knew not where she lay or even how she got there. Nothing about her looked familiar and the traumas of the previous day hung heavily on her mind. She raised her head. A thick horse-blanket, dotted with morning dew, covered her body. Other than this there was not much else to see. She was in a clearing surrounded by a thicket of trees, the air hung heavily on the ground, and everywhere was veiled in a thin layer of hazy mist. The morning sun, low in the sky, penetrated the canopy high above her head and radiated down in narrow beams to touch the moss-covered ground at her feet; and where the heat of the sun did touch the ground, steam rose adding a swirling mist to the already shrouded forest air.

The Abbess felt her wrists. They were bruised and sore, but her hands were no longer bound. She fingered the rope burns about her wrists to remind her that this was no dream. She felt her side where she had been kicked. She was sore and no doubt, heavily bruised.

Bardolph shook the Abbess gently by the shoulder and spoke softly.

"Holy Mother, it is time for us to leave," he said.

The Abbess gasped and sat upright with a start. To find someone so close, had come as a complete surprise. She had not detected another's presence and considered herself to be alone. She turned her head to see a man kneeling by her side.

Bardolph handed the Abbess a small piece of bread and water from a small wooden bowl.

"Holy Mother, pray eat and drink a little," he said, "Salopsbury is a good three hours ride from here. This will see you through."

The Abbess gazed towards the tall, elegant stranger kneeling over her, then looked about the glade at her unfamiliar surroundings. The events of the previous evening came flooding back. She was being held captive by a band of brigands from across the border. She considered them to be wicked men and had wished evil upon them. She had prayed for deliverance, and God had answered by sending the Angel Gabriel to smite them down, and the last thing she remembered was being carried away in the arms of an angel.

But this was not the Angel Gabriel kneeling beside her. This was a mortal man, dressed in the greens of the forest and offering bread and water. She studied the man's face and found his looks familiar. She furrowed her brow.

"I know your face!" she said. "Our paths have crossed before, but where I cannot recall."

Bardolph pressed the bread and water to her hands.

"Yes, Holy Mother, our paths have crossed. It was at the abbey at Wistanstow. It was there I delivered an injured soldier to your Holy Order. Now pray eat and drink. We must ride."

Memories of that encounter came flooding back and she nodded her head. Now she remembered.

"You! You are the King's falconer!" she said.

Bardolph gave a gentle nod and replied, "Yes, Holy Mother, it was I. I am indeed that very person."

The Abbess looked about the glade, her eyes wide and staring. Her surroundings were more familiar now. She was in a clearing. The dying embers of a fire rested near the centre and a white horse champed the grasses to the far side. One thing was for certain, this was not the brigand's campsite. There were no rocks or overhang here. Her eyes turned to the old gnarled oak between which roots she rested and she gained comfort from a familiar sight. This oak was hollow and she had hidden here as a child. This tree and this glade were at least two miles from the brigand's campsite and a good distance from the road.

Feeling more at ease, the Abbess returned her gaze to Bardolph.

"We are in the woods at Longnor!" she remarked. Then with an apprehensive glance about her, she questioned, "But where are the brigands? The Welsh marauders that did'st capture and bring me here?"

Bardolph could see the Abbess remained deeply troubled and tried to put her mind at rest.

He told her, "Fear not, Holy Mother, the brigands from across the border have either been slain or chased away by soldiers of Salopsbury. You are safe now. No harm can befall you."

The Abbess looked about the glade, her eyes searching for soldiers, but there was no one else, just the King's falconer.

She furrowed her brow and questioned, "The Welsh brigands, you say they are either slain or chased away by soldiers of Salopsbury? But where are these soldiers, these men-at-arms? Why are they not here with you?"

Bardolph returned a wry smile. On this point he had quite a tale to tell, but stories of skulduggery and treachery were not for the Abbess, or for that matter anyone else. For the time being, he was keeping all this to himself.

"Our paths have never crossed," he replied simply.

The Abbess closed her eyes in an attempt to recall the final moments leading to her rescue, but her recollections were vague and confused. There had been mayhem and shouting, this much she remembered, and she recalled the deaths of three brigands shot by arrows. But after this, she must have fainted, for all she could remember was being cut free and falling into the arms of the Angel Gabriel.

The voice of the man knelt by her side brought the Abbess back to the present and she opened her eyes.

"Holy Mother, pray eat and drink for we must be away. It is to Salopsbury we must ride, for I have important despatches to deliver. We must ride together on my horse. If our journey goes well we will be there by noon."

The Abbess gave thanks to God for sending the Angel Gabriel to rescue her and delivering her safely into the company of this man from the King's court at Winchester.

Bardolph, riding his white horse, and with the Abbess in the saddle before him, rejoined the road to Salopsbury at a point just north of the woods at Longnor. A milestone indicated that there were fifteen miles to go. This was now open countryside, with meadows of grazing sheep and cattle, and the occasional field of golden wheat dotted amongst the rolling hillsides. Trees were few and orchards none existent. This was north of cider country and a place where good old English ale was still brewed and respected.

Bardolph rode with his arms about the Abbess and holding the reins. For a while they travelled in silence, the white horse moving at a steady canter.

The Abbess broke the silence.

"Tell me good sire," she asked, "once your pledge to the fallen herald is fulfilled and the despatches entrusted into your keeping delivered safely to Salopsbury, will'st thou be returning to Lodelowe and standing in judgement at the trial of the Lady Adela?"

Bardolph considered the question. However his answer was simple. He had no intention of standing in judgement against anyone. He was already much delayed and had to be moving south. But he was also intrigued. During their brief encounter at the abbey he had mentioned little. He had talked of the Abbot, saying they were known to each other, but this was about all, and he could not recall ever mentioning Lodelowe or the Lady Adela. Their talk was about her signet ring bearing the crest of the Fitzgeralds, and she had revealed that she was the sister of the new Earl of Salopsbury. He had also mentioned his reason for being at the abbey and his pledge to Corporal Egbert, the fallen soldier, but at no time did he mentioned standing in judgement against the handmaiden. Their discussion had been brief and conversation light. Eventually, he replied.

"Why do you enquire of such things?" he asked.

The Abbess, sensing she had spoken out of turn, felt an explanation in order. She apologised.

"Pray forgive me good sire, for I do not wish to pry," she said before going on to explain, "After your departure from the abbey, the Abbot did'st come to the church. We meet regularly on either side of the partition to discuss the affairs of the abbey and we talk of many things. On our last occasion he did'st talk of his recent visit to Lodelowe, and that whilst there he did'st stand in judgement against the handmaiden of the Lady Adela; he did'st also mention that by his side sat a falconer from the King's court at Winchester. I assumed good sire, this falconer to be you, and that you would be returning for the forthcoming trial of the Lady Adela. Pray forgive me for talking out of turn. It is not a woman's concern to pry into the affairs of men. I will do penance for my sins."

Bardolph understood.

"Holy Mother, do no penance for my part, for indeed it was I that stood in judgement alongside the Abbot and dignitaries of Lodelowe," he confirmed. "But as for future trials, the Baron hath exonerated me from further judgement. The road south beckons my call. I have the King's birds to deliver and I am already much delayed."

The Abbess placed her hands on Bardolph's as he held the reins around her waist.

"Then once more good sire, pray my forgiveness for prying into your affairs. I will ask no more," she answered.

But Bardolph remained curious.

"You show much concern for the Lady Adela?" he said.

The Abbess answered the best she could.

"Lady Adela is kin," she said. "She was our Countess and a Fitzgerald by marriage. So naturally I show concern."

"She may hang for her crimes," stated Bardolph matter-of-factly.

"She may," the Abbess replied, "but I believe she will not. Her innocence will be proven. I have prayed for her safe deliverance constantly since hearing of her imprisonment. God will save her for I know her to be innocent."

Bardolph said no more and for the rest of the journey they rode in silence.

At the gatehouse to the bridge that spanned the River Severn they were waved on without challenge; the Abbess being recognised by the guard.

Once across the bridge and negotiating the narrow streets of Salopsbury, no one gave them notice, and it was not until the white horse reached the portcullis to the castle did a challenge come.

The guard lowered his pikestaff across the path and in a loud voice called, "Halt, who goes there? Who seeks access to the castle of Salopsbury?"

The Abbess, sat to the fore, did the talking. Her voice loud and authoritarian, she told the guard, "I am the Lady Elizabeth Fitzgerald, Abbess of Wistanstow and sister to Herbert Fitzgerald, Earl of Salopsbury. Now let us pass."

On hearing the Abbess's words, the guard raised his pikestaff and stood rigidly to attention. Inwardly, he was trembling but he tried no to show it. No one of this much importance had ever approached the gates whilst he was on duty.

Bardolph kicked at his horse and moved beneath the portcullis and through to the courtyard beyond. No sooner had they entered, the Abbess spoke.

"Good sire, pray pull up your horse. I will'st get down here," she said.

Bardolph pulled up his horse, dismounted and helped the Abbess to the ground. He looked around. Already from different directions a stable lad and a pageboy were heading to greet them.

To Bardolph's right, in the near corner of the courtyard, stood the family chapel of the Fitzgeralds. The Abbess pointed towards the chapel.

"It is to the chapel I must go first," she told Bardolph. "I have a lot to thank God for. As for you, your duties lie elsewhere. Go seek the Earl. Deliver the despatches from Lodelowe and fulfil your pledge to the fallen soldier."

She raised her hand to Bardolph. He kissed the Abbess lightly upon the knuckles.

"Then enter the chapel, Holy Mother," he told her, "and may God go with you. Perhaps someday our paths will once again cross, but if this proves not to be our destiny then I will always remember our meeting at Wistanstow and our ride this day to Salopsbury. Fond memories never fade."

The Abbess curtsied and raised her head.

"And I too will never forget that I once were privileged to ride with a King's falconer," she said. "This memory too, will remain with me forever."

A pageboy and a stable lad arrived from two different directions almost simultaneously, the stable lad taking the horse's reins, and the pageboy bowing low before the castle's visitors. Bardolph smiled and addressed the pageboy. He decided he would introduce himself for what he was; a man travelling under warrant from the King of England. The dispatches from Lodelowe would only be revealed once in the presence of the Earl.

"The Abbess wishes for solitude," he said firstly. "She goes to the chapel to pray. But I have important business to conduct with the Earl. Run immediately and inform him that an officer from the Royal Court at Winchester, travelling under warrant from the King hath arrived and seeks an immediate audience."

The pageboy straightened and set off immediately across the courtyard, continually repeating Bardolph's message in the hope of not getting it wrong.

Bardolph turned to the Abbess. She too was wishing to leave. He smiled and waved her on. She returned the smile, gave a final curtsy, and set off for the chapel. He waited for the pageboy to disappear and the Abbess to enter the chapel before turning to the stable lad.

Collecting the despatches from his saddlebag, he told the boy, "Lead my horse to the stables. Feed him fresh hay and water and treat him well."

He then waited for the pageboy to return and lead him to the Earl.

Chapter Forty-Three

At the best of times news from Lodelowe was slow to reach Salopsbury. Even serious issues such as the abduction of the Abbess were late in coming. So on the morning after the event, as Herbert Fitzgerald sat alone in his chamber, news of his sister's desperate plight had failed to reach his ears. Similarly, an account of the midnight rendezvous between two of his officers and the leader of the Welsh brigands had as yet not materialised.

With noon approaching and the midday sun beating in through the narrow slotted windows of Salopsbury Castle, the only thing on the Earl's mind was the arrival of a rider bearing despatches from Lodelowe. For only when the herald appeared and his despatches handed over, would he then be in a position to act.

The Earl was sat deep in thought, his elbows resting on a table and head in hands, when a small pageboy escorted by a guard entered the chamber and knelt down by his side. The boy was much out of breath and had obviously come running.

The Earl raised his head and looked down upon the pageboy. Could this be the news he awaited? Could this be news of the herald?

"What is it?" he asked curtly.

The pageboy, not looking up and staring down upon the feet of his master, said in a trembling voice, "My Liege, an officer from the Royal Court at Winchester and travelling under warrant from the King, hath arrived. He seeks an immediate audience."

The Earl sighed. This was not the herald. He shook his head in despair. If only this could wait, but an audience with anyone purporting to be travelling under warrant from the King could not be ignored. He rose to his feet and clapped his hands. A servant appeared as if from nowhere.

Striding briskly towards an adjoining chamber, the Earl called, "My official robes. I must hold audience with this holder of a King's warrant. Get ready the reception hall. A formal greeting is needed. I will hold audience with him there."

Not long afterwards, Herbert Fitzgerald took his seat in the reception hall of Salopsbury Castle. Grand tapestries adorned the walls, fires blazed in the inglenooks, and more than a hundred candles burned, making the hall both warm and bright.

For the occasion the Earl wore a cloak hemmed in ermine. On his left breast he wore the insignia of an Earl Marshal of the Crown, a pale blue and red quartered shield bearing the three lion heads of Salopsbury and the three passant lions of the King of England. With a single clap of the hands he summonsed the castle's royal visitor to his presence.

Bardolph entered the hall and strode briskly across the floor. He came to stand before the Earl and dropped to one knee.

The Earl acknowledged the arrival of the royal visitor with a single nod to the head.

"Greetings o' bearer of a Royal Warrant," he said. "Welcome to the house of Salopsbury. Now pray enlighten me, what brings a lone traveller under warrant from the King to my humble castle?"

Bardolph held four documents in his arms. Three were scrolls, sealed with the crest of Lodelowe, the other a folded parchment. Bardolph handed over the folded parchment. It bore the great seal of King Henry III, King of England.

He explained, "My name is Bardolph and I hale from the ancient Kingdom of Wessex," then indicating the parchment now in the Earl's hands, he added, "This missive and seal will'st explain the authority the King hath invested in me."

The Earl unfolded the parchment and read the contents. On completion, he nodded his head with approval. The man stood before him was a falconer to the King, a position well thought of in royal circles and always held in high esteem. As Royal Falconer he would ride regularly alongside the King and be regarded as a man of high rank.

The Earl handed back the parchment.

"Then Bardolph of Wessex, you are most welcome to my castle and the hospitality it may afford," he told him. "Now, pray tell me, what brings a Royal Falconer to Salopsbury?"

It was always Bardolph's intention to keep his explanation to a minimum.

"I bring despatches from Lodelowe and the court of Baron de Clancey," he told the Earl. "Their deliverance was not put in my charge, but I did'st encounter the herald entrusted with their safe delivery. Alas, he did meet with an accident. He did'st fall from his horse. I found him lying in a ditch, his leg broken, and I did'st take him to the abbey at Wistanstow. It was there I did'st swear a solemn oath to complete the herald's journey, and to deliver these despatches to Salopsbury."

Bardolph handed over the three scrolls. The Earl placed them on his lap and made no effort to read the contents. He was already aware of their contents and would only read them once alone.

"Then my thanks go to you for the safe deliverance of these despatches,' he told Bardolph. "Now I offer you the hospitality of my castle. I will'st get my servants to prepare a room and a bed, and you must be hungry from your travels. I will'st have a table laid for you."

Bardolph bowed his head in thanks, but as far as he was concerned a room and a bed were not necessary.

"Perhaps a little food," he told the Earl, "for I have not eaten this day, but not a room nor a bed, for I must be away. I am already much delayed and the King eagerly awaits my return."

The Earl clapped his hands and beckoned a servant to his side. A servant arrived almost immediately.

"Go to the kitchens and see to it that a goodly table is laid before this good servant of the King," he told him. "Offer him my best wine, or ale if he prefers, and offer him any other comfort he so desires, for he is a most welcome guest to my castle."

Bardolph bowed low.

"My thanks go with you for your most gracious and extended hospitality," he said. "But my task here at Salopsbury is complete. Lodelowe's despatches are delivered. Now I must beg of your leave."

The Earl acknowledged the falconer's dismissal with a single wave to his hand. Bardolph rose to his feet, gave a final nod to the head, then turned and walked from the hall with the servant assigned to him, following in his wake.

His plan for the rest of the day was simple. He would enjoy the few small comforts of the Earl's kitchen, then once he had partaken of a meal, return as quickly as possible to Ralph and his birds. With what daylight remained, he could be halfway back to Onneyditch before nightfall.

A little while later Bardolph wiped away the grease of freshly cooked goose from his mouth and sipped a little more ale from a pewter tankard.

He was sat alone at a table in a room above the castle's kitchen, and before him was spread far more than he could eat. Around him hovered several serving wenches, all eager to please. Every time he looked up they would spring to attention ready to serve his every need.

The door opened and a male servant entered. Immediately, the serving wenches retreated to stand with their backs to one wall. Even in the kitchens, there was a social order and everyone knew their place. The servant approached the table and bowed his head.

"Sire, there is a lady here who seeks an audience," he said. "She was the handmaid to the Lady Adela, the late Earl's second wife, and hearsay tells that you hold word of the Lady Adela and her imprisonment at Lodelowe."

Bardolph wiped his mouth with a cloth and gave a wry smile. He was a little surprised as to how quickly rumours spread here at Salopsbury. The Earl would only have read the despatches some half an hour ago, and now the entire castle was awash with rumour.

But there was something else that puzzled him and it raised his curiosity. Since arriving at the castle he had not mentioned anything about the Lady Adela or ever having visited Lodelowe. Furthermore, he had deliberately introduced himself as a servant of the King, and no more. The scrolls he conveyed were sealed and he could quite easily have met with the stricken herald whilst journeying south to Lodelowe. So how did this woman, that now sought an audience, learn of such things?

Bardolph nodded his head. He wanted to find out how such rumours began.

"Yes, bring her to my table," he said. "I will grant her the audience she seeks."

An elderly woman, wheezing and much out of breath stood in the open doorway. The servant signalled that all was in order and she entered the room. She came to stand before the table and curtsy the best she could considering her age and condition. She was wearing a green dress, very similar to those worn by both the Lady Adela and her handmaiden, and on her head she wore the white bonnet of a serving wench. Most noticeable, however, was a brooch pinned upon her dress. It was a large green emerald, dewdrop in shape with a gold surround. Bardolph was keen to learn more about the brooch, but formalities needed to be observed first. This woman had asked for an audience and protocol meant that he was obliged to listen firstly to what she had to say.

"You seek an audience with me?" enquired Bardolph.

The woman, remaining curtsied, looked up.

"Good sire," she said, "my name is Mary and I was handmaid to the Lady Adela whilst she resided within these castle walls. Rumour hath it that my Lady is now held at Lodelowe and that you hold word of her imprisonment. Is it true you have seen her? And is she in good health? Pray good sire, do tell me, for I am most desperate to learn of my mistress's grave misfortunes."

Bardolph detected much discomfort in the woman's voice, and that her concern for her mistress was real. The problem was, he had not visited the Lady Adela whilst at Lodelowe, and now he wished he had. Their only contact had been at the ford and later in the stables at Onneyditch. On arrival at Lodelowe, she had been confined to a room in the north wing and he had no reason to visit her. However, hearsay told him that she was being well looked after and remained in good health.

"Alas, I did not see the Lady Adela whilst at Lodelowe," he said sadly. "But I am told she remains in good health. She is held under guard by order of the Baron, but she has a good room with a fire, a comfortable bed on which to rest, and is served wholesome food from the kitchens. She has also been afforded a bible so that she can pray and take comfort from God."

A look of relief spread across Mary's face.

"Then my Lady is safe and not put to any test?" she asked.

Bardolph thought this to be an odd question and stroked his beard before answering.

"Lady Adela is safe and she has not been put to any test," he confirmed. "It is Baron de Clancey's wish that she should be treated with all the dignity that doth go with her status of noble birth. So fear not, the Lady Adela will not be put to any test."

Mary curtsied low and thanked Bardolph.

"Then, good sire, I thank you for granting me this audience," she said. "I shall not rest easily knowing my mistress's desperate plight, but I will'st take comfort from knowing that she remains comfortable and enjoys good health."

Bardolph smiled and watched as Mary took one step backwards towards the door.

"Wait, one more question," he said.

Mary stood waiting.

"Tell me, Mary, from where did'st you get that brooch," he asked and pointing towards her chest.

Mary looked a little surprised at the question and raised a hand to grasp the brooch.

"This was a present from my Lady. I was given it as a fond and lasting farewell," she explained.

Bardolph mused upon the revelation. He had half expected this answer, but he needed to be sure. On leaving Lodelowe he had seen a brooch very similar to this one pinned to a dress being carried across the courtyard by Sergeant Cuthred. The dewdrop shaped emerald also matched the one worn by the Lady Adela at the ford. He pondered over the significance for quite some time before giving Mary permission to leave.

"That will be all Mary," he told her after a long wait, "You may go now."

Mary curtsied as low as her aging frame would allow, then turned and made for the door.

As the door closed Bardolph stood up and walked to a window. He watched as Mary appeared in the courtyard below and hurried away to the other side. She was heading straight for the Earl's chambers.

He nodded his head.

At least now he knew the instigator of the rumours. It could only have been the Earl.

This revelation, coupled with Mary's brooch, he found most interesting indeed, and he mused upon what he had learnt.

Chapter Forty-Four

Bardolph having partaken of his meal, was ready to leave. Thanking the kitchen maids for their services, he set off for the stables. The efficiency here pleased him. Nothing seemed too much trouble. News of his departure had already preceded him and he had been informed that his horse was saddled and ready to ride.

The walk to the stables took Bardolph past the small family chapel of the Fitzgeralds. With his saddlebag slung over one shoulder Bardolph hesitated then turned and made for the chapel doors. There was a chance the Abbess would still be there and he had something that belonged to her. A signet ring, tossed away by the captain and picked up in the woods remained in his possession, and this was his last opportunity to see it returned.

Bardolph entered the chapel and closed the door. He bowed low towards the altar and made the sign of the cross before his chest. The interior was dark and it took time for his eyes to adjust; the light only coming through two small stained glass windows to the rear of the chapel. He looked about him. The Abbess was knelt before a raised tomb set against one side of the chapel. On top of the tomb lay two stone figures; a man and a woman resting side by side and clasping their hands in prayer. The figures were gilded and brightly painted, and the colours were fresh suggesting a recent laying to rest.

Bardolph moved to stand alongside the Abbess.

On the side of the tomb, chiselled deeply into the stone and gilded in gold leaf, were the words; *'Guilliam et Catherine – Concilius et Pacis'*. There were also the dates *'1172–1235'* and *'1174–1230'* beneath each person's name.

Bardolph, well versed in Latin, translated the inscription. In Anglo-Saxon it would read; 'United and at peace'.

He understood. This was the final resting place of William Fitzgerald, the late Earl of Salopsbury, and also that of his first wife Catherine de Say.

Bardolph knelt down beside the Abbess and clasped his hands in prayer. The Abbess acknowledged his arrival and they prayed together, reciting in Latin several thanksgivings. On conclusion, Bardolph took out the signet ring from his purse and handed it to the Abbess.

"Holy Mother, I believe this ring belongs to you," he said. "I found it in the woods at Longnor. You must have dropped it."

The Abbess took the ring from Bardolph and kissed it gently. She rose to her feet. Bardolph was expecting a few words of thanks, and even the need of an explanation as to how the ring came into his possession, but nothing was offered nor asked. Instead, the Abbess placed the ring next to the hands of Catherine's stone image resting on top of the tomb.

"*Ex voto*," she told him as she returned to kneel by his side.

Bardolph understood and returned a small nod of approval. The ring was a token offered to Catherine on account of a vow.

After a moment of silence and another small prayer, the Abbess spoke again.

"The ring belonged to Catherine when she was alive," she explained, "It is a family tradition here to pass down heirlooms. The ring was given to me on her death some five years past. It is now returned to its rightful owner. I think she deserves it more than I. A mother superior has no need for such refineries, and the nunnery has its own seal for despatches."

Bardolph nodded his head slowly and thoughtfully. The mention of passing items of jewellery down the family made him think of other possibilities. After a short pause, he returned to speaking to the Abbess.

"Then, Holy Mother,'" he replied, "it is good, like you say, that the ring be returned to its rightful owner."

The Abbess turned to Bardolph. She knew the real reason for his coming. The ring could have been left with a servant. This was to be their last encounter, their final farewell. A little tear welled up in the corner of one eye. She desperately wanted to learn more about the handsome young man that had saved her life. But she refrained. It was not a woman's calling to ask of such things, and certainly not her right to pry into the affairs of men. Bardolph's business was with her brother the Earl and nothing to do with her.

Her question to Bardolph was therefore simple.

"You are finally away then?" she enquired of him and adding, "You return to Wessex and the King?"

Bardolph nodded his head.

"Aye Holy Mother, my work here is done," he confirmed. "Lodelowe's despatches are delivered, and now the King awaits his birds and I must be away."

"Then before you go, is there no favour I can repay?" asked the Abbess, "Money perhaps? The abbey has a small income, and we sell fruit and vegetables, and honey at the market."

Bardolph shook his head.

"Nay Holy Mother, I require neither favours nor money," he told her, "Knowing that you are safe from danger is my reward. I will always treasure these memories."

The Abbess smiled and held out a hand.

"Then God speed good servant of the King," she said. "May you ride safely and may St. Christopher go with you."

Bardolph took the Abbess's hand and kissed her lightly upon the knuckles. Together they said a final prayer.

"Now, Holy Mother, I must bid you a fond farewell," said Bardolph on rising, "for the time has come for me to leave."

The Abbess smiled.

"Then farewell my Angel Gabriel," she replied. "You will always be remembered in my prayers. And may God go with you."

Bardolph rose to his feet, and as he did so he looked down upon a memorial stone set into the floor where had been kneeling. He assumed this to be the resting place of a Fitzgerald since it bore an inscription. However on further inspection, he could see this resting place to be a little different from all the others in the chapel, for the stone bore just one date and no name. At the top of the stone was carved the year *'1154'* and below in Latin were the words; *'Illi mens est misera qui ne vivit ultra annus'*. Bardolph translated the inscription. The words on the gravestone read; 'A wretched soul is he that does not live beyond a year'.

Bardolph pointed to the memorial stone at to his feet and enquired of the meaning.

"An unusual inscription," he said. "Is this the gravestone of a Fitzgerald?'"

The Abbess, still kneeling and with hands clasped tightly together in prayer, looked up to Bardolph then down to the tombstone set in the floor. It was strange, but she had taken no notice of this inscription before. She read the Latin and answered him with what little she knew.

"They are all Fitzgeralds entombed here in this chapel, these and those within the graveyard," she said. "The body of my dear cousin William, who died some weeks past, is here in this tomb and now lies alongside his first wife Catherine, united at last in heaven. There are places reserved for both my brother and I when the good Lord decides it is time for us to join him. But as for this memorial stone, I am sorry but I know not whose body it holds except to say that it must be kin."

Bardolph pondered for a while then decided that time was pressing.

"Then I must tarry no longer, for I must be away to Wessex and the King,' he told the Abbess.

The Abbess made the sign of the cross before her body.

"Then farewell, good servant of the King," she said. "Perhaps one day our paths will cross again and perchance, under more congenial circumstances."

Bardolph tossed his saddlebag over one shoulder and bowed a final farewell. But as he turned he saw something that set him thinking, for alongside the tomb of William and Catherine stood another tomb.

This was the resting place of Sir Rupert Fitzgerald and his wife Eleanor of Montgomery, and on it an inscription read, *'Rupert et Eleanor – Semper Paratus'*. He recalled the name Sir Rupert Fitzgerald. How could he forget it? This was the knight who once served in battle by Squire Henry Stokes, the man that had stood in judgement alongside him at the trial of the handmaiden.

This set Bardolph thinking. But it was not the inscription that intrigued Bardolph. It simply translated as, 'Always Ready', and most probably this was Rupert's personal motto. Instead, it was a certain year that held his attention. Beneath the word *'Rupert'* were inscribed the dates *'1154–1219'*. He pondered long and hard. There was something about the year 1154 that seemed important to both the Fitzgeralds and the de Clanceys. Could this be just a coincidence? Or had he stumbled on something far more significant and something that might even save the lives of the Lady Adela and her handmaiden?

Bardolph turned to the Abbess. She remained facing his way and following his departure from the chapel. She waited for him to speak.

Sounding much thoughtful, Bardolph asked, "Holy Mother, did you not enquire of me whether there is some favour you can repay?"

The Abbess managed a small smile.

"I did'st, my angel," she replied, "and I ask of you again: Is there no favour I can repay?"

Bardolph turned pensive. Was he asking too much of the Abbess? For what he required had to remain a secret from both the Earl and the Abbot.

"Holy Mother, can'st what I say remain within these four walls of the chapel and not pass beyond?" he asked.

The Abbess gave a slight nod to the head in agreement.

"What is spoken between us this day will not pass from this chapel; may God be my witness," she swore and speaking with hands together as if in prayer.

Bardolph was satisfied. The Abbess would be true to her word. He never doubted this anyway, but it had to be said.

"Then perhaps, Holy Mother, there are two small favours I ask of you. Firstly, will'st you attend the trial of the Lady Adela and be willing to testify if called upon? And will'st you also take with you Mary, formerly the handmaid of the Lady Adela? Ask her to bring with her the brooch given to her by the Lady Adela on her departure for Normandy, but to keep the brooch concealed and not to show it to anyone. Keep it hidden from all eyes. For I think, this brooch may be the saviour of both the Lady Adela and her handmaiden."

The Abbess held no objections to what was being asked, but why the secretive nature of this action? She was curious. There had to be something else; something more important and most secretive.

"Gladly I will'st do this small favour for you," she said. "It is the least I can do. I will'st gladly attend the trial of the Lady Adela, and I will'st take with me Mary the handmaid along with her brooch. It will be my pleasure to return such a small favour after all that you have done for me. But you said two things. What else does't you require of me that requires such a furtive nature?"

Bardolph looked the Abbess in the eyes.

"Yes, Holy Mother, there is one more favour I ask of you," he said, "And this you must do alone. No one must know. The Abbey at Wistanstow must somewhere retain records of past disputes between Salopsbury and Lodelowe. In particular, the resolving of the boundary dispute that took place in the year eleven-hundred and fifty-four, when the boundary was moved from Onneyditch to Marsh Brook?"

The Abbess thought for a while. She did the maths. This was eighty-one years ago, and if anything was recorded then it was long forgotten.

"There are records kept in the vaults," she confirmed, "and I can gain access, I have the keys and can go there alone. What year did you say, eleven-hundred and fifty-four? I will look and see what I can find."

Bardolph bowed low.

"I would be most obliged if you would, Holy Mother, for I think I may have stumbled upon the answer to all these riddles," he replied. "But please, it is important that you tell no one and bring anything you find to the trial."

"I will do as you bid. If the records are there I will find them, and I will tell no one," she said. She then went on to ask, "You think this will save the Lady Adela?"

"It may well do," he replied.

"Then I will return to the Abbey on the morrow, and this I will do," she replied and adding, "How else could I repay my Angel Gabriel?"

Bardolph bowed one final time.

"Then, Holy Mother, I must hasten away," he said. "I go next to the Abbey at Wistanstow. For within the abbey walls there does't reside an injured soldier that eagerly awaits news of the despatches entrusted to my care. I must put his mind at rest. But whilst I am there, I will'st pass on news that you are safe at Salopsbury, and that you will'st be returning shortly."

The Abbess returned a nod of approval.

"Then God speed to Wistanstow, good servant of the King," she said, "and once again my heart filled thanks, and perchance we will meet again at the trial of Lady Adela?"

Bardolph on this occasion gave no reply. His plans were for him alone. With a final lowering of the head he turned and walked from the chapel. He had no intention of giving away any of his plans, not even to the Abbess of Wistanstow, for he was beginning to learn just how fast rumours spread in this corner of England.

Chapter Forty-Five

As dawn broke, Captain Clarence set out from the lodge at Longnor. With him rode eleven soldiers of Salopsbury, all protected by mail and identifiable by their pale blue uniforms and three yellow snarling lion heads upon their chests. There was, however, one man missing from the party. Sergeant Godfred was no longer with them. His leg wound was serious and it would be several weeks before he would be fit to ride again.

The campsite of the brigands' was not easy to locate. The woods around the lodge were extensive and the layout unfamiliar to those in the party. Captain Clarence knew the brigand's campsite to be somewhere to the far side of the road, away from the lodge, but its exact whereabouts were unknown to him. For this reason he split his party into three groups of four and sent them off to search left, right and centre. The call of the hunting horn was to be the signal to congregate once more.

In the end, it was Captain Clarence's party that located the campsite and the call of the horn was not used. To begin with, it was thought the sound would only alert the brigands. But after observing for several minutes from behind a thicket of trees, and noting the camp lacked any activity, Captain Clarence considered there to be no point in calling the others. All that could be seen were three bodies and five very agitated horses tethered to a nearby tree. One body lay with his face in the remains of a campfire; a second on the ground not far away and the third slumped in the mouth of a large cave.

After sending in two men to check out the campsite, Captain Clarence walked to the centre and with his boot rolled away the body from the ashes. The man's face and hair were gone, but he recognised the Welsh brigand from the bulkiness of his body. This was the one they called Dewi.

Captain Clarence snapped the arrow from his back and examined the flight. This was a well-crafted arrow. The shaft was straight and true, and the feathers a most distinguishable reddish-brown. He knew these feathers. They were the feathers of the red kite.

With the broken arrow in his hand, Captain Clarence moved to the body that lay a little way from the fire. Again, he rolled the body over with his boot. He recognised this man too. This was the brigand Ifor. There was an arrow in his chest that had pierced his heart. He snapped it away and put the two arrows together in his hand.

The captain moved to the cave entrance and rolled the third body over with his boot. This brigand too, he recognised. This was Daffyd, and he had been struck dead by an arrow to the top of his skull.

Standing close to the entrance of the cave, Captain Clarence looked up. The arrow that killed Daffyd would most certainly have come from the top of the overhang. He turned his gaze to the campfire and the body of Dewi. That arrow too would have come from the overhang; as would the one that killed Ifor a short distance beyond.

He bent down and examined the arrow embedded in Daffyd's skull. The shaft and flights were identical to those in his hand. From the evidence he concluded that one man, shooting arrows from above of the overhang, had been responsible for all three deaths.

Captain Clarence rose to his feet and moved into the cave. Against the rear wall rested a large gilded crucifix, and to the centre five bedrolls were laid out upon the floor. Two looked like they had been slept in. The crucifix reminded Captain Clarence of the Abbess and suggested that she too was once here.

Deep in thought, Captain Clarence walked back into daylight. His men had no knowledge of the Abbess. This was a secret held between him and Sergeant Godfred. On entering the camp he had been hoping to discover the Abbess's body and was ready to appear shocked at the discovery. However, on finding no Abbess, he concluded that she remained alive and in the hands of either a Welsh brigand or possibly their assailant. He had no way of telling.

However, Captain Clarence did his sums. It was not difficult. Originally the brigands numbered five, and the bedroll count confirmed this. He had personally slain one brigand at their midnight rendezvous and a further three now lay dead here at the campsite; this therefore, left just one brigand not accounted for. He recalled all five names and the ones he knew to be dead. He concluded the one still alive would be Maredudd, the brigand's second-in-command. He looked to the horses and recalled the time when he first joined up with these men. Their mission back then was to waylay and slaughter the Lady Adela and her party, and the brigands were in possession of six horses, five to ride and one spare. But now only five horses remained, so one was gone and his sums did add up.

From the evidence Captain Clarence concluded that the one remaining brigand must have flown the campsite and taken the Abbess with him. They would be sharing the horse, and in all probability heading for the Welsh border.

This left the captain with a big problem. If the Abbess was to ever reach Dolwyddelan, then the Lord Llywelyn would no doubt hold her captive until the one hundred golden sovereigns were handed over. At this point the Earl would certainly want to know the whereabouts of his money, and why it was never handed over.

And there was something else that worried him. A third party was now involved. Someone had been responsible for these men's deaths and now posed a physical threat. The evidence suggested one man did this, but on this point he could not be certain. There was also the possibility that this man now held the Abbess.

Captain Clarence considered this second option. He looked about the campsite and then to the broken arrows in his hand. Three arrows had been released and all were identical. All were finely crafted, with shafts straight and true, and all with very distinctive reddish-brown kite feathers for flights.

So one thing was for certain, whoever did this was a deadly marksman, and he knew of no one from Salopsbury or the surrounding area capable of such deadly accuracy.

The call of the hunting horn was the signal to regroup at the campsite. Once all were gathered, Captain Clarence detailed six of his men to gather up the bodies, horses and possessions and take everything to the lodge. The remaining five were then to go with him.

But where to go, he was not sure. Instinct however, told him to leave the woods at Longnor and head for the Welsh border. One thing was for certain,

Maredudd, the last of the brigands had to found and killed. As for the Abbess, dead or alive, it did not matter. Found alive he would get praise. Dead, he would blame the brigands.

Chapter Forty-Six

Captain Osbald pulled his horse to a halt and looked to the sun. At most there was one hour of daylight left. He was in a valley that ran almost due north to south. To the west lay the *'Long Mynd'*, a long narrow whaleback ridge of high ground that ran almost the full length of the valley. To the east lay other hills, but these rose and fell with sharp peaks and dales. The captain recognised the highest peak. He knew the name given to it by the locals. In the Welsh tongue they called it the *'Caer Caradoc'* or in Saxon the, *'Hill of Caratacus'*. Rumour had it that it was here on this hill in 50 A.D that the King of the Britons, *'Caratacus'* fought and died in battle and in so doing ended any of Britons' resistance to Roman rule.

But legends of long ago were far from the captain's mind as he surveyed his surroundings. His distance from Salopsbury and the time of day were the only two things on his mind. The unmistakable landmark, however, was of great use. On seeing the steep-sided hill he knew that he was midway between Lodelowe and Salopsbury. He turned in the saddle and looked to the road he had just travelled. No one was following him. He had left word at the abbey for his men to follow, and to head north, but knew this unlikely to happen until the morrow. Knowing that he was on his own, he returned his attention to the road ahead. This too was deserted, but the signs were good. Fresh horse droppings told him that a party of travellers had passed this way only an hour before. The trouble was, he was not sure whether they had been left by the Welsh marauders or by a group of innocent travellers.

He took heart from what had led him to this point and his reason for taking the road north to Salopsbury, and the reason for not turning west for the Welsh border at a junction in the road some five miles back. He was following a positive sighting of the Abbess by peasants working the fields. They gave an account of six horses being ridden strongly and in a line. And of the riders, five were men, the sixth a nun. Captain Osbald was no tracker, but six horses travelling in line left many clues and proved not too hard to follow.

He thought back to a junction in the road. It was here he decided to continue heading north, for the trail showed signs of the brigands taking the road to Salopsbury. This, at the time, he did not understand. By rights the brigands should have turned west and heading for the Welsh border. But for reasons unknown to him they had chosen to carry straight on, taking the road north and running parallel to the border some thirty miles to the west.

Captain Osbald kicked at his horse and moved on. He was now deep in the estates of the Fitzgeralds and had no authority here, but neither had the Welsh brigands. However, the Council of the Marches held sway over these borderlands and if challenged, he would refer the matter to the overlords.

At a point some five hours ride short of Salopsbury, the captain pulled up his horse. Darkness was almost upon him and there was a thicket of trees nearby. He moved for cover. Here in the thicket, out of sight from the road, he would rest for the night, but come first light he would be ready to continue with the chase. From the lead the brigands had over him, he reckoned they would be entering the woods at Longnor about now, and in all probability making their own camp for the night. He was a cautious man and recognised the folly of riding blindly on and entering the woods after nightfall. He considered it more prudent to wait until daylight before moving on, since there was no knowing what dangers awaited him.

As dawn broke he moved on, but at a more sedate pace. Wary of what may lie ahead, he rode with caution; looking both to the front for impending danger and behind for signs of his own men, for they should surely be following by now.

For most of the morning the captain passed through what was mostly farming country, with rows of cultivated vegetables or fields of dancing wheat. By noon, he found himself approaching a densely wooded area. He kept on going at the same sedate pace whilst continuously looking behind for signs of approaching horses.

At about the same time Captain Clarence, accompanied by five soldiers of Salopsbury, set off along the road that ran centrally through the woods at Longnor. They rode two abreast. There was only one thing on the captain's mind; Maredudd, the one remaining Welsh brigand, had to be caught before he reached the border with Wales. It was imperative that the Lord Llywelyn should never get to hear of the treachery that befell his men in the woods at Longnor, even though three deaths were none of his doing.

As the party rode south with the woods behind them and with wide open cultivated fields to either side of the road, Captain Clarence called a halt. A rider approached from the south. Even from a distance it was obvious this was a fighting man, and by his chainmail hood and by his red and dark blue uniform, a soldier of Lodelowe. They waited for the rider to come to them.

"Halt and state your business," called Captain Clarence as the rider came within hailing distance.

The two men knew each other from a series of previous meetings. Both were captains over their own separate armies; Clarence for Salopsbury, Osbald for Lodelowe, and for this reason they had met on several occasions when the two great estates were attending conference at the Council of the Marches.

Captain Clarence spoke once more as soon as the identity of the approaching rider became known to him.

As the rider came to a halt, he said to him, "Osbald, what brings you here? These estates and surrounding lands belong to the Earldom of Salopsbury and you have no right to be here."

Captain Osbald steadied his horse before explaining his presence.

"I chase five Welsh marauders," he told Captain Clarence, "They have done a foul deed. They have broken into the abbey at Wistanstow and abducted the Abbess. I have followed their trail and they are heading this way. The Earl of Salopsbury must get to hear that his sister is in grave danger."

Captain Clarence considered his position and the quandary he now faced. There were five men with him and all had heard the Captain of Lodelowe explain the reason for his presence. Up until now, no mention of the Abbess had occurred. The only thing his men were aware of was the presence of a band of Welsh marauders somewhere in the area. They also knew that four were killed and their orders were to seek out and kill the one remaining brigand. No one, other that their captain was aware of the presence of the Earl's sister. He decided to act ignorant of this fact and look surprised at the revelation.

Clarence told his fellow captain, "The Abbess you say? We are aware of the Welsh marauders; that is why you find us travelling this road. There were five in all. Four are slain and a fifth has escaped us. I have men scouring the woods at Longnor and we head for the border with Wales in the hope of cutting him off if perchance he has fled the cover of the woods. But we have not seen or heard anything of the Abbess. This news is new to us."

Captain Osbald could only go by what he had heard from the peasants tending the fields.

"I have been reliably informed that six horses came this way as the sun began to set," he explained and added, "Five were men, the sixth dressed in a nun's habit. I have followed their trail thus far, and they have not returned by this road. If you say there is still one brigand alive, then it is my belief he will be holding the Abbess; for he will have no reason to let her go. He will be holding her captive as a safeguard for returning across the border."

These were precisely the same thoughts held by Captain Clarence, but for a completely different reason. Captain Osbald was quite rightly concerned for the Abbess's safety; whilst he preferred to see her dead. For there remained a chance that the Abbess would have learned from Maredudd, the one remaining brigand, that treachery was afoot and the captain was the main instigator. He decided on the course of action that suited him best. If Maredudd had not come this way, then in all probability he remained in the woods. He had the authority to turn Captain Osbald away, since this was not his territory. He decided that he would do this and return to scour the woods along with the rest of his men. He nodded his head then hoped that this gesture was not seen.

"Then we will go no further," he said. "We will turn around and head back to the woods at Longnor. As for you, Captain, you have no authority here. I demand that you turn your horse around and head back to the estates of Lodelowe. This is our problem. After all, it is the Earl's sister that has been abducted and no one from Lodelowe is in danger. We are quite capable of handling the situation without outside help. So turn around and go back across the border between our two estates."

Captain Osbald considered the ultimatum. In a way his fellow captain was right. This was none of his business, and now that someone from Salopsbury had been informed, then perhaps his job was done. After all, he had problems of his own. As he spoke he had all available men scouring his own woods for the whore Madeline. His Baron demanded this, and this should be his top priority. He conceded and agreed it best to turn around.

"I will do as you command. I will turn around and return to Lodelowe," he responded. "But pray assure me that you will send one of your men forthwith to the Earl at Salopsbury with news of his sister's abduction. He must get to know forthwith."

Captain Clarence gave a wry smile and answered, "If what you say is true, then I will'st send one of my men to Salopsbury straightaway with the news. You are right, the Earl must get to know of this treacherous deed."

Captain Osbald turned his horse, and looking over one shoulder responded by saying, "Then goodbye, fellow captain. Perhaps we will meet again under more pleasant circumstances and that the Abbess is found safe and well."

"Goodbye, fellow captain," responded Captain Clarence as Osbald's horse began to move away.

As the captain disappeared into the distance, Captain Clarence turned his horse in the opposite direction.

"Come, let us return to the woods at Longnor," he told his men. "Let us track down the one remaining brigand and slay him."

Chapter Forty-Seven

Maredudd, sole survivor of the band of Welsh brigands, was no fool and refused to rush blindly from the woods at Longnor. He knew that by rights, he should be dead. He had witnessed the death of all four of his comrades; his leader at the hands of Captain Clarence, and the other three by some mysterious night-time visitor to their campsite. This man, whoever he might be, had somehow managed to creep behind his back inside the cave, without being seen. He had held a sword to his back, but instead of striking him down had allowed him to go. This mysterious man demanded answers, and after relating all he knew, Maredudd was let go on the pretence of conveying news of this treachery back to his Lord Llywelyn.

He considered this to be a trap however, and his astuteness told him not to rush headlong for the border. Daylight was only a couple of hours away and the last place he wanted to be was out on the open road with Captain Clarence and his men on his tail. Instead, he bided his time, moving slowly, staying within the woods at Longnor and keeping himself hidden amongst the trees.

As dawn broke he found himself on the edge of the woods, close to the road, and looking out across open fields of ripening wheat. Some thirty miles west lay the border with Wales and safety. But even though the distance was easily reachable on horseback, he realised that to travel in daylight was folly. His plan, therefore, was to spend the daylight hours concealed somewhere in these woods and only when darkness descended for a second night would he set off for home. The moon was full at present and hopefully he could see his way along what was a well-trodden road.

Remaining thoughtful and not wanting to be found during daylight hours, he considered it dangerous to stay this close to the southern edge of the woods. It was here the search parties would most certainly be concentrating all their efforts. His other big problem was his lack of arms. He had no way of defending himself. Both his sword and dagger were gone. The dagger sunk deeply into the thigh of Sergeant Godfred, and his sword dropped to the floor of the cave. With all these thoughts weighing heavily on his mind he mounted his horse and set off back into the woods. He was looking for someplace to hide and only venture out once the sun went down.

For several hours Maredudd moved deeper into the woods, and all the time keeping a keen ear to the wind and listening for sounds of any activity. It was not long before he found himself completely lost. These woods were all new to him. He had never been here before. In fact, he had never been out of Wales before, and only Idwal, their leader, had occasion to visit these woods on one previous visit. It was therefore, by chance that he found himself on the edge of a clearing that looked all too familiar. Here were remains of a campfire and beneath an overhang of red sandstone rock, there stood the mouth of a cave.

Immediately his thoughts turned to his sword. He had dropped it to the floor of the cave and a possibility remained that it was still there. He dismounted, tethered his horse to a tree and crept on hands and knees to the very edge of the clearing. From the cover of a low bush he looked out. This place had been his campsite the previous night, of this he was certain, but it was now deserted and there was evidence that someone had gotten here before him. Gone were the horses, as were the bodies of Ifor, Dewi and Daffyd. But these were all activities outside the cave and there remained a faint possibility that his sword still lay on the floor where he had dropped it. In his mind he just had to have a look to see if his sword was still there. There was also another possibility. There were still the bedrolls, and at least two of his comrades had swords and daggers which, when sleeping, were kept by their beds. It was in bed he had found two of them on his return to camp the previous night; so there was a chance, just a faint chance that a weapon of some sorts remained in the cave.

Seeing no sign of activity he broke cover and stepped into the clearing. Feeling vulnerable he made quickly for the cave. Disappointment followed immediately on entering. The cave floor was completely clear. Gone were the five bedrolls, and gone too, was the crucifix that he recalled had been left propped against the rear wall. But biggest disappointment of all was his sword; it was no longer there. Everything the gang possessed had been taken away and not one single item remained.

Feeling downhearted he wandered back to the mouth of the cave. Suddenly, he stopped and cocked and ear. He was sure he had heard a horse whinnying. He listened hard and on the wind he heard another whinny, and this quickly followed by another. This told him that there was more than one horse out there, and by the sound of it they were heading his way. He thought about going for his own horse, but he had left the animal at a considerable distance from the clearing. It was also in the direction of the approaching horses.

Maredudd was at a loss, unsure of what to do next. Initially, his thoughts were to retreat to the back of the cave and hope he would not be seen. But the cave was bare and offered nowhere to hide. Furthermore, once trapped inside, there was no way of escape. Therefore in his mind there was only one feasible option left available to him; if he was to survive he had to get out of there fast, and on foot. He set off running, circling the sandstone outcrop and disappearing into the woods to the rear of the clearing.

Chapter Forty-Eight

Bardolph, on delivering the despatches to the Earl and the partaking of a meal, set out south from Salopsbury Castle with the intention of at least reaching the Abbey at Wistanstow before nightfall. He rode fast and hard until reaching the edge of the woods at Longnor, here he slowed to a steady walking pace. He knew there to be a hunting lodge and many soldiers of Salopsbury in these woods; and for the next five miles extreme caution was required.

It was not long before he heard the clatter of fast running hooves coming towards him. The sound told him that it was just one horse approaching, but at great speed. Instinct told him to get out of the way and he moved to hide alongside the edge of the road. As he looked out from a thicket of trees, he watched as a soldier of Salopsbury sped by. He could tell this from the pale blue coloured uniform and the three golden lion heads emblazoned upon the chest of the rider. Bardolph was not to know, but this was the messenger sent by Captain Clarence to inform the Earl that his sister, Elizabeth, was being held captive by brigands from across the border.

With the rider out of sight, Bardolph rejoined the road and moved on. Eventually, he came to the twentieth milestone marker. Here he stopped momentarily to survey the scene of the previous night. All looked very different in daylight. Here the road widened and, for the first time since entering the woods, clear blue skies were visible above the clearing. Opposite the milestone marker he identified the branch in the road that led to the hunting lodge.

Remaining seated upon his horse Bardolph looked to the ground. Gone was any evidence of a skirmish. The body of Idwal, the leader of the brigands, had been taken away and either buried someplace nearby, or taken to the hunting lodge. If there had been any blood spilled, then Bardolph could see no evidence. The ground beneath the spot where Idwal had died, and the ground to the side of the road where the sergeant had received a stab wound to the thigh, had both been swept clean by branches from a nearby bush. All this was evident to Bardolph's trained eye.

Bardolph was about to move on when he heard a disturbance away in the woods. The noise was coming from the side of the road opposite the hunting lodge. His keen senses told him it was the sound of one man moving fast through the trees and breaking branches as he ran; and there was something else; behind him but at a distance there chased a number of horses. Sensing danger, he moved quickly for cover and dismounted.

"Move to cover, Whitewind," he told his horse. "Keep well out sight. Do not come unless I call."

Whitewind whinnied and moved away. Soon he was out of sight. With his horse gone, Bardolph crept to the road and to duck low behind a thicket of low bushes. He put an arrow to his bow and waited.

It was not long before the runner burst onto the road and out into the open. He stopped, bent forward and put his hands to his knees. It was evident that this was a man very much out of breath. He was dressed in the brown tartan plaid of Wales and his hair were long and plaited. After regaining his breath he set off again across the road. But the centre of the road was about as far as he got before being challenged.

"Stop or I shoot," issued a command from the side of the road.

Maredudd pulled up immediately and looked around. The language spoken was that of the Welsh. The man had spoken in his own tongue, and there was something else; something about the voice that sounded familiar.

"Who are you? Show yourself." said Maredudd much out of breath.

Bardolph remained cautious and out of sight. He had recognised the man the moment he burst into the open. This was Maredudd, the Welsh brigand he had released the previous night. But he could see the man was unarmed and without his horse, and by the sound of approaching hooves, about to get caught by soldiers of Salopsbury. He had a decision to make, and make it quickly. Should he remain under cover or step out into the open? Reluctantly, he decided to reveal himself. If he was to save the Welshman then he saw no other option open to him other than to take a great risk. Somehow, he had to stand between Maredudd and the men on horseback. Hopefully Captain Clarence was not one of them and he was able to talk his way out of this.

Bardolph stepped from cover, his bow pulled taut and arrow primed and ready to shoot.

Maredudd watched as a man appeared from the side of the road. He had stepped out from a spot nowhere near where he had heard the voice, and marvelled as to how he had managed to move so far without being detected. Or perhaps, he had not moved at all and had a trick of throwing his voice.

"Stay where you are and do not move," ordered Bardolph.

The voice was the one he had heard in the cave, Maredudd was certain of this.

"You're the voice in the cave!" he remarked on seeing the man appear. "You're the man who let me go!"

Bardolph stepped closer, an arrow pointing at Maredudd's heart. There was no time for pleasantries.

"What brings you here? Where is your horse?" he demanded. "You should be well on the way to Wales by now."

Maredudd gave a look of despair and held out his arms.

"I am parted with my horse," he said with a sigh, "and now I am chased by soldiers of Salopsbury."

Bardolph could hear the soldiers' horses quite clearly now. They were very close and getting nearer by the minute. He counted five being ridden hard, and a riderless horse trailing behind. This set a problem. His express wish was for Maredudd to cross back over the border and explain to the Lord Llywelyn the events of the previous night, and why only one man managed to return.

He moved close to Maredudd and braced himself for the soldiers to appear. This was going to be a difficult situation and hopefully he could talk his way out of it.

"Stay close to me," he told Maredudd in the language of the Welsh. "I will'st do the talking. You are my prisoner."

Maredudd accepted this, for he had very little option other than to run. Both men stood to the middle of the road; both listening to the sound of breaking branches and clattering hooves getting ever closer through the trees to the front of them.

It was not long before the first rider appeared, and this quickly followed by another and then another. In total five soldiers, all wearing the pale blue tunics of Salopsbury, rode one by one into the clearing. At the head of the column rode Captain Clarence. To the rear, and led by the fifth soldier, there trailed a riderless horse. By the look of the tartan blanket saddle this was a brigand's horse, and in all probability that of Maredudd's.

On seeing the two men stood to the centre of the road, the emerging soldiers formed a circle around them and drew their swords. Captain Clarence stepped down to confront the pair. He was well aware of the identity of the stranger. This was the Royal Falconer that had stood in judgement at the trail of the Lady Adela's handmaiden. The captain had been present at the trial along with Sergeant Godfrey. But he was not to reveal this fact, for this would give the game away. To him this man in green, stood next to the one remaining Welsh brigand, could quite easily be deemed to be an enemy of Salopsbury. With the slaying of Maredudd his one and only priority, he was quite willing to sacrifice this second man if he stood in his way. No doubt there would be repercussions, but he was sure he could talk his way out of it. Anyone shielding someone from across the border could quite easily be deemed a traitor. He would say he was only doing his duty. This was his reasoning as he moved to confront Bardolph.

"Drop your bow. You are both under arrest," he said in the Saxon tongue.

Bardolph too, recognised the captain, for this was not their first encounter. He had observed him standing to the rear at the trial of the handmaiden. Furthermore, he had broken a branch over his head in the Forest of Wyre when rescuing Madeline; overheard his conversation with his sergeant at the top of the rise that led down to the hunting lodge and observed from this very spot the captain's clandestine meeting with the leader of the Welsh brigands. So he knew a lot about this captain of Salopsbury and knew him to be a man not to be trusted. But he, like the captain, was not willing to reveal any of this.

Reluctantly, Bardolph placed his bow and arrow on the ground at his feet.

Captain Clarence watched as the bow and arrow went down. The action brought back memories of something that occurred earlier that day. The flights of the arrow bore the distinctive feathers of the red kite. This set him thinking. Surely this was not the same man that had slain the three brigands at their campsite? But if he had, why was he protecting the life of the last remaining brigand? Did he really want him to go free and report back to the Lord Llywelyn? If so, this was really bad news and there was no way he was going to let this happen.

Bardolph, on surrendering his bow, stood upright to come face to face with the captain.

"You cannot arrest me for I travel under the command of a King's warrant," he informed the captain. "This Welsh brigand is my prisoner. I have arrested him under the powers invested in me by the King of England."

"Then show me this warrant," snapped the captain.

The warrant was in Bardolph's saddlebag and his horse had moved to cover some distance away. There was no way he could go for it, for if he did, then surely they would slay Maredudd whilst he was away. He whistled. Whitewind would have to come to him.

But strangely, nothing happened. He could hear no sound of Whitewind responding to his call. He whistled again and still no response came. He decided to bluff his way out.

"The warrant is in my saddlebag and my horse is too far away to hear my call," he informed the captain. "Yet, I need not show it to any soldier of Salopsbury, for I have already presented the King's warrant to your Lord, the Earl of Salopsbury and he has given me the authority to do as I will'st in all of his estates."

"But not to protect Welsh brigands, of that I am sure," retorted the captain, raising his sword towards Bardolph. "So stand aside and let us take this man prisoner. Else you too will be deemed a brigand, for I know not whether you speak the truth."

Bardolph put a hand to his own sword held in his scabbard.

"The prisoner is mine, by order of the King of England," he stated flatly.

Captain Clarence simply laughed.

"Men, dismount," he called. "We take the Welshman prisoner. If either man resists, then slay them."

For Bardolph, everything was going wrong. None of his bluffing had worked and this man was determined to kill the Welsh brigand at all costs, and to kill him too, should he get in the way. He felt helpless. All he could do was look on as the four soldiers on horseback dismounted, joined the captain and formed a five-man circle around both him and Maredudd.

With swords raised and pointing towards the two men at the centre, the captain issued his final demand to Bardolph.

"Hand over the prisoner to the authority of the Earl of Salopsbury, or die, for I shall deem that you too have resisted arrest," he said with a noticeable touch of venom to his voice.

Bardolph moved his hand away from his sword and to a dagger he kept in his belt behind his back. If it was to come to a fight, then he would attempt a strike at the captain. But the man wore chainmail and he could not guarantee a fatal strike. And Maredudd was no help. He bore no weapon at all. He decided to have one more go at reasoning with the captain.

"By taking this action you and your men face the wrath of the King of England. I order you to put down your swords and let us go on our way," he said, speaking in a voice in authority.

Captain Clarence, however, was having none of it. He simply laughed and thrust his sword close to Bardolph's throat.

Bardolph's hand moved further behind his back and to touch his dagger. It seemed there was no way out of this predicament other than to fight. But with five swords drawn and raised, he knew that the odds were stacked against him.

"Move aside and hand over the Welshman," Captain Clarence demanded. "This is my final order. Resist and you will die along with the Welshman."

Bardolph rested his hand upon the hilt of his dagger. At the same time swords moved closer to his and Maredudd's throats.

Bardolph was prepared for action, as were the soldiers of Salopsbury. A fight to the death was only seconds away. Bardolph said a little prayer, grabbed the hilt of his dagger and drew it from his belt. In the same instance, Captain Clarence readied his sword, as did the other four soldiers.

But this was as far as anyone got as all eyes turned to the road south. The sound of thundering hooves were coming their way. Within seconds, they appeared from around a bend in the road. The half dark blue and red tunics told Bardolph that these were soldiers of Lodelowe; but what was more surprising was the horse in the lead. It was white and riderless. It was Whitewind.

Within seconds the riders were upon them. Now Bardolph could identify them all. Captain Osbald was there along with another eight soldiers of Lodelowe. But these were not the normal guard under the captain's command. These were Baron Clancey's elite riders, for they wore no chainmail. These were his archers, eight men that accompanied him on hunting trips to the Forest of Wyre. With bows and arrows already primed and remaining upon the saddle, they quickly formed a circle around those stood to the centre of the road.

"A welcome appearance," Bardolph called towards Captain Osbald as he dismounted. Then turning to Captain Clarence he added, "It seems we have a stand off. I suggest you put down your swords and surrender to the soldiers of Lodelowe."

"You have no authority here," stated Captain Clarence. "These woods belong to the Earl of Salopsbury and you have no right to be here."

"Perhaps not, but they are here, and by the authority invested upon me by the King of England, I give them the authority they require. So tell your men to put down their swords and surrender to the King's men."

The four soldiers under the captain's command looked at each other. They nodded to each other and agreed. This was no time to disobey an order from a servant of the King. They laid down their swords on the ground. Captain Clarence, on seeing his men's action did likewise and placed his sword at his feet.

"The Earl shall hear of this wicked treachery," spat the captain. "You have exceeded your authority here at Longnor."

Captain Osbald stepped through the circle of soldiers to greet Bardolph and the two men embraced.

"A timely appearance," remarked Dardolph, "but what brings you to my aid, Captain. And why my horse? I thought him lost."

"We were travelling this road with the intention of going all the way to Salopsbury. I had encountered the captain earlier before my men arrived, and I did not trust him to send word to Salopsbury. So when I was joined by the Baron's archers, I turned around and came this way. As for your horse, he came to us. He was waiting in the middle of the road. I could see he was agitated and by his actions he wanted us to follow. He set off at a gallop, and we did'st follow at the same speed. And this is how we got here, and just in time by the look of it."

Bardolph patted Osbald on the shoulder.

"And a timely intervention at that," he said. "For without it, I may well have been dead by now."

Osbald laughed heartily.

"Then my friend, one good deed deserves another," he replied. "You saved my life at the ford at Marsh Brook. Now consider my debt repaid."

Bardolph laughed too.

"The debt has truly been repaid and I for that I thank you with all my heart," he confirmed.

With all the pleasantries over, Bardolph looked to Maredudd and then towards Captain Clarence's horse. His saddlebag was there. He brushed past the soldiers of Salopsbury and moved to the horse.

"Come, join me, Osbald," he called. "Let's see what we have in here."

He unfastened the straps to the saddlebag and felt inside. He found what he was looking for. It was a large purse. He tested the weight. It was heavy and he tossed it up and down in his hand.

"I think here we will find one-hundred golden sovereigns destined for the Lord Llywelyn," he remarked, then pointing to Maredudd still stood to the centre, he added, "Osbald, my dear friend, will'st you do one more thing for me? Will'st you escort this Welshman safely to the border, and take this purse with him. For the money doth rightly belongs to the Lord Llywelyn."

Osbald looked to his circle of archers and then to the men stood at the centre.

"I will'st do that gladly. I will escort the Welshman to the border and see him on his way," he replied. He then added, "But what of the soldiers of Salopsbury? What must be done with them?"

Bardolph managed a little smile. With the one-hundred golden sovereigns now in the hands of its intended recipient, there was little the Captain of Salopsbury could do. He could now go back to the Earl and report that the money had been handed over. He could also blame the deaths of the brigands on the Royal Falconer. Well, at least three of them. How he got around the fourth would be tricky, but he was sure he would think of something.

"Let them go," he told Osbald, "The track yonder leads to the lodge. Give them back their swords and send them on their way. I don't think we'll have any more trouble from them."

Osbald turned to his men still seated upon their horses and with bows primed and ready to shoot.

"See the soldiers of Salopsbury on their way. Let them take up their swords and remount their horses. Then send them back to their lodge down the track opposite. The Welshman's horse remains here with us," he instructed.

As the soldiers of Salopsbury recovered their swords and moved to mount their horses, Osbald turned to Bardolph.

"But what of you, my dear friend? I now find you even further from Wessex and the King's New Forest. Where next will'st you go?"

Bardolph whistled Whitewind to come to him. He patted the white horse on the neck before responding to Osbald's question.

"My friend I have many plans, and it seems the King's birds must wait a little longer. But on your return to Lodelowe there is something I want you to do. For I think I know where we can find the Baron's stolen treasure."

Osbald looked a little stunned by the revelation, but said nothing. At the time horses were being mounted and ridden away towards the lodge. As the last solder disappeared from view, he turned once more to Bardolph.

"Then, my friend, I assume you are planning to remain at Lodelowe for a while," he said.

Bardolph turned pensive.

"It seems that fate dictates I remain until after the trial of the Lady Adela," he said solemnly, "I shall ask of the Baron that I be permitted to stand in judgement at the trial of the Lady Adela. After that, who knows? God willing I shall be free to return with my birds to Wessex and the King of England."

Chapter Forty-Nine

The day of the trial arrived. The Great hall of Lodelowe Castle was prepared and ready. The long table that normally ran lengthways down the centre of the hall, had been moved to the rear and turned to run the full width. Because of the great size, one end needed to be butted against a side wall, allowing a small gap at the other end to let people by.

Behind the table there stood eight chairs with their high backs to the far wall. In front of the table and to either side of the hall there stood many rows of chairs. Here, the two families would sit; the de Clanceys to the left as you enter, the Fitzgeralds to the right. The centre of the floor was clear except for a solitary chair placed centrally and facing the table. It was here that the defendant, Lady Adela Fitzgerald, would sit throughout her trial.

Even though the trial was to take place during daylight hours, and the windows permitted some light to enter, it was considered not enough, and as a result no expense had been spared. Candles burned everywhere. There were several candlesticks resting on the table, each holding six or more candles. There were also candles in their hundreds arranged in great chandeliers that hung from the high vaulted rafters, and many more in brackets against the side walls. It was true to say the Great hall glowed with light.

Six of the chairs to the rear of the table were reserved for those that would sit in judgement. The seventh and eighth chairs were for two scribes. For it was considered appropriate to have one recording in Anglo-Saxon, the other in the Norman tongue. This was to ensure that proceedings of the trial be available for the Duke d'Honfleur should he wish to know his daughter's fate. The Lodelowe scribe was to be one, the other provided by the Council of the Marches. It was agreed the two scribes were to take up their seats at the end of the table that abutted the wall.

Of the six remaining seats, three of those that sat in judgement over the trial of the handmaiden would sit again. These were Squire Henry Stokes, the Abbot of Wistanstow and the young Edwin de Mortimer. The remaining three seats were for three newcomers; for it was deemed inappropriate for Baron de Clancey and Captain Osbald to officiate in what was considered a family matter. As for Bardolph of Wessex, he had been asked to sit in judgement but had declined, saying he would prefer to observe from the sidelines.

Of the three newcomers, one was a trader in wool; he was Raymond de Clees of Titterstone, for he was a man of immense wealth and well respected in the area. The second newcomer was also a well-respected trader, this time in wheat and flour. He was Arthur Miller of Clungenford.

The sixth and final seat however, was reserved for someone far more senior. He was the father of the young Edwin de Mortimer. He was Earl Simon de Mortimer, Lord of Powys and Overlord of the Council of the Marches, and it was he who would preside over the whole proceedings.

The seating was agreed as follows; from the scribes' positions and working along, next to them would come Squire Henry Stokes, then Raymond de Clees, then Earl Simon de Mortimer, followed by his son Edwin de Mortimer, then Arthur Miller of Clungenford and finally, the Abbot of Wistanstow; for it was considered the Abbot should be free to move to the front should his blessings be required.

It was hoped that enough space be afforded between wall and end of table for the Abbot to squeeze past. But just to make sure in the case of difficulty, two servants would be placed on standby to assist, should help be required.

There were also a few places available to the paying public. But they would not be in the Great hall. For them, it would be the minstrel gallery. For the exorbitant price of one silver crown there would be a limited number of seats for thirty-six people. The high price being deliberately set to keep out the peasants. With twelve silver pennies to a silver shilling, and five silver shillings to a silver crown, and with earnings of most peasants no more than two silver pennies a week, then one silver crown was far beyond the means of most people in the area. However, it was still expected all seats to be taken.

One final thing had been agreed between the two parties. There were to be no knives, no daggers, no swords and no weapons of any sort allowed into the Great hall during the trial. A precaution, deemed necessary should the proceedings become heated.

The trial was set for midday. Those members of the paying public lucky enough to obtain one of the thirty-six well sought-after entrance permits were allowed to climb to the minstrel gallery well before this time. Most taking up their seats some one hour before the trial began.

Some half hour before the trial was to begin the hall began to fill with the de Clanceys and the Fitzgeralds; both families taking their allotted places to either side of the hall. Noticeably on the Fitzgerald side, there sat the Abbess of Wistanstow, and by her side sat Mary the handmaid that had cared for the Lady Adela for five years before her departure. Opposite, on the other side of the hall, sat Bardolph of Wessex.

With just a few minutes to go, the two scribes entered and took their seat behind the long table. Their escritoires, ink and quills, along with a great number of scrolls and parchments already laid out and waiting.

The trial began with the call of the hunting horns announcing the entrance of the six that were to sit in judgement. Silence fell and everyone rose from their seats as the six men entered through the large double doors to the front of the hall. With Earl Simon de Mortimer at the head, they walked in line. The line being formal, and in what was considered each individuals importance and position in society. Behind the Earl came his son Edwin de Mortimer, then the Abbot of Wistanstow, this was followed by Squire Henry Stokes, and then the wool merchant Raymond de Clees. At the end of the line came Arthur the Miller of Clungenford for he was considered the least senior of the six.

Each in turn moved around the table and took their seats in the order allocated; the Abbot being the last to sit down. As expected, he needed assistance to squeeze past the end of the table.

On entering the hall, Earl Simon de Mortimer had carried with him three jewels; these being an emerald necklace, an emerald brooch and a gold signet ring. He placed all three objects on the table before him, arranged them in a neat row and then looked up to address all those assembled in the hall.

"You may take your seats," he told everyone, "this court is now in session."

After the rumble of chairs had died down he spoke again.

"Bring forward the accused," he said loudly so that those at the doors at the far end of the hall should hear.

A few uneasy minutes followed before Lady Adela Fitzgerald entered the hall accompanied by two guards. The guards were not armed and wore no chainmail, and they wore the claret and light blue quartered tunic of the Council of the Marches.

Lady Adela walked gracefully between them and took her seat at the centre of the hall. The two guards then bowed low, turned and marched out of the hall, leaving the Lady Adela to sit all alone in the centre of the floor.

Once she had settled, Earl Simon de Mortimer looked to the Abbot.

"Let us pray," he said.

Having already struggled to get around the table, the Abbot rose from his chair and made no attempt to move to the front. He made the sign of a cross, recited a few prayers in Latin and immediately sat down.

On seeing the ending of the prayers, Earl Simon de Mortimer held out a hand towards the nearest scribe. Not a word was spoken as a scroll was passed down the line. He unfurled the scroll and looked to the Lady Adela. He began to read in the language of the Saxons, and not that of the Normans. The language having been previously agreed by all parties since the Lady Adela was known to be well versed in both languages.

He read, "Lady Adela Fitzgerald, Dowager to the late Earl William Fitzgerald of Salopsbury, you are brought before this court this day accused of robbery and murder, in so much that on the fifth day of August, in the year of our Lord twelve hundred and thirty-five, you did aid and abet in the theft of property from his Lordship, the Baron de Clancey, and also aid and abet in the murder of Richard, son of Frederick, guard to the Baron de Clancey, and thereafter did wilfully partake in the concealment of property stolen from their rightful owner."

Then, looking up from the scroll and addressing the accused, he asked her directly, "Lady Adela Fitzgerald, Dowager to the late Earl William Fitzgerald of Salopsbury, how do you plead to these charges, guilty or not guilty?"

Unlike her handmaiden before her, Lady Adela had been briefed as to proceedings and was well aware of the charges. Remaining seated with back straight and head held high, she gave her reply.

"Not guilty, my Lord," she said in a loud and clear voice with a hint of a Norman accent.

The Earl waited for the plea to be duly recorded before continuing.

"Your plea of not guilty has been recorded," he informed her. He then went on to ask, "Lady Adela, do you wish to speak in your own defence, or as is your right, you may nominate someone to speak on your behalf?"

Although well briefed, having someone to represent her had not been mentioned. It turns out that both Baron de Clancey and Earl Herbert Fitzgerald of Salopsbury had agreed beforehand that the Lady Adela be left to defend herself. This suited both parties. Baron de Clancey was desperate to save face, and for him only a guilty verdict would do. As for the Earl, he too desired a guilty verdict, but for more sinister reasons.

A silence fell whilst the hall waited for Lady Adela's response. She was about to speak when up stood Bardolph of Wessex and took one step forward onto the floor. He turned to the table and with one hand across his stomach and the other out at his side, he bowed low.

"I, Bardolph of Wessex, Royal Falconer to King Henry, King of England, will'st speak for the Lady Adela if she does't agree and this court permits it to be so," he said whilst remaining stooped and looking upwards.

Earl Simon de Mortimer looked to all those seated in judgement, turning his head from side to side, and all in turn nodded a favourable response. It was clear no one held any objections. Satisfied, he turned to the Lady Adela.

"Then Lady Adela, does't you agree to this man, Bardolph of Wessex, to speak in your defence?" he asked.

Lady Adela turned and looked to Bardolph before returning her gaze to the front. She was unsure as to what to answer. Memories of their first encounter at the ford at Marsh Brook came flooding back. It was here that this man had shot an arrow and killed one of the guards protecting her. But then she recalled their second meeting at the stables at Onneyditch. It was here that he had been kind to Gwyneth, her handmaiden. He had cut her down, given her water to drink and laid her on the straw by her side.

After giving the Earl's question much thought, she nodded her head and gave her reply, saying, "Yes, my Lord, I give my consent to this court. I will'st allow this man, Bardolph of Wessex, to speak in my defence if he so desires."

Earl Simon de Mortimer listened, then turned to his scribes. He waited until they had both finished writing before returning his gaze to the front and to Bardolph in particular.

"Then Bardolph of Wessex, Royal Falconer to King Henry, King of England, you have this court's permission to speak in the Lady Adela's defence," he said.

Bending slightly lower in an act of respect, Bardolph replied, "Then I thank this court for the authority it has vested in me."

"Your thanks are received. I'm sure we that sit in judgement eagerly wait to hear what you have to say," responded the Earl.

Bardolph rose and crossed to the lone chair placed centrally on the floor. He kissed the awaiting raised hand of the Lady Adela.

"Pray do put all your faith in me, my Lady," he told her softly and away from most ears in the hall. "If God permits, then I will'st have you freed of all charges levelled against you."

The Lady Adela smiled.

"Then I put all my faith in you, dear servant of the King," she replied. "For I know not what to answer this court other than to continuously declare my innocence."

Bardolph returned the smile.

"Of your innocence I am certain, and if God willing I will have you free of all charges levelled against you. In the meantime, pray to God and hold faith my dear Lady, hold faith," he whispered.

He kissed her lightly once more on the back of her hand before moving to stand by her side and face the table.

"Pray continue with the trial, my Lord. We are ready to answer all charges," he told the Earl.

The Earl, having been briefed beforehand, recognised that the one piece of damning evidence held against the Lady Adela was the emerald necklace found in her possession. By all accounts, this item of jewellery belonged to the Baron de Clancey and was stolen from his strongroom some three weeks earlier. He collected the necklace laid out on the table before him and held it high for all to see. He looked to the Lady Adela.

"My Lady, is this the necklace found in your possession at the ford at Marsh Brook?" he asked. "And if so, then this court requires an explanation as to how it came into your possession. For by rights, this necklace does belong to the Baron de Clancey and is part of his father's legacy."

A short silence followed as Lady Adela collected her thoughts. As far as she was concerned, she was given the necklace by her husband, the late Earl William Fitzgerald, shortly after their marriage, and that was some five years ago. She was about to relate this when Bardolph stepped forward.

"If this court does't so agree, may I be allowed to inspect the necklace you hold before the Lady Adela answers what has been asked of her?" he requested of the court.

The Earl looked back and forth down the table. Once again, no one objected. On seeing their response he turned to the front and held the necklace out for Bardolph to collect.

"You may inspect the necklace. This court holds no objections," he said.

Bardolph stepped to the table and leaning across, took the necklace from the Earl. He turned it over and inspected the back.

"Ah!" he exclaimed. "It is as I thought. These marks tell me this necklace was made by monks and craftsmen at Cluny, a monastery well to the south of the Norman's lands. I have seen this jewellery before at the King's court at Winchester. It is in nearby mountains that the emerald stone is mined, and the gold would have come from Rome, for it is the Holy Roman Church that controls all the gold in these parts."

Bardolph turned to the Abbot seated at one end of the table.

"May I ask the Abbot," he said. "Of what Holy Order does't your Abbey belong?"

The Abbot gave a look of surprise at being asked such a question. But he answered anyway.

"It is true. We are of the Cluniac Order and belong to the Holy Order of Brethren of Cluny."

"Thank you, Abbot," said Bardolph as he returned to stand before the Earl.

"Where is this leading?" asked a curious Earl. "For it is not customary for a member of this court to be asked to speak."

"Leading to the truth, my Lord," Bardolph replied, and holding up the necklace went on to say, "For it is my belief that in establishing the origin of this jewel, the truth will come out. If my Lord agrees then may I continue with my questioning? For I have more to ask of the Abbot."

The Earl looked to the Abbot who responded with a shrug of his shoulders.

"Let him ask, for like you, I am curious as to where this is leading," answered the Abbot.

"Bardolph of Wessex, you may continue," said the Earl who was also curious.

"I thank you, my Lord," replied Bardolph.

He bowed, turned and walked the floor towards the Abbess of Wistanstow, seated to the Fitzgeralds side of to the hall. She was waiting for him with a scroll in her hands.

She handed the scroll to him, smiled and whispered, "Good luck my Angel Gabriel. Hopefully what this scroll contains, will help you save the Lady Adela from the gallows."

Bardolph bowed low, smiled and returned with the scroll to place before the Abbot.

"This document is written in Latin. It is the language of the church and not understood by most assembled here. I therefore, ask of you to read out the date," he said

The Abbot unfurled the scroll and read the date as asked.

"This document is dated, '*Anno domini deciens centum quinquaginta quatuor*'," he said, then without being prompted went on to translate by saying, "It reads; 'In the year of our Lord eleven hundred and fifty-four'."

"And the day and the month?" asked Bardolph.

"*Diapente october*," read the Abbot, adding, "The fifth of October."

Bardolph was satisfied, but there was one more thing he needed the Abbot to verify before he could carry on.

"Now, can you tell us of the three seals on the document," he asked.

The Abbot unfurled the scroll completely and looked to the seals at the foot of the document. He checked them closely.

"These are the seals of the Fitzgeralds, the de Clanceys and of the Abbey at Wistantow," he said.

"And what of the document itself? Can you tell us of its purpose?" asked Bardolph.

The Abbot read the contents and took his time before replying.

"It is an agreement between the Fitzgeralds and the de Clanceys over a boundary dispute. Here all parties agree that the boundary be moved from the River Onney in the south, to a stream to the north that runs through the ford at Marsh Brook,"

Bardolph acknowledged the Abbot's contribution with a bow.

"I thank you kind Abbot for displaying your excellent knowledge of Latin, and explaining to this court the nature of the agreement," said Bardolph, leaving the scroll in the Abbot's hands. "The scroll that you now hold is the property of the Abbey at Wistantow. May I ask that you retain it, let it be used as evidence if this court so desires, and whence this trial is concluded, return it safely to your vaults?"

Bardolph stepped away and moved to a position where he could address the whole of the court.

"Gentlemen, permit me to explain in more detail the agreement now in the Abbot's possession," he said. "I'm sure he and the scribes will verify all I have to say."

He began to explain by saying, "My Lord, eighty-one years ago this coming October, the boundary dispute between the Fitzgeralds and the de Clanceys was resolved by direct arbitration from the Abbey. For it was also in the Abbey's interest that the boundary be moved. The Abbey's main commodities being both cider apples and wheat. Then, as is now, both commodities being more marketable to the south. Cider being the drink preferred by those living to the south of the Onney, whilst Salopsbury retains the taste for good old English ale. Wheat on the other hand, holds no boundaries, but the milling of flour always did. The watermill at Onneyditch being on the lands of the Fitzgeralds meant flour was under the control of Salopsbury. The agreement therefore, was for the present Baron's father, Edwin de Clancey, to pay the sum of two-hundred gold sovereigns towards the construction of a new mill closer to Salopsbury. In return, it was agreed that the boundary be moved north to the stream at Marsh Brook, and that, my Lord, is the basis of the agreement. With the boundary changed, the Abbey moved to the estates of the De Clanceys', and Salopsbury profited from having flour ground much closer to the city."

The Earl intervened.

"That's all very well, but how did Lodelowe benefit from this agreement?" he enquired.

Bardolph explained, "The benefit of Lodelowe's market, my Lord, for the market now thrives and people from miles around does't flock to the town. And there was one more benefit gained. In recognition of the late Baron's honourable gesture, a gift from the Abbey was presented to the family of the de Clanceys. That gift was in the form of items of jewellery. Jewellery made by the monks and craftsmen at Cluny and passed on to various abbeys of its Holy Order. One Holy Order in particular, being that of the Abbey at Wistanstow."

The Earl interrupted once more.

"By saying gifts of jewellery, I assume you are referring the emerald necklace and brooch that now lies as evidence before this court?" he suggested, for he could see where all this was leading.

Bardolph acknowledged with a slight bow.

"You are quite right to believe this, my Lord," responded Bardolph, "but not just the two items laid before this court, but other jewellery too."

"Other jewellery?" quizzed the Earl.

Bardolph paused. The time was right to introduce his first witness.

"My Lord, if I may be permitted, I would like to call upon someone who can enlighten this court on the exactitude of this jewellery," he said.

Once again, the Earl looked back and forth along the table and to all those seated in judgement, and once more no objections were raised. All were curious as to where all this was leading.

"This court holds no objections. You may bring forward your witness to stand before this court," he said, giving his permission.

Bardolph signalled towards the large double doors away over on the far side of the hall. Whilst everyone waited anxiously to see who this mysterious witness would be, there came a hubbub of noise from both sides of the floor, and this joined by further rumblings from the minstrel gallery above.

Then suddenly, the mutterings turned to great gasps of breath as the witness entered. Striding boldly into the hall marched John Smith the blacksmith of Onneyditch, and in his arms he carried his great-grandmother Agatha.

As John Smith came alongside Bardolph, the King's falconer turned to the Earl.

"My Lord, my witness is Agatha of the inn at Onneyditch," he announced; "Sadly her advancing years make it difficult for her to walk, so she is carried into this court by her great-grandson, John Smith of Onneyditch. I hope this court holds no objections to his presence, but other than hold this lady firmly, he will take no part in the proceedings. As for this dear old lady's recollections of events some eighty years past, her memories of the evening of the fifth of October, in the year of our Lord eleven-hundred and fifty-four remain sharp and clear, and this court will find no difficulty in appreciating all she has to say."

The Earl managed a compassionate smile.

"You may continue," he said simply.

Bardolph turned to Agatha.

"Agatha, before we begin will you kindly tell this court your age," he said.

With a mouth displaying a single tooth, she replied saying, "I am in my ninety-third year; I'll be ninety-four next month."

Bardolph turned to the Earl.

"My Lord, at the age of ninety-three this woman would have been born in the year eleven-hundred and forty-two. In eleven-hundred and fifty-four, when the agreement to move the boundary was signed, she would have been twelve years old. It is as a twelve-year-old girl that I now ask of her to give witness. For events that unfolded on the evening of the fifth of October of that year hold a vast significance to the outcome of this trial," he explained.

He then turned to Agatha.

"Dear lady, can you tell this court, as a girl of twelve, exactly where you were on the evening of the fifth of October, in the year of our Lord eleven-hundred and fifty-four?" he asked of her.

Agatha grinned, her one tooth showing. She knew exactly where she was that evening, for it was a tale she had told many times sat in her rocking chair before the hearth at the inn at Onneyditch.

"I was at my parents inn; the Golden Lion at Onneyditch," she said.

Bardolph cut her short for he considered a little explaining to the court necessary before Agatha began to relate her tale.

Quickly interrupting, he said, "Thank you, Agatha." For another tale was to be told; a tale of events that took place earlier that day.

He turned to the court.

"Before Agatha tells her tale of the events of that evening, I must explain to the court the events of the day," he said.

He waited a while, and on seeing and hearing no objections he went on to explain, "A special ceremony took place that day at the Abbey at Wistanstow. Baron Edwin de Clancey, his wife Lady Caroline and their two newly born children, the twins Edmund and Edward travelled to the Abbey to receive a gift of gratitude. However, the Baron had all along insisted that no reward be given to him or his wife, but instead to his two sons. Once gifts had been presented, prayers said and the ceremony concluded, they set off back to Lodelowe. But the hour was late and it was pre-arranged that the Baron and his entourage should stay that night at the inn at Onneyditch."

He turned to Agatha.

"Now, Agatha, tell us what happened not long after the Baron and his party arrived at the inn," he said.

She grinned once more, for she loved telling this tale.

She began: "The hour was late and it was getting dark when the party arrived. We had been warned in advance at what hour the Baron would be arriving and their rooms were prepared. I was at the door with my mother when the Baron and Lady Caroline arrived. They were accompanied by several guards who, on seeing the Baron and his wife enter, moved on to stable their horses. My mother escorted them upstairs to their room, and I followed on to help."

At this point Bardolph interrupted.

"But, what about the twins? You make no mention of them. Were they not with their parents at this time?" he asked.

Agatha shook her head.

"The Baron and his wife arrived first along with the guards," she explained. "The twins were to follow on behind in a carriage. It was some time later when the carriage arrived. The twins were sleeping in their cots. There were two guards driving the carriage, but that was all. One guard got down from the carriage, took up one of the cots and carried it into the inn. My mother and I were waiting inside to greet the babies. It was at this point a great commotion broke out with shouting and screaming coming from outside. It was raiders from across the border, arriving on horseback. The guard with us, on seeing what was happening, ran quickly out and by calling loudly to the stables he raised the alarm. He took up arms, but before help arrived the raiders had already attacked and killed the guard that remained with the carriage. On seeing the guards running towards them from the stables, the raiders quickly remounted their horses and rode away into the darkness. Then to everyone's horror, when the carriage was inspected, the second cot was gone. A splash in the river was heard as they rode away. The river was searched both that evening and the following day, but only the cot was ever found. Poor Edmund, for that was the twin that was lost; must have drowned that night, and all our prayers went with him."

"Thank you, Agatha, for that very vivid account," said Bardolph. "Now will'st you answer just one more question. Edward, the twin that survived, how was he dressed that evening, and was he wearing jewellery of any kind?"

Agatha smiled again. She was enjoying all the attention she was receiving.

"Edward was but eight months old, but all the same he was dressed in a small but regal suit, braided in gold and lined with ermine. And yes, he was wearing jewellery. Around his neck was a gold chain and pendant, and on his suit there was pinned a brooch. Both jewels bore matching stones. They were large, green stones in the shape of pear."

Bardolph had earlier returned the necklace worn by the Lady Adela to the table. He collected it along with the brooch and presented them both to Agatha.

"Tell me, Agatha," he said, "were these those jewels?"

Agatha peered closely at the items, for her eyesight had seen better years. A toothless smile appeared.

"Yes, those are they. Those are the jewels worn by Edward. How could I forget them?" she said.

"Thank you, Agatha," said Bardolph.

He then turned and placed the necklace and brooch back on the table in front of the Earl.

"My Lord," he said, "a long tale has been told, but a very necessary tale, for it was not only Edward invested in jewellery that day, but also his twin brother Edmund. Not just one necklace and brooch were presented that day, but two necklaces and two brooches. At the ceremony at the Abbey at Wistanstow earlier that day, both Edmund and Edward were presented with a matching necklace and brooch."

The Earl rubbed his chin.

"Have you evidence to substantiate this claim?" he asked.

Bardolph nodded.

"Yes, my Lord, I have the evidence," he said.

Bardolph turned to Mary, the handmaid of Lady Adela, who had been seated alongside the Abbess of Wistanstow throughout the trial.

"Mary, will'st you bring forward your departing gift from the Lady Adela and present it to the court?" he asked.

Mary rose and walked towards the table. It was an unsteady walk and her chest wheezed as she ambled across the floor. On reaching Bardolph, she placed a large emerald brooch in his hand.

Bardolph collected the second brooch from the table and held both brooches high, one in each hand. He showed them firstly to the court, and then turned to reveal the brooches to both sides of the hall.

Immediately, there came great gasps of amazement; firstly from those seated at the table, and afterwards from all those seated in the hall, as everyone found themselves staring at two identical brooches.

Bardolph waited for the hubbub to die down and for Mary to return to her seat before returning to the table and to stand before the Earl. He laid down the two brooches and then organised them so that the necklace and Mary's brooch stood together, with the second brooch resting a short distance away.

"My Lord," Bardolph began, pointing to both the necklace and the brooch, "here we have the necklace found in the possession of the Lady Adela and the brooch presented to this court by Mary, her handmaid."

His hand moved across the table to the lone brooch a short distance away.

He continued, "And here we have the second brooch, this time found upon the dress of a whore plying her trade at the local tavern here in Lodelowe. So, what is missing? It is the second necklace that is missing. But my Lord, I also have the answer to this. For earlier this day I asked the captain of the guard here at Lodelowe to search a certain room within this castle. I now ask permission of this court for the captain of the guard of Lodelowe to enter and bring with him what was found."

The Earl, full of curiosity, replied without consulting the rest of the bench, saying, "You may bring the captain of the guard of Lodelowe before this court. Let us all see what he hath found."

Bardolph turned to the main doors at the far side of the hall. He signalled with a wave of his hand and waited.

The doors opened and in marched Captain Osbald. He was dressed in the uniform of Lodelowe but wore no chainmail and carried no weapons. Behind him followed four servants each carrying a weighty sack. The four servants placed the sacks down before the table, bowed low then turned and departed the hall, leaving the captain standing alongside Bardolph.

"Captain, will you please tell this court what you have been doing and were you have been," said Bardolph.

Captain Osbald turned to the court.

"I have been searching the rooms of Sergeant Cuthred, this castle's sergeant-at-arms. Hidden beneath his bed, were these four sacks and in one of those sacks I found this," he said, placing a single item of jewellery on the table before the Earl.

The Earl took up the offering, unravelled the gold chain and let a large pendant fall to the end of the chain. He held it high for all to see. He was holding a gold chain from which hung a large emerald stone mounted on a pendant of gold. Having shown everyone, he placed it down on the table alongside the lone brooch. He then looked to Bardolph and waited for an explanation.

Bardolph moved closer to the table and pointed firstly to one set of jewellery and then the other.

Addressing the Earl, he said, "My Lord, here we have the evidence. Here before this court there now lies on the table two necklaces and two brooches. One pair presented to Edward, the other to his twin, Edmund."

The Earl rubbed his chin and for while remained in deep thought.

"Then we have been deceived all along," he replied speaking slowly, "there were two of everything; two necklaces and two brooches, and I assume these four sacks contain the Baron's stolen treasure? And can we assume it was this castle's sergeant-at-arms that took the treasure?"

"You are quite right on all counts, my Lord," responded Bardolph, "and it was indeed Sergeant Cuthred that alone did the robbery. I am told that he now resides in this castle's dungeon, having been arrested and taken there once the treasure was uncovered."

"Alone, you say? Has he confessed to this crime?" asked the Earl. "And why would he commit such a hideous crime? Surely a man of his position would not stoop to such a thing."

Bardolph responded by attempting to answer all the Earl's questions in turn, saying, "My Lord, the sergeant did indeed do this alone. However, I know not whether he hath confessed. No doubt a separate trial will reveal all. As for why he would commit such a hideous crime, then I would say he needed the extra wealth to sustain his daughter Anne's residence at the Abbey at Wistanstow, for she is a novice there and is being schooled in the ways of this most Holy Order. I believe it was something she always wanted since her mother passed away some short time ago. But as you very well know, my Lord, enrolment in the Holy Order doth come at a great cost and remains a place for the daughters of the landed gentry. My Lord, I also have further proof of Sergeant Cuthred's guilt. If this court permits, then I will'st present it as further evidence to the innocence of the accused."

"You may present this further evidence," agreed the Earl.

Bardolph turned to Captain Osbald and collected a folded piece of parchment paper. He then turned to the Earl.

"My Lord, here is final proof that it was indeed this castle's sergeant-at-arms that did'st this crime. This missive was found in his room along with the Baron's missing treasure."

He unfolded the parchment and with a hand flattened it out on the table before the Earl.

"My Lord, note the pale blue ink," he said, "this ink is that used by the Abbess in her missives to relatives of the Order's Holy Sisters. I'm sure, if asked, she will'st confirm this. This missive is addressed to Sergeant Cuthred confirming Sister Anne's acceptance into the Order. Now please note that the bottom of this document hath been torn away and a piece is missing from the corner. Well, here I have that missing piece."

From a pouch on his belt Bardolph extracted a small piece of paper.

"My Lord, I give you the missing piece," he said, and placing the two pieces together to show that they matched.

Taking up the gold signet ring that had lain on the table all along, he then went on to explain, "This gold signet ring is that of the Baron's father and was reportedly found by Sergeant Cuthbert in the shoe of Lady Adela's handmaiden. It was found wrapped in this very piece of paper, for it was I who retained it after the handmaiden's trail. I put it to the court that it was indeed Sergeant Cuthred that placed this ring, wrapped in this piece of parchment, inside the shoe of the handmaiden at the time of her search within her cell. I also put it to this court that the brooch found upon the dress of the whore at the tavern in the town, was also put there by Sergeant Cuthred, for it was he that found it and brought it before the Baron. My Lord, it was Sergeant Cuthred, acting alone, that entered the

Baron's strongroom that night and did'st kill the guard on duty, and that both Gwyneth the handmaiden and the whore Margaret are innocent of all crimes. My Lord, they are due to hang tomorrow on the day of the market. It is within your power as Overlord of the Marches to pardon these prisoners and set them free. I pray that this will be done and the innocent not punished."

The Earl rubbed his chin once more. He was not one for rushing into things without giving the subject some consideration.

"I will'st consider what you say whence this trial is concluded," he said, "but first, we must agree a verdict on the trial that now stands before this court. But before we convene to consider our verdict, there remains one thing that still bothers me. An explanation is surely needed as to how the necklace and brooch that once did'st belong to the twin Edmund end up in the possession of the Fitzgeralds of Salopsbury?"

Bardolph had the answer. It was however a topic he hoped would remain unquestioned, but now that the Earl had asked, he felt compelled to give an explanation.

"My Lord, it is a tale that can only be speculated on. It is quite possible that the jewels found their way into the possession of the Fitzgeralds by fair means, possibly by a sale or gift, or even a chance find of abandoned booty, for the exact means will'st by now be lost in the annals of time. But I can put forward one other possible explanation, for I have one further piece of evidence."

He then turned to the Abbess of Wistanstow and called across the floor, "Holy Mother, please hand to this court the second document in your possession."

Bardolph crossed the floor to the Abbess and took a scroll from her hands. He then returned to the table and addressed the Earl.

"My Lord," he said, "this document was signed and sealed at the same time as the agreement reached over the boundaries issue."

He unfurled the scroll to show two seals at the bottom.

He went on to explain, "My Lord, this document is dated the same day; the fifth of October in the year of our Lord eleven-hundred and fifty-four; and contains two seals, those of the de Clanceys and the Fitzgeralds. It is written in the language of the Normans, and not Latin as with the agreement of the church, for this is consent between the two families, as required by law at the time. If I may, my Lord, rather than read out this document in full, instead I will'st offer this court a brief translation. For I am sure anyone schooled in the language of the Normans will confirm what I have to say."

The Earl nodded.

"Go ahead, I will have the document verified once this session is concluded," he said.

Speaking slowly, Bardolph began his explanation, for the tale was long and complicated, and remained in some parts pure speculation on his part.

"My Lord," he started and sounding deep in thought, "this further agreement, signed and sealed at the Abbey at the same time and some eighty year past, covers the future appointments to the Abbey of both the abbot and the abbess. It was agreed the abbot to be appointed by Lodelowe and the abbess by Salopsbury. And this agreement still applies to this day; for indeed, Father Monticelli, the current abbot of Wistanstow, and who sits with you in judgement today, did'st get appointed by the grace and favour of Lodelowe; and likewise, the Holy Mother, Elizabeth Fitzgerald, the Abbess of Wistanstow was appointed by the grace and favour of Salopsbury. But let me read to you just one line from this document. It concerns the appointment of the abbess by Salopsbury. This, I will'st translate into Saxon for the benefit of this court."

Bardolph unfurled the scroll and translated one particular line, "*By the grace of God the new baby daughter recently born to the Lady Joanna de Bohan, whence she becomes of age, will'st be the first of the Fitzgeralds to be appointed to the Holy Order.*"

Bardolph held the document across the table so that the Earl could see.

"You see, my Lord, the word here definitely reads '*fille*'." he said, pointing to one particular word. "This in the Norman tongue is the Saxon word for 'daughter', and with the agreement being for the appointment of the abbess, there is no doubt in my mind that in the year eleven-hundred and fifty-four there was born a baby girl to the Fitzgeralds."

Bardolph took a deep breath and waited for the hubbub to settle; for he was creating quite a stir amongst all those present in the hall.

"My Lord," he continued, for he had a lot more explaining to take place. "The year is important here. Eleven-hundred and fifty-four also happens to be the year of the twins' birth. It also happens to be the year of the birth of Sir Rupert Fitzgerald. This, I find most curious. For how is it possible for Lady Joanna de Bohan to have both son and daughter in the same year that is already ten months gone? Possibly they were twins, both boy and girl; but this was never recorded. In fact, nothing about the baby girl was ever recorded, for it is my belief that this girl died shortly after birth. My Lord, in the chapel of the Fitzgeralds there lies a grave within the walls of the castle of Salopsbury. On its stone is written the solitary year; '*eleven-hundred and fifty-four*' and beneath lies an inscription in Latin stating that whoever was buried there did'st not live beyond a year."

Bardolph waited once more for the crowd to settle, for there was much talk amongst both families.

"My Lord, I put it to this court that Sir Rupert Fitzgerald, Knight of the Order of St. John of Jerusalem, was in fact the twin Edmund. I put it to you that he did not die that night at Onneyditch, but was taken away to become the child of the Fitzgeralds. My Lord, this can then explain how Edmund's jewellery came into the possession of Salopsbury. It stayed with the child and was kept with the family."

Bardolph moved along the table to stand before Squire Henry Stokes.

"Squire," he said to him, "you did'st once serve Sir Rupert Fitzgerald in battle in the Holy Lands. And I believe that on a few occasions you did'st attend the company of the Baron's late father Edward here at Lodelowe. Tell me, did'st you ever notice any similarities between Edward and Sir Rupert?"

Squire Henry gave the matter some thought.

"Now that you come to mention it," he said. "There was a great similarity between the two men. Both had the same facial features and the same stock of thick red hair. Yes, there were similarities, but it was something I never connected; for Sir Rupert was a brave knight and fought alongside the good King Richard in the Holy lands, whilst Baron Edward de Clancey ignored the King's call to arms. It was for this reason the coat of arms of the de Clanceys was frowned upon and considered 'craven'. But the more I think about it, you could very well be right. It is quite possible that Sir Rupert and the late Baron Edward de Clancey were indeed twins."

Bardolph turned to the Earl.

"My Lord, there you have it. It is my belief that Sir Rupert Fitzgerald was indeed Edmund de Clancey, taken from his cot at Onneyditch and handed to the Fitzgeralds of Salopsbury. My Lord, it is my belief that the present Baron de Clancey and Salopsbury's Earl, Hubert Fitzgerald, are both sons of the twins and are in fact, cousins. With this, my Lord, I rest my case, and in so doing have proven beyond a doubt that the Lady Adela is truly innocent of all charges held against her."

And with that Bardolph stepped back and bowed low. His job was done. Now it was up to the court to reach their verdict.

The verdict did not take long, for all that sat in judgement were of one mind.

"Will everyone stand," said the Earl and standing himself. "This court finds the accused, Lady Adela Fitzgerald innocent of all charges. She is free to go."

A cheer went up from certain sections of the crowd. But others stood stony faced.

Bardolph walked up to Lady Adela seated alone in the centre of the hall. She was holding up her arm as he arrived. He kissed the back of her hand.

"Dear servant of the King, how can I ever thank you?" she said. "For without your intervention I would surely have faced the gallows. For what you did hypothesise was true. It was a family secret that Sir Rupert was indeed a de Clancey. One day I happened to overhear a conversation between my late husband and the current Earl. My husband learned that I overheard and made me swear on the Holy Bible that I reveal this secret to no one."

"So I was right," said Bardolph. "Perhaps now that the secret is out you will convey this knowledge to the Earl. There is no more I can do. My job here is done and I must be away. The King awaits his birds and I cannot tarry here in Lodelowe a day longer. Tomorrow, at the break of dawn I will be away. But for you, my dear Lady, may your journey south continue, and that you become once again united with your family in Honfleur."

And with that Bardolph kissed the back of her hand and retreated. He gave a final smile then headed for the doors. He was to retreat to his room, get a good night's sleep and be away at the break of dawn.

As he walked from the hall he heard the head of the court say, "Earl Hubert Fitzgerald, and you Baron de Clancey, come with me to my chambers, we have some important matters to resolve."

Bardolph smiled and kept on walking. Hopefully the two families would come to some agreement.

Chapter Fifty

On the morning following the trial Bardolph rose well before dawn. It was still dark outside and this suited him, for this is what he wanted. The previous night he had left instructions with the stables to saddle his horse and prepare his donkey in readiness for departure at first light. He was hoping he could just drift quietly away from Lodelowe whilst everyone was still asleep.

But how wrong could he be?

As he entered the courtyard carrying his falcons in two separate cages he could see that his horse and donkey were prepared and awaiting his arrival. The two animals were standing at the centre, their reins held by stable lads. But there was something a little disconcerting about the rest of the sight that greeted him. Grouped in small huddles about the courtyard, there stood gatherings of both men and women. And what was more alarming, they were all looking his way.

It was Ralph that greeted him first. He had stationed himself close to the door that opened out into the courtyard in readiness for the falconer's arrival.

"Let me take the birds, sire," he said to Bardolph holding out his hands. "I will'st tie them to your donkey whilst you say your fond farewells. For I am sure those gathered here at this early hour have a lot to thank you for after yesterday's trial."

Bardolph handed over the cages. Already he was feeling slightly embarrassed. "Ralph, you are a good lad," he said to him, and from his purse he took out a silver crown. "Here, Ralph, this is for you. Accept it from the King of England, for it is his birds you have tended so well whilst I have been pre-occupied on business that did not concern the King."

Ralph took the silver crown and touched his forelock.

"Thank you kind sire," he said. "I am honoured to have had the privilege to serve the King in such a small and humble way."

"Go, tie my birds to my donkey," said Bardolph. "It seems I have people awaiting my presence, and my departure could well be much delayed."

Bardolph moved on.

The first group awaiting him were three women. They stood remote from the huddle gathered around the horse and the donkey. They were the Lady Adela, the Abbess of Wistanstow and the ageing handmaid Mary. On reaching them, Bardolph bowed politely and the three women curtsied. The Lady Adela held out her hand. Bardolph took her hand and kissed her lightly on the knuckles.

"My Lady, this is not necessary," said Bardolph sounding apologetic. "You should not be out in the cold, and as for fond farewells surely these were all said on conclusion of your trial?"

Lady Adela shook her head and responded by saying, "Nay, kind sir, surely it is only right and proper that I be present at the departure of a man I hold dear. A man that hath spoken on my behalf and in so doing hath saved me from the gallows. Bardolph of Wessex, Royal Falconer to the King, I wish you safe journey and may St. Christopher go with you."

Bardolph kissed her hand once more.

"Then I too must wish you safe journey home to Normandy, and may the winds be kind whence you cross the English Channel," he said releasing the hand.

Bardolph moved along the short line.

Mary was next in line. She stood between the Lady Adela and the Abbess. Mary curtsied and stayed in that position; remained low and with head facing the ground, for she was only a serving wench and knew her true station. Bardolph bent low and spoke to Mary in that position.

"Mary, I have nothing but praise for you. If it was not for you I would never have unlocked the key to all these riddles," he told her. "If you had not worn that brooch when you came to me in Salopsbury's kitchens, then I would never have known that there were indeed two sets of jewellery. Mary, by bringing that brooch here to Lodelowe, it was you not I that did'st save your mistress's life."

Mary feeling embarrassed, her head remained low and facing the ground.

In a quiet voice she said, "Thank you, my Lord, for your kind words. Have a safe journey home, and may St. Christopher go with you."

Bardolph straightened to stand upright.

"Thank you, Mary," he said.

He moved on to greet the Abbess of Wistanstow who stood to the end of the short row. Again, a raised hand awaited him. He kissed her lightly on the knuckles, looked up and their eyes met. There was a sparkle to them and the Abbess was smiling.

"Holy Mother," he said, "it seems more thanks are in order. The finding of the two scrolls in the abbey's vaults proved vital for the trial. Without them I would have had no case to defend. If thanks were in order from the Lady Adela, then they should go to both you and Mary. Without your presence, and to do what you did, I could not have spoken in the Lady Adela's defence."

The Abbess's smile broadened.

"My sweet Angel Gabriel," she replied, "there was nothing I would have done without your guidance and blessing. I know where true thanks should lie and it is not with me. Go with God's blessing. Ride safely to Wessex and may St. Christopher go with you."

Bardolph took hold of the Abbess's hand. But before saying his final farewell there was something he still would like to know.

He asked of her, "Pray tell me, what of the novice Anne? What fate awaits her now that her father is charged with the theft and murder of the guard?"

A look of sadness appeared on the Abbess's face.

"She will be allowed to remain with the order. She is a good girl and hath served her penitence well and put all her faith in the Lord. If further money for her training is no longer forthcoming, then I personally will fund her. It is the least I can do," she answered.

Bardolph's face too reflected the sadness. But if it were not for that chance moment of seeing Anne at the abbey and learning that she was the sergeant's daughter, then one small piece of the puzzle would be missing. Perhaps things would have been much different; he had no way of telling.

He raised the hand that he still held.

"Then offer Anne my blessings, and I hope all goes well for her in the future," he told her.

"I will do just that as soon as I return to Wistanstow," she said and then repeated. "So go now, my Angel Gabriel, ride safely to Wessex and may St. Christopher go with you."

It was time to move on. The Abbess smiled and Bardolph kissed her hand for a final time. He returned the smile and bowed low. Another group awaited him, and this time gathered around his horse and donkey. He recognised them all except one woman, but it did not take much sorting. This was the whore Margaret, for stood with her were John Smith the blacksmith, also Madeline, whom he had rescued from the forest, Gwyneth the handmaiden and Ralph, who on tying the cages had moved to join them.

If there was one person missing then it was Agatha, and this was Bardolph's first question as he arrived to greet them.

"Where's Agatha?" he queried, for if there was anyone that needed thanking, then it was this dear old lady.

John Smith was ready with the answer.

"She returned to Onneyditch yesterday whilst light remained," he explained. "It proved to be a most tiring day and she does't so like to sleep in her own bed. But she sends her best wishes, and hopes that one day you will'st return and talk with her besides the fire. For these are the fond memories she holds of you."

Bardolph gave a slight nod of his head in recognition.

"Then give Agatha my best wishes," he said, "for once again, I could not possibly have achieved the verdict that did'st go our way."

John Smith threw an arm about Madeline and drew her close to him.

"We are to get married," he announced, "and Madeline's daughter, Gwyneth, is going to stay with us. She will be a good sister to Ralph. Once more the stables at Onneyditch will be run by a family, and you never know, perhaps one day we may hear again the patter of tiny feet."

Bardolph laughed, as did John.

Madeline acknowledged John's proposal by saying, "Yes, John hath asked me to be his bride and I have accepted. He a good man, kind and gentle, but that is not why we are here today. We come as a family to give thanks to a man who did'st save me from a great beating, and possibly death, for who knows what those men were capable of?"

Having met those men, the two soldiers of Salopsbury, and witnessed their ruthlessness, Bardolph knew exactly what evil deeds they were capable of. But he said no more on the subject. Madeline was safe now and this was all that mattered.

"Then my best wishes to both you and John upon your forthcoming marriage," he told Madeline. "May God look favourably upon your Holy union," then turning to Gwyneth and Ralph he added with a smile, "and of course, to your ready-made family."

It was Gwyneth's turn to greet Bardolph, for she was next in the row, and she wanted to give her own personal thanks to the man that had saved her life. However, as a mere serving wench she knew her station and curtsied low before speaking.

"Dear sire, I must thank you for what you did for me. Without you I would have faced the gallows this very day. You dear sire will always remain in my thoughts," she said.

"It grieves me to see injustice done. I did what was necessary and asked your pardon of the Earl, that was all," he told her.

With time pressing Bardolph really wanted to move on, but not before he had a final word with Margaret. The ravages of her torture remained. She remained thin and ashen faced, and stood with a stoop to her body. Gwyneth put an arm around her shoulders to hold her steady.

"And you must be Margaret," said Bardolph, for they had never met.

She acknowledged with a slight nod to the head.

"Yes, good sire, I am Margaret," she confirmed, "and I could not see you go from here without thanking the man that did'st save my life. I thank you dear sire for what you did for me, for without your intervention, this day, on the day of the market, would have been my last. From the bottom of my heart I thank you."

Bardolph felt embarrassed.

"Thank you for your kind words," he said, "departing Lodelowe in the knowledge that I did'st manage to save innocent lives will'st remain with me forever."

Bardolph smiled and moved on quickly, for there were two more people awaiting his presence. He walked over to them. They were both dressed in the red and dark blue uniforms of the soldiers of Lodelowe.

First in line stood Corporal Egbert. He stood supporting himself with a staff and had a leg heavily strapped with splints. Bardolph reflected that the last time he had seen the corporal was back at Wistanstow Abbey on his return from Salopsbury. At that time it was considered by the monks that Egbert needed a few more days for his leg to heal sufficiently before returning to Lodelowe.

"Egbert, you are back at Lodelowe and looking well," said Bardolph and added, "and how does the leg go, does it heal straight and strong?"

Egbert smiled and nodded his head.

"Good sire, my leg is healing well. Soon the splints will be away and I will be walking again without the aid of this staff. And from the bottom of my heart I must thank you for all that you did for me that day. Without your timely intervention my dispatches would never have reached Salopsbury and I would have remained a cripple for the rest of my life," he said.

Bardolph reflected on what happened that fateful day.

If Egbert had not fallen from his horse, then he would have never had cause to pay a visit to Salopsbury, and to encounter the Welsh brigands in the woods at Longnor, then subsequently rescue the Abbess from their clutches. But more importantly, he would never have visited the chapel and seen the date on those graves, and furthermore never held audience with Mary, Lady Adela's faithful servant, and seen the brooch she wore upon her dress.

If anybody needed thanking for saving the life of Lady Adela, then it had to be Egbert. For without his untimely accident then, Bardolph would most certainly have been well on his way back to Wessex and not knowing anything of the outcome of the trial. He was thinking perhaps it was the Abbess's prayers and God's intervention that saved all those innocent lives.

The two men embraced, patting each other on the back.

"Then heal well my friend and return quickly to being a true soldier of the Baron. For he holds a good and honest man in his service," said Bardolph.

Egbert smiled and nodded.

"Be reassured, I will serve the Baron with all my heart," he said and added, "Good sire, go well with all my blessings, and may God and St. Christopher go with you."

Perhaps with a small tear in the corner of his eyes, Bardolph moved on to greet the second soldier that awaited him.

The two men embraced.

"Captain Osbald," said Bardolph, "Of all the friends I have made during my brief stay here at Lodelowe, you must truly be the one most indebted to my very existence. Your intervention in the woods at Longnor proved most timely, and without your appearance I would in all probability be dead by now."

Captain Osbald laughed heartily and he said, "It was not I, but your horse, Ventabli, you must thank for that timely intervention. But do not forget that it was you that also saved my life at the ford at Marsh Brook. My dear friend there will always be a welcome here at Lodelowe for you. Now go, mount your horse and be away from here. Dawn breaks and you have a long ride ahead. So may God and St. Christopher go with you."

"Thanks friend," said Bardolph, slapping Osbald on the shoulder. "But you are right on one thing. It is time for me to leave. And I go with a heavy heart at leaving all these good folks behind. Perhaps one day, I will return. Who knows what the future may bring?"

Having spoken in turn to all those awaiting his departure, Bardolph, with the help of the two stable lads, mounted his horse and tethered his donkey to his saddle. From the saddle he looked down upon the small crowd gathered to see him off. They all stood together now.

"Goodbye to every one of you," said Bardolph, "and goodbye my friends, goodbye Lodelowe. Goodbye the Marches. Perhaps one day I will return. But for now I must be away, for I have some urgent unfinished King's business to attend to."

And with that he kicked his heels and set off to pass beneath the portcullis and out into the streets of Lodelowe. He did not look back, for if the truth be told, there remained a small tear in the corner of each eye.

It was left to Captain Osbald to have the final word.

"I wonder if we will ever see the return of the Royal Falconer?" he said as he and all those gathered in the courtyard waved goodbye.

The End

Glossary of Terms:

Abbey – In the Christian church, a monastery (of monks), and sometimes combined with a nunnery or convent (of nuns), though strictly segregated and dedicated to the life of celibacy and religious seclusion, and governed by an abbot and/or abbess respectively.

Anjou – This was a former province in northern France, capital Angers. In 1154 the Count of Anjou became King of England as Henry II, but the territory was lost to King John in 1204. Today Anjou is famous for its wine production.

Calvados – This is an apple brandy made from distilled cider, and the name taken from a region of Normandy. Cider making in Britain was known to exist during Roman times, but before 1066 remained limited to farmers and families and never produced commercially. Apple orchards were unknown in Britain and only wild crab apples were used. Apparently, William hated the English ale. He said it tasted foul. So he changed all this by planting extensive cider apple orchards from saplings brought over from France. Most cider apples growing in Britain today are descendants of trees transported from Normandy in the years following 1066. These trees were planted mainly in the West County, (Somerset and Herefordshire.).

Today, cider making remains a major industry in these counties, thanks entirely to the Normans. Cider making also remains a strong industry in Normandy, as does the production of calvados. Ale, stout and porter are the correct names for English brews of the time, but not beer. The word beer comes from the French *bierre*, and refers to a brew made from hops. Hops did not grow in Britain until the 15th century when they were imported from Flanders. English ale before this time was based on malt and wheat.

Cinque Ports – Five harbours in Kent, (SW England), and closest to France. These are generally accepted today as Sandwich, Dover, Hythe, Romney and Hastings, though Pevensey, Rye, Winchelsea and others still stake a claim. Probably founded by the Romans when it was a bit hit-and-miss as to where they would come ashore in rough seas. The Cinque Ports only rose to promenance after the Norman invasion.

Council of the Marches – A council established by local barons to bring law and order to the Marches (an area that bordered Wales) and to oversee a common judicial system. Although created in William the Conqueror's time and in existence at this period in history, the council itself did not officially become recognised until 1470, with headquarters at Shrewsbury. The council was abolished in 1689 in the reign of William and Mary.

Craven Arms – A term applied to the Coat of Arms of families that for various reasons failed to serve the king or country during wars or crusades, and roughly translates as 'faint-hearted' rather than coward. There are several Craven families, Craven areas and Craven places in England. An example being the Craven District: an area of Yorkshire just north of Skipton. There is also a village in Shropshire of this name that lies on the road between Ludlow and Shrewsbury.

Crusades – European wars against non-Christians and heretics, sanctioned by the Pope. There were a series of eight wars in total; held between 1096 and 1291, and undertaken by various European rulers in order to recover Palestine from the Muslims. 1189 to 1192 saw the Third Crusade led by Philip II Augustus of France and Richard I of England. This crusade was not a great success and failed to capture Jerusalem, which had been seized by Saladin.

Danelaw – When during the 10th century the viking settlers recognised the authority of the English kings, they were allowed to follow some facets of their own traditional laws. By the 11th century the term *Danelaw* was being used in law codes to indicate that customary English law was influenced by Danish practice.

Deheubarth – An area of central Wales bordering the English Marches (now mostly the Welsh County of Powis).

Dolwyddelan – The capital of a region in West Wales, (now mostly the Welsh County of Gwynedd) where the Lord Llywelyn resided and ruled. Born in 1173 and reigned from 1194 until his death in 1240 and therefore, alive in 1235 when this story is set. (Also see Llywelyn ap Iorwerth).

Ex voto – Latin *'as, in fulfilment of, a vow'*. Something offered on account of a vow. A thanks-offering placed in a church after safe return from a voyage, recovery from illness, tumultuous ordeal, etc.

Forest of Wyre – Remnants of the Wyre Forest exist today, lying west of the banks of the River Severn mainly between the towns of Bridgnorth and Bewdley. In the 13th century this forest was much larger, stretching for most of the way along the west bank of the River Severn from Shrewsbury in the north to Worcester in the south, and in parts reaching westwards almost to the Welsh border.

Hunting Lodges – In the 13th century the call to hunt was strong. Hunting lodges were a place of gathering for noble lords. Even royal guests may have come for the chase. A hunting lodge in Clun Forest (a forest of the Marches which unfortunately does not exist today) is recorded that at one time there were 160 horses stabled at the lodge. There was also water gardens present with associated pavilions so that noble lords could entertain their guests whilst their ladies whiled away their time in the gardens.

Llywelyn ap Iorwerth, (Llywelyn, son of Iorwerth), 1173–1240 – Recognised as Wales' paramount overlord from 1218 to his death in 1240. Never actually called king, but took the titles Prince of Aberffraw, Lord of Snowdon and most notably, the Lord Llywelyn. He married Joan an illegitimate daughter of King John. He was therefore, related to King Henry III in as much that he was married to his half-sister. A gentleman's agreement existed between Llywelyn and Henry not to encroach on each other's territory. In the year 1235 when this story is set, any organised or pre-meditated raid across the border into England would need to have been sanctioned by Llywelyn ap Iorwerth.

Marches – The frontier or borderland country between the English Shires of West Mercia and the unsubdued Welsh kingdoms. This border area was troublesome throughout the whole of the 11th to 13th centuries. Welsh incursions were frequent and the Anglo-Saxon inhabitants of the area were not happy to be subjugated by the recently arrived overlords from across the channel. The Normans therefore, wished to assert military power. William the Conqueror and his successors created a militarised buffer zone in the Marches by rewarding his loyal French supporters with gifts of land and titles in the area. The building of numerous castles showed clearly the invader's strength and their intention to control the inhabitant's tendency to brigandage and revolt with military force if necessary.

Matins – The first canonical hour, the time for Morning Prayer. It could be at a set time, or as dawn breaks, depending on the order and time of year.

Mercia – Land of central England settled by the Saxons. Lichfield, founded in 669, was the capital. Today West Mercia is generally considered to encompass the counties of Shropshire, Staffordshire, Worcestershire and Herefordshire.

Milestones – Mile from the Latin *mille* meaning one thousand, and milestone, a stone indicating the miles on a highway to or from a given place. Milestones came to Britain with the Romans. The Roman mile being 1,000 military paces, about 1,620 yards. The statutory mile of 1,760 yards (or 80 chains to be more precise, a chain being 22 yards) was not officially standardised until the 15th century, so in 1235 when this story is set, the shorter distance of 1620 yards would be the most likely distance measured by the milestones.

Motte and Bailey – A fortified hill, introduced by the Normans soon after the invasion in 1066, its purpose to look out and defend. Over 600 were set up all over England in the first 20 years of rule. The motte was a central hill most often manmade with a wooden defensive structure on the top, whilst the bailey incorporated an outer defence circle of ditches and stockades.

Novice – Newcomer to a religious house who is still under probation. This could be up to five years.

Nunnery – In the early Anglo-Saxon period, monastic life for women was almost always in double houses. In most of these, monks and nuns shared a church, though always kept strictly apart. An abbess ruled over the female community. She was often of noble birth and for many centuries nunneries remained places for noble women.

Pean – Heraldic term: An ermine fur that has gold spots, usually on a black background. Normal ermine fur is white with black spots.

Plantagenet – Dynasty began with Henry II (1154–1189), son of Geoffrey IV the Handsome, 9th Count of Anjou, and Matilda daughter of England's Henry I. The name Plantagenet is said to have come about from Geoffrey IV who often wore in his hat a sprig of broom. Latin *'Planta Genista'*.

Poultice – Derived from the Latin *'pultum'* meaning pap or porridge and the early French *'poultis'*. A hot moist mass of meal etc. applied to an inflamed or painful part of the body. This type of cure was practised widely by the Normans and seen as a panacea for most illnesses. Similar remedies may have been in use in Britain before the invasion, however, the word *'poultis'* and a general acceptance of what a *'poultis'* was, only came about after the arrival of the Normans. Many recorded herbal recipes for poultices remain and were not necessarily restricted to humans. Horses, cattle, sheep and even pigs and dogs were subjected to this treatment. There are no records to say whether any animals survived.

Rhys ap Gruffydd, (The Lord Rhys), 1133–1197 – Welsh king, born 1133, reigned 1155–1197. Ruler of an area of central Wales known as Deheubarth and bordered the Marches. He is known to have successfully exploited the departure of Norman barons to Ireland (from 1169) and to extend his domain into Dyfed, (an area of South West Wales), rebuilding Cardigan and Dinefwr castles. He is buried in St. David's cathedral with his raven emblem.

Signet Ring – This is a finger ring bearing a crest, coat of arms etc. Used as a private seal for sealing documents etc. with or without a signature. When the owner of that seal died the seal usually went with him. If titles were passed down then a slight variation would be put on the new seals to distinguish the owner. (Also see Wedding Ring)

Soldiers and Rank – In this period of history no regular army existed. Most soldiers simply enlisted for a campaign, mainly called upon by the king. They signed up for what they were best suited, mainly man-at-arms (a foot-soldier), archer (or crossbow-man), or cavalryman. They were paid for a specific campaign and were expected to supplement their income by looting and pillaging. When the campaign was over, these men simply went back to doing what they did before.

Knights, on the other hand, were recognised professional soldiers and maintained their own code of chivalry. Captured knights were usually ransomed until their family paid for their release. Private armies with full-time soldiers were small in size, usually no more than a dozen men, and their rank and structure varied from shire to shire. Generally a baron, or any man of wealth, maintained his own private army mainly for his own protection, and for the purpose of collecting taxes. The lowest ranking foot soldier would be a man-at-arms.

The Latin *'Decurio'* meaning divided into companies of ten was used right up to the 14th century to indicate a spokesman from the lower ranks. This position is now accepted as corporal and being the lowest non-commission rank in the army. Likewise *'Centurio'* was the leader, or head of one hundred. This is now recognised as captain. A sergeant would be intermediate to these in any 13th century structure.

For the purpose of this story the ranks corporal, sergeant and captain are not strictly true and are merely used to depict an order of seniority. Rank in the 13th century was indicated in many ways. Sometimes a coloured plume on the helmet, sometimes a badge or even coloured ribbons. Coloured epaulets or tassels on the shoulders were another popular means of depicting rank.

Squire – The name squire can be traced back to 10th century England and applied originally to a young man attendant on a knight bearing his shield, and by the late 14th century entitled to his own coat of arms. Chaucer's squire from Canterbury Tales, written in the 14th century, was a dapper young man serving his father. In the 13th century when this story takes place the title squire remained with that person way after service was ended. These men, who generally gained the title from service in the Crusades, were highly respected in later life and invariably, through looting and plundering, held a position of power and wealth.

Surnames – Derived from the French *'surnom'* meaning nickname. The use of surnames came to the fore with the arrival of the Normans. Before this time people were generally known by one name, most often biblical. Second names usually depicted a status, such *the Great*, or *Unready*, or followed some sort of relationship such as *son*, or *brother*. Harold II defeated by William I at the Battle of Hastings was known as Harold *Godwineson* after his father *Godwine*. The *Domesday Book* (1086), the *Magna Carta* (1215), and the Normans' paranoia for supreme control changed everything by insisting that everyone should bear a second name in order that people with common first names, such as Matthew, Mark, Luke and John, could be more readily identified. Surnames took many forms. These could be either from parents with the ending *son*, as in *Godwineson*, or occupations such as *Fletcher* and *Smith*, or area or town such as *Mansfield*, or even as a nickname which the French were quite willing to add. King John for instance was called *Lackland,* (or in French *'Sans Terre'*) from the lands he lost in Normandy.

Watling Street – A Roman road that ran from *'Viroconium'* (*Wroxeter, Cheshire*), near the Welsh border, to *'Londinium'* (*London*), and still one of the main arteries of communication during the 13th century. Someone travelling from the Marches to the Cinque Ports would almost certainly have used this road.

Wedding Ring – The wife of an earl or a baron would hold her own ring. In heraldry a ring offered in marriage would show both sides of the family. The male line would be to the left; or *dexter side* when viewed, the female line on the right; or *sinister side* as it is termed. The downward vertical line dividing the two halves is called a *'party per pale'*. (Also see Signet Ring)

Wessex – Land to the south of England, today encompassing the counties of Dorset, Wiltshire and Hampshire. The New Forest lies mainly within Hampshire today.

Winchester – The City of Winchester on the border of the New Forest was the capital of England before the Norman invasion and remained so for at least the next 150 years. There is no official date when London took over from Winchester. But Henry III, on the throne when this story is set, had a lot to do with the move. He set up an English Parliament that based itself in London, and instigated the rebuilding of Westminster Abbey.

End of Glossary

DISCLAIMER

The Latin and translations may not be accurate. It is the best the author could manage from his limited knowledge of Latin and the use of a Latin/English dictionary. (Two years of Latin at senior school before opting for English Literature as an alternate. Something he now regrets).

Also events of the year 1235 and the characters depicted are totally ficticious. Some names did exist in history. Certainly King Henry III was on the throne, the Lord Llywelyn ruled Wales, and the Council of the Marches did hold considerable sway when it came to law and order in the area, but these are about the only things of any accuracy to the story.

Of the names and places mentioned, Marsh Brook, Longnor and Winstantow are villages that exist today, but may not have existed in the year 1235. Some geographical names such as the Clee Hills, the Long Mynd and the Wyre Forest also exist. (The Clee Hills being mentioned on the *'mappa mundi'*). However, there is no abbey at Winstantow, or the village of Onneyditch, but the River Onney does exist. Some rivers mentioned such as Severn and Teme also exist today.

The actual distance between the towns of Ludlow (Lodelowe in the story) and the city of Shrewsbury (Salopsbury) is about thirty miles. The story exaggerates this distance by at least two fold, maybe three, giving the distance a good twelve hours ride at a gallop. Admittedly, the roads in those days were rutted tracks, but with modern roads (the A49) and by car the distance can be covered without rush within 45 minutes.

* * *